CW00500801

LOCK ON

by

Paul Curran

Wyvern Print

This novel is entirely a work of fiction.
The names, characters and incidents portrayed in it are the work of the authors imagination. Any resemblance to actual persons, living or dead, events or localities is entirely coincidental.

Published by Wyvern Print
PO Box 816, Taunton, TA1 9EH, Somerset
www.wyvernprint.com

A catalogue for this book is available from the British Library

ISBN 987-0-9555258-0-3

Printed and bound in Great Britain by
The Fast Print Network, England

For Dad

ONE

Blue on Blue

One

Shamiya Desert – South Eastern Iraq
January 15th 1991, 01.45 hours.
.........[**Targetconfirmed**]...[**Al.Muharraq.24'42,52' 18**]......[**Transmission ends**]...............
The de-coded message was still warm from the printer, the Iraqi lieutenant staring at the buff coloured sheet in his sweating hands. The significance of the target registered with a stark clarity. He immediately made his way forward towards Fire Control, other bodies busying themselves within the cramped confines. The previous firing, two days ago, had shaken the intelligence officer, Kamal having always classed himself as a patriot. The order to bomb the suburbs of Tel Aviv had caused him to question the wisdom of others much greater than himself. The Scud unit had been in the field for seven days before the first contact from high command in Baghdad had been made. Some

one hundred miles from the Saudi border the unit had waited patiently for its first mission. With radio contact kept to a minimum, Kamal had found it difficult to gauge the progress of the Coalition assault. Hidden in a deep canyon, the unit's personnel could only venture from their vehicles by night. It was possible to hear the allied jets over fly their position and to the east the horizon had glowed with a pulsating light for three consecutive nights.

With the first launch, Kamal had sensed a change of strategy from the Ba'athist regime. In a desperate bid to unite Arab nations against the West, Saddam had struck out for Israel, not at the great allied military machine, but the very heart of the Jewish capital. Kamal was the only Shia in the unit but he had not been alone in feeling ill at ease with the new direction the war was taking. He was a career soldier first and foremost. Attacking civilian targets was for butchers and madmen but he knew only too well that such thoughts were dangerous. He had a family. The first launch had proceeded without delay and the unit had received a short communiqué soon after confirming a successful strike. With the rumour of Allied special forces at large in the area, the convoy of vehicles had immediately set course for a new launch site.

Scanning the new print out, Kamal checked for confirmation of the designated payload. Each man in the unit was well aware of the contents of the smaller of the two tankers in the convoy. The sand coloured Volvo bowser was parked some two hundred metres from the main convoy. On its back was a small cylindrical tank containing seventy five litres of Sarin nerve gas. Kamal seriously questioned his allegiances should the gas ever have to be used. He had been one of the few Iraqis ever to see the pictures of the devastation the gas was capable of. His nights were still plagued by visions of Kurdish villagers, the mothers curled around their young, the roads littered with the grotesquely distorted, victims of their own countrymen. He knew what their death had entailed, the nausea and vomiting, progressing to convulsions and eventual respiratory failure by a prolonged and steady asphyxiation. An unspeakable way to die. This time however, the nose cone of the Scud C would be carrying 120 Kg of high explosives. Kamal offered up silent prayer.

'Al Muharraq is a large airfield in northern Bahrain, sir. Reports indicate American and British bombers with supporting units.' Kamal spread the large map over the table, his finger tracing a line to the target. The commander of the unit sat hunched over the map for several minutes. Kamal positioned the small angle poise lamp to give a clearer view. The main control cab of the MAZ-543 transporter unit was cool from the air conditioning that hummed gently in the background. Finally the commander stood.

'Very well, you can begin a preliminary survey of the site and ask Lieutenant Yawad to deploy his troops. I want tp launch in one hour from now.'

'Sir.' Kamal saluted and ducked through the doorway into the cold night air. The potential launch site would need to be carefully surveyed to ensure a safe, accurate firing. Several of Kamal's section had already taken readings from theodolites around the site. As a weather balloon was being released by the unit's meteorological officer, the convoy's ZIL tanker pulled up alongside the transporter. Liquid propellant would be pumped into the main fuel cell and the conventional warhead armed. The unit was well drilled and figures ran silently between the small group of vehicles. On the surrounding high ground the twelve men of Yawad's group were fanned out around the perimeter of the site. Each man was heavily armed, with three using passive night goggles to scan the flat, featureless horizon.

Masil Yawad blew into his cupped hands, the chill of the night biting into his flesh. The deployment of his Republican Guard unit had been a direct response to earlier Allied attacks on launchers. He felt confident as he gazed down on the convoy, the smaller vehicles grouped around the transporter like suckling pigs. The Scud was still lying on the back of the giant launcher as figures climbed about it. He adjusted the definition of his PNG unit, tiny servo-motors humming in the silence. He knew that the Allied Special Forces units usually operated in eight man teams. His training in Britain in the late seventies had prepared him in a way that he could never have envisaged. Part of him was intrigued at the prospect of his own unit taking on his former tutors from all those years ago. He remembered the training on the bleak moor land of North Wales, the live firing exercises, the pursuit and interrogation, and the field craft lectures by a masked sergeant from Hereford. He wondered if he could out there tonight Yawad was snapped from his thoughts by the crackle of a voice in his earpiece.

'Stand by. Centre to all units. Event in T-minus ten minutes. Out.'

In the wadi below, the flurry of activity died down as men disappeared into the cluster of vehicles that surrounded the launcher. With the last of the doors locked shut, the site fell silent. A full four minutes passed before the Russian built transporter began to pulse with sound of activity. The steady rhythm of the motors increased as hydraulic rams started to raise the missile into the firing position. With an overall height of forty feet, the Scud took a full two minutes to become vertical. The process completed, the launcher once again became silent. In the main control cabin, located at the centre of the launcher, the darkness was punctuated by the glow of the tracking console. Two operators sat at the controls monitoring the results of the survey unit together with the planned trajectory of the missile. Kamal stood between them, his eyes reflecting the cool glow of the main satellite tracking display. LED indicators flickered as the status of the Scud was displayed.

'Begin firing sequence.' The commander, a tall broad shouldered Sunni Muslim from Al Mawsil sat back in his swivel seat and adjusted his headphones. From deep within the launcher, systems began to activate filling the control cabin with a constant drone. The countdown entered its final minute. Kamal confirmed the status.

'Initial sequence activated, tracking affirmed and T-minus twenty…nineteen….
eighteen.'

The commander sat forward in his seat, hands clasped together. Kamal anchored his back against a bulkhead and steadied himself. Outside, Yawad resisted the temptation to turn and witness the increasing crescendo of noise that was erupting from the wadi below.

The propulsion unit shook as the liquid propellant ignited. For a brief moment the missile was held in check as the power increased, sending great gaseous plumes streaming from the rear of the launcher. The pitch turned to a roar as the Scud slid from the launch rail, slowly at first, then powering its way up into the night sky. Inside the control unit the thunder of white noise changed to a steady pulse as the Scud pushed through the cloud cover. The rocking of the cabin eventually ceased, the missile appearing on the monitoring system as a small flicker. Telemetry was reporting that the trajectory was good. The relief on the face of the commander was mirrored by all in the cabin as headphones were removed and words of congratulations offered. It was then that Kamal heard the muffled sound of gunfire from outside.

Al Muharraq Coalition Airbase.
Bahrain, 02.00 hours.
Joe Ferrelli stumbled as he tripped over the cable. Hot coffee spilled over his hands causing him to drop both cups.

'Shiiiiit.' The cry was more guttural than a shout. He might have been burnt, but with the airfield on general alert he would have to suffer in silence. Ferrelli kicked the cups away and held his hands under his armpits. 'Jesus that stung', he thought. It was half a kilometre from the British NAAFI tent to the engagement control van. With the base in total darkness it had taken Farrelli a full five minutes to edge his way over the rough, boulder strewn ground. As their station was at the end of the main runway, he had been able to make some progress under the light from the tailpipes of departing bombers. Now that the aircraft were long gone the surrounding area had again been plunged back into grainy darkness.

He readied his excuse as he approached the squat rectangular shape of the control van. In the shadows to the left he could just make out the angular outline of the missile canisters. The battery of rockets consisted of eight four-tube launchers. Thirty-two Raytheon Patriot surface-to-air guided missiles of the 52nd Louisiana Air Defence Battalion defended the airspace above the Al Muharraq Coalition air base. Ferrelli paused at the main hatch into the cabin, gave the password and entered. Inside, the fetid air was rank with sweat and cigarette smoke. Ferrelli decided to go on the offensive.

'Who lit up ? If Barnes catches ya, we're all in the shit, guys.' Two figures turned towards him. A short, crop haired youth hurriedly stubbed the remains of a smoke under his heel.

'Jesus, you scared the life outta me, Fez.'

The youth stood up, his head just clearing the low ceiling. 'Barnes ain't due for another half hour, an' where's the coffee, man?' Ferrelli took off his helmet and sat in one of the bucket seats next to the control console. The unit was the size of a small freight container and could be transported on the back of a flatbed truck. To the members of the battalion it went by the unflattering nickname of '*The Meat Wagon*'.

'No coffee tonight Louie. That Brit store shut down when we went on alert'.

'Then how come you got coffee stains all down your pants?' Louis Glover, the battery's guidance operator raised an accusing finger. Ferrelli held out his arms.

'Ya got me. I dropped em when those bombers took off. Blacker than your ass, Nunk. I couldn't see my hand in front'a my face.' The third member of the fire team, a small bespectacled Georgian leant back in his seat and took a long draw from his cigarette.

'And you had trials for Baltimore? My ass Fez. You couldn't catch a cold.' The three men began to laugh as the base klaxon blared into life. The unit radio crackled with chatter as the operators jumped from their seats. Noah 'Nunk' Clay was first to his console, at the same time adjusting the headset and throat mike that put him in contact with the Muharraq radar.

'This is Tango Seven requesting trade, over.' The reply was instant, the accent pure Bronx.

'Ah, that's affirmative Tango Seven. We have one confirmed, possibly two incoming guided on 245, copy ?'

'Roger control. Maintain comms.'

Glover hauled the thick steel hatch closed and threw the locking bolts. Behind him Ferrelli swung into the second seat and activated the target engagement system.

'I may have bunked Baltimore, Nunk but I'm gonna catch me a Scud tonight.'

Located at the eastern perimeter of the airbase, the medical centre at Muharraq was a sprawling single storey mix of portable units and tented storage space.

Assembled in a little under a day by Dutch sappers at the beginning of the conflict, the hospital was staffed by a mix of Coalition personnel under the direct command of the US Army. As the warning sirens echoed across the base, medical staff began a pre-determined evacuation of patients to nearby blast shelters. Only one ward would remain occupied. As the last of the patients was removed one of the civilian medical staff sprinted back into the building. The only occupied ward was at the far end of a narrow corridor at the rear of the complex and would take valuable seconds to reach. Together with her team of four nurses, Sister Anna Pearson was part of the remaining staff tasked with the care of the patients who could not be moved. The small ward contained eight beds, six of which were occupied. All were considered too ill to be evacuated.

With all of the windows covered and lighting kept to a minimum, the ward was still as Anna arrived. William Daines, the burns unit specialist looked up from his desk. He spoke in a whisper, his thumb pointing over his shoulder.

'Any chance of getting those bloody klaxons turned off?' He grinned, the Australian accent barely perceptible. Anna picked up a clipboard from the table and turned several pages.

'You and me both. I hope that's the only noise we get tonight.' Anna smiled, her mind drawn to the events of the last four hectic days. Arriving from London's St Thomas' Hospital, the whirlwind of circumstances had almost overwhelmed her. The travel had been arduous but she had immediately been put at ease with the realisation that she would be working with some familiar faces. She had been allowed to hand pick her immediate staff and she had known Bill Daines from their training days together in Bristol. He was a good doctor and she had a lot of time for him. A bit of a devil with the ladies but once you got past the front he was a nice enough guy.

'I've just checked out the American lad in Seven. He'll need a new drip and I'd like to change the bandages on his left leg again.' Daines stood and took the clipboard from Anna. His six foot plus frame towered over the petite Londoner. His eyes motioned towards a nurse at one of the windows. She was peering through a gap between the curtains, moonlight cutting a line across her face.

'I think one of your angels is a touch nervous.' He winked as he turned towards the window. Anna smiled again. He was what her father called 'a character' and in any other circumstance the sort of man she would avoid. He was, however, an optimist at heart and good to be around. The nurses liked him and the team spirit on the ward, after only a short time, had been excellent. Anna could remember her grandparents talking about the sense of togetherness during the war. 'I suppose this was the same feeling,' she thought.

While Daines was busy with young Debbie, Anna walked past the sleeping flyers towards the last bed. Mitchell Walker was propped up on his pillows, the lower half of his body covered by a sheeted tent. Although conscious, his wounds were serious enough that any unnecessary movement could be dangerous. Both of his legs had been badly burnt in a helicopter crash three days earlier. Brought down by small arms fire on the Kuwaiti border, Walker had been dragged from the burning wreckage of his Apache by a passing Saudi patrol. He was the only crew-member to survive.

Awake but heavily sedated, Walker struggled to recognise the blurred figure before him. He managed a wide toothy grin as Anna came closer.

'That you, Whitney ?'

'Typical squaddie,' she thought.

'Sorry Mitch, just me tonight.'

'Tell me it's another bed bath, Anna. Pleeease !' His laugh made him wince as his scorched legs moved under the bandages.

'Settle down Mitchell, you need rest, yes ?'

'Wha....whats the alert ?'

'Don't you worry. I'm sure it's another false one. All clear soon.' Anna kept her voice low and slow as she wiped his brow with a cooling cloth. In two nights of seeming constant alert status, she had had grown expectant of the piercing wail of the klaxon. It had made sleep a virtual impossibility. The last four days had been run on adrenalin alone. As she changed the drip next to the pilot's bed, the distant roar of jet engines caused her to pause momentarily. She looked at the window closest to the source of the noise. Walker noticed Anna's distracted gaze.

'You got someone up there tonight Anna ?'

The question took her by surprise.

'Possibly,' she answered, 'but I hope not.'

Nunk's eyes played over the circular screen in front of him as he searched for the incoming threat. His right hand moved the tracking ball that allowed him to scroll through the airspace display before him. To his left, Glover monitored the readiness of the Patriot system. One of the benefits of the MIM 104 missile was that it was stored, transported and fired from the same sealed, canister without the need for maintenance. In seven live firings, Glover had had the relatively simple task of monitoring the missile until the target was destroyed. In the event of a malfunction however, he would be responsible for aborting the mission and destruction of the SAM. Glover was edgy. This was their first engagement and tonight was no simulation. Without warning, the low humming of the console was augmented by a shrill, piercing tone. The array lit up like a vast city scape, lights flashing in rhythm with the pulsing alarm.

'Contact on 240. Big contact, 12 clicks closing fast.' Nunk hit the final sequence of commands on the console and waited. All eyes were now on the main array display as the automated guidance system took over. The incoming Scud appeared as a bright white rectangle on the soft green of the screen. The contact appeared large to Nunk, and was moving fast.

'Is that one contact?' Ferrelli shouted. Glover wheeled forward on his seat.

'Could be two.'

Nunk's finger flicked the safety-catch over the fire button. He hesitated.

'Going for a two shot.' He pressed two buttons in rapid succession. There was a momentary pause before the cabin was rocked by a double explosion. Two Patriots, nanoseconds apart, roared from their launch tubes. The white-hot glow of their tailpipes skipped and pranced as the automatic guidance system made minute adjustments to the rockets trajectory. From the centre of the tracking console two small white dots appeared. Immediately they diverted towards the much larger contact at the top edge of the screen.

'Two clicks and closing. Gonna be close.'

Nunk realised that the closing contacts would meet close to the perimeter of the airfield, at the very least showering lethal debris from above. He pulled the rim of his helmet lower. The three men stared silently as the first SAM closed in, making much faster progress that its fellow Patriot. As the two contacts merged the sound of a large explosion rumbled through the cabin with a dull 'crump'. The merged contact glowed brightly before fading from the screen. Ferrelli let out a war cry as he leapt from his seat. He stopped in his tracks as he noticed Nunk's quizzical expression. The second SAM had reached the point of impact. It should have ignited.

The white dot continued through the contact.

'No ignition Louie. We gotta rogue.'

With a dread that sent ice racing down his spine, Glover wheeled round to his console.

He was breathing in great gulps of stale air.

'Shit. Abort. Abort !' He held out his hands, as if frozen in his seat. His mind began to race through the sequence of instructions, his lips silently mouthing the words as he punched commands into the keyboard. Nothing happened. Lights continued to flash in front of his eyes. He had done everything. There were no other procedures. He began to panic.

'No abort Nunk,' he screamed.

'Try again.'

'I have. I got no manual and auto went dead. We gotta go for a shoot down.'

Glover knew that the chances of intercepting their own supersonic missile where virtually impossible. Nunk's fingers frantically rolled the tracking ball to locate the new target. The cross hair danced on the screen as the operator tried to lock on to the erratic path of the

SAM.

'Come on, come on you son of a.......'

'Too late, we got free fall,' Glover screamed. With the rocket motor burnt out, the Patriot was now a gliding bomb. The stabilisers now dead the missile began to arc back on its path. At an altitude of just under 300 feet the missile would hit the ground in seconds.

Glover stabbed vainly at the destruct button until his finger became a whole fist, slamming into the console. Sweat was pouring down his face. He was screaming.

'Explode you bastard.......explode.'

The detonation of the Scud had shaken the medical centre, smashing several windows and setting off the fire alarms. Water cascaded from the ceilings as the sprinkler system was activated. In Ward 8, Anna Pearson was finishing bandaging Walkers legs when they were both soaked by water spray. Through the shrieks of surprise Anna called out to Daines.

'Bill! Shut off the main valve. Its over the doorway.' As she turned back towards the flyers bed she felt a sudden surge of pressure in her head. She put her hand up to one ear as the high-pitched scream caused her to wince. The Patriot entered through the wall at the far end of the ward. The high explosive fragmentation warhead detonated on impact. In an instant the air was torn from her lungs before the shock wave hurled Anna Pearson across the ward, the plate glass window of her office shattered as her body catapulted through the glass. Liquid fire engulfed the confined space as the remaining occupants were vaporised. Finally, the fabric of the building could resist no more and gave way to the explosive pressure.

Ward 8 was blown apart sending debris arcing through the air. The black of the night changed briefly into day, illuminated by rolling clouds of flame that billowed up into the sky. Secondary explosions sent gas canisters snaking across the ground and overhead, power cables collapsed into the remnants of the Unit, bright white sparks crackling like lightning. As the roar of the explosions began to subside, fragments of wreckage began their slow descent back to earth.

Very suddenly, but for the crackling of flames, the air became silent again.

Two

Gulf of Bahrain, 02.30 hours.

Rob Latham eased the throttle lever forward, the twin engines of the Tornado GR3 responding with a surge of power that forced the Squadron Leader deep into his ejection seat. The bomber began a gradual ascent, at the same time increasing its speed to 600 knots. The night sky ahead was clear and brightly lit by starlight. To the north the horizon glowed with an orange hue, the result of earlier Coalition attacks. Latham scanned his instruments, the low glow of the luminous dials leaving his night vision unaffected. Directly in front of him, reflected onto the interior of the windshield, more information appeared as if suspended in thin air. The artificial horizon projected onto the head up display, gently glided to the left as Latham took his six-ship formation through a slow turn to port before settling back to the horizontal. The cockpit was silent apart from the low rumble of the engines and the hiss of static from his headset. Fifty minutes out off Muharraq the formation of four Tornado bombers and two Buccaneers had maintained a strict radio silence. Occasional bursts of chatter from supporting missions had interrupted the concentration but Latham had generally been pleased by the tight formation that the aircraft had maintained. Talk needed to be kept to an absolute minimum. Somewhere high above them American fighters were spoiling for a fight and with Iraq reluctant to launch aircraft during night raids, to the British bomber crews, the sense of frustration was palpable.

Latham's headset crackled.

'Mother One, 22k at One o'clock.' Latham's navigator, Mark 'Tommo' Thompson was first to visually identify the tanker rendezvous.

'Roger, Delta One closing.' Latham replied. High and to starboard he could just make out the silhouette of the Victor tanker, the distinctive high tail plane and four-engine plume confirming the identification. The one hook-up would ensure that, without further fuel, the formation could at least make friendly territory by the return leg of the mission. The refuelling would be made in silence. Latham opened his eyes wide, stretching his facial muscles. Night-time refuelling was notoriously taxing as well as potentially dangerous. The formation had had plenty of practice on the flight from England.

Latham lined up with the port wing of the large tanker

and slowly glided forward towards the drogue basket, the forty-foot long hose slowly extending from a fairing beneath the large crescent shaped wing. The drogue undulated gently in the slipstream of the Victor. Latham could hear the rhythm of his breathing increase. The large conical housing was lit by an array of tiny lights into which the pilot had to aim the refuelling probe. Making contact at the first attempt, Latham watched as the set of lights housed under the tankers fuselage turned to green to signal the successful flow of fuel. At that same moment his Number Two was taking in fuel from the starboard drogue. Latham drew back on completion and held formation on the wingtip as Max Ronson in Three slowly edged towards the dancing basket. The Tornado twitched constantly as Ronson made slight adjustments with the stick. Latham smiled as he recalled his wingman's description of in-flight refuelling as 'trying to poke fog into a bottle with a stick'. The irony was that he couldn't recall Ronson ever needing more than one attempt. Tonight was no exception. With the fourth Tornado replenished the bombers withdrew to allow the Buccaneers to approach.

Twenty-five miles from the Iraqi coast was the signal to break with the tanker and descend towards the sea. The Victor gracefully arced away to the south, its job for the night done. Latham envied the warm beds that the crews were heading for. At fifteen miles the formation dropped to 100 feet to avoid long-range radar. The zigzag flight path would add to the confusion as the aircraft headed in-land towards the first target north of Basra. One hundred miles out and the formation dropped to what had commonly become

known among the squadron as 'camel height'. The handle was the crew's method of dealing with a practice that had already taken the lives of two squadron colleagues in earlier missions. Latham eyed the desert floor as it undulated below his aircraft. The occasional Bedouin encampment flashed by as the moon shadows of the bombers raced across the arid terrain.
Nine minutes to contact.

An hour earlier the formation had pulled out of Muharraq, the radio chatter falling away as the heavily laden bombers climbed slowly up to altitude. In his rear station, Tommo had finished programming the on-board computer and armed the two Paveway guided bombs that hung from the Tornadoes belly. On the outer wing pylons two Sidewinder missiles were carried for self defence. All twelve men had received a comprehensive briefing two hours before on the two targets that would make up their mission. The cramped interior of the intelligence room had belied its former guise as a freight container. Surrounded by sand bags piled up on all four sides, the container was situated away from the aircraft in an attempt to look as inconspicuous as possible. With all of the crews present the air had soon grown thick under the heat of the spot lamps. Latham had poured over the cluttered briefing table that dominated the centre of the room. The intelligence boys had provided detailed maps showing each target, mixed with enlarged colour photocopies of aircraft, buildings and assorted Iraqi armament. This particular target, a large airfield had been attacked two days earlier, the main runway partially destroyed and the control tower knocked out.

That most of the images seemed to have been taken from *Janes* military manuals was a fact that had always amused Latham in previous briefings. The cold reality was that much of this information was relevant, largely up to date but unfortunately also available in most high street book shops.
The formation was to attack the heavily defended airfield at Jalibah before proceeding north to destroy a road bridge that spanned the Euphrates at Al Nasinya. Max Ronson and Geoff Halliday in Three would be tasked with that attack alone, the other aircraft providing cover. Latham eyed the black and white image of the bridge, the old box girder construction giving it a heavy, over-engineered look. A newer, concrete structure would have required more firepower to bring it down. One hit on the central arch, he calculated. And then get the hell out.

As the briefing drew to an end a WRAF officer had begun to move silently among the flyers as if collecting at a Sunday service. This was the moment Latham dreaded the most. As he handed over his personal effects he paused as he pulled at his engagement band. He tried to picture Jenny's face but the image was clouded. The last evidence of his identity dropped into the plastic pouch and it was sealed shut. All that he had now was the number and name he wore around his neck. He had considered wearing the ring around his neck, but the opportunity for a switched on Iraqi interrogator to exploit, presented too much of a threat. Tommo had run through the final equipment check with his pilot, tightening straps, checking pouches and generally encouraging each other. Latham could feel the slight pressure from the Walther PPK that was strapped to the inside of his left calf. Around his waist was £5000 worth of gold sovereigns wrapped in one of two silk escape maps. In the event of a capture the money could be used to buy a man out of trouble, but if this failed each pilot carried a note written in English and Arabic promising a reward of £20,000 on the safe return of a downed airman.

02.45 hours.

Six minutes from the target and Latham eased the control column back to begin the climb to 15,000 feet. At the same time every navigator in the formation activated his aircraft's electronic countermeasures. The Iraqi airfield defences comprised Soviet built surface to air missiles together with older radar guided anti-aircraft batteries. The RAF had already lost two aircraft to this wall of fire. With a high cloud base the Buccaneer boys would have little difficulty in marking the target for the Tornadoes. Each of these elderly bombers carried laser designators that would reflect a beam of light from the target, allowing each of the Paveway bombs to glide to a direct hit. The navigators in each aircraft now had a responsibility of delivering the weapons while still monitoring the very real threat of detection by the enemy.

Latham scanned the immediate horizon for a visual identification of the target. His headset began to pick up a pulse.

'PLB boss. Sounded English.' Tommo adjusted his receiver as the signal from the personal locator beacon drifted in and out of range. Somewhere in the darkness, several thousand feet below, was a stranded airman.

'Mark it and send it on the return leg, Tommo.' The instruction was immediate, Latham briefly allowing himself the thought of a fellow flyer, stranded many thousands of miles from home and staring up at the distant and disappearing lights of friendly aircraft. The Iraqi's would have heard him too. He shivered and stretched himself in his harness.
Three minutes.

The Buccaneers now eased ahead of the formation and climbed to 20,000 feet. The Tornadoes would await confirmation of each designated target before beginning a shallow dive to deliver their bombs. In Buccaneer Delta Five, navigator Gary Mills searched the airfield below on the black and white monitor between his knees. A familiar shape came into view on the screen.

'Target acquired, Delta One away.'
Latham immediately eased the stick forward and dived. In the rear seat, Tommo could monitor the target as the Tornado bucked and pitched in the turbulence. The large Antonov transport filled the frame, the thin cross hair of the designator hovering over the centre of the fuselage. His thumb held steady over the release button.

'Bombs gone.'
Latham felt the aircraft buck as Tommo released the 1000 lb Paveway. He pulled hard on the stick and applied full power. High above, the Buccaneers held a steady course to maintain contact with their targets. As the lead Tornado pulled a 4g turn and climbed away from the airfield, Tommo's eyes remained fixed on the monitor. With a blinding flash the screen turned white

before the image was restored to a scene of smoke and debris. The navigators voice was calm and business like.

'Delta One, splash one transport.'

One by one the Tornadoes delivered their munitions unhindered, the main runway taking more direct hits as well as many hangars and outer buildings. Latham looked back over his shoulder. In the far distance, the explosions started as small pin pricks of white light before billowing into the sky in an orange cloud of tangled wreckage. As the bombers departed to the north, debris could be seen snaking its way skywards before gracefully arcing its way back down to earth. There was no celebration, no contact and no acknowledgement as the final target had been despatched. There was no need.

With dawn breaking to the east, the formation began to accelerate to altitude, each navigator returning his attentions to the threat of retaliation. The extra height would decrease the possibility of a missile successfully acquiring a heat source. Something clipped Latham's vision, his head snapping to the right. The tell tale white plume of a missile exhaust was snaking up from below. Before he could call out, his headset exploded with noise.

'SAM, SAM, SAM !' Tommo screamed. 'Five o'clock low'. Warning klaxons filled the cockpit, the tell tale whine of a designated missile filling Latham's ears. He pulled the control column back as far as it would go, at the same instant punching the throttles forward and sitting the Tornado on its tail. The aircraft rocketed towards the higher cloud cover, both men pushed deeper into their ejection seats. Anti-gravity corsets inflated around their legs to counter the violence of the 5g turn, the blood being forced to remain in their upper bodies to prevent a blackout. Tommo forced a gloved hand down onto his console, his fingers stretched wide to make contact. He hit the switch. From beneath the rear of the fuselage, a flare canister immediately burst into a shower of phosphorescent light. Tommo wrenched his head backwards in an effort to find the SAM when an explosion threw the Tornado forward. The aircraft shook violently as shrapnel beat a tattoo against the fuselage. The canopy above Latham cracked but, miraculously, held together as more debris rained against the aircraft. The control column whip-lashed between his legs as the bomber went into a turbulent spin. Latham grabbed at the stick with both hands with his world spinning about him. As he wrestled with the controls a fleeting shadow flashed across his vision. A Tornado spiralling in a desperate attempt to out manoeuvre another SAM. In his headset, he heard the scream.

'Locked onto me!' It was Max in Three. Latham regained control as the bomber settled into a shallow dive. At three thousand feet he pulled into a climb and began to search for the rest of the scattered formation. Contact was soon made with the two Buccaneers. They had been able to monitor the progress of the SAMs and climb to a higher altitude.

'Delta One, this is Delta Five, over.' Gary Mills voice was calm as he surveyed the scene from on high. He had identified the first SAM an instant before the formation had scattered, Mark Thomson's warning filling his ears.

'Delta Five, this is Delta One. We have slight damage but systems are live, over.' At that moment two sand coloured Tornadoes formed on Latham's starboard wing, each bathed in the golden glow of a rising sun. Two and Four had been able to dive away to the south and had escaped the strobes of the missile battery. Max Ronson was still missing. As the ten remaining aircrew searched the skies around them, the bombers began to accelerate north. A familiar voice invaded the airwaves.

'Delta Three playing follow my leader, over.' For once Latham was relieved to hear Max's informal chatter over the intercom.

'Another few seconds and you would have been looking for a new best man, boss.'

'OK Three, stow it and make a visual.' Latham smiled with relief. Forming on the rear aircraft, Ronson's Tornado appeared from below. As the aircraft drew level with his own, Latham surveyed the length of the fuselage searching for any signs of damage.

'Sorry boss, had to go low for a bit of canyon dodging.' Latham could see the whites of Ronson's teeth as he gave the thumbs up from his cockpit. Max was a good pilot and more than capable of looking after himself. His natural ebullience, however, had frequently found him at odds with the strict protocol of a wartime situation. Senior officers had had many occasions to consider Ronson as dangerous, but his sheer talent for fast jet flying had tilted the balance in his favour. With Max, thought Latham, the pros far outweighed the cons.

The bridge at Al Nasirya, as far as the latest

intelligence had reported, would not be defended but would require a different method of attack. Unlike the soft ground targets at Jalibah, the bridge was a solid, well built structure. Delta Three would have to attack from a greater height to give the Paveway more penetration. In the early morning haze, the formation was soon circling the target. Far below, the Euphrates meandered its way through the town of Al Nasinya, largely a sprawl of single and two-storey residential buildings. The bridge stood at the northern end of an industrial site and joined the town with the main highway to Basrah in the east. There was little sign of life on the early morning roads, but with a large civilian population, the delivery would need to be accurate. The designator Buccaneer soon acquired a fix on the central span of the bridge, the two-lane highway empty as Delta Three began its dive. At fifteen thousand feet Ronson released his last bomb and the Tornado climbed away on full reheat. High above, the Buccaneer navigator waited for the impact. As the five remaining bombers re-formed on each other, a calm voice relayed the message.

'Check one bridge.'

The return route had taken the formation over the Shamiya Desert at minimum height and at full speed. At such low levels the Buccaneers came into their own. Originally built for naval carrier operations, the reinforced structure of the bomber was ideally suited to the intense buffeting encountered during ultra-low level flight. Latham felt slightly envious of the smoother ride that the older bombers were getting. The airways remained silent as the six aircraft zigzagged their way towards the Saudi border. A second rendezvous with a tanker was swiftly refused when the threat of Iraqi aircraft in the vicinity became apparent. The formation dropped lower. After a further hour of flying Latham broke radio silence. With fuel becoming an important factor, the news he received from Muharraq was not good.

'That's a negative Delta One. We have a missile alert in progress. Request that you re-route to Al Baduyi immediately. Good luck.'

Some thirty miles to the west, Al Baduyi had been a small Saudi Air Force transport field before the war. Taken over by the Americans, the base was being used for covert operations behind the Iraqi border. It also acted as a relief landing ground for Muharraq. Latham brought the formation straight in and taxied immediately off the runway. There would be plenty of other aircraft diverting tonight. As soon as the aircraft had come to a halt, technicians ran towards the bombers. Latham sat back in his seat, his head tilted back and eyes closed. In his headset he could hear Tommo's whooping war cries. He leant forward to loosen his straps, the whole of his back soaked in sweat. Cold morning air flooded into the cockpit as the canopy was raised. The air tasted good. Latham removed his helmet and mask, the latter leaving an angry red imprint where the rubber lining had been pulled tight against his face. As he began to run through his sequence of post flight checks, rendering the aircraft safe, he noticed a tall figure in an American officer's uniform standing in the shadow of one of the flood light towers that surrounded the apron. Intelligence, he thought, watching a technician removing the mission video cassette from beneath his aircraft. The officer stepped forward and, receiving the tape, motioned to Latham a squat building at the side of one of the larger hangers. Latham waved back and, before shutting down the main consul, checked the fuel gauges. Empty.

The small base had doubled in size in the build up to the ground offensive in late December. Aircraft seemed to inhabit every available space on the tarmac dispersal areas. There was a constant movement of men and traffic, the large double rotor Chinooks particularly conspicuous by their distinctive thudding signature. With the extra traffic of the night, the base would be stretched to capacity. After a shower and a change of clothes, the British flyers were shown to the main Officers Mess. The brightly lit bar was empty except for a Chinook crew recently returned from a mission. Ronson wandered over to the four men.

'You boys part of the dirty tricks brigade then?' Max waved a bottle of Budweiser in their general direction. The load master, a large Texan, studied the British flyer over the top of his glasses.

'Sorry sir, I'm afraid that's on a need to know basis.' Max turned and winked at Latham before offering a hand to the American. A large grin appeared across his weary face.

'Of course, of course. Stupid of me to ask. Max Ronson, Royal Air Force, Muharraq. That's my Spitfire parked outside.' The American hesitated before slowly shaking Ronson's hand.

'You guys know about Muharraq?' The look of concern concentrated the attention of all of the British flyers. It was Max who answered.

'Should we ? We knew they had an alert on, that's why we dropped in on you.'

The Texan slowly removed his hand.

'Jeez sorry guys, but they took a coupl'a Scuds tonight.' Ronson's face dropped.

'Casualties?'

'No word yet, but we heard they were hit pretty bad. Nothin' else come through yet 'cept a lot more planes than we're used to here.'

The door to the mess opened and the tall intelligence officer entered. He was brisk in his delivery.

'Gentlemen, we are ready for your debrief. Would you please follow me.' Latham was still looking at Ronson's dazed expression when the officer approached him.

'Sir, there is a telephone call for you from you base. If you follow me, I'll take you to the office.' Latham swigged the last of his beer and left with the officer. The remaining crews were taken through a maze of stark white corridors before they found themselves in a small projection room. Several rows of seats faced a large screen at one end. As they took their places, the American officer appeared through the door and took his place behind a lectern at the front of the screen. He began with a briefing on the known situation at Muharraq.

The men sat in silence as they listened to the details of the raid. Although the casualties were initially reported as light, there was an air of despondency among the flyers. The mission tapes began to roll as a resident RAF intelligence officer ran through the two raids. The usual bravado of previous missions was missing as the black and white images direct hits played on the screen. Ronson's navigator, Geoff Halliday took notes on his knee-pad as the film continued. Ronson sat silently in his seat, the images of destruction playing

before his tired eyes.
Finally the footage of the bridge was shown from a more detailed viewpoint. The nose of the Paveway bomb also carried a colour camera, which would show the path to the exact point of impact. On a split screen, the aerial view of the target was augmented with a view from the nose cone. The footage started with a view under Ronson's Tornado before a sudden jolt revealed the release and freefall. The Paveway took twenty-one seconds to reach the target. The crewmembers watched in silence, the bridge growing ever larger on the screen. At seven seconds from impact Ronson sat bolt upright in his seat. From the bottom left of the screen a large vehicle could be seen making its way onto the bridge. As the bomb homed in, the bus revealed more of its detail. In that final second before detonation the yellow, American-style school bus loomed large. It was full.
The screen went black.

'Noooo!.' Ronson stood and turned on the Buccaneer crew sat directly behind him. He was across the seat and holding the navigator by the throat before hands could drag him away.

'You bastards. Why didn't you abort ? Why didn't you tell me?' Ronson was hauled back, the navigator gasping for air.

'I…I..didn't have time Max. You saw how quick it was.' It was Halliday who grabbed his pilot and forced him out through the door and into the narrow corridor. Ronson was shaking.

'What the fuck were they doing there at five o'clock in the bloody morning?' His eyes were wide, his hands outstretched. Tears streaked his reddened face.

'Just..just stow it Max. We all feel the same mate, but there was little we could have done. You can't blame the Bucc boys.' Halliday stepped back as Ronson slumped against wall of the corridor. At the far end Rob Latham stood silently, his hands placed on his hips, head slightly bowed. Slowly, he began to make his way down the passageway towards the group.

Ronson looked up. He saw the eyes. He knew.

Latham held out a hand.

'I'm so sorry Max. It's Anna

Three

Al Kut, Central Iraq
2nd November 1993,
02.01 hours

The car was late. Abdul Kamal angled his Rolex towards the yellow glow of the street lamp. Ten minutes now and the narrow alleyway had remained silent. He searched for the crumpled packet in his shirt pocket. The glowing ember of the previous cigarette lay at his feet, several butts scattered nearby. He felt sick. He knew that the nicotine would only heighten the nerves but the rush felt too good, too comforting. He would need to bathe before returning home. Halah hated the smell. She said it reminded her of the war, when everyone had smoked. She would know that there was something wrong. The beam of headlights cut across the cobbled stone of the wall opposite Kamal. The car was large, the sides barely clearing the walls as it edged its way up the alley. 'This was it,' he

thought. The Service favoured the imported four-wheel drive vehicles that gave them an air of menace. It would also be black.
Kamal moved from the doorway he had been sheltering in, the powder blue folder he carried conspicuous in his grasp. Lights were dipped three times and the Shogun drew level with the doorway. The windows were tinted black. Kamal tried the rear door handle and climbed up into the cab. The interior had a new car smell of leather and air freshener. Although he could see the eyes of the driver reflected in the rear view mirror, he knew that no contact would be made. The journey to Baghdad would take some two hours. Kamal settled back into the deep, cushioned seat and gripped the folder on his lap. He opened the window a couple of inches, conscious of his own smell of tobacco and stale sweat. His shirt, clean on not an hour earlier, now seemed to form a second skin. He grasped his fists tight. It had been three years, and now the Mukhabarat wanted him again.

Since the end of the war, the Iraqi intelligence services had suffered in wake of the defeat. Part of many who were blamed for the capitulation to the West, the Mukhabarat had been purged for any perceived weaknesses. Many officers were executed in the months following Saddam Hussein's pledge to avenge the 'betrayal of the people' in a route that destroyed many families. Saddam vented his rage at the very heart of the military. Armed troops came in the night, houses raided and many hundreds of men interned at the Al Nihiya prison in central Baghdad, the former royal residence known as '*The Palace of the End*' for its murderous reputation. Kamal had lost many colleagues that night, including his brother-in-law. Hassan had served with the Republican Guard and had formed part of the personal protection that had surrounded the regime at the time of the Iraq-Iran war in the early Eighties. A number of unpublicised assassination attempts, all of them made by Iraqi militants, had failed to kill Saddam. Two of his rumoured doubles had been killed, and this only served to fuel an increasing distrust of those around him. The first raids took those closest to the top of the chain of command and, as head of Saddam's travel protection, Hassan became one of the earliest victims.

Kamal tried to picture his brother-in-law as he gazed through the darkened windows. The hair and clothes were clear. He could even hear Hassan's distinctive cackling laughter. It was the face that did not register. His grandmother had always said that the eyes were the first to be forgotten once friends had parted. Kamal doubted that he was still alive. The Shogun jolted as it crossed a single rail track. The road straightened, beginning to shadow the path of a wide river. The driver tuned the radio randomly, a cacophony of music and talk between the bursts of static interference. After a few frustrating minutes he settled on a banned US Forces station, the alien sounds of Western rock music turned up to fill the interior of the Shogun. Kamal shifted uncomfortably in his seat. The music reminded him of the war, the dark star lit nights deep in the desert, the radio operator eaves-dropping on Allied music stations. It was banned, as it had always been but Kamal imagined it was a practice all sides were guilty of.

Kamal saw little sign of life as the once busy Tigris flowed past. To the north west the horizon began to give up the darkness of the night and the distant mountains began to gain ominous silhouettes. Gradually the desert plain revealed random pockets of humanity. Scattered settlements merged as the outskirts of Baghdad grew closer. Traffic began to slow their progress as they approached the centre of the urban sprawl. Kamal had not visited the capital since the beginning of the war. Gazing out through the gap in the window, he was struck by the sense of normality. There were few signs of the damage inflicted by the air-raids and American cruise missiles. Municipal buildings had risen from the ruins with an obscene alacrity that had angered many who had lost their own property. While the very fabric of the state was re-assembled, much of the squalor of suburban Baghdad remained unchanged. With little sentiment for the country at large, the centre of the city had been restored to symbolise the opulence of the Al Takriti regime. It had cost millions.

Although the hour was early, the streets were already busy with trade. Buses and taxis began to slow their progress further. At the southern end of Zowrah Park the Shogun passed under the Victory Arch that had been erected to commemorate the victory over Iran in 1988. Kamal gazed up at the towering crossed swords, each scimitar held by a colossal bronze arm, said to have been modelled on those of the President. In the increasing light of the dawn sun the monument looked suffused with blood. Kamal had fought in the eight-year war, which had cost the lives of over 400,000 of his countrymen. More lost comrades flickered through his memory, hazy, bloodied faces and the twisted bodies of yet more victims. He tried to block the thoughts out by focussing on familiar landmarks. Another half mile and the Shogun would pass into the Al-Mansur district. Once past the now empty Western embassies and his journey would finish at the gates of Mukhabarat headquarters. Kamal drummed his fingers along the walnut sill of the door as the traffic lights remained on red. He lowered the window an extra inch. His gaze settled on the drivers hands as they gripped the steering wheel. No signal, Kamal thought. He should be turning left at this junction.

The Mansur Miliyah Hotel stood at the end of a long tree lined avenue. The Shogun's wheels had spun as it darted down the narrow side streets that snaked between the Ahrahr and Sinak bridges. Kamal had been forced back in his seat at the traffic lights. He knew that this was an evasion route in case of pursuit. His mind raced as unfamiliar road signs flashed by. He could feel the sickness in his stomach returning. His temple ached. After back tracking through the market sprawl of the Al-Ishbiya district, the car began to slow. Several of the large hotels so favoured by Westerners before the war, passed by before the Shogun turned into Haifah Street. The smell of orange blossom filled the air, in stark contrast to the stench of the market streets. As the car slowed to walking pace, Kamal realised his destination. The white paint had begun to fade from the once bright façade, the Miliyah now a pale imitation of the venue that had attracted so much wealth in the Sixties. Built in the high rise style of the period, the more it became run down, so the clientèle became less particular. Once used as a sanctuary for high- ranking Ba'thist officials and members of the Al-Takriti family in particular, those who wished not to be seen had increasingly used the hotel. It was this knowledge that terrified Kamal. Drawing level with the lobby entrance, the door of the Shogun was opened by a tall, bearded man in a Western style black double-breasted suit. The expensive American Rayban sunglasses only served to emphasise the wire that trailed behind his left ear. As the car glided silently away the man gestured for Kamal to enter the hotel.

The ride in the lift had taken place in complete silence, the Mukhabarat agent staring only ahead with his hands clasped across his abdomen, the legs planted firmly apart. On the seventh floor Kamal was shown into the bedroom suite of a large penthouse. Still no words were spoken. He waited for the agent to leave before approaching the large double doors that led to the rest of the apartment. Muffled voices from beyond indicated at least three men in the next room. He heard the agent enter but could not hear his voice. Kamal quickly returned to the side of the large bed as the sound of approaching footsteps grew louder. He could feel his pulse rate increase, the throbbing in his temple causing him to wince. The doors slowly opened.

The tall figure of Uday Saddam Hussein al-Takriti paused briefly before entering the suite. Dark, piercing eyes slowly scanned the room before settling on Kamal. The lean frame was dressed casually in expensive Western designer labels, all unavailable to the Iraqi on the street. Kamal stood his ground as the aroma of strong aftershave filled his nostrils. Uday pulled a gold cigarette case from his jacket. He snapped it open in a melodramatic movement calculated to impress. Kamal stood motionless as the Gauloise was lit.

'You are Kamal?' Uday spoke through a cloud of acrid smoke.

'I am.' Kamal answered before fear invaded his reason …….sir.'

'You know me?'

'All of Iraq knows you as the son and rightful heir of our great and exulted leader.'

Kamal bowed slightly as he eyed the most hated man in Iraq.

'You think so Kamal?' Uday sneered as he blew a slow stream of smoke from his nose.

'It is the will of the people sir. You are the chosen….' Uday held up a hand.

'Spare me your platitudes, Kamal. You don't convince me.' A humourless smile crossed Uday's face. Kamal could feel his temples burn.

'Come, let us discuss business.' Uday beckoned a figure from the shadows of the penthouse. The small, overweight man was dressed in a rumpled cream coloured suit that tried, unsuccessfully, to hide the bulge of his stomach. The air conditioning had done little to freshen the air around him. He looked more nervous than Kamal felt, a shaking hand constantly wiping at his brow. He carried a brown leather attaché case.

'You know Hamdani?' Uday drew deeply as he spoke, the gesture almost dismissive.

'I….I don't think that we have met, sir.' Kamal lied. Hamdani had been one of the head guards at the Al-Nahiya when Kamal had tried to find out more information about his brother in law. This was the same nervous grin that denied all knowledge of his whereabouts, the same darting eyes that betrayed so much more. Within the ranks of the Mukhabarat, Hamdani was also known as Uday Hussain's personal fixer. No job was too dirty for Hamdani. Many who had crossed the Iraqi leaders son would end up in his hands. Arriving in the dead of night, the suspected rivals, enemies and anyone perceived as a threat to Uday's rise to power, would be met by Hamdani and his guards. Rumours had circulated that these killings were actually sanctioned by his father. These theories were supposedly quashed in the summer of 91 when Saddam was forced to act on his son's predilection for rape. Although similar in many ways, Sadaam had often been angered by his son's seeming lack of restraint around women. Usually drunk, Uday would often patrol the deserted streets of Baghdad by night. His red Porsche, together with carloads of bodyguards would move from club to club. The dance floors would clear as the entourage swept in, pausing only briefly before leaving with the chosen entertainment for the night. If unsuccessful Uday would take to kidnapping women from the streets, the victims then being abandoned out in the desert and left to make their own way back to the city, all dignity shattered. Very few spoke out. Those who did were not seen again. Saddam himself, on two separate occasions, had had to pay off the families of men his son had murdered in sudden piques of rage.

The situation came to a head when Saddam discovered that one of his most senior Air Force officers had been shot and seriously wounded by Uday in a nightclub fracas. Uday was summoned to the Presidential palace and once again a family was paid to keep its silence. This time the actions seemed to bring about a change in Uday. Chastened, and mindful of his brother Qusai's increasing affection in his father's eyes, he laid low for several weeks before continuing his pattern of destruction. Despite being surrounded by sycophants, Uday became wary of his father's attitude. No longer was the oldest son certain of his future. For Uday a new challenge was needed, something that would harness his energy and prove beyond all doubt that he, and he alone, was the rightful heir to his father's dynasty.

Uday took a folder from Hamdani's case. Kamal could see printed sheets and photographs as Uday leafed through the document. Without looking up he spoke.

'By all accounts, a hero of the State, Kamal.'

'You honour me sir. I was…am...fortunate to serve.' Kamal stammered. Uday read aloud from the report in his hands.

'The sole survivor of a launch unit wiped out by British butchers, I see. Refresh my memory Kamal. How did you escape?' Kamal coughed to clear his parched throat.

'May I be allowed a glass of water, sir?' Uday held up a hand.

'That won't be necessary. Please proceed.'

'I was…I mean.. my detachment had just launched our round when we were ambushed by a British unit. I heard their shouts. I was trained in Britain in the Seventies. I…I knew that the accent was not American. I ran from a floor hatch in the control unit. The gas tanker was parked at the edge of the wadi and I made for that. From the cab I watched my unit destroyed. Every man. They took no surrender. It was annihilation. I was spotted but they came no closer than fifty metres. They seemed to know. No firing. They just stood and watched me.'

Uday was handed another file by Hamdani. More photographs and anonymous faces were fleetingly glimpsed. Kamal was hesitant but continued to speak.

'Th…the keys were still in the ignition. They just watched me as I escaped, made no attempt to follow me. It was the Sarin, they knew about the gas. I was very…..'

Uday held up a hand.

'Allah was indeed merciful that night. It seems that you were destined to serve him further.' Kamal bowed slightly and was about to speak when Uday changed tack.

'I see that your daughter is about to start school next month.' The smile was cold. Kamal felt his shoulders slump. The reference to Milay caused his heart to race. He could feel his face draining of blood. The room suddenly felt icy cold. Uday continued.

'And I see that your wife has returned to teaching in…where was it?' He leafed through the papers in his hands. Kamal worked his mouth, the delivery hoarse and monotone.

'Al Kut.'

'Ah yes, indeed. A noble calling.' Uday was still smiling. 'A genial existence in which to raise a family. I see that your war pension allows you to live in some comfort.' An A4 page was pulled from the file and held up. The colour photograph was an enlarged view of the Kamal residence in the wealthy Aradah district of Al-Kut. Taken from the air, the washing was visible hanging in the roof garden. Uday held the glossy image just long enough, until he saw the desired reaction in Kamal's eyes. Again, the cold smile.

'Good, good. Now that I seem to have your full attention I would like you to tell me who this is.' The image was of a superior quality, a carefully posed portrait of a woman in her mid thirties. Her black hair was short, the cut expensive and Western. The large dark eyes wore little make up. Such a striking gaze needed little to enhance it. Kamal had not seen Aisha Taraz for five years. The image before him was more contemporary. He was shocked to see her face, the memory of her had begun to fade over the past two years.

The brief, but exhilarating affair had shocked him at first. He had always considered himself contented with his lot. In Halah he had all he could have wished for in a partner. The birth of his child had only served to enhance the sanguine nature of his life to date. In Aisha, however, other instincts overtook him. They had trained together as part of a new intake to the Mukhabarat. As the elite of the secret service, operatives were trained to suit all surroundings. With her traditional black abaya removed, Aisha became an added distraction for the men of the academy. Her striking appearance, she had a poise and natural grace of movement that displayed her toned body to the full, had deemed her unapproachable by many men on the campus. Kamal had also been struck by her calm confidence. She also seemed devoid of the arrogance often present in one so physically attractive.

As they trained together, Kamal found that Aisha was

beginning to work her way into his existence. For some reason, he had been chosen. The occasional meetings in corridors, in the silent restraint of the library, even along the route to his Baghdad flat seemed to have been pre-meditated. Kamal gradually felt overwhelmed by the exhilaration of being pursued. In the end it had taken little to ignite the inevitable. A not so chance meeting in the cool evening air of Zowrah Park had led to the quiet confines of a small hotel on the outskirts of the city. The affair lasted three short months before guilt drew Kamal back to his family. And there she was before him. Five years on. She had grown into the sophisticated beauty that Kamal had always predicted. Fully formed. No match for a mere man. She looked as if she had gained that missing attitude. The eyes looked serious, cold even.

'Yes I know her.' He answered.

'Of course you do. What was it? Three, four months back in Eighty eight?'

Kamal nodded slowly as Uday approached him. A firm hand was placed on his shoulder.

'How would you like to work with her again Kamal? Eight, ten months overseas. Purely professional of course, your wife may never know.' There seemed little choice.

'You were such a team in Algeria, Kamal. What an opportunity to continue the partnership.' Kamal nodded silently.

'And the mission, sir?' Uday's face visibly brightened. He gripped Kamal's shoulder.

'Ah yes, the mission.' He turned away, as if deep in thought. After a pause he turned to face Kamal again, his head tilted to one side.

'My father is a great man, Kamal. And great

men require great gestures to honour them. Aisha Taraz will brief you fully but suffice to say that I am placing in your hands the opportunity to prove, once again, that my fathers dominance is all-powerful. You are on a world stage, Kamal. You have greatness at your fingertips' Uday gripped Kamal by both shoulders. In an instant the smile was gone.

'I will leave Hamdani to brief you further. You will leave for Paris tomorrow morning. Tell your wife what you like - except the truth.' Uday turned to leave. As he reached the doorway he paused. Without turning he spoke.

'We will not use you again, Kamal. The rewards will be beyond your comprehension.' He turned. The face was impassive. 'And I will personally guarantee the safety of your family.'

It was the last declaration that decided Kamal's next move.

December 3rd

The flight from Damascus had taken a little over five hours to reach French airspace. The Air France 757 had landed in Greece to refuel before continuing over the Swiss Alps. Kamal had spent much of the flight with his eyes closed as his mind ran over Hamdani's briefing. As was usual with Mukhabarat policy, the information was kept to a minimum. Kamal was to make contact with Aisha through a Paris contact. She and Kamal would head a cell of five operatives, each a specialist in their own field. The nature of the mission would remain unknown until the cell had been fully assembled. It did not do to dwell on the nature of such missions. Kamal had long given up trying to second guess. Piecing the puzzle together clouded your

judgement and Kamal preferred to know little until he was needed. What he did know for certain was that if his involvement was needed, it meant the presence of some form of guided weapon system.
On the decent into a rain swept Paris-Orly, his thoughts were of Halah. She had taken the news with a calm acceptance that had betrayed her sense of inevitability. Another sudden departure with little in the way of explanation, her eyes looked tired as a look of resignation crossed her face. There were few tears as he left. He didn't wake the child.

Customs were a formality. He was always stopped. They knew he would never be caught carrying anything. Previous trips had been interspersed with meaningless family breaks to the capitals of Europe. He despised using his family as a cover, but the ploy seemed to work. Travelling alone, he would be tailed as soon as he left the terminal. Pursuit, boredom, even a sarcastic wave as he boarded the aircraft. On this occasion, he was kept in a side room for forty- five minutes before an abrupt inspector allowed him a three-month pass. Easily long enough for a person to disappear.

Laden with luggage and clasping his passport between his teeth, Kamal began a deliberate slow walk out onto the congested scrum of the main concourse. Only one case contained his personal effects, the other three would be dumped later. He was now tagged. Stopping to light a cigarette, Kamal glanced up at the large analogue clock at the far end of the hall. Five minutes. Pausing by the main entrance to buy a *Paris Match*, Kamal continued on through the sliding doors and out onto the wide expanse of the Taxi rank. To his

right a large line of passengers queued, while a steady stream of coaches embarked groups bound for central Paris. The stairway to the Metro link lay to his left. Orly was busy tonight.
On the far side of the traffic queue, a white Citroen taxi nosed its way into the flow and joined the slow procession towards the terminal entrance. A powder blue folder lay on the dashboard. Kamal began to feel inside his pockets as if to appear distracted. From the corner of his vision he could see the white car, the bright *libre* lamp lit, edging its way closer. In one movement Kamal swept up his luggage and made for the taxi. The lamp flashed off and after a brief exchange, the luggage was loaded and journey to Paris begun.

As in the Shogun, there was no communication with the driver. Nor was there anything other than eye contact with the body double that crouched in the foot well of the rear passenger cabin. Kamal gazed down at himself. The same deep brown eyes, long Arab nose and carefully trimmed moustache, if a little fuller in the face, he thought. The hair had been shaved back to mimic Kamal's bald pate, but the illusion was still unnervingly realistic to Kamal. The taxi began to pick up speed as it entered the outer suburbs of Paris, Kamal preparing himself for the switch by occasionally bending forward, as if searching through hand luggage. During a turn at a busy intersection close to the Sacre Cour, the switch was made. The doppelganger was dropped at Gare de L'Est together with Kamal's luggage. Only one case was swapped and Kamal's possessions remained in the spare tyre well of the boot. By nightfall the rogue Kamal would be approaching Vienna. For the next two hours the taxi toured Paris picking up predetermined fares. From the cramped confines of the foot well Kamal recognised some of the faces as experienced operatives. Others were newer, younger and unknown to him. Eventually the Citroen entered an underground car park close to the Left Bank. Kamal was dropped and after a change of clothing, left to make his own way.

Four

North Cornwall, England
December 27th
The small boy cupped his hands over his eyes, the low winter sun making him squint. From his cliff top perch he scanned the distant horizon. He had lost them.
The low afternoon cloud had broken from the grip of the sea, allowing a thin strip of blue sky to line the horizon. Still the boy searched. Some hundred feet below, the North Atlantic swell sent plumes of water crashing against the jagged coastline. The sea hissed as each wave dissolved back into the depths.
Again. There they were, two small dots travelling just above the line of the horizon. The boy climbed slowly to his feet, his eyes fixed seaward. As he watched the dots began to move closer to each other as they approached the distant peninsular of Trevose Head. For a few brief seconds they seemed to merge into one and come to a halt. The boy frowned. The dot seemed

to be getting larger. He could just make out the dark smudge of jet exhaust against the lighter sky. A smile appeared as he realised that the aircraft were approaching, fast.

From the west the two jets banked, hugging the coastline towards the mouth of the Camel Estuary. Dark grey in appearance, the first fighter roared low across the flat sands of Polzeath beach and headed inland. The boy stood motionless, momentarily lost in the spectacle before him. The crackle of disturbed air caused him to turn, his senses shattered as the second aircraft banked low over his head. He instinctively ducked, his hands vainly protecting his ears from the assault. The fighter levelled before pulling into a steep climb, thunder echoing across the bay. As if mirroring its twin, the first jet, by now a distant speck on the horizon, began a near vertical ascent. The fighters converged as they rose higher until, at five thousand feet they disappeared into the cloud cover. The boy followed them as far as he could until only a distant rumble belied their presence. When he was sure they had gone he turned to search for his bicycle in the tall grass.

The large slab-sided fighter appeared from the clutches of the dense cloud and held formation on the starboard side of his wingman. Twitching from the slight adjustments of control, the dark grey English Electric Lightning F6 slowly edged forward until both aircraft were level. From the cockpit, the pilot eyed the second fighter. Brilliant in its natural aluminium finish, the second Lightning seemed of an older generation, the fuselage streaked and weathered by age.

Some forty minutes into a training sortie from Warton

in Lancashire, both aircraft carried large over-wing fuel tanks and were each armed with a pair of dummy Red Top air-to-air missiles.

As the fighters began to climb higher, a double pulse appeared simultaneously on each aircraft's radar screen. Nearing the end of their fuel range, the chances of a simulated attack by RAF Tornadoes increased with each dying minute of the sortie. The fighters immediately split formation and increased power, the silver Lightning diving away towards the sea, leaving the grey fighter to climb.

In the cockpit of the grey, the pilot's gloved hand pushed the throttle levers forward. The fighter would need to gain valuable height from his potential attacker. With the Tornadoes registering at twenty miles on the radar, the Lightning swung in a wide arc to face head-on to the aggressor. The dogfight was on. Through the viewing cowl of his Ferranti radar, the defender monitored the trace for deviations in speed and altitude, the modern Tornado enjoying a more impressive manoeuvrability and avionics that had rendered the Lightning visible far earlier. Seconds counted as the pilot constantly scanned a 360 degree sweep of the sky. At 16,000 feet the silence was broken by the aggressor.

'Contact. Target acquired.' In the cramped confines of the grey Lightning, the pilot searched through the canopy for any sign of contact. The cockpit suddenly filled with sound of screeching static, the pilot desperately fumbling for the volume control on his headset. The radar was dead. Through the interference, the same calm voice.

'Vis-ident, gaining for a lock.' The defender

strained to see over both shoulders. Nothing. No visual and no contact. Time for evasive action. The pilot lowered the nose of the Lightning and deployed the airbrakes. Below the large tail plane, on either side of the rear fuselage, two large panels were hydraulically raised to disrupt the airflow. Packed in small bundles in the well left by the brake panels, thousands of silver foil strips were caught in the slipstream forming a billowing cloud behind the fighter. The Lightning regained speed as the brakes were closed. It was a last gamble, but a deceptively simple ploy. Any aggressor radar screen would now be filled by multiple metallic contacts as the foil strips reflected the signal in their slow descent. An incoming missile could easily mistake the cloud for a larger target giving the defender valuable seconds.

As the pilot twisted and turned in a desperate search for contact, a dark grey blur flashed overhead. The noise in the cockpit ceased immediately as Rob Latham felt his fighter buck in the jet wash. This time the voice carried an edge.

'Lost lock. Repeat, lost lock. Probable gun kill.' Latham grinned as he caught sight of the other aggressor Tornado closing fast from the left. He hauled the large fighter onto its back and deployed the air brakes again. It was one bluff too many with the silver chaff a low tech' one-shot trick. The whine of a locked-on Sidewinder soon filled Latham's ears. End game.

The whooping noise that punctured the maelstrom in his headset jolted Latham. In an instant he knew what was happening.

'Hasta la vista, knob jockeys!' The scream mixed with the distinct bass growl of a Red Top acquiring its target. Max Ronson came spearing out of the cloud base in the near vertical and cut through the Tornado formation causing thc fighters to break hard.

'Fox Two and probable Fox One. Ronson claimed a missile kill and a possible shoot down with guns. Only development of the cine film at Warton would give him a confirmed double kill. With the Tornadoes breaking for RAF St Mawgan in the west for valuable fuel, the sortie was abandoned. Latham levelled out and searched the upper atmosphere for the telltale glint of polished steel. Ronson brought his fighter around in a slow arc and formed on his wingman. Soon the fighters were level at 15.000 feet. Latham could see the wide grin, bright white teeth framed by an impressive moustache. Then the familiar thumbs up.

'Look at those bastards run. One steam-driven beast taking out forty million quid's worth of state-of-the-art junk. Where were you Lathey?' Rob Latham raised a middle finger and stuck out his tongue. A bit of the old Max, he thought as he grinned to himself.

Latham had seen precious little of his friend's distinctive personality in the months that followed the Gulf War. The trauma of the loss of Anna, together with the Al Nasiriyah bridge incident had all but broken Max Ronson. Latham had volunteered to escort Ronson home from Bahrain on a VC10 that contained injured and former POW crewmembers. The two spoke little during the five-hour flight. At Brize Norton the air crew and their escorts had been separated as the medical teams took over. It would be four months before Ronson would reappear from counselling. In that time, he had changed. Gone was the ebullient centre of attention that had made Max such a popular and valuable member of the squadron. He and Latham had been due to marry their respective partners that summer. The wedding to Jenny had been overshadowed by Ronson's presence. It was too soon and Ronson had spent most of the day in the hotel bar. He had always liked a drink, but it now seemed to control him. Several brushes with the Military Police at Brize Norton had given his commanding officers enough ammunition. Ronson was damaged goods and the Air Force wanted him out.

At thirty-seven, Latham had fully expected to see out his remaining commission with an airline job in Civvy street the natural progression. The treatment of Max had changed all that. A year after the Gulf War, Flight Lieutenant Max Ronson, holder of the Distinguished Flying Cross and a veteran of thirty-two missions over Iraq, was discharged and paid off. They said that he was unfit to fly. Despite the gnawing realisation that the brass were right, the Forces lack of loyalty and the haste with which the case was dealt with sickened Latham. He had resigned his commission the following day. Jenny had shown understanding but it was clear that his friendship with Max was causing a strain. The rehabilitation that had begun slowly was often painful with Ronson becoming more and more isolated, his volatile nature stripping away the patience of friends and colleagues alike. Soon only Latham met with him on anything like a regular basis, Jenny having long since banned him from their home.

With many contacts made over the past fifteen years in the trade, Latham had wasted little time in advertising his availability within the aerospace industry. Through a former boss on his Tornado squadron, Latham was contacted about a couple of flying vacancies with the testing division of British Aircraft Limited. Flying out of Warton in Lancashire, the company was using two former RAF Lightning fighters as high-speed targets for a new radar system. The contact knew of Latham's departure from the Force but little of the circumstances. It was during a late night 'phone call to Warton that Latham tossed Ronson's name into the frame. When the contact revealed not even having ever heard of him, Latham took the chance. At first Ronson was reluctant to fly again. He was in no fit state to begin with, but with Latham's perseverance and a raw talent he could do little to suppress, the two signed contracts for a year of intensive testing. Ronson was in his element again.

High above the North Devon coastline the formation made contact with Warton for a course to return to base. As Latham increased throttle, his Lightning surged ahead of his wing man. Ronson did not follow. Latham searched for him in his mirrors. A mile behind, the silver fighter began to lose height. From the tail pipes a dark smudge of vapour left a Morse like pattern across the sky. Ronson pulled the nose higher.

'Target two, I have power loss in engine One. Fire warning. Am attempting re-light.'

Ronson's voice was calm over the intercom. Latham instinctively banked towards his wing-man and throttled back. The Lightning was struggling to maintain a nose-up attitude.

'I have negative re-light with fire warning confirmed.' Latham could hear the increased rhythm of Ronson's breathing through his headphones. The nose was dropping.

'Hold it Max. You're smoking, but no show on external fire, over.' Latham pulled under the rear of the fighter. The upper tail pipe was belching thick black smoke.

'Shutting down One and making for emergency landing. I'll need a heading, over.'

'Roger, contacting Exeter.'

Ronson began to bank his aircraft inland, the high ground of Exmoor passing below. Air traffic control at Exeter immediately cleared all channels and gave Latham a heading Distance was given at forty-two miles with two possible alternative landing grounds should they be required. To the south east lay the Fleet Air Arm station at Merryfield, east of Taunton. To the south, high on the Blackdown Hills, the former war time fighter base of Templemere offered one serviceable runway. On one engine, and with a high landing speed, Exeter was the best bet for the fighter. Latham maintained a safe distance from the starboard side of the slowing fighter. Twenty miles out, with the nose rising higher, Ronson lowered his wheels and opened the airbrakes to provide valuable drag. His voice remained calm.

'Two flaming out Rob. Losing fuel. Gotta go for a landing now.'

Latham knew that if Ronson lost the second engine now the big fighter would be virtually unflyable. Fifteen tons of dead metal gave Ronson mere seconds to select a crash site before ejecting.

'Gonna go for Templemere.' Ronson was now breathing hard.

The silver Lightning banked gradually to the east, the M5 motorway passing below as it snaked past through the Vale of Taunton. In the haze of the evening sun the plateau of the Blackdowns dominated the skyline. Ronson was losing height rapidly. With no control from the disused airfield, Ronson was relying on information from Exeter. Only one runway remained serviceable and that, at under two thousand feet would be perilously short. Latham gave himself more distance from the ailing fighter and lowered his own gear. Ahead, from a break in the woodland, a familiar triangular pattern of runways slowly appeared from the haze of dusk. They looked so small to Latham. Only one gave any impression of being used, the other two almost blending with the overgrown scrubland that made up the remainder of the airfield. Ronson would only get the one chance and the odds, as well as the runway, looked too short.

'Forget it Max. Climb and bang out.' Latham implored his wingman. No response.

With the tops of pine trees flashing ever closer, the two fighters continued their descent. Latham could see the disused control tower at the centre of the converging runways. The dark silhouette of two hangers lay off to the left of the airfield.

The silver belly of Ronson's Lightning cut through the treetops at 150 knots. As the perimeter of the field was crossed the runway threshold rushed up towards the fighter. Tyres bit heavily into the scarred tarmac. Dust and debris from the runway immediately entered the jet intake, at the same moment that the port tyre of the main undercarriage exploded. The control column was yanked from Ronson's hand as he fought to keep the fighters nose in line with the faded white lines strobing beneath him. His left fist grasped the throttle handle and shut the remaining Rolls Royce engine down. He then activated the engine bay extinguisher system.

Five hundred feet above Latham banked his Lightning over the airfield in a slow, wide turn. He had seen the tyre burst and now watched the fighter snaking its way along the runway. Ronson pulled on the break parachute release and the fighter bucked violently. Behind, the 'chute billowed in the slipstream before fully deploying. The speed was too fast. The silk canopy wrestled briefly with the huge forces being exerted on it before the steel hawser connecting it to the tail-plane was torn from its housing. Ronson felt the release with a sudden surge of speed. Both legs locked as he pulled hard, both hands grasping the break lever on the control column. The Lightning began to slide as the perimeter fence loomed large in Ronson's vision. Two hundred yards from the end of the runway, the fighter left the tarmac and ploughed into the soft grass of the verge. The nose wheel folded sending a great plume of earth into the intake and over the cockpit. Ronson instinctively raised his arms to protect his face. The fuselage briefly levelled as the nose raised, the underbelly rupturing as the fighter slewed sideways. An embankment brought the slowing Lightning to a gentle halt. Latham brought his machine low along the centre line of the runway. Below, the landing had gouged an ugly wound across Templemere's once sleepy surface. The stricken Lightning lay partially embedded in the embankment. Smoke hung thick in the air.

'Max, get out now. Can you hear me? Get out.' The head piece crackled with static. After what seemed to be an eternity, Latham saw the canopy slowly rise. Ronson struggled to haul himself from the cockpit before sliding, feet first down the fuselage. He hit the ground in a crumpled heap.

'Max, you bastard!......Whaaaoooooo!' Latham was screaming into the intercom, his fist punching the plexiglass of his canopy. He ripped his oxygen mask from his face.

'You beauty!' Cleaning up the undercarriage he lit both afterburners as he crossed the end of the runway and rocketed skywards. Coming off the top of a loop in a slow victory roll, Latham dropped the power for another pass. With the undercarriage lowered he began to radio Exeter for assistance. As the Lightning came in over the crash site, Latham could see Ronson walking away from the fighter. His head was bowed as he removed his helmet. Slowly he sank to his knees, his whole frame shaking as he began to sob uncontrollably.

Five

Somerset, England.
February 5th 1994

The traffic out of Yeovil had been relatively light. At seven thirty on a damp, late Winter morning the majority of the flow was headed into the town. This was one part of his job that made life interesting. Passing the rows of bleary eyed commuters, Latham had always enjoyed knocking off while the rest of the world was dragging its weary carcase back to another nine-to-five day. Twilight flying forced the body to adjust to nocturnal surroundings and for Latham, night missions still held a fascination. Some two hours earlier he had gazed down on the sleeping towns from an altitude of twenty thousand feet, the twinkling neon street lights gradually blinking off as the murky dawn light cleared the horizon. The aircraft had done all that was asked of it, the earlier flights having long since proved the stability of the design and Latham had returned the prototype to the Westfields 'drome as the first shafts of sunlight broke over the treeless expanse of Salisbury Plain. The programme was ahead of schedule and would soon bring to an end a four month long period of intense flying. Latham would soon be able to concentrate on matters more domestic in nature. Jenny had long been desperate to leave the company quarters at Yeovil and had taken it on herself to search a large area across central and western Somerset for what she wanted. Village life was what they had both promised each other and the small hamlet of Culmhead, nestling high on the plateau of the Blackdown Hills, seemed to be the ideal escape from an urban existence. It had also helped that they had discovered Tannery Cottage on a clear blue summers evening, the cream walls bathed in a golden glow. It was small, Latham thought, but it had been Jenny's call. It had to be.

As Latham passed through the outskirts of Yeovil he eased down on the accelerator, the Jeep beginning to eat up the long stretches of tarmac that ran out through to the Blackdown Hills. In the warm interior Latham felt relaxed, he enjoyed driving, it was a chance to be alone with his thoughts. It was during these routine drives that Latham found himself thinking of the past and of his father in particular. From a faded early colour photograph, the boyish grin of a young man in his prime. The 26 year old Flight Lieutenant George Latham in full dress uniform, the guard of honour, swords raised as the young bride and groom emerged from the porch of the small Lincolnshire church.

Latham had been three when his father had died, his memory a vague presence in those early years. It was always the same picture in his mind, the hot summers day, probably in 1963 was his nearest estimation, the three of them on a vast, empty beach in southern Ireland. He remembered playing, of rock pools, buckets and spades, his younger sister Sarah and of the smiling presence of the only father figure he had ever known. And in a year, he was gone. After Aden, his mother had distanced herself from the service, Latham and his seven-month-old sister kept away from other families. Rob could remember the uniformed officer at the door of their home in Germany, the calm silence of his mother as she was told. Her husband had been posted to Cyprus, his squadron flying daily reconnaissance missions over the Aden territories. It was during one of these sorties that George Latham's Hunter jet had been hit by a hail of anti aircraft fire from warring militias in the south of the country. The inquiry had later concluded that, although he had had plenty of time to eject, the seat firing mechanism had failed, damaged by shrapnel from the incoming fire. George Latham had died trapped in his own funeral pyre. Caroline Latham told her children a different story, the truth only emerging many years later as Rob decided to join the service his mother had grown to loathe so much.

Latham reached inside his jacket pocket and opened a small wallet, holding it over the steering wheel as he drove. The dog-eared wedding photo, the colour from the late Fifties blurring at the edges, was tightly folded. His eyes flitted between the smiling faces and the road ahead. He had studied it many times over the years, the minute details of a day captured in time. The guard of honour had been made up of members of his father's squadron, gleaming swords raised aloft, the laughing faces and Brylcreamed hair complementing the assorted beehives and Jackie Kennedy clones. To the left of the gable, the vast bonnet of a Ford Zodiac nosed into view, the polished chrome bumper catching the early Spring sunlight, creamy silk ribbons fluttering across the windscreen. Latham turned the photograph over. A date was written in immaculate copperplate script; April 23rd 1960. He carefully folded the print and placed back into the wallet. He had one other reason for treasuring the image. His mother was smiling, a broad, joyous beam that came from a different era, a time when life was full and the future held no fear. It was the last evidence that he had of his mother's life before her world changed. She had never fully recovered, her health slowly deteriorating, in sharp contrast to the blossoming of her children. Relationships were few and she soon resigned herself to providing as stable home environment as was possible on a widow's pension.

By the time Latham had finished his training, with his life focussed and settling into a self-sufficient future, fractures had began to appear between him and his sister. His mother, by now largely housebound and increasingly frail, had begun to become ever more reliant on Sarah who had moved in to care for her. Latham would be overseas for months at a time; his training taking him to the distant edges of a bygone empire and communication could be difficult. Slowly the resentment began to increase and by the time Latham became fully aware of the situation, it was too late. Soon after his mother's death in 1988, Sarah had simply stopped calling, her life slowly rebuilt with a new partner in Scotland. Latham tried, but she simply was not interested. He cursed his own ignorance. His single-minded determination to emulate his dead father had forsaken the only two people who had ever been as close. That he could be so selfish had shocked him, the self-loathing surfacing as he closed himself off from everything but his work. For nearly two years he denied himself any contact other than that of his squadron colleagues. Eighteen months of hedonism were beginning to take their toll when Max Ronson had fixed him up on a double date.

Her name was Jenny Turner.

The Air Force had trawled them around some of Britain's farthest flung outposts in the years before Westfields had made Latham an offer he could not refuse. To Jenny, teaching forces kids had never been rewarding. The turnover was high, you might only see a child for a matter of weeks before a new posting came through and they were gone. There was little time for a solid grounding. As a couple, both had decided that the RAF offered little in the way of educational stability should they have any children. When the Warton job came up Jenny wasted little time in securing a post at a small Primary on the outskirts of Preston. It had been a happy eight months for her, a small reception class and the chance to build a relationship with minds that were still eager to learn. She soon made an impact. Then came Westfields. Latham battled with his conscience as he realised that the offer would force his hand. It would be his final move, the prospect of work that would guarantee their financial future. It was during this period of upheaval that they lost contact with Max. He had resigned from the test programme before an enquiry was started. It seemed ungrateful at the time. Many friends had rallied around and plenty of time and effort had been given. In the months after the crash at Templemere Latham was not the only one to see the change. The fragile mask had been broken away. It was just as before, the explosive rages that hit without warning and with such severity. And the drink. Always the drink.

In the months immediately following the end of the war in the Gulf, Max slowly started to unravel. With Anna, he had found a serenity that few friends thought possible. The pregnancy had not been announced. Max had tried to dissuade her from the posting to Muharraq but eventually relented to the forceful energy that had initially attracted him in the first place. The marriage would be in the summer if all went well. It had been hastily arranged, Latham returning the best man favour. Anna's death, and the manner of it, started a rapid disintegration. The school bus bombing, of which Ronson was quickly exonerated, had been suppressed by the Allied command. The propaganda value to the Iraqi's was deemed as too sensitive. In the light of later events, the raid on the bridge had had little effect on the inner demons tearing at Ronson's shredded conscience.

Six months after the war, the US Army concluded that the second Patriot missile had suffered a catastrophic telemetry malfunction rendering it uncontrollable. The three members of the fire control team had all been cleared by an internal enquiry. It was through an exchange-posting colleague in the USAF that Ronson had learned the truth. Two of the men had quietly been discharged after a number of re-assignments designed to throw the press off any scent. The word was that at least one had failed a drug test. To Ronson, the whole investigation had been a sham. A cover up. The earlier 'blue on blue' incident in which the crew of a British armoured carrier had been destroyed by an American ground attack pilot had been a public relations disaster that the US government was not eager to revisit. The Patriot incident rapidly became a sideshow of the war and, with forces co-operation, was soon a distant memory in the eyes of the public. A British tabloid had briefly championed the memory of the ten victims in Ward 8 but was soon relegated by the latest Royal scandal.

For Max Ronson, the Lightning episode had finally broken any last vestige of recovery. The company inquiry had concluded that an in-flight fire had been responsible for the engine failure. The board had commended Ronson in his absence, although one member questioned the merits of staying with his aircraft given that ejection had seemed a safer option. Although the airframe was deemed salvageable, the cost of recovering a thirty-year old fighter, nearing its fatigue limit, proved to be uneconomical and the Lightning was sold to a local scrap dealer for a nominal fee. The matter was over. Another rung broken, another nail hammered with clinical precision, and eighteen months of silence.

Latham forced himself to concentrate on the ever-narrowing country lanes that now wound their way up towards the Blackdowns. He was tired now and just wanted to see Jenny. He could just catch her before she left for school. The road began to climb as the Jeep left the Vale of Taunton far behind.

Paris, Les Lilas district.
21.20 hours
Kamal pushed the doorbell six times in rapid succession. The small landing was dark, the only light emanating from the narrow lift shaft at the centre of the stair well. The building was suitably drab and nondescript, a safe house that had been used on previous occasions. People kept their own business, the comings and goings from Flat 12 warranting no more than idle interest. The three months Kamal had spent in Paris had been deliberately low key. He preferred to take sole responsibility for the planning stages. Slowly, he had made contact with the other members of his group and dates and times were discussed. Only when the group came together would he reveal the true nature of their work. For now, he would be working with two others in Paris. The time to leave would come soon.

High above, in the upper floors of the tenement block raised voices echoed through the ceiling. Quite an argument, Kamal thought. His gaze settled on the eyehole of the door. A large eye blinked back at him. The door opened slowly and, without speaking, Yasan Rana al Takriti beckoned him in. The living room was spartan in its furnishings, a single light bulb throwing shadows across the interior. A large window was covered by a heavy black curtain and at the centre of the room, a fold-out dining table had been covered by a large map, paper weights holding each corner. Kamal

paused to light a cigarette. He turned to face Rana. The image before him was a familiar one. Expensive designer clothes, the short, styled jet-black hair and the neatly trimmed moustache gave Rana the very appearance of his paymaster. Uday Hussein had plucked Rana from death row, the murder charges immediately dropped as the Presidents son signed the release forms. He had long surrounded himself with a carefully chosen bodyguard of hired Sunni thugs. He enjoyed the reaction they encouraged, each man sworn to a loyalty that only a reprieved killer could guarantee. The Fedayeen knew only one master.
Each member of the guard possessed a unique talent that Hussein could call upon when the desire effect was needed. With Rana the carefully tailored image disguised a darker talent. His own particular speciality was with the blade. He was proud of his silent killing skills and in particular, his persuasive methods in matters of interrogation. Kamal had heard of his fondness for torture and of how his victims suffered at his hands. Rana liked to toy with prisoners, his stiletto blade cutting at the body, between fingers, around the eyes, each wound made with psychological precision. Information or not, the victim was dead from the moment that Rana was assigned to them. This sickening theatre would often last for hours, the slow demise occasionally viewed for pleasure whenever Uday was entertaining. He would frequently bring women to witness Rana's handiwork. He appreciated the precision. Rana was a psychopath. Uday liked that.

Kamal eyed the stocky, broad shouldered figure before him. His voice registered with barely disguised malice. He had worked with Rana on two separate occasions and each time had been appalled by the man's seemingly endless fascination in causing pain to others. He was a killer, no more and no less, but he was also a very accomplished one and this mission needed a cleaner. Kamal turned his attention to the map.

'The stores. You have a location?' Smoke momentarily clouded his vision as Rana moved towards the table. He turned to face Kamal. The delivery was slow and deliberate.

'The direct route to the north is out. Too much traffic. Phase two is now in use. Marseilles. The boat is available to leave on the third of next month. The pick up point will now be at…….' Kamal raised a hand.

'Brest, yes I am aware of that Rana. Now tell me, how many?' Rana seemed hesitant as he moved to Kamal's side, the two men staring at the map of western Europe. Kamal persisted. Stale sweat filtered through his nostrils.

'How many?'

'Two.'

'Two?' Kamal spun to face him, his face failing to mask the shock.

'Why?….how can this be. I was promised a minimum of four.' His arms were raised in exasperation. Rana backed away. A thin smirk spread across his face. He seemed to enjoy Kamal's anguish.

'The Taliban originally had three but one was damaged in transit. Turkish authorities. This is all we have.' Kamal was massaging his forehead, his shoulders slumped.

'No spare? Totally unacceptable. Without the guarantee of proper support we have to terminate now. I am not going to risk our lives without full backup'

Clenching his fists into tight balls, Kamal began to pace the length of the room. Rana was still smiling.

'You know that we are too far gone to pull out now, my friend' A look of anger flashed across Kamal's face. He knew in an instant that Rana was right. The smile slowly dropped from Rana's face.

'Failure means that we do not get home. You know that.' Kamal faced the large window and pulled the curtain aside. As he stared out across the neon haze of the Paris skyline he found his thoughts returning to Al Kut, to Halah and Milay. The resentment boiled inside him. Rana, for all of his twisted nature, was right. It was a job, and only its success would bring Kamal's release. The sound of sirens passing in the road outside snapped Kamal from his thoughts. He blindly grabbed at the cigarette packet on the map table.

'England?' He asked as he lit up.

'Latest contact from Taraz confirms all priorities are on schedule.'

'And our driver?'

Rana grinned, revealing a gleaming gold tooth.

'Finally starting to succumb to her charms. He starts the next course this week.' Kamal's face remained still.

'And the equipment?'

'Roughly one month from testing. Countermeasures are being fitted within days.'

'Already?' Kamal seemed surprised.

'In practice we will be able to jam any radar surveillance, but the confirmation will be in the testing.' Kamal moved away from the window and began to fold the map. Within the hour they would be leaving to rendezvous in Brest. If all of the components came together, Kamal's unit would be assembled within the month. He would then have just under three months to prove to Baghdad that the unit was operational and able to achieve its objective.

Straddling the Devon and Somerset border, the plateau of the Blackdown Hills is over 900 feet above sea level. To the occupants of the dozen or so villages that are scattered about the area, the high altitude gave the hills a sense of isolation from the surrounding towns. Climbing up out of the Tone valley had always given Latham a feeling of invigoration, of leaving the stresses and strains of working life behind at the end of another day. They had taken to village life in a short space of time with Jenny busying herself on the village hall committee and helping out with the local toddler group. Rob had wasted little time in sampling the pub social life and had joined one of the many skittle teams. Life was slower down here, and much improved for it. Latham felt more content than he had for many years. The forces and the Gulf in particular, were becoming a distant memory.

The Cherokee ground to a stop on the gravel drive. Latham could see that Jenny's Volvo was not in the garage. He cursed under his breath. He had missed her. As he retrieved his flight gear from the tailgate, his ears picked up a familiar drone. From the west, a lone aircraft was approaching at low level. The silver grey blur banked as it roared over the cottage at little over tree top height. Latham shielded his eyes from the glare of the sun to get a better view. As suddenly as it had appeared, the aircraft was gone, a distant noise on the eastern horizon. Piston-engined he thought, and

old. It had sounded like the unmistakable roar of a Merlin engine.
The tailgate slammed shut and he fumbled for the keys. The aroma of toast filled the air as he entered the hallway and dumped his bags on the stairs. In the kitchen a yellow Post-It note contained Jenny's usual 'breakfast in dog' message. She wouldn't be back until late. Staff meeting followed by a parents evening. So much for knocking off at 3.30, he thought. The early morning sunlight had begun to filter through the low kitchen window. The day was his own. He had never slept after a night sortie. It was better to run right through the day and get an early night. He had tried cat napping in the early days but that tended to confuse the body clock in a similar way to jet lag. He drummed his fingers on the large oak table. Coffee, toast and a shower. Then a little bit of exploring.

The Blackdown Hills has always enjoyed its own unique weather system. Snow bound winters and thick fog dominated the colder months, with the beginning of Spring bringing the rich blue sky's of an English summer. A land of extremes. This particular day had begun with rain, but from the west, fragmented clouds had begun to disperse leaving an early morning sun. Latham allowed himself to roam, the Jeep eating up the long straight roads that criss-crossed the hills. Each village seemed much like the last, the square towered church, the small local, the linear pattern of dwellings. At another crossroads sign a familiar name appeared. Templemere.

The land seemed to rise as he approached the perimeter, the twisted MOD pattern barbed wire rusting away at the airfields edge. He parked at the eastern end of the main runway, the great expanse of concrete stretching for a mile. Memories swam back into his conscious. Only the distant cries of a predatory buzzard accompanied the gently gusting breeze that carried the slightest scent of aviation fuel across the airfield. Latham leant against a faded wooden crash gate and shielded his eyes from the sun. The derelict wartime control tower shimmered in the mid-morning haze. Close by, two large hangers revealed the presence of activity, a lone tail fin silhouetted against the blackness of the shed walls. Latham's gaze returned to the runway. The faded piano key markings carried the scars of numerous landings. He searched for the tell- tale skid marks. There was no sign of the ploughed furrow left by Ronson's landing. All was quiet.

From the west, a distant sound caught his attention. It was the growl of an aircraft engine. His eyes strained as he scanned the far end of the runway. As the aircraft made its approach, Latham began to recognise the familiar pitch of the engine. The Merlin again, or was the tone deeper, he thought. Before he could decide, the pale blue Spitfire appeared low over the perimeter of the field. It banked as it passed over the control tower and pulled into a sharp wingover. Latham caught his breath as he realised what he was looking at. The Spitfire Mark 19 had been the fastest variant of the type, the wings clipped, a single piece Perspex bubble canopy and the fuselage stripped of all outer protuberances. Designed specifically for photographic reconnaissance, the aircraft was required to fly at high altitude to its chosen target and, with the information gathered, the Spitfire would then use its un-matched speed in a dash for safety. Latham's doubts about the engine proved correct, the later mark machine being powered by the more powerful Griffon, the sound a deeper, more bass like rumble.

Latham followed the slow loop over the main hanger complex before the Spitfire levelled off to begin a slow circle of the airfield. He still had the buzz. That unique feeling that only such an aircraft could give a pilot. The summer of 1985 had given Latham the break of his life. A posting to the Battle of Britain Memorial Flight, based at Coningsby in Lincolnshire had given him the chance to fly the very aviation legends of his childhood. His initiation on the Hawker Hurricane was to be cut short by a sudden vacancy on one of the flights two Spitfires. Latham had made enough of a nuisance of himself to be selected and had spent a memorable three months touring Britain as part of the escort for the flight's sole Lancaster bomber.
The Spitfire completed its slow circuit of the field, wheels lowered and wing flaps down. Latham followed the final turn and listened for the change in engine pitch. The Spitfire glided low over the parked Jeep, the propeller feathering as the engine was throttled back. The landing was light and the 'plane was soon taxying towards the distant hangers. Latham stood, hands in pockets, for a further minute before returning to the warm interior of the Jeep.

Six

Devon, England,
February 8th
22.19 hours
Detective Inspector Ronald Thursby blew into his cupped hands. The windscreen in front of him misted slightly, momentarily clouding his view of the main road. As his gloved hand wiped the condensation away, the car radio crackled into life. Sergeant Iain Hart reached out for the hand-set. Thursby raised a hand.

'Leave it son'. He could see the sergeant's hesitant look in the dim glow of the instrument panel. He knew he was not the best role model in the force, but tonight was not the night for overtime. Three hours in a dark lay-by in a cold car were more than enough.

'Sir?'

Thursby removed his glasses and massaged the bridge

of his nose.

'How long until we knock off son ?' The eyes were closed as he did his best to appear tired.

'Eleven minutes sir'.

'Exactly. You young lads can have all the extras you want, but it's way past my bed time and besides, you know what the reception is like this side of Exeter.'

Hart sat back in his seat. He knew that it would be pointless to argue. Two years into his first posting with the Devon and Cornwall CID had seen little in the way of incident. Honiton was a sleepy rural town close to the Somerset border. Far too genteel after the streets of his probation in Bolton, he thought. The radio crackled again. Thursby looked at his watch.

'Eight minutes.' He glanced at Hart over his glasses. 'You know what it will be. Punch up outside Albi's Kebab, or at best a joyride into the metropolis that is Exeter.'

Hart could not help but smile. Thursby had been a decent enough cop once, even a few tales of derring-do in his youth. The death of his wife had seen a change, less of a career path, more of a means to keep him occupied. He had passed up any further promotions despite a number of high profile cases that had seen experience out manoeuvre the cock-sure swagger of new blood. He was now ten months from retirement and the clock was winding down.

Hart had been different. After an initial weariness, he had been good to the lad in the beginning, showing him the ropes on his patch. Rural crime came with few surprises. Thursby blamed the cold winter months for the drug culture that seemed slightly misplaced outside of an urban setting. Theft tended to be on a smaller scale but involved a greater value, the odd £50,000 Combine disappearing across the fields at night. Interspersed with the domestics and drink driving, there were a few local villains to be kept an eye on.

Thursby of course, had seen it all. Apart from a brief sojourn in Bristol, he was a local man who had spent his entire career with the force. The partnership with Hart had developed over the first year, the older man seemingly refreshed in the company of the college graduate. For Hart it had been his first experience of a *working* DI, the occasional bursts of activity punctuating the mind numbing hours of paperwork and routine. The dry sense of humour caught him out at first, but he soon became used to the wind-ups. Hart vowed to make the most of this source of experience before Thursby hung up his badge.

From the shadows of the lay-by the unmarked Ford appeared invisible to all but the most powerful of headlights. The gloom would be accentuated to anyone situated on the brightly lit forecourt of the petrol station opposite. At ten-thirty at night, there were few customers. Hart started the engine and, keeping the headlights off, turned the heating up to full. Thursby blew his nose long and hard. Hart winced.

'Suppose that's our cover blown then sir ?'

'Very droll son, very droll.' Thursby finished the elaborate wiping of his nose before carefully folding and replacing the white handkerchief in his breast pocket.

'Two more minutes and then a cuppa. He's not on tonight. I'll wager your little snout at Templemere is down the Crown right now, laughing his cock off. Remind me what it was supposed to be

this time ?'
Hart shifted in his seat. Three hours of surveillance had played hell with his back. As he glanced at Thursby's shadow he could see the gleaming whiteness of a broad smile.

'Russian contraband sir. Reckoned he was bringing in a fair whack with his aero parts. Two containers from Belarus.'

'Oh yes, I remember now. Twenty four tons of caviar and enough vodka to flatten Oliver Reed. Right ?'

'Look sir, he was right about the videos and computer parts. All knock off.'

Thursby retrieved a pipe from the dashboard. Hart wound his window down as a cloud of musty tobacco began to fill the interior.

'Small fry son. Not enough to do him. You won't get the likes of Roly Whittaker with a few mucky porn flicks in his boot. The blokes too switched on for that. He's bigger than……'

Thursby stopped as Hart held up a hand. From the east, a set of headlights was slowing, the indicator flashing a slow wink. As the car approached the neon glow of the station, Thursby recognised the familiar shape. The silver Mercedes rolled silently onto the forecourt, the bright lights reflected in the tinted windows.

'Bingo', Hart hissed.

The drivers side door opened and a heavy set man rose into view above the roof of the car. Dark shoulder length hair and a two-day stubble told Hart all he needed to know.

'Driver, bodyguard ? Where's Whittaker ?'

'Still inside, maybe. Just be patient son. I saw someone in the passenger seat.'

The Mercedes refuelled, the man made his way into the shop and disappeared from view. The two policemen waited silently. Three minutes passed before the passenger side door opened. From the black interior the tall figure of a woman slowly rose into view. Before either man could study her face, the pair of sunglasses that had perched on the woman's head, were lowered. The jet-black hair was cropped short in an expensive cut that mirrored the charcoal grey of her trouser suit. She lit a cigarette with slow, careful precision.

'Naughty girl,' Thursby whispered.

'I wouldn't say no to one sir.'

'The Merc, the girl or the fag?' Thursby was grinning as he reached for the radio hand set.

'Charlie Quebec, this is Blue Two, over.' The radio hissed with static. Hart reached forward and lowered the volume.

'Charlie Quebec….ceiving, go ahead.' The voice was breaking up.

'We've got a car but no target. Two unidentified players. Confirm that you saw Whittaker leave the ferry, over.' More static.

'Definitely saw him on at Dieppe and…aw the car off….Newhaven. No confirmed sighting this side though…….moked windows, over.'

Thursby acknowledged the message and signed off.

On the forecourt the woman was leant against the bonnet of the car, arms folded and taking long, slow draws on the cigarette. Her dark, honey-skinned features now filled the viewfinder of Hart's camera. He held his finger down. Five shots in rapid succession. Next he zoomed in on the door of the shop. As the man reappeared, the slight electric whine of the shutter motor broke the silence again. More shots.

'Do you want me to follow, sir?' Hart asked as he focussed on the car's number plate.

'Nah, not tonight.' He paused, fumbling for his tobacco pouch in the foot well. 'When you're eight months out from the big heave ho, retirement suddenly becomes a deciding factor, know what I mean? Looks like we've lost Whittaker anyway. I want those developed and some names put to faces first. This could be getting a little more interesting.'

As the Mercedes disappeared into the grainy black of the duel carriageway Thursby stretched in his seat and yawned. His brow furrowed as he sucked his cheeks. His pipe had gone out.

Paris,
23.15 hours

Jubal was certain he had been followed. It was only his second duty, but Kamal knew that he had an understanding of the French security services. It was unfortunate if he was correct, but not entirely unexpected. Kamal could be confident that his own departure from the country had been ratified, but Jubal was a long term resident and had to maintain a certain routine. In Paris, the threat of compromise was always extreme. Kamal ushered Jubal through the door of the apartment and called Rana from the second bedroom. In turn, the two men embraced the youngster.

'This was to be expected on at least one account, and we all knew the risks.' Kamal stared at the floor, his hands on his hips. As he glanced up at Jubal he saw, more than ever, the slight and stooping frame of the bespectacled twenty year old. The faded jeans and T-shirt together with the scuffed canvas of his baseball boots completed the guise of a student. He looked so *ordinary*, he thought. And that was why he was needed so much. Kamal waited for him to sit at the table.

'You realise that you are now working alone? Communication only, and you stay in Paris. The usual channels.' Jubal would now have to rely on an ally to pass all outgoing information. Iraq had not been without its sympathisers during the war and Jubal had cultivated contacts in two Paris embassies. Kamal was not overly concerned with the morning's events. He had allowed for such a possibility and was confident in the boy's ability to work alone. The callow youth had a genius for covert communications born of an almost obsessive knowledge of computers. As if conscious of being heard, Jubal spoke in a hoarse whisper. Kamal strained to hear the soft tones of his voice.

'I have two possible outlets to *Host* and Baghdad. If compromised, and I miss my allotted time, you will have to communicate direct with *Host* via the designated London embassy. Do you wish the latest communication sir?' Jubal reached his hand inside the old rucksack and, before removing it, looked up at Kamal. The eyes showed fear. Kamal nodded before receiving the typed message from Jubal's outstretched hand. He read the short paragraph in silence before handing it to Rana. His gaze returned to Jubal. He smiled.

'Relax my friend. The first phase is over. We leave tonight.' Rana was also grinning but the sight caused Jubal to tense every muscle in his small frame. Kamal was older, wiser and had been more of a mentor to the younger operative over these past months. Rana's reputation preceded him and, much closer in age Jubal had detected an edge of competition between the two. He would be grateful that he was staying in the capital. Rana burned the note-paper and allowed the embers to float to the floor before he ground them with the Cuban heel of his boot. He caught Jubal's eye. Again, the grin and this time the hint of a curled lip. Jubal turned away, eyes closed, he clenched his fist as visions of Hassan filled the inside of his eyelids.

Hassan had lost his left ear when he had refused conscription at the height of the Iraq/Iran war. To his younger brother, Hassan had seemed the very essence of free spirit, that brittle combination of teenage cock-sure confidence and the uncertainty of youth. He had frequently clashed with his parents, in choices of education and later, women. To a nine year old Jubal he was a figurehead, a mentor free in his guidance and always there in times of uncertainty.

The war with Iran had already claimed the services of his father and three uncles. Hassan knew that the advent of his seventeenth birthday would bring with it the shadow of compulsory service at the front. He had planned for the day long in advance, storing provisions for the journey south to his grandmother's house in Naazir. The departure had been in the still of a moonlit night, Jubal the only member of the household to be woken. The boy fought back the tears in the dim shadows of his room, convinced that he would never see his brother alive again. Hassan had smiled warmly, pulling his brother into a long embrace. Promises were made and oaths exchanged. As his brother slipped into the night, Jubal sobbed under the cover of his sheets, sleep now impossible. He remembered the calmness of his mother in the morning, her abject acceptance of his brothers actions. It was his father who reacted badly. In future days Jubal was to question his fathers actions that day, the phone calls and the arrival of strangers to their house.

Hassan had made good progress over the three hundred mile journey, but the men had been waiting as he turned into his grandmother's street. Despite his deliberately dishevelled appearance he was recognised with ease, his schedule and route seemingly well known. He surrendered calmly as the Mukhabarat men came out of the doorways, the large Toyota waiting down a side alleyway. Before the day was out Hassan would make his first encounter with Yassan Rana.

The empty grocery van left early the following morning, taking a minor road south of the city. The route would take in various pick-ups and deliveries along the way before heading north west towards the Brittany coast. By the next sunrise they would be in position. Kamal had tried to sleep in the cramped confines of the cab. The cold, combined with intermittent glare of on-coming headlights made rest a virtual impossibility. He shifted uneasily as his mind replayed the concerns over Jubal. He had not expected the tail so soon. Jubal was known for his obsessive preparation before moving about the city. Could he have been mistaken, a touch of youthful paranoia perhaps? Kamal forced his tired eyes open. Beside him, Rana was a study in concentration as headlights illuminated his serious features. He was taking the final shift before sun up. The dashboard display showed just after three as the van joined Route N23 to

Alencon. Kamal pulled the blanket back over his shoulders and curled himself tighter against the seat. In just under two hours he would know whether his services would be required.

Rue du Montparnasse, Paris
04.15 hours
The Paris skyline glowed under a neon haze that gave the air an orange tint. From his third floor office, Colonel Gilde Tressor gazed out over the sleeping city. The roads below were quiet, save for the occasional newspaper van on its first delivery of the night. From its modest, nondescript headquarters in the south of the city, the Departement Generale de la Securite Exterieure provided the only signs of life in the otherwise deserted commercial district. Several floors of the six-storey block were lit. For the men and women of the DGSE, the security of France was a continuous exercise. As the Colonel returned to his desk his attention again focussed on the two black and white photographs lay on top of a black box folder. He sank slowly into the large leather chair positioned behind the impressive expanse of the mahogany desk and reached for the nearest picture. The face was familiar. Tressor reached for the intercom switch and asked for a coffee to be brought into him. He lowered the angle poised lamp that also held a magnifying glass. The grainy image filled his vision. Jubal al-Rikabi stared back at him.
There had been something about the young student that had held Tressor's attention. When the immigration authorities had first alerted him of al-Rikabi's presence in March of 1991 it was far more than physical attraction that had alerted the security

agent. He was wary of allowing personal feeling to cloud his judgement. With al-Rikabi there was much more. A number of innocent inquiries at the engineering college at Parc Monceau provided Tressor with enough doubts as to why the so-called Saudi student was enrolled with the college. The three-year marine electronics course was in little doubt. Subtle plying of his tutors revealed a precocious talent for electronics. He was achieving the highest scores in his year. The student had been tailed over a random pattern of days throughout the first months of his residency. It was towards the end of the third month that a number of night-time visits were made to the Syrian embassy close to the Monmartre. Al-Rikabi always travelled light, the same battered khaki rucksack that seemed to be so obligatory to student life, casually slung over his right shoulder. The visits were short, but enough for Tressor to feel confident that an operative was at work.

From inside the box file Tressor pulled a second set of photographs. Also black and white, these images were small and taken from a great distance. They showed a youth entering, and then leaving the entrance to a residential block in the Les Lilas district. With a sharp rap on the solid, oak panelled door Xavier Pinon entered with a tray of coffee and rather limp looking baguettes. Under his left arm he clutched another box file. A large man, his over-weight frame filled his inexpensive suit, red braces straining over a protruding belly. From beneath the large moustache the deep voice echoed around the high ceiling of the office.

'Home made I'm afraid, sir. Salad or venison?

Tressor gazed over the top of his spectacles at his subordinate. The corners of his mouth were turned down.

'Euch. I think I'll pass on that. What else do you have?'

'That final confirmation on Kamal sir. Austrian police had him leaving the train at Vienna and taking a flight to Istanbul. They didn't get close enough to him though.' Pinon knew of his boss's doubts. 'You're not convinced are you sir?' Tressor rubbed his tired eyes long and hard. He was still to be convinced but there was something more, something long ago that he was struggling to remember.

'About Kamal? No. They've used doubles before and I've too suspicious a mind to allow a seven year sleeper to seemingly drop in and immediately take off again.' He removed his glasses. 'It's the propulsion specialism that concerns me. Tell me about his Gulf record again, will you?'

Pinon carefully placed the tray on the desk and retrieved the folder from under his arm. He leafed through a thick sheaf of papers before answering.

'Weapons officer on two Scud units inside the Iraqi border between October 90 to January 91. Sole survivor of the unit that reputedly hit the Muharraq hospital.' Tressor held up a finger.

'Tried to hit Muharraq. Remember, it was the Americans who hit the hospital.' Pinon continued.

'I'm still in contact with MI6 about that operation, but they are being somewhat evasive to say the least.' Tressor reached out for the file, his voice betraying ill concealed disappointment.

'They never make it easy, do they? So much for the bloody Union. Keep on at them, tell them that he was hovering near a British Airways check-in at Vienna if you like, but keep on pestering them.' His hand hovered over one of the baguettes before he finally sat back in his chair. Pinon had no such hesitation in devouring his venison.

'And al-Rikabi, sir?', he asked through a mouthful of meat.

'Full, round the clock until Sunday. Then we pull him in. Is he still making his trips on the river?' Tressor was referring to the frequency with which the student had been taking the river boat taxi on the Seine.

'Fairly regular but no discernible pattern. We really need to get someone closer. He seems to spend at least part of the time below deck. We've got quite a gallery of passengers, but no match yet.' Pinon shook his head slowly. 'I still think it's too random for a contact.'

'Could be a drop off point.' Tressor sipped at his coffee. 'Then again, it could just be an engineering student travelling around Paris. We need more Xavier. See what you can do.' He began to roll up the sleeves of his shirt. As Pinon turned to leave Tressor remembered what had been troubling him about Kamal. He snapped his fingers to gain attention.

'Black September.' Pinon's brow furrowed at the mention of the Palestinian terrorist group.

'Sir?'

Tressor continued. '....Orly, 75. Tried to shoot down an El Al 747 with an RPG from the end of the runway.' Pinon was now nodding in agreement.

'Crude, but at least they hit something. A Czech plane if I.....'

'Yugoslav.' Tressor interrupted. 'Two minor casualties. Scared the hell out of the government.' He rose from his desk, a finger pointing at the photographs spread out in front of him. 'It can't be the major airports, not with the levels we have now, but I'll bet that it's something to do with Kamal's interest.'

'Surface to air?' Pinon asked as he returned towards the desk.

'A distinct possibility, but what is our target? We've got the G7 summit in a year and the D-Day anniversary before that. Either one would hit the jackpot.'

Pinon picked up a copy of L'Equip that lay on Tressor's table. He turned to the back pages.

'Sports? We've got several Cat A fixtures coming up. Roland Garros in May.'

'Tennis? No I don't think so. Certainly a high media profile, but too soft politically. I think they want something big, something that amounts to retribution on a grand scale.' Tressor picked up a photograph of Jubal al-Rikabi in the Rue des Bruyeres. It was in the east of the city, the same direction of Kamal's departure. He suddenly swivelled in his chair and rose in one swift moment. On the wall behind lay a large map of the country. Coloured marker pins were scattered across its expanse. Tressor allowed his fingers to trace a path across northern France to the western seaboard. His hand stopped at the northern tip of Brittany. Placing his glasses on the top of his head he leant forward and reached for the intercom on his desk.

'Giselle? Get me Pierre Lisi in our Brest office.'

Seven

Devon
February 11th
Jenny held out her hands in despair.

'You must be kidding. We're just not ready Rob.' Her pale, china-blue eyes pleaded. 'We've still got half the furniture in your Dad's garage, and the bedroom's are in a total mess'. She was having an effect. The visit had been planned months previously, two of Latham's oldest Air Force friends invited to an unofficial house warming. The idea had been for a small reunion, to catch up on service gossip and introduce new partners, but Jenny was right. The house was a wreck. Old mates willing to crash on a sofa, yes, but with their partners? Jenny wanted desperately to show off the one house that had been bought specifically to be called a home.

'I just want to do it properly. It's too late to

cancel them. It's next week for goodness sake. Just this once Rob, please. There's bound to be guest houses up here.'

Her hands were outstretched in asking. 'Find them a nice farm B&B. They sell a guide in the shop' Jenny's arms wrapped around Latham's waist as she nuzzled into his neck. He flicked soapsuds over his shoulder causing her to cry out. He turned from the sink and caught her by the wrists, gently pulling her towards him.

'OK, OK but it'll cost you. Something gratuitous and prolonged, candle lit and scented sticks. The full works.' He smiled. Jenny blew the suds from the end of her nose. The accent was pure West Country.

'Certainly, master. Is it to be the haywain or the four poster, sire.' She laughed. Her face was radiant in the early morning light. Latham pulled her closer. She kissed him lightly, letting her lips play across his. Latham lowered his hands to knead the firm roundness of her buttocks. She began to grin at the touch of his exploring hands.

'Enough, horny toad or you'll get me started.' She pulled away and made as if to run.

'Last one to the shower goes up against the tiles'.

Latham had enjoyed the brief sabbatical. Two days had passed since the night flight and he was not due to fly until the end of the following week. The time allowed him to relax in between compiling flight data and report writing. Latham had explored more of his newly adopted parish, the village shop selling him a guide revelling in lore and legend. Latham was also on a mission. Jenny was right and with a free day, the search was on. The guide had given several addresses and in the warm morning air, the Cherokee had seen a great deal of the narrow lanes of the Blackdowns. The high hedgerows afforded precious little in the way of views, the occasional gateway flashing a view of the undulating skyline. Latham smiled as he recalled his wife's instructions. This time it was Jenny who was calling the shots. With the constant Air Force travel, she had never been allowed to become overly house proud. He feared losing her. It would have been easy. He had seen it happen constantly in the Force, the obsessive nature that bit deeply into a relationship. The wives called themselves single mothers for all the time they had with their partners, the jokes about OMO soap packets appearing in kitchen windows, signalling 'Old Man Overseas', were the lighter side. In truth, few marriages were longstanding, the shear geographical logistics of an occupation that was subject to the whims of a fragile political climate decreased the odds somewhat.

At the second attempt Latham found his country retreat. Culmholt Hall was a small Jacobean mansion house hidden in one of the many small wooded valleys that only the well and truly lost could find. The steep road that wound down through the dense foliage of the grounds made Latham thankful that he had chosen the Jeep rather than Jenny's battered old Volvo that morning. As the roadway twisted its way lower into the valley, the darker and more oppressive the vegetation seemed to get. Just as it seemed that he had taken a wrong turning, the house appeared through a large clearing in the canopy. The sweeping gravel road took Latham past the cultivated lawns of a garden that was more Georgian in its layout. The dark stone fascia of the house rose though three stories with the two outermost wings standing proud of the main frontice. The cars parked around the edge of the circular drive confirmed his feeling for quality. After the requisite long wait, Latham's tug on the door ring was answered and a menu acquired. The fare was impressive, if wildly overpriced, but with his and Jenny's second wedding anniversary looming, Latham congratulated himself on his find. It was as he was making towards the Jeep that the shrill roar of an idling jet engine broke through the air. The noise held its note for several seconds before dying away to nothing. The east, he thought and thumbed the guide that had lain furled on the warm dashboard. Latham started the engine and after studying the pages of the guide momentarily, checked his bearings and spun the wheels of the Jeep.

It took only five minutes to climb to the perimeter of the old airfield, the familiar shapes of the main hangers appearing on the shimmering horizon. Passing the old crash gate at the end of the main runway, the road wound its way around the edge of the base until a derelict guardhouse appeared in a break in the rust covered fencing. The windows were gone, the brickwork pitted with random patterns of holes, some large enough to put a fist through. A large wooden board hung at a lazy angle across the top of the doorway. The letters, faded and peeling, bore witness to a more glorious past.

ROYAL AIR FORCE STATION
TEMPLEMERE

An eagle crest lay beneath the writing, the Latin motto almost obscured by the blistering paintwork. Newer, plastic signs gave warnings of private property and of the presence of aircraft movement. Tall grass grew between the cracks in the concrete pattern of the taxiway. Latham gunned the engine of the Jeep and sped past the 5 miles per hour sign. As he drove he began to recognise the layout of the base, his mind returning to eighteen months ago when Max Ronson had lost several of his nine lives on that cold, overcast day in February.

Latham had circled his wingman many times before a lack of fuel had forced him to break for Exeter, some twenty miles to the west. The emergency services arrived en mass as the fighter left the scene, but it was the sight of the slumped figure by the side of the crashed Lightning that would stay in Latham's memory for years to come. That day he witnessed fate shaking the last vestige of hope from an already broken man. Within days Ronson would be gone.

The site had changed little, a touch more overgrown in places, the clear skies enhancing the green of the vegetation. Latham slowed the Jeep as the twin boom tail of a Vampire jet appeared in a break in the grass ahead of him. The matt grey fighter was taxiing slowly towards the end of the same runway that Ronson had landed on. Latham stopped completely and killed the engine. From his vantage point at the side of the runway he watched as the small jet powered up to full throttle. The brakes released, the little Vampire leapt forward and gained speed rapidly. Drawing parallel with Latham's vehicle the fighter left the runway, the undercarriage retracting almost immediately as the pilot pulled up into a steep climb. Within seconds a small dot against the blue of the sky, its movement only betrayed by a barely discernible smudge of exhaust trail, disappeared from view into the blinding glare of the sun. The smell of kerosene invaded the air-conditioned interior of the Jeep. Latham inhaled deeply. The smell was comfort.

At the approach to the two hangers situated at the eastern end of the airfield, another Vampire jet, this time a single-seater, was parked alongside a familiar sight. The powder blue Spitfire, the curvature of the fuselage catching the sun, only the uniform pattern of rivets breaking the smooth lines, sat brooding alongside it's later counterpart. Latham still felt the same awed reaction on seeing the aircraft. It was something that would never leave him. Only one of the hangers seemed in use, the open doors revealing a further piece of British aviation history. A relic of the Fifties, the De Havilland Devon transport was sitting on raised supports, the most part of the rear fuselage missing. Three figures could be seen working on the dismembered airframe. Above the hanger another sign, this one distinctly modern, revealed the identity of the operation.

WHITTAKER VINTAGE AIRCRAFT RESTORATIONS Ltd

Latham parked the Jeep at the side of the main hanger and grabbed his leather jacket from the back seat. His old RAF identity card was in the inside pocket. As he walked around to the front of the hanger, the sound of hammering echoed from within the cavernous interior. He stood at the entrance, hands thrust deeply into his pockets and savoured the history on display. One of the men perched atop the wing of the Devon looked up. The accent was thick Glaswegian.

'Can ah help you pal?'

Brittany, 10.50 hours

Henri du Blayac had few qualms, if any, when it came to immigrant labour. It amounted to little more than slavery, but for the past fifteen months a steady supply of Middle Eastern workers had harvested in his orchards. A small, slouching frame, his face like an unmade bed, the old farmer stood at the top of his own valley gazing down on the massed ranks of pickers slowly working their way through the vines. If du Blayac had been present in Paris on the day that Abdul Kamal had originally arrived in the country, even his tired old eyes would have recognised that many of the passengers who shared the agents taxi that day had made an appearance at his vineyards over these last few months. Workers came and went, one work force blurring into another. He let that fool of a manager Grestain deal with the pickers. Who the hell cared where they came from in the first place? And these boys had been as good as gold, no pilfering, and no complaints from that bitch up the road. This lot were thorough.

The extra rent from the Arab boys had been an added bonus. They usually found cheap board in St Pol-de-Leon on the coast, but if a bunch of them wanted to rent on his land, then what the hell. It was all money. He would have a root around while they were out picking tomorrow. Always good for a haul, some money, a little hash and on the odd occasion some interesting reading matter. He took the briar from his mouth and belched loudly. A clear sky. Good picking weather for tomorrow, he thought as his eyes caught site of a small van bumping it's way over the gravel roadway that led to his farm, the wheels stirring up a small dust cloud in their wake. Du Blayac reached for the small wire framed spectacles in his waistcoat pocket. His vision barely improved, he could just make out the two figures in the now halted van. He began to hurriedly make his way back to the Citroen pickup that was parked behind him on the brow of the hill.

Yasan Rana stretched his sinewy frame, a long exhalation of breath belying the relief of freedom from the cramped interior of the grocery van. Kamal remained in the passenger seat of the cab, his eyes taking in the landscape before him. The gently undulating topography rose on either side of the small cluster of buildings on the floor of the small valley. Vineyards stretched away in uniform ranks with a strong crop clearly in evidence. The farmhouse itself was as nondescript as it was plain. Small out buildings were situated towards the rear, with two large storage buildings lying just outside the perimeter fence of the house gardens. The larger of the two barns, its roof giving every appearance of imminent collapse, had no doors, revealing a crammed miscellany of farm machinery. The smaller, and more stable looking building had strong oak doors that where padlocked shut.

As Kamal slid the cab door back, du Blayac's battered Citroen bumped down the track and pulled up in front of the van. Rana turned to face the old farmer, his French suitably faltering.

'You…you..sir Monsieur du Bayac ?' Rana bowed slightly as the wheezing farmer approached.

'My brother and I are very hard workers.

We…we hear that you have much work for hard workers, yes?' The bow was deeper.

'Names Du Blayac. You two from Alencon ? Mustapha said you'd be here yesterday'
There was a touch of anger in the rumbling voice.

'Very…sorry..sir. My brother here got us lost and then a wheel ..we lose.' Rana pointed at the van. A third bow, and this time mirrored by Kamal in the cab. The farmer gazed silently at the old Peugeot before raising one of his enormously impressive eyebrows. Turning to face Rana, he loudly cleared his throat before landing a huge ball of spittle at the labourers' feet.

'That may be but I've got a harvest to land and standing round here ain't gonna get it done. You're in the barn with the rest of them. I pay by the load and any shit from either of you and I'm onto the Customs at Brest, understand?'
Kamal did not wait to answer what sounded like the standard welcome. Starting the engine, he swung the wheel of the van and headed for the out buildings. Rana sprinted after him, but not before the obligatory bow. Kamal caught sight of him in the wing mirror and smiled to himself. He played the peasant well, he thought.

As the van bumped its way along the dusty farm track, Kamal scoured the vineyards for recognisable faces. Again, he recognised a number of the labourers as the taxi fares from Paris. None caught his gaze as he passed them, each man struggling under the weight of large baskets brimming with grapes. At the far end of one vine he found them. Working together, Salam Mawsil, Latif Nadar and Asil al Takriti were stooped among the overflowing vines. On Kamal's approach they all made a show of greeting each other and embraced. Backs were slapped and there was much laughter as travellers were re-united. As one by one the men returned to work, two figures detached themselves from the group and walked a short distance to the edge of the field. Latif, the tall, sinewy Basran turned his back on Asil and the remainder of the group. Only Kamal could now see his eyes. The voice was a barely audible whisper.

'Jubal confirms that the cargo is past Gibraltar. Three nights, on the ebb tide on the Pointe du Raz peninsular.' Kamal nodded before speaking.

'Shola is due within three days and will confirm the status of the delivery system.'

The two men then stood silently as they gazed over the figures working silently before them. There was no need for any other dialogue.

Templemere

The initial reception was not as cordial as Latham had hoped for. Aviators considered themselves part of an exclusive club, and as with all inward looking cliques, there was an unwritten sense of protection amongst its members. It was usually the mention of his former career that had opened doors for Latham, from the odd favour, a good table at a restaurant, through to the furthering of his career with Westfields. Latham had felt little guilt for the Masonic side to this network of convenience. Hell, he had put his life on the line too many times to remember and he was determined to mine any seam rich enough to secure his future. It was with this in mind that made the frosty reception at Whittaker's harder to fathom. The large Scotsman had been working on one of the Devon's engines when he had noticed the stranger at the hanger door. It was as if Latham had been caught in possession of stolen goods for all the warmth of the welcome he received. The man slowly made his way towards the hanger door. Behind him the remaining mechanics continued to work. After being informed of the private nature of the property he was supposedly trespassing on, Latham had hardly time to retrieve a business card from his jacket and introduce himself, when he was being asked to leave. Short of being frog marched to the door of his car, the test pilot managed to hand one of the cards to the reluctant looking mechanic before deciding to retreat. Making his way back to the Jeep, he had to step briskly aside as a large silver Mercedes drew up beside the hanger. The honey-skinned woman who got out did not seem to notice the stranger or the presence of the Jeep. As he drove off towards the perimeter, reflected in his rear view mirror, Latham could see the man standing motionless in the open hanger doorway as if to ensure that the invader was vanquished. The well-dressed woman was also looking in his direction. Latham shook his head in disbelief. The whole episode, from entering the hanger, to starting the Jeep, had taken less than two minutes. So much for the local hospitality, he thought.

It had not taken Jenny Latham long to deduce that her husband was troubled. Over a light salad supper he told her of his discovery of Culmholt and of the subsequent reception at Templemere. She smiled as she poured him a second glass of wine.

'Old boy network not working then?' The fake sympathy caused a smile to flicker across

Latham's face.

'Aw c'mon Jen, you know that I'm nowhere near as bad as some of the lads. It's not me that wangles flights abroad like Dave Dakin.' Jenny finished pouring.

'More's the pity, I could do with a holiday'.

'What really got me was the aggressiveness of it all. You'd have thought that I was about to try and waltz off with one of their prize assets.'

'Did you mention Westfields?'

'Just about. I managed to blurt out that I was former aircrew but it was like talking to a brick wall. Hadrian's wall at that, bloody Jock.' Jenny began to laugh and reached out for Latham's hand.

'Go on, admit it. You wanted to play with their Spit' didn't you?'

'Yeah, you got me. I was just curious about the place, you know, what with Max's crash, and seeing the Spitfire. I just thought I'd drop in. Sod it now.'

'Now, now fly boy, don't sulk.' Latham scowled in mock anger.

'You're not taking this seriously are you Mrs Latham.'

Jenny grinned as she slowly shook her head.

'Sorry, but I'm more concerned with our guests. You're certain about this Culmholt place then?'

'Certain. It's like some sort of time warp down there. Steve and Lisa will love it even if it does cost a fortune.'

'Well, I'm not concerned with the money. This weekend's on us, okay?'

Latham squeezed her hand lightly.

'Sure, but just one favour. If they do offer to

pay, turn them down twice and if they still insist, give in on the third offer.' Latham managed to duck the first bread roll as it flew across the table.

Eight

Cherbourg, Northern France
February 14th, 08.50 hours.

Gilde Tressor adjusted the gold tie pin and smoothed the lapel of his double-breasted suit in the faint reflection of the two-way mirror. The suit was new, something he insisted on when his budget allowed. It was an extravagance that was in part intemperance, part camouflage. The illusion was of a wealthy businessman, a throwback to the boom years of the eighties and certainly a soldier of the private sector, anything but an agent of the State. Through the glass he could see Pinon sitting at the end of one of the rows of plastic seating that filled the arrival hall, the slowly revolving baggage belt beginning to disgorged its load. Pinon was wrestling with his usual copy of the sports pages.

The early morning ferry had docked fifteen minutes

earlier and the first passengers would be due through the arrival lounge in five minutes. Tressor stepped back from the pane of glass that separated him from the main concourse. He was still affected by the chance stares of those who confronted the two-way mirrors of the line up rooms. They were always unsighted but it was uncanny how many felons had met Tressor's gaze over the years. He checked his watch as the first passengers made their appearance at the end of the hall and reached for the clipboard on the table in front of him. He turned to the uniformed customs officer beside him.

'What have you for me today Lisi?'

'Nothing from our side today I'm afraid, the only trade is from the British. Mainly smuggling. We've got a positive ID on one suspect vehicle, one Roland Vincent Whittaker, wanted on the other side on several counts of low grade smuggling, Videos and alcohol mainly. Drives a top range Mercedes. Very expensive.'

Tressor traced his finger down the list. Familiar terrorists, names real and assumed mixed with the usual assortment of couriers and felons. Abdul Kamal was the second name on the list.

'No visuals among the passengers yet?' Before the officer could reply, his lapel microphone crackled into life. The message was brief. Lisi retrieved the clipboard.

'None from this list sir, but it turns out that our English smuggler is not driving his car. Some woman. Middle Eastern appearance. We've pulled the vehicle in down stairs.' Tressor walked over to the mirror without answering and rapped on the glass three times. Outside, Pinon rose quickly from his seat.

Within minutes the three men were taking a lift down to the main customs vehicle compound.
The silver Mercedes stood at the far end of the hanger-like structure, four customs officials already in the process of a thorough search. On the ground at the rear of the car the back seats were neatly laid beside the contents of the opened boot. Lisi led the two DGSE agents past the car and showed them through an office door. The small room contained a single table and four chairs. On the table a telephone and tape recorder sat side by side. A single strip light gave the interior an unforgiving brightness. Behind the table, a woman was sat impatiently tapping a small notebook on the faded melamine surface. Tressor was immediately struck by her presence. The clothes, hair, jewellery and make up made a powerful impression. Self made or aristocratic, there was an underlying arrogance to the obvious frustration the woman was feeling. As the three men entered, she looked up. It was not a face that Tressor recognised. He immediately felt that he should have, however. This was a face that demanded recognition, even if it was only in the most exulted of company. After letting Lisi introduce them as Customs officials, Tressor and Pinon sat opposite the woman while Lisi remained standing. He began the questioning.

'Madame, your passport says that you are one Halah Akief from the United Arab Emirates. Is this correct?'

Tressor watched as the woman raised her head. Her expensive aroma filled the small room. The brown eyes showed little fear as she cleared her throat to speak. The smooth, clipped delivery betrayed a European connection.

'That is correct. May I know why I have been

stopped?'

'I'm sorry Madame, you will have to speak up for the tape.' Lisi indicated the cassette deck at the side of the table, the tape revolving silently inside. She answered again, this time more than a faint trace of anger in her voice. Lisi continued.

'From your earlier passage through customs it would appear that you are staying in our country for a week and that you intend to visit friends in the east. Is this correct?'

'Yes' The voice was firm and clear. She raised her head fully and placed the notebook on the table before clasping her hands. 'I am representing a client in Oman and conducting business in England. I am in France purely to visit some old friends in Strasbourg. May I ask, again, why I have been stopped?'

Pinon leant forward placing his hands on the table and continued.

'And your business, Madame? Your passport says that you deal with antiquities. Could you please elaborate.' Akief sighed as she sat back in her seat. She crossed her black stocking clad legs and pulled the hem of her skirt towards her knees. Again she cleared her throat before answering.

'I represent a collector of antique aircraft. We are in negotiation with a restorer in England to purchase one of his collection. You will find all of the details in my case.' A bejewelled hand casually pointed towards the door. She met Tressor's eyes for the first time and held his gaze briefly. As she did he took a small photograph from his clipboard and slid it across the table. Akief did not look at it. Lisi continued.

'Can I ask you to look at the photograph Madame, and tell me if you recognise the man as the owner of the Mercedes?'. As she picked up the black and white image there was a sharp knock at the door. Tressor recognised the face as one of the officials who he had earlier seen searching the silver Mercedes. Lisi looked up from the table. The officer was brief.

'Nothing sir'.

Devon, England
09.10 hours

It was the one aspect of the job that Latham loathed. In the service it had been commonly known as 'flying a mahogany bomber', which was a rather grand title for the mountainous paper work that, evermore, seemed to conclude each flying sortie. In the business of test flying the written aspect of experimentation was that much greater. The flight of the previous week had determined important information concerning the pitch and yaw of the new *Skua* aircraft. In-flight data, recorded by the banks of computers that filled the intended bomb bay of the aircraft, had been assimilated over the course of the fifty-minute flight. Down-loaded via disc, the data now appeared on Latham's computer in his small office at the Westfields headquarters. Having worked through the night, Latham's eye's blurred as he looked away from the screen towards the large clock that hung above the door of his office. The ringing of his mobile broke his concentration.

'Latham'.

'Only me, Biggles. How's the paper work going?'.

It was Jenny. Latham stretched back in his seat, the tilting mechanism creaking under the weight.

'Oh, okay I guess. I'm starting to see double

though. I think you're right about glasses. You're home early, have you been expelled again?'.

'Yup, I head-butted the Chairman of Governors.' Jenny was laughing. 'I'm on a training course today, remember? I'm just about to leave.'

'I'm going to call it a day soon love, is there anything apart from the wine for tonight? I'll get two red and two white.' Latham's friends were due that evening and he could sense a slight air of anxiety in Jenny's voice.

'Great, that's fine. I'm pretty sure we've got everything. I would have just about finished the cleaning but I've been on the phone with some American bloke. Says that he's from Templemere and that he'd like to talk with you. I've got a number.'

'Templemere?' Latham sat forward in his seat. 'So the card got through after all. OK, I'll finish up here and drop into town'.

Curiosity shortened the journey home by at least fifteen minutes, as Latham was eager to make the call. The number got him through to a secretary who put him onto a mobile to Belarus. The voice that boomed down the line caused Latham to remove the handset from his ear. The American accent was South, he thought. Deep South.

'Roland W Whittaker's the name. I'm pleased to talk to you Mr Latham, always a pleasure to talk to a fellow flyer such as yourself. So you got my message then?'.

'And you got my card?'. Latham replied.

'Ah yes, I must apologise for my chief tech'. I'm afraid that you got one of his famous Scotch welcomes. He's my number one when I'm away on business you see. Very protective of the site at Templemere, Mr Latham. We get all sorts up there nosin' around and not all of them are interested in the work we do. Damn kids mostly.' The line crackled with static.

'I see from your card that you fly for Westfields, Mr Latham'.

'I've been there six months, freelance. Testing mainly, but a bit of occasional ferry work.'

'Are you ex service Mr Latham ?'.

'Fast jet crew and props.'

'Well that's just splendid Rob, can I call you Rob? I'm always on the lookout for pilots with experience. I'm strictly a prop jock ma'self and you jet boys are hard to come by'

'So what exactly do you do up at Templemere. Is it just renovations?'.

'Mainly, son. We do the occasional contract work for your MOD, but mainly I buy and sell war birds. Flying, non-flying. US mainly but I'm looking to open up in Asia and the Middle East. That's what I'm doing here, tryin' to buy a coupla' Migs from this shitty little air force.' Latham could not help but grin.

'I'd certainly like to come up for a visit sometime.'

'Hell, sure you do. Listen son, I've gotta go talk with some Ivan General now. You leave your work number back with Emma and I'll get back to you sometime next week. That a deal?'.

Before Latham could reply, the whirlwind that was Roland Whittaker had been replaced by the clipped English tones of his secretary.

Cherbourg

'No I do not recognise this man. Is this why you have stopped me?'

Aisha Taraz sat ramrod straight in her chair.

'Please Madame, just confirm the identity for us first'. Pinon was insistent.

'I have already told you, I do not know this man. The car is owned by Mr Roland Whittaker, the gentleman I am dealing with in England.'

'May I ask why you are driving his car?'

'Of course. It has been loned to me for the duration of my visit to France. I would rather not hire a vehicle if it can at all be avoided.'

'Do you make a habit of borrowing things from your business acquaintances Madame?' Tressor shifted his weight in his chair as Pinon went on the offensive. 'Could you confirm your relationship with Mr Whittaker? An acquaintance perhaps, a boyfriend?'

The bait was duly accepted as Akief rose from her seat, the anger clearly registering. Momentarily she seemed exposed, before regaining her composure and slowly lowering herself back down. The classical features were suddenly distorted.

'What right do you have to question me like this? I am in negotiation for a deal that you would have to work twenty years to earn.' She spluttered. 'I accept the kind generosity of a true gentleman, something I do not expect the likes of you to understand, and I am being treated like some common drugs mule'.

It was the use of the word 'mule' that Tressor picked up on. Why not smuggler? Just too much knowledge for a Lady, surely? He entered the conversation for the first time.

'Madame Akief, I must apologise for my

colleagues' line in questioning but we just have to clear up a couple of important points.' It was now Pinon's turn to receive the disdainful stare, before the Akief turned her gaze to the newly conversational third official.

'And they are?'

'Firstly Madame, you have been loaned the car by Mr Whittaker for the duration of your visit to France, to wit, no longer than two weeks.'

'That is correct'

'Secondly, that you packed the car yourself before leaving England'.

'Again, correct.'

Tressor got to his feet and moved towards the door.

'In that case Madame, I must apologise for wasting your time. A purely routine procedure, I assure you. Please, if there is anything I can do to ensure a quicker passage to Strasbourg, you have only to ask.'

Akief grabbed the notebook from the table and thrust it deep into her Prada handbag. The voice was full of bitterness.

'May I leave now?' Tressor nodded slightly before showing the way.

'Certainly Madame, just the formality of collecting you luggage from customs. A brief moment, I assure you.'

With that Akief was ushered from the room leaving the three men alone, the last traces of her scent hanging in the air. Tressor picked up the telephone and punched an internal number.

Thirty minutes after the interview, from Lisi's second storey office, Gilde Tressor watched Halah Akief and the silver Mercedes leave the terminal building. Pinon turned from the window as the car disappeared from sight. Walking towards Lisi's desk he retrieved the clipboard from the official.

'Who did you show her sir?'

Tressor did not respond instantly, holding his gaze on the exit road from the terminal. Without turning to face Pinon he answered.

'Somewhere near the bottom, an Algerian dissident I think.' He turned to face the two men. 'I'm not sure about her. The Arab connection is too obvious, but there was something about her that was too much bluff.' He tapped his fingers on the edge of the mahogany desk, deep in thought. 'Best not to let her know that we're on to this Whittaker, though.' He looked up at Pinon. 'Bug placed?'

'Rear off side-wheel arch. GPS at Rouchelle have just confirmed a strong signal. She's on the N 13 heading for Valognes.'

Tressor turned back towards the window and loosened his tie.

Aisha Taraz waited until she was on the open road before allowing herself time to process the events of the last hour. Whittaker's loaned Mercedes had provided an added flourish to her deliberate guise as a successful businesswoman. The attention was to be expected, as was the search at the Customs building. What troubled her was the, albeit brief, interrogation. Of the three men in the small room, the taller man, Lisi, could almost certainly be taken as Customs. The other two, Taraz was not certain of. The fat one she could handle, she was well used to the third degree tactics. As always, it was the quiet one that you needed to watch. The expensive suit and calm manner gave

little away. If they were DGSE agents, they were dressing well these days, she thought.
The first drops of rain began to hit the windscreen as the Mercedes joined the main route out of Cherbourg. Taraz selected the wipers, the slow lazy arc of the telescopic arm reaching out for the farthest corners of the windscreen. She eased her foot down on the accelerator noting the barely audible change in pitch as the engine pushed the Mercedes into the third lane of the motorway. The surface water was causing a spray that enveloped the surrounding cars. Taraz eased back and selected the cruise control at a steady ninety. She smiled as she thought of the large American and his capitalist ways. Although he had been resident in Britain some fifteen years, Whittaker still held on to some vestiges of the homeland. To many, the fat cigars, leather jackets and air conditioning were little more than the expected stereotype, but to Whittaker they were a little taste of home, a capitalist fat cat writ large in the 51st State. And he *was* the consummate businessman. The smile evaporated from her face as she remembered the interrogation. What was Whittaker?'
She knew the car was wired, either bugged or a transmitter. If not, then she had a tail. The Glock Seven handgun had remained undetected within the roof cavity, the porcelain body impervious to x-ray. The mission paper work was still strapped to her back, the stiffness of the binding beginning to rub into her flesh. What she could not be certain of was the reason behind the stop and search. If they were tailing the car and not her she would still need to travel to Strasbourg to allay any suspicions surrounding her story. If it were she alone, then the rendezvous with Kamal would be

postponed. Either way, she would be at least a day, if not more, off schedule. Any phone calls would have to be public and not mobile. A truck stop would provide the opportunity. A hire firm in Strasbourg from the phone book. She would park up and remove her cases before losing herself in the city centre, rush hour even better, before doubling back to the rental car and exiting to the south. It would be at least two days before anyone got suspicious.

Taraz smiled as she tuned the radio. She had never been to Strasbourg.

Nine

Culmholt Hall, Blackdown Hills
February 15th, 20.30 hours
With Jenny agreeing to drive, Rob had not hesitated in breaking open the first of what would be many bottles over the course of the night. Steve and Lisa had taken little time to recover from the journey down from Lossiemouth in Scotland. Reaching the end of his commission, and coinciding with the retirement of an aircraft type just marginally younger than himself, Steve Lomart had served in the Gulf and had flown two missions supporting Rob's squadron in target designator Buccaneers. He and Lisa had been married for five years and although their visits were infrequent, the Lathams considered the couple to be among their oldest friends. Latham was looking forward to the *'rumble'* as his Irish friend so enthusiastically called their infrequent gatherings.

He knew that he would have to make it up to Jenny. She and Lisa enjoyed each other's company and knew what to expect from their husbands in such circumstances. These former warriors found it impossible to shake the habit of the last chance saloon. When they partied, they partied hard and tended to make the most of what time was afforded them. Thus had it always been and, in particular, during those searing days in the Gulf.

As Jenny's Volvo swept up Culmholt's floodlit drive, the former aircrew were already in high spirits in the rear seats. Steve looked over his wife's shoulder as the mansion house loomed up ahead of them. He let out a slow wolf-whistle.

'Bloody hell Lath', no wonder you got us in these penguin suits. Will the Maharaja be in tonight?' As Steve laughed Latham could smell the whiskey on his breath and suddenly realised how drunk they already were. The car was met at the entrance by the matre'de, Latham catching the reflection of Jenny's eyes in the rear view mirror as the door was opened. Maybe this wasn't the most suitable of venues.

Feeling slightly overdressed the foursome made their way into one of the large dining rooms and were seated. Drinks were ordered and Lisa was the first to raise a toast.

'To friends and a new start.' She smiled, holding the thin-stemmed glass at arms length. Steve stood and filled his glass. The words were slightly slurred.

'Jen and Lath. Two escapees from the firm who managed to find their rural idle.'

'Don't you mean idyll?' Jenny began to laugh as Steve

continued.

'I know what I mean.'

From his seat Latham raised his empty glass to his former colleague.

'Just as Ringo wasn't even the best drummer in the Beatles, I give you the man who wasn't even the best pilot in his aircraft and who, on a certain winters' night five years ago, was in no way connected with the flying of a Bucc' through Fifteen Squadron's hanger.'

Jenny's eyes widened as the grinning Lomart sat back into his seat.

'Not guilty Your Honour.'

Jenny looked across at Lisa. Her slowly nodding head and broad smile told everything.

'He didn't?' It was Rob who answered.

'He bloody well did. Took a layer of paint off the hanger doors and nearly incinerated a couple of poor linies. It was only the darkness and lack of witnesses that he got away with it.' Steve was now holding up a hand as if on oath.

'I can prove that I was at a children's hospital doing charity work that night'.

Before any more innocence could be professed, a waiter arrived at the table. The laughter subsided and menus passed around. The table fell silent.

Brittany 10.00pm

The lamplight threw long shadows that ran the full length of the old barn. Around the table at the far end, four men sat at either side as the woman, known to all except Kamal, only as Host, stood. Silently, she removed a number of identical folders from her portfolio case and distributed them. Rana disappeared briefly into the gloom before returning with a small rust covered pitcher that he placed next to the oil lamp. His distinctive leather bound filofax was placed carefully on the table, his pen at the ready. Taraz finally sat as the folders were opened. Silence ensued as pages were slowly turned and photographs removed. It was Asil who broke through the quiet with a low, drawn out whistle. Taraz looked up from her document.

'I take it you have reached our intended target, Asil'. The stare was cold.

The younger man shook his head slowly, his eyebrows arched in an air of bewilderment. 'I…I mean…we, all realised that the air-to-air system meant an airborne target but….' Kamal cut him off.

'Does Air Force One frighten you, Asil?' Again, the stare was impassive.

'No sir, it does not'.

'Good. Then we may proceed.' Kamal carefully placed his papers in an arc on the table in front of him. 'I realise that many of you are concerned at the apparently complex nature of our task. As you know it is the wish of our superiors that we inflict so much more than a statement of intent. With the current state of security surrounding out target, the possibility of a close-in kill is limited at best, suicidal at most.' He nodded towards Salam at the far end of the table as he continued. 'I realise that there are many among us who bring very capable means to the table, but our superiors require global recognition of their intent. This is why you are all here.' Kamal began to hand out papers around the table.

'Jubal was maintaining communication as of 9.00am GMT, but I am prepared for those lines to be

severed, should he be compromised. In that event Host, here and myself have been fully briefed and the mission will become self governing.'
Taraz continued. 'The main purpose of my visit, gentlemen, is to brief you on the status of my operation. At present the proposed delivery aircraft is in an airworthy state and final preparations are being made for test flights. I am awaiting imminent confirmation as to the willingness of the British Civil Aviation Authorities to allow those flights, but Jubal is confident that enough influence can be achieved. As far as our originally stated window of opportunity is concerned, the clock still ticks.' She held up a photograph to Latif.

'This is your pilot, Latif. You will only meet him on the day, at the arming rendezvous at Coudeville-sur-Mer. Code name is Steel. You have this for five minutes before burning it.' As she handed him the photograph Rana looked up from his file.

'Contact with our sea bound cargo was made last night and the landing should be on time. Three units instead of the promised four.' He glanced at Kamal before continuing.

'I am still not convinced with the delivery method. Surely surface to air would be a less complicated option. Why not?'
It was Kamal who answered.

'Far too inaccurate. If you can get within two miles of the target, an air launched kill is statistically more probable. It's all a matter of proximity. Your little pea shooter would run out of steam way before our target's altitude. We estimate that our best chance is at thirty thousand feet before the aircraft descends to meet the French escort.'

Rana raised his eyebrows, still to be convinced. As he sat back in his chair, Asil spoke for the first time.

'Jubal said something about a Navy airfield ?'

'Lessay, to the west. Mainly old Crusaders from the French carriers but this is where the escort of Mirages will fly from. Take off time is very close to our intended rendezvous so we need to neutralise the threat or at the very least, delay them getting airborne. There is also Lanveoc further south but that's mainly 'copters.'

Aisha was silent, her cigarette glowing in the half light as she took another slow draw. A long stream of smoke billowed from her mouth as she spoke,. 'Yes, I want it looked at.' She glanced at Rana through the haze.

'Take a drive up there tonight. I want a layout of the base and a report of comings and goings. If they're switched on, and they will be, that's where the quickest reaction time will be.'

Kamal replaced the sheets in his folder. He ran his fingers along the edge of the spine.

'Jubal also has unconfirmed reports of a land based American Patriot battery close to the Normandy beaches where the main ceremony will take place. This is standard procedure with so many Heads of State in one place at the same time. It is well outside the range of our target intercept area but needs to be checked out nonetheless.' Heads nodded silently as Taraz rose from her seat. 'And Salam, be sure that your little diversion at Caen looks like an accident. We don't want to scare them off now, do we?' Rana nodded silently

'If there are no further questions gentlemen.' She turned to face Kamal.

'A word in private if you will.' As the two of them left by the rear of the barn, Rana began burning sheaves of paper in the rust covered pitcher.

The meal was all but over when Jenny excused herself from the group. The food had been excellent, if a little rich for her taste. As they awaited the final course she used the opportunity to check out the bathrooms and freshen up. Even more opulent than the restaurant décor, the cloakrooms provided a safe haven from the testosterone fuelled banter of the table. That said, she was enjoying herself. She had always got on well with Lisa and found Steve one of the less demanding of Rob's friends. It was good to see him unwind. The move and the last month of testing had visibly worn him down to the extent that, if this weekend had not taken place, she would have insisted on a break anyway.
As she left the cloakroom curiosity made her turn left into the larger, more opulent space. At the far end a bar stretched across the entire width of the room, several guests could be seen taking pre-meal drinks. It was towards the farthest corner of the room, huge bay window doors open to the vast arboretum that stretched from the rear of the house, that Jenny's attention was drawn. There again, the laughter that seemed to fill the great yawning expanse of the vaulted ceiling.

Staying close to the edge of the oriental screen that partitioned the two rooms, Jenny tried to focus through the cloud of cigar smoke that filled the far corner. The laughter was coming from a heavy set man who seemed to be dressed far too casually for the surround. With his back to her, Jenny squinted through the haze but the face was hidden from view. The hair was longer she thought, but the broad shoulders wore the trade mark leather jacket that had seen better years, let alone days. The man seemed deep in conversation with an older man sat directly opposite him. The leathery, tanned features were offset by sharp blue eyes that belied their older surroundings. Barrel-chested and looking fit despite the enormous cigar rolling around the corner of his mouth, Jenny estimated that the man was a well preserved sixty something. His groomed but casual appearance also seemed at odds with Culmholt's more formally dressed clientele. As Jenny edged forward, exposing herself from the cover of the screen, a distant memory halted her progress. A memory of conflict, and of a life she had striven to forget. She paused momentarily before slowly edging her way back behind the screen and, turning gracefully, walked back towards the smaller dining room.

It was Steve who noticed her first.

'That was quick Jen. Changed your mind ?' He grinned from behind his glass.

Lisa hit him on the arm. 'For god's sake you beast, you're not in the Mess now. Give a girl a chance.' Rob laughed as Jenny took her seat, but not before he had noticed her slightly forced smile. He reached out and squeezed her hand, as he mouthed an 'Okay?'

The slightest of nods before she poured herself another glass from the water pitcher, Jenny winked at Lisa. 'I suddenly remembered what bores you two turn into. What was it Lisa, big metal flying things or football ?'

'Both, and something about sorting out some Scottish bloke up at an airfield?

I must admit though, they're not as bad as they used to

be. I mean it's after nine and they've both still got their trousers on haven't they?' Lisa smirked.
Kamal led the way through the rear doorway that took them out into the bright, moonlit courtyard. He could hear Aisha's heels rapping across the cobblestones. He made for the van, which was parked at the side of the larger of the two barns. Without speaking, each got into the front cab. There was a brief silence before Kamal spoke.

'Your journey. You were compromised?' He could see Aisha's slight smile in the shadow of the unlit interior. He was now close enough to breathe in her aroma. The vision of distant memories heightened his senses.

'Still able to second guess me, Abdul' There was little emotion in her voice. She now looked directly at him, before continuing. 'Whittaker, I'm afraid. I was stopped in Cherbourg by Customs. The car was bugged, of that I am certain. That is why I was late.' Kamal's brow furrowed.

'Whittaker ? He knows of us?' Aisha held up her hand immediately.

'No,no…I have no reason to believe that he knows anything of the operation. I think that it was his car, or rather him that they were after. For what reason I need to find out. I will leave tomorrow and collect the Mercedes from Strasbourg. My main concern is that the French now have me in the system. If they put you and me together at the DGSE they will know that we are operational. Our masters may have short memories, but the French, however do not.'
For the first time since he had known her, Kamal saw anger in Aisha's eyes. She was referring to an operation in the mid Eighties that had taken them both

to Algeria to liase with a faction of political dissidents. It would be only through their brief affair three years later that they would realise that they had both been posted on the same mission, albeit in different locations. Over the space of three months the mission had been compromised by the presence of an unknown French DGSE agent. By the time she was discovered the identities of many of the main players had been put at risk. Kamal changed tack.

'And Steel? The drugs, they are working?' Aisha nodded slowly.

'It is a delicate balance, but he is becoming more reliant on me. The combination of the heroin and his own rage guarantees his co-operation.' Kamal raised an eyebrow.

'And for the flights?'

'I give him 18 milligrams of Codelphene over a three day period before each flight. It is essentially a sensorial stimulant, the rationalisation sharper, the reaction times accelerated. He suspects nothing.'

'And the side effects?'

'With his current heart rate, the next four months, should he live, will begin a gradual disintegration of the aorta and the surrounding tissue. Dead within a year.'

Kamal rested his hands on the top of the steering wheel.

'But in good shape so far?'

Oh, he has his moments. The drink doesn't help but I have other methods.' She looked away. Kamal studied the backs of his hands, a small grin of remembrance playing across his face. He tried to clear his head.

Kamal made to take her hand in reassurance. She

flinched at his touch before continuing. ‘There was an agent at Cherbourg, I’m certain was not Customs. They will be waiting for me tomorrow so I will have to travel clean. From then on it may be that we communicate only through Jubal.’ She gathered the portfolio case she had purchased in Strasbourg and opened the cab door. She stopped.

‘Abdul’ He turned to face her. The voice was softer. ‘My code name, Halah. I know it is your wife’s name but I can assure you that it was a coincidence. I don’t know if our superiors are playing with us’ She tried a weak smile as Kamal silently nodded his acknowledgement. She continued. ‘And watch Rana. He’s dangerous.’ With that she turned and began her way back across the courtyard.

Despite his wife’s apparent unease after the meal the rest of the evening had proved to be an enjoyable affair, Jenny eventually livening up enough to join in with the late night drinking. The party ran out of steam in the early hours. Jenny had relented earlier in the day and agreed to Steve and Lisa staying in the undecorated spare room. The tired couples made their way to their respective rooms.

Rob waited until all sounds had subsided. From the gap beneath the bedroom door Latham saw the landing light go out. He listened as the last of the muffled voices faded into the night air. The house was quiet. Jenny sat in front of the mirror removing the last of her make up. Latham walked up behind her, placed his hands on her shoulders and squeezed gently.

‘A penny for them.’

Jenny glanced up at him in the mirror. ‘For what ?’

‘Tonight. You looked like something was on

your mind when you came back from the cloakroom.'

'That ?....I...I thought that I saw someone in the bar. Turned out to be a false alarm.' She looked away from his concerned gaze. He persisted.

'Are you sure love, you looked pretty shaken up.'

'Yes, I'm sure. You remember that bad parents evening I had back along ?
I thought it was the father of that restraining order lad I taught. Sorry , I guess it brought it all back a bit suddenly.' She rose from the chair before her husband had a chance to pry further. She hated lying to him but this was one sighting that she hoped would not raise its head again. Rob had taken the bait.

'God, I'm sorry Jen. Of all the places.' He paused remembering the tearful nights and threatening phone calls that had lasted for over a month before the police managed to track down the boy's estranged stepfather. The sudden thought that the situation might have followed them from Preston was chilling. He left it at that as Jenny climbed into bed and turned onto her side. Climbing in beside her he leant over and kissed her gently on the temple before turning the light out.

Ten

Honiton, Devon
March 7thth 1994,
09.10 hours

Iain Hart managed to cup his hand over the mouthpiece of the receiver before the spluttering cough that sprayed his desk with breadcrumbs. The noise echoed in the high ceiling of the large office. Ronald Thursby looked up from his paper work at the gesticulating Sergeant, gazing through the glasses perched at the end of his nose. The look was stern. He valued the first half hour of every day in the station as a time for quiet contemplation and a chance to catch up on the pile of paperwork that forever seemed to litter his in-tray.

'Promotion through is it son?' Hart cleared his throat, his eyes watering from the effort to speak.

'Red phone sir. It's the Deputy Commissioner, in person.'

Thursby paused before lifting the receiver. His finger hovered over the connect button.

'Relax son, me and Ronny go back about a hundred years or so.'

Hart held up a hand.

'Not Mr Draycott sir, the DC from SI6 in London.' Thursby's hand froze over the button, his brow furrowed. A call from the hush-hush boys, he thought. A rarity indeed.

He composed himself before punching the button. His Devon accent was barely perceptible.

'DI Thursby sir, how can I be of service.' Hart had managed to digest the remnants of his sandwich and settled down to earwig on the conversation.

'Certainly sir, but I must emphasise that this man is strictly small fry, in the scheme of things. In the rural context he is certainly a face in these parts but the evidence points to minor league smuggling.' Thursby gestured for a pen and paper from Hart. He began to scribble notes onto the pad immediately.

'The car is certainly a match sir, and the woman could be a possible confirmation from an earlier observation. Do we have any pictures ? Uh huh, that will be a big help sir.'

Hart made his way to the large stack of filing cabinets that filled one corner of the office and began to search through the alphabetically listed compartments. The location of the thin folder was easily remembered. Thursby was listening with intent, his head nodding occasionally.

'I see sir, and will I need to get in direct contact with the gentleman? Very well sir, I would expect a result within the day and will contact Paris

directly.'
The receiver slowly replaced in its cradle, Thursby circled the first line on the note pad several times before looking up. Hart, holding the file out at arms length, pre-empted his superior's line of thought.

'Roland Bradley Whittaker?' Thursby spread the contents of the file over his desk.

'Possibly, but its his motor, or rather the woman who's driving it, that could be interesting. You remember that classy piece out at Stop Gate services?' Hart nodded as he retrieved the photographs from the nights operation. Thursby continued.

'It seems that our friends over in France have a rather more pressing interest in her. One Halah Akief from the Emirates. Possible terrorism connections. At present it's only a hunch, some bloke by the name of Tressor that I've got to contact tomorrow. The boss wants us to take a closer look at Whittaker's operation before then. Plymouth warehouses, Templemere, the works.' Hart held up a second set of photographs. 'We never did get a positive on the second face either.' The muscular, dark haired man from the filling station fore court had remained an illusive figure.

'Certainly, but I'll still wager that he's ex forces.' Thursby rose from the desk and retrieved his trench coat from the rack in the doorway. 'Get yourself over to Exeter data store at Middlemoor and onto that mainframe. Scan him in and see what floats to the surface.' Hart gathered the pages from the desk and placed the file in his leather brief case. As it clicked shut he looked up.

'This serious sir?' Thursby looked back from the open door.

'Don't worry son, we have all the back up we need at a moments notice, but for the present we're on the local yokel. Low key and on the look out for nothing more than a small scale ciggy smuggler Got it?' Thursby tapped the side of his nose as he winked.

Strasbourg,
12.00 hours
The car seemed to have been left untouched. Taraz opened the capacious boot and filled it with the results of a busy morning's shopping. The umbrella was still placed diagonally across the matting that covered the spare wheel bay. The handle, coated in a thin of film of lubricating oil, remained untouched. She waited until the car was stopped at traffic lights on the outskirts of the city before she adjusted her hair in the rear view mirror. As her hand teased and preened, she felt for the bulge of the Glock in the ceiling cavity. It was still there. That would need losing before Cherbourg, she thought. The surveillance seemed to be keeping at a discreet distance.

The traffic moved at a faster pace as the early afternoon hustle of the city gave way to the wide-open sprawl of the Alsace countryside. Despite the delay caused by the customs episode, Taraz was satisfied with her progress. All relevant information had been directed and she had been quietly assured by Kamal's preparation. She had wanted to stay aloof, which she had. She knew of Kamal and the situation with his family. It was unfortunate for him but the need for his expertise demanded his absolute attention. She may not have agreed with her master's methods but what could not be denied was the way in which blackmail tended to concentrate the mind. He had lost weight, she thought. The same deep eyes, the smooth, low tone of his voice had all remained. She had been relieved that the feelings of the recent past had seemed easy to control. She had moved on. Changed even. Her work had made relationships virtually worthless. She had learned to control her feelings, learned to become less reliant on the warmth of human contact.

Her thoughts were concentrated by a road sign for the Cherbourg terminal. She drove for a further two kilometres before the Mercedes turned onto a small country road. She would bury the Glock and contact Jubal for further supplies. Cherbourg was no longer an unknown quantity. She knew what to expect.

Devon and Cornwall Police Headquarters,
Middlemoor, Exeter, 13.40 hours

The computer hummed with life as Hart allowed the cursor to play across the screen. His finger hovered over the mouse as the arrow came to rest on the rectangular red icon at the top of the page. He hesitated briefly before double clicking.

The password that Thursby had given him had failed the first time, the system automatically shutting down. The audible chime from the consul had caused heads to turn in the unit. Only a few of the consuls were occupied in the long, newly refurbished computer suite at Middlemoor. The high temperature in the unit emphasised the smell of new carpets and freshly painted walls. Finding an empty consul at the far end of the room, Hart had hoped to complete his task in private and present Thursby with a name before anyone higher up the chain became involved. He tried the password again, this time in capitals. The screen ran through a series of security warnings before eventually revealing the required database. Hart reached out for the plastic coffee cup to his left. Still too hot. He opened the military files and began to search.

The Q, or 'Questionable' file, revealed those members of the forces who had, for whatever reason, left the service under unconventional circumstances. Hart set his parameters before initiating a trawl. He would start with a twelve month period from the present day and cast the net over a greater time frame should the first sweep be unsuccessful. The target's association with Whittaker made the RAF an obvious starting point. The computer took seconds to compile a list of forty seven suspects from the last year. Starting alphabetically, Hart began to run through the profiles, records and mug shots of these personnel. Before long he was scrolling through many of the files on a visual basis alone. It was as he was approaching the end of the list that a distinctive face stared back from the console. The eyes had a haunted look about them, he thought as the serviceman's career details scrolled across the page. As the image gained clarity Hart knew that he had found what he wanted. The hair was much shorter, trimmed to military precision and the moustache did little to change the general structure of the face. Hart held up the blow-up of the garage forecourt still next to the monitor screen.

'Got him', he whispered through clenched teeth as the printer at the far end of the room began to disgorge the files valuable information.

Templemere,
15.05 hours
Whittaker's secretary had called on the Monday after the Lomarts had returned to Scotland and although he was mindful of the official invitation to visit, Latham still felt wary of previous welcome he had received. The Scot on the other end of the phone could not have been more genial when Latham contacted Templemere to arrange a visit for later in the week. As the day approached, Latham left work early - he had yet to reason why he had not told Jenny of his second visit and did not want to arrive home at a later hour.
Arriving at the airfield, a familiar scene greeted him. The small Vampire was once again aloft, spiralling and darting between the high clouds that were scattered above. The clear blue of the remaining sky allowed the sunlight to occasionally catch the bare metal skin of the rolling fighter. As Latham allowed the Jeep to glide to a halt outside the main hanger entrance, a familiar figure appeared from between the great hanger doors.

'Iain McCleesh. Pleased to meet you.' A huge oil stained hand reached out towards Latham as the mechanic lumbered towards him in the hanger entrance. The grip was as vice like as to be expected. Latham removed his Barbour and left it on the back seat of the Jeep.
'I saw that you were ex crew.' McCleesh held the card that Latham had earlier given him. One eyebrow raised as he read the contents at arms length.
'Westfields ya say? Och you should have said at the time son. I'm sorry if I was a bit short with you last week, but we get quite a few anoraks up here who want a nosy around, you know what I mean?' The large Scot unzipped his overalls and tied the arms

together around his considerable midriff. The grubby T-shirt bore the Whittaker logo. McCleesh pocketed a large wrench and wiped an arm across his sweat stained brow. 'It's always good to meet fellow trade, albeit slightly more modern.' The laugh echoed around the interior of the hanger. 'So you've just moved into the area then?'

'Culmhead, been here just over four months.'

'Ye not a local then like me?' Again, the huge guffaw bounced it's way overhead. Latham smiled.

'No not at all, Sunderland actually, but I do feel that I know this place.' Latham gazed up into the roof trusses high above.

'D'ye know Mister Whittaker then?'

'Actually no I don't but I've spoken to him. That's why I'm here. I was here last year when you had a mate of mine drop in on you. I was wingman to the Lightning that crash landed here.'

McCleesh's eyes widened. 'Ma God, we've got the set'.

It was Latham's turn to look surprised.

'Sorry, I.....'

'You just missed him. Did you see the two-seater Vampire take off ? That was Mr Ronson. He's flyin' fer us now. Over a year now, tests all the renovations. He does the jets, while the boss does the props. Bloody good pilot.'

'Max? You mean Max Ronson?'

'Ay, the very same'

Latham shook his head slowly and raised his eyes to the roof. He looked around him at the interior.

'My God. I thought that he had had it with flying. How the hell did he end up here?'

'Well you'd have to ask the boss about that

one. All I do know is that he bought the Lightning for spare parts and Max got in contact with him a few months later. He's only up for half an hour. Do you want to wait for him?'

Latham tried to answer but stopped. This was sudden news. He paused before answering.

'Yes…yes of course.'

McCleesh placed his hands on his hips. 'You seem a little shocked laddie?'

'I…I am. I haven't seen Max for almost two years. It was that crash that grounded him for good, or so I thought.' Latham began to replay those final few weeks of their friendship before all contact had been lost. At first he had felt an initial guilt at not intervening to help his friend further, but this had been tainted by the memory of that last drunken evening at Latham's married quarters in Warton. Ronson had been disgraceful that night, reducing Jenny to tears as she became caught in the crossfire of his venom. The memory of having to restrain his own friend, before throwing him out onto the streets of Manchester caused Latham to turn away from McCleesh. After a brief pause he looked up and turned to face him.

'The flying……is he, I mean, has he still got it?'

'Ay, top drawer. You should see him go, son. Are you sure you're OK?'

'Yeah sure.' His head cleared. He pointed to the interior of the hanger. 'Do I get the guided tour?'

'Jeez, of course son, where are my manners' McCleesh held out his arm to show the way. The interior seemed less cluttered than Latham's previous visit although the presence of the blue Spitfire in a far corner was an addition.

'We got rid of another Devon last week. She's on a freighter bound for Texas now. Three month strip down for static display. A valet job really.' McCleesh pointed at the Spitfire. 'That there is the boss' pride and joy. Mark 19 reconnaissance job. Stripped down smoother than a baby's arse, that one. She goes like shit offa greased shovel.' Latham could not help but smile.

'Four hundred and fifty in a dive, or so the boss reckons. And there's only one other like it and that's in Australia. He paid seventy five thousand for it back in eighty four and now reckons it's worth close on quarter of a million.'

'I've a got few hours in these things, but never in one of these clipped wing jobs.'

Latham was up on tiptoe as he looked into the cockpit. McCleesh was grinning.

'I didn't have you down as being that old son.'

'Thanks very much. I had a year on the Battle of Britain Memorial flight. Mark 9.

Nothing quite as impressive as this though.'

'Well, if you're good to the boss he might let you polish her one weekend'. As they walked along centre line of the hanger, several mechanics busied themselves on the remaining two aircraft.

'Over there we've got another Vampire and that's hopefully going to be airborne

by the new year. Single seater, and staying fairly local, down at Hurn near Bournemouth.'

Approaching the rear wall, Latham recognised the shape of a small, tired looking Tiger Moth biplane sitting in several large pieces on the concrete.

'And that's my winter homework' stated

McCleesh, his words partially drowned by the familiar sound of a Vampire engine. 'That'll be Max. He always beats up the hanger on his return. Causes a few dropped spanners but you get used to it after a while.' He grinned as he trotted towards the hanger entrance.
Outside, in the early Spring sunlight Latham shielded his eyes as he followed the progress of the Vampire as it approached on finals. He felt like a nervous schoolboy about to meet a former bully. As the fighter taxied to a halt, the canopy already raised, the pilot held up a gloved thumb to the ground crew who were waiting at the edge of the apron. A small ladder was attached to the starboard side of the cockpit. From his viewpoint at the side of one of the vast hanger doors, Latham watched silently as the pilot unstrapped himself from the ejector seat and made his way down the ladder.
The frame seemed to have lost a little in weight, but the shoulders remained impressively broad. Before removing the helmet, the pilot crouched under the starboard wing and kicked one of the main undercarriage tyres. Words were briefly exchanged with an approaching member of the ground crew before he began to make his way towards the hanger entrance.
Latham stood his ground and waited for the first signs of recognition. The pilot undid the chinstraps, before raising the smoked visor and removing the matt green flying helmet. Sweat soaked flying gloves were peeled off and a hand forced through the flattened tangle of dark hair. It was the features that Latham recognised first. The sparkling eyes that had once so expressed a thirst for life carried a serious, somewhat remote look. Gone also was the trademark moustache, the once

neatly trimmed staple of British flyers, seemingly replaced by a haphazard three day growth that was offset by shoulder length hair which had looked so out of place protruding from beneath the back of the flying helmet. A single bead of sweat trickled from his greying temple. Together with McCleesh, Max Ronson strode purposely towards the office at the side of the hanger. Passing almost parallel to Latham, it was McCleesh who had to break Ronson from his concentration.

'Do you no recognise your old oppo, Max?' Ronson stopped and turned. The look was penetrating before recognition finally dawned.

'Rob?...Rob Latham?'

'Hi Max. How are you?' Latham held out a hand. Ronson stared at it, his face a mask of confusion. It seemed a long pause before he managed to find the words.

'What the hell are you doing here?' The reply threw Latham somewhat, or rather the tone of Ronson's voice. Surprise, certainly, but with a barely discernable edge of anger in the tone. The brief silence was broken by a visibly uncomfortable McCleesh.

'Mr Latham's down at Westfields now, Max. Boss invited him over for a look.'

Ronson sensed the atmosphere created by his words. The smile, somewhat forced, was accompanied by a rigorous handshake.

'How'd you know Whittaker then?' Ronson held the grip.

'I didn't at first. I just came up out of curiosity. If truth be told, it was seeing that Mark 19 in there that really whet my appetite.' Latham pointed a thumb in the direction of the main hanger.

'Do you need work then, Lath'?'

'No…no not at all, just curiosity. Like I said, I saw you flying around and….'. Latham stopped when he realised that Ronson was staring over his right shoulder, his attention focussed on the far distance. From behind, a metallic silver Mercedes was making its way around the perimeter fence towards the hangers. It was impossible to see through the smoked glass of the windows as the car purred onto the apron.
The large figure of Roly Whittaker climbed stiffly from the passenger side door, the Mercedes' suspension lurching under the weight. Latham did not have to be introduced to recognise the American. Chomping on a huge, unlit cigar, Whittaker made his way over to the group.

'Rob Latham? Pleased to meet you, son. I hope this moody Scot has been taking better care of you this time.' The laugh was loud enough to echo through the doors of the hanger. Whittaker slapped a large hand across Latham's back and pulled him in the direction the second, smaller hanger. Behind them came two sharp horn blasts from the Mercedes. Ronson glanced over at the parked car before looking back at Latham.

'Look..I've gotta go Rob. I'll get your number off Mac and give you a bell, OK?' This time the tone was more conciliatory.
Whittaker pointed a wary finger at the two men.

'You two guys know each other?' Latham was about to answer when the driver side window of the Mercedes began to lower. The same honey skinned woman he had seen on his first visit removed her sunglasses and stared at the approaching Ronson.
The woman seemed impatient. Latham watched as his

former colleague walked silently around the front of the car and got in to the passenger side door. The woman became aware of Latham's scrutiny and raised the window. The car glided away from the complex and towards the taxiway, soon disappearing from view on the grassy horizon.

'You two flew together? Jeez son, this must be like the High School reunion. He's a good pilot. Does all my jet testing. I tell you, it was a blessing in disguise the day he put that Lightning down here.' The two men approached the smaller hanger, it's doors bolted shut. Whittaker stopped to light up his cigar before wrestling with the giant padlock that secured the small entrance that was cut into the left hand door.

'You remember the F6? I bought her for scrap. Cost me five hundred bucks ' He hauled the door open. From the darkness fluorescent lights flickered overhead, the interior of the hanger briefly resembling a light storm as the tubes kicked in. The strobing flashes of illumination caught the Lightning along the lines of its slab sided fuselage, the matt finish of the dark grey paintwork doing its intended job in absorbing much of the glare. It was a sight Latham knew well. What shocked him was the condition the fighter. He could almost smell the fresh paint.
Gone was the classic natural Sixties finish of polished steel, replaced by camouflage of the late Eighties when the fighter was in its final throws as a cold war warrior. Latham turned to face Whittaker, his hands held up in front of him.

'When you said scrap, you were taking the piss, right?'

'Sure, she's a bit of a sight ain't she?' The shit eating grin was wider than ever.

Latham dug his hands deep into the pockets of his jacket as he walked under the starboard wing. Even to his experienced eye it was obvious that the fighter had received hundreds of hours of expensive attention. He let his hands play along the rivets of the leading edge panels.

'Does this get any better ?' Whittaker stared at the concrete apron before answering.

'Oh yeah, I intend her to fly all right. You remember you couldn't contact me all last week? I was up at Gatwick with the CAA. Reckons we're weeks away from a permit to fly. Friends in high places, if you know what I mean.' Whittaker tapped the side of his nose with a nicotine stained finger as he winked. Latham continued to make his way around the fuselage, unconsciously mirroring his pre-flight check of the past. Safety pins were tugged, ailerons pulled down and skin gauges checked as habit took over. The condition astounded him. This was caring love and attention on an obsessive scale. Never had he wanted to fly an aircraft so much in his life.

'Is she ready?' The question was as simple as it was direct. Whittaker smiled before answering, his hand patting the nose cone above him.

'She sure is. We've had both engines fired up. Both at reheat. I think they heard us in Bristol that day. We've got some work to do with the navigation system but when that's complete Max'll be takin' her up' Whittaker drew long and hard on the cigar and thumped the side panelling of the cockpit.

'I believe you guys call them Rag and Bone men over here? Making something outta nothing. I gotta Arab millionaire who's gonna give me eight hundred thousand bucks for this baby.'

He grinned at Latham and winked.
I oughta' be locked up.'

Eleven

Houses of Parliament, London
March 21st, 13.50 hours

The terrace was quiet save for a smattering of newly elected faces showing their families the sights. The children milled about the tables and chairs, boredom etched into their faces. Sir Giles Cardew snorted audibly as he made his way towards the covered area at the far end of the terrace. Why they ever allowed the little menaces into the palace was beyond him, caused nothing but a bloody nuisance. He used his bulk to force his way between the chairs scattered about the terrace, his reddening face glinting in the early afternoon sunlight. Amilnas was his usual punctual self, his small, immaculately dressed frame partially obscured by the large awning that threw a shadow over the far corner of the seating area. The slim, silver brief case that he was never without was on the table in front of him. A pretty waitress had just delivered a jug of iced water and was making her way back into the interior of the restaurant. Cardew cursed the climate of the day. Three weeks of rain and the first day of sun brings him out in a bloody sweat. Arabs, of course could control themselves. Numerous visits to the Middle East had taught him that. Money also helped. The more a man had the less he sweated, or so it seemed. Cardew drew a damp handkerchief from a pocket and clenched it in his right fist. He knew Amilnas' hand would be chalk dry, his own palm feeling like a Turkish bath house. The Syrian businessman looked up from his newspaper and removed his sunglasses as he rose from the seat. The cream coloured suit was pressed to perfection, in stark contrast to the British politician's crumpled pin stripe ensemble.

'My dear Sir Giles, how wonderful to see you' Amilnas gestured towards the sky. 'A wonderful day don't you agree ?'

Cardew removed the handkerchief and offered his hand. 'Quite so Mr Amilnas, a pleasure to be in your company again. I must apologize for my lateness. The PM does tend to ramble in his briefings'. The two men smiled as Cardew sat his large frame into the terrace seat. It was incorrigible name-dropping but Cardew knew that these little snippets of parliamentary life helped to grease the wheels of negotiation, and with four hundred thousand at stake he needed all the grease he could muster.

Amilnas poured a tall glass with water, several ice cubes splashing droplets over the table's surface. Cardew unbuttoned his suit jacket and placed his cigar pouch on the table in front of him. He fought to keep his breathlessness inaudible. The voice was controlled.

'A tolerable flight I trust?' Amilnas finished sipping his water before answering.

'El Al, ironically, but I do find the service to be most agreeable. And my chances of recognition much decreased.' The smile revealed the only imperfection in the Syrians appearance, the nicotine stained teeth betraying a virile habit.

'Good, good I'm glad to hear it.' Cardew leant forward in his seat, the large stomach straining over a leather belt. He was eager to continue negotiations.

'The PM is absolutely thrilled by your donation, Kalid' he lied. 'As you know, the party, and obviously now the Government, has always held your organisation in extreme regard. In particular the aid you afforded us during our little spat with the Argentinians.'

Amilnas held up a hand.

'This is nothing my dear Sir Giles. As you are well aware my masters are ever eager to cement relations with a country we have only ever considered as the very best of allies. Think of this as a mere gift of gratitude.' He raised his glass and tilted his head to the side, his last words drowned by the rumble of a jet inbound for Heathrow.

The Englishman leant further forward, waiting for the roar to subside before speaking.

'The usual channels, I take it?'

'Of course. A discreet press release would not go amiss. The usual platitudes.

I take it that you will be dealing with the matter personally.' Amilnas steepled his fingers, holding them in front of his mouth. His eyes narrowed as he stared at the MP.

'Certainly, certainly, you have no worry on that score my dear fellow. I will be making the visit myself, however. The PM regrets that his timetable for June allows little time for fund raising. As you know, he's a very busy man. The summer schedule will involve the official visits to Canada and the States, before returning for the D-Day Anniversary in June. The UN conference in France will follow on from that.'

Cardew could see that Amilnas had expected the news, as he had on a number of occasions. He smiled and raised the glass to his lips before pausing.

'Ah, yes, the chains of office. I would fully understand any head of state finding the prospect of visiting an armament manufacturer a, how shall we say, public relations minefield' Cardew knew that he had been rumbled.

'You are a shrewd man indeed, Kalid. The PM feels, with every justification I am sure, that the rest of the world does not have the capacity to view our very special bond in its entirety. He calls them peasants.' The smile was broad.

'I myself would be delighted to represent Her Majesty in the summer.' His mind fleetingly remembered the previous visit to the isolated armament complex on the Lebanese border, two years before. The corporation had pandered to his every whim, the very best in travel, accommodation and above all women. The sensorial nights had awoken him in ways he could not contemplate. He knew why he was being used, and he allowed himself to become compliant in every way. He was going at the next election, he had no qualms. Parliamentary privilege provided anonymity beyond the term of office, and ancient and arcane legislature would allow him to cover any tracks.

In return for lobbying on their behalf, FLR Ordinance had benefited the party to the tune of 2.5 million dollars over the past four years. Cardew had creamed what he considered to be his fee percentage and if anybody knew of this, then they had revealed nothing. The Englishman lit himself a slim Cuban cigar and allowed the smoke to roll in rings under the canopy. It was then that Amilnas changed tack.

'It seems that I am not the only beneficiary of your immense talents, Giles. I only realised this week that we have a mutual colleague. I believe that you know of Roland Whittaker?' The reference took Cardew by surprise. He preferred to keep his lobbyists as separate entities. He had heard of conflicts of interest being sniffed around by the gutter press. Better to keep such matters separate.

'Roland, you say?' He wondered how much to give away. Before he could answer he had his mind made up for him.

'Friend of mine is an aviation enthusiast, bit of a hobby really. Oil, you know. Spends ridiculous amounts on old aircraft. Whittaker renovates them for him.'

Cardew was hesitant before he answered.

'Yes, yes of course. His business is in my constituency. Colourful fella, being a yank and all. He recently approached me about a small matter with our Civil Aviation Authority, and being on the board myself, he felt that might be able to assist him.' Amilnas replaced his sunglasses.

'Quite remarkable man, I must say. He has

had connections with FLR over the years and has proved to be a valuable ally on more than one occasion. No doubt your legendary powers of persuasion will work for him as well'.

'Well I, er can't go into any details you trust, but obviously one likes to look out for colleagues.' The lugubrious wink was all that Amilnas needed. He raised his glass and toasted the British politician.

'I quite understand Sir Giles. Now, what news have you of Blind Eye.

M5 Motorway Services, Exeter
19.40 hours.

Thursby blew into the polystyrene cup between his chilled hands. Hart was late. The jumbo hotdog lay gently steaming on the counter top of the truck stop van. He would prefer the time to eat it in peace, but the urgency of the situation required Hart's presence. Thursby made his way back to his car and reached in through the open window for the radio receiver. He had just made contact with Exeter control when a familiar navy blue Ford Orion pulled into the lay-by. Hart flashed his lights as he drew up alongside. The Detective Inspector winced as several heads turned towards them from the crowd of drivers gathered beneath the awning of the burger van. He turned the collar of his coat up before he got into the car. The interior was warm, but it would be some time before Thursby would feel the chill begin to dissipate from his bones.

The previous month had been a frustrating sequence of non-events as the Whittaker surveillance had gone cold. Whittaker himself had failed to leave the country while the operation at Templemere, including the activities of the woman Akief, had squared with every line of inquiry. Thursby's superiors were beginning to question the legitimacy of budgeting for an operation at the behest of the French.

'Mr Draycott trying to balance the books is he sir?' Hart had sensed his gaffer's conflict with the constraints of the financial restrictions that every costly surveillance operation was up against. Templemere wouldn't be the first or last operation pulled through a lack of funding.

Thursby seemed more irascible than usual.

'Oh he'll pull it alright. Three weeks, and he starts to get cold feet. Says he's got big football matches coming up. Derby games and potential trouble.' He turned to Hart.

'Plymouth verses Exeter. I ask you? Not exactly First Division is it?' Hart shrugged his shoulders.

'Sorry sir, I'm a Newcastle United fan.' Thursby raised an eyebrow .

'Still, it's not funny is it. A bunch of tractor driving hoolies having priority over an Interpol job.' Thursby tapped his pipe on the dashboard, the contents disappearing into the passenger foot well. Hart motioned to open the ashtray but came up short, his thoughts envisaging old dogs and new tricks.

'So why the rush, sir ?' Thursby answered in between sucks on his newly lit briar.

'My little snitch down Honiton way says that the mystery lady up at Templemere is shacked up with our former Gulf war veteran. Saw them canoodling in some wine bar last week. A classy piece like that sticks out a mile down here.'

'Well I thought that was obvious, sir. The

amount of time spent in that Merc, I didn't think that they were saving on petrol.' Hart grinned through the tobacco smoke.

'Fair enough son, they're both attractive enough young bucks but I would have thought that a Middle Eastern maid was a non starter for Ronson.' Hart looked confused.

'Sorry sir.... I don't follow.'

'I've got an old mate in MOD records over at Swindon, we were in Aden together when I did my National. Anyway, he looked up our friend's record and it turns out that the reason for his questionable crack up was a bit more that shell shock.' Hart lowered his window and gulped in a lungful of air.

'You remember that hospital unit that was hit by a rogue Yank missile? Several killed, a bit of a diplomatic cock-up for a time and a rushed through enquiry.'

'Rings a bell, sir.'

'Well it turns out that Ronson had a girlfriend, or should I say fiancée, killed in the blast. They were apparently to be married that summer. That, coupled with some sort of botched bombing raid...' Thursby waved a finger at Hart. '...and I want that checked out.....sent him over the edge.'

'Interesting sir but I don't see what you're getting at?'

'Think about it. You've just lost your woman in an accident in some Middle Eastern conflict. The last thing you would want is to start knobbing some Arab princess, is it?'

Hart could not help but grin. He struggled to remain straight faced in the stern gaze of his superior.

'Grief works in many ways, sir. She's probably the

first relationship he's had since '91.'
Thursby shook his head slowly. 'Too....too....' He struggled for words. 'Too much, too soon.
I might be jumping to conclusions but it just doesn't make sense.'

'Forgive and forget, sir?' Thursby turned slowly to face Hart.

'You what? Is that the best your university educated brain can come up with. Sorry about the little spat with my fellow countrymen and the death of your wife to be, but why don't we start something, big boy.' Thursby was wide eyed as he studied Harts face.

OK sir, I was only trying to cover all possible angles.'

'No, no son, its not on. I need to see more of this blokes file. What effect did his Gulf service have on him, and so on ? Then I'll make up my mind, but until then it still looks dodgy.

DGSE Headquarters, Paris
March 22nd 18.30 hours
The photographs were pinned up along the length of a portable notice board that had been set up in front of Tressor's desk. Xavier Pinon chewed on the frame of his spectacles as he silently studied the montage before him. Several mugshots were scattered about a central cluster of photographs. Many were joined by line of red string held in place by coloured map pins. Central to all of the photographs, Abdul Kamal stared impassively back at the French agent. The large oak panelled door echoed as it shut behind Gilde Tressor. He did not look up as he entered the room, his attention focussed on a telephone number. He studied the piece of note pad paper at arms length.

'Interesting.....have a look'.

Pinon replaced his glasses and turned to face Tressor who handed him the paper.

'That's the number of a local inspector from Roland Whittaker's neck of the woods. An area called the Blackdowns in the West. It seems that our antiques dealer is indeed doing business with the man and all of her connections in the trade are legitimate.'

'Are we still picking up a signal from the Mercedes ?'

'Only small local routes. Nothing of any distance since she arrived back in Britain.' It was Tressor's turn to study the notice board in detail. He stepped forward and unpinned the photograph of Kamal. Pinon sat at the large desk and leant back in the leather seat.

'You still think that there could be a connection between these two ?'

Tressor shrugged his shoulders.

'A hunch, just a hunch. Of course it would help if we knew Kamal's exact whereabouts. If he's safely tucked up in Baghdad, then we've been wasting our time. I need either proof of his location or a connection with a known operative in the field.' He turned to face Pinon and gestured back towards the photographs.

'Please, Xavier. I would value a second opinion.' Pinon stared long and hard before answering. As he did, he held out a finger to emphasise each point.

'OK, first we have an Iraqi face we have not seen for a good number of years turn up and immediately disappear. Not just anyone but a senior agent and a propulsion expert at that. Secondly, we have been monitoring the student Jubal and his regular visits to the Syrians, one of a number of supposed Middle Eastern students under observation, a definite and sustained rise in the numbers of suspects. Third, we have an unconnected smuggler, albeit one with a questionable link with the arms trade, suddenly showing links with another possible suspect.' He paused. 'That link does need proof, though.' Pinon held the three fingers before slowly lowering them.

'It's a delicate balance, Xavier. Take it higher and risk ridicule, or ignore it and risk….risk what?' Pinon tapped the photograph of Halah Akief.

'Why her, sir?' Tressor looked up. He shook his head slowly.

'I honestly don't know. A feeling, a glimmer of recognition. I'm sure that I have never met her, and your trawl hasn't flagged up any positives. It's just …' He failed to finish the sentence the distant wail of a siren echoed across the rooftops. He snapped out of his torpor.

'Has the fax come in yet?'

Pinon held up the grainy image.

'Former RAF pilot. A Gulf war veteran with a history. He was caught up in that…' Tressor held up a hand. His thoughts immediately turned to Kamal.

'But a pilot none the less'. Tressor interrupted. 'I don't like the pattern of this set up. We lost Kamal and gained this Akief woman, and now we seem to have arms dealer connections in at least one area.' He pulled open the desk drawer and removed a solid silver letter knife. Tressor stood in front of the notice board and allowed the point of the blade to trace a circular pattern over the assembled photographs. Slowly the knife settled on the young features of Jubal.

‘We’ll make this a priority for the time being. Leave the Algerian link on hold for now. Time to pull that young student in, I think.’

Twelve

Pointe du Raz peninsula, Brittany
March 26th, 21.30 hours
The *Luna* rose and fell in the slight swell. The small cove made it a tight fit for the fifty-foot trawler, the steep rock cliffs that rose on either side seemed to increase the sense of claustrophobia. Further along the coastline the slow, pulsing light of the Vieille lighthouse picked out the dark outline of the Pointe du Raz peninsular. The landing site had been chosen for its isolation, it needed to be suitably rural, and out of range of the two naval bases, Brest to the north and Lorient in the south.
Apart from the gentle slap of waves against the boat's hull, only the faint sound of foot falls could be heard from the shingle beach at the head of the bay. Against

the backdrop of luminous, fast moving clouds, the occasional figure could be seen silhouetted on the cliff top. Each man moved silently among the outcrop of rocks that led down to the water. PNG units were strapped to each head giving the men a green tinged view of proceedings. From the shore, an inflatable Gemini was launched, the two crew paddling silently towards the anchored trawler. Behind them they towed a cluster of large flotation buoys. On either side of the *Luna* a pair of large pulley beams had been lowered into the water. Chain links tightened one by one, only the occasional glimpse of a masked head on the surface giving any indication of the activity taking place beneath the hull. With a silent signal from one of the divers, the low hum of a winding motor thrummed the air. The winching was deliberate and slow. It would be a full ten minutes before the long, rectangular objects simultaneously broke the surface on either side of the trawler. As the winches were silenced, the crew of the Gemini began to secure the buoys to the sides of each container. Under tow, the cargo slowly made its way towards the shore. A further fifteen minutes passed and the three cases were secured in the back of the small grocery van at the cliffs edge. Without further contact the *Luna* slipped her anchor cables and allowed the tide to take her back out to sea. The route to Tripoli would take in many ports of call.
The van waited until it had joined a main road before using full headlights. Thirty-two minutes and forty seconds in total. And no contacts made.

The nails squealed in protest as the wooden lid was levered upwards. Inside, beneath layers of plastic sheeting lay the missile. A single arc light illuminated the interior of the main barn. Kamal quickly slit the cover away with his knife. The slender steel casing of the body was eleven feet in length with four paddle like fins just aft of the centre. A protective Perspex cowl covered the rounded nose sensor. A folded piece of paper was taped to the casing. Kamal paused to read the prayer that had been hand written. It was Russian and deliberately avoided any Muslim syntax. He smiled as he handed the paper to Rana.

The remaining sheeting was removed allowing Kamal to feel his way along the underside of the missile. It was dry, the airtight seal having done its work. The discarded fibreglass containers lay at the far end of the barn. They resembled elongated life raft capsules of the sort carried by passenger ferries. Each had been sealed by plastic welding and had had to be cut open with power saws. The halves would soon be buried along with the Gemini craft. Kamal let his fingers trace over the aluminium data plate riveted to the upper side of the body casing. Although the date appeared as 1975, the appearance was as new. His hand smoothed along the length of the missile before pausing at the nose sensor.

'A beautiful sight, is it not? A 68 lb proximity fragmentation warhead with a seven mile range at a speed of over Mach 3' Rana peered into the crate and shrugged his shoulders.

'As long as it performs, but I would have been happier with Sidewinders'.

'Age brings with it the bounty of experience Rana. Remember that. Besides, I find the irony of using a British missile, liberated from the Kuwaitis, too rich an opportunity. Admittedly the range is somewhat limited but it is as much a matter of availability as it is compatibility.' Kamal began to manoeuvre the lifting trolley that would be used to remove the missile from it's housing. Chains swung from the pulley as the frame was positioned over the casing. Rana's gaze was fixed firmly on the Red Top.

'I have contacts Kamal. A Sidewinder is not totally out of the question.'

Kamal turned to face the Basran. He held up a hand.

'Enough Rana, you have your work to do, now go.' The dismissive wave clearly angered Rana who momentarily stood his ground, dark eyes boring into Kamal's turned back. Suddenly he smiled, his eyes betraying his genuine feeling.

'Of course you are right my friend.' Kamal spun to face him.

'That's Sir to a superior officer.' He barked. The reply was slow in coming. Another grin.

'Sir.' A slight bow before Rana disappeared into the shadows of the barn. It was only then that Kamal noticed the silence. All work had ceased as the rest of the recovery party had paused at the sound of raised voices. All eyes were now on Kamal. He turned to face them. He spoke in a low voice.

'If you would proceed, gentlemen.'

Blackdown Hills
March 27th, 19.05 hours

The syringe was sitting in a silver ashtray on the far edge of the mantelpiece. He could feel his hand trembling as he reached out. He paused, his outstretched fingers hovering over the glistening phial. He needed it badly. He caused his fist to clench tight and held it until the tendons in his wrist began to pulse. He had to wait. It was so much better when Halah injected him, or rather the aftermath as he descended into unconsciousness. Placing the bottle onto the shelf, he grabbed at his fist with the free hand and pulled his arm away. He took great gulps of air through his mouth as another wave of nausea swam through his head. Leaning back against the chimney breast, Ronson heard the lock in the front door being turned. A familiar shadow played across the doorway into the hall. She was back. Max Ronson moved silently towards the foot of the stair case, a loose floorboard belying his presence. He winced. It was futile to think that she had not heard him.

'Is my man ready yet?' The seductive tone caused him to pause. He turned to face the doorway, his eyes darting to the ashtray. Halah Akief rounded the door frame and paused, her dark eyes searching the room.

'Naughty boy Maxy, you know we are seeing guests tonight and I need you on top of your game.'
She approached the fireplace and picked up the glass phial. The amount it contained seemed to elicit an immediate change. She rounded on Ronson holding the phial in her right fist.

'You bloody fool. There's enough in here to sedate an ox.' She moved towards him.

'I want a lucid, credible test pilot and not some gibbering idiot shooting his mouth off.'
Ronson backed away, his hands held up above his face. He looked away from her eyes.

'P….P..Please, Halah. This was none of my doing. You said yourself that Latham was a one in a million shot. What can I do?'

'What can you do? For a start you can get yourself shaved and dressed. We're due there in an hour.' Ronson pulled his bathrobe together. A glint caught his eye over Halah's shoulder.

'Just one small shot, please.' His hand outstretched, he motioned towards the mantle piece. Halah moved forward and held his outstretched hand. She gently smoothed his cheek. In her eyes Ronson saw the same sensuous, slightly vulnerable woman he had allowed into his life some eighteen months previously.

Halah Akief had invaded his conscience at a vulnerable time in his supposed recuperation from the discharge from the service. The week in Nice had done little to shake him from his increasing feeling of desperation. The warm sun on his skin and hustle of the French Riviera were supposed to distract him sufficiently, particularly from the drink. He was not a beach dweller. Too much time to stew in his own juices, the endless replays of the last eighteen months eating away at his stability. He had tried to busy himself with meaningless tours of monasteries and vineyards in the hills to the north of the city, but would always find himself in the same beach side bar come the evening. The combination of the sunset and wine took little time in reviving memories of Anna. It was during one of these evening sessions when he caught the eye of a woman sat several tables away. She seemed to be alone, her fingers rolling the stem of a single glass of red, a Weimaraner lying at her feet, it's mink grey coat flawless in its sheen. She was reading and on the occasions that she gazed over the tops of her sunglasses, Ronson caught a glimpse of the dark, almond eyes.

Two nights later the same woman, the same dog and for all Ronson knew, the same book appeared at dusk. He stayed sober and played ignorant of her existence, trying not to seem interested. The occasional stolen glance reciprocated no exchange but Ronson enjoyed that the frisson the situation created. With the lowering of the sun, the shades were removed, the eyes fully revealed. Ronson had armed himself with a local paper and played the waiting game. When it came, the glance was fleeting but with enough of a pause to confirm an interest. Ronson gave his best smirk, half of his mouth raised slightly, the faintest of nods. He saw the smile and the immediate lowering of the eyes. He had not looked at another woman since Anna's death, and the feeling had taken him by surprise. He took his time finishing his drink before carefully folding the newspaper and summoning the waiter. As the bottle of 78 Montrachet arrived he rose slowly from his seat and made his way through the maze of tables to the far side of the veranda. The greeting had been cordial and she had allowed him to join her.

He had been surprised by her willingness to listen. He had been wary of revealing the recent past, the source of so many broken friendships back in the UK. Slowly at first, he had given more and more away. Halah just sat and listened, the occasional soothing interjection and the slowly nodding head. He had to stop himself on a number of occasions as he felt the conversation becoming maudlin. He would change the subject in an attempt to find out more of this calm, darkly alluring woman. But every time, she would steer the talk back to him. They spent consecutive evenings walking along the edge of the harbour, the gin palaces moored along its length glowing in activity with the party season in full swing. With her interest in him leaving little in the way of garnered information, Ronson only had the profession of antiquities and nationality of Oman as any clue to her identity. It would be the third meeting before he learnt her name.

In Halah's presence, he felt more at peace than he had at any time since the Gulf. He'd tried the Air Force's method of counselling and had had a bellyful of shrinks in uniform, the skewed justification of all acts of war and the inevitable necessity of death. It was corporate sanity and it stank. He had never considered drugs, not least recreationally, not until he had met Halah. His method of relaxation had been standard squadron fare; numerous bars in Cyprus, Germany and even a windswept crofters cottage in the Falklands had witnessed *his* method of counselling. With Halah, the first hits had seemed to last forever, time standing still and, more importantly, reality suspended. He enjoyed the release. Soon the craving had started and he found Halah to be a willing supplier of his needs. It was during one of his worst bouts of depression that she had made her move. The probing and prompting had been gentle at first, surgically precise in it's sparring with Ronson's fuelled state. Once in the roller coaster of emotion, he found it virtually impossible to recount his thoughts or actions. By the end of one particularly long weekend in the fall of 1993, Halah had begun to draw him in. She worked at his anger, the one side of his nature the cocaine seemed unable to change. She seemed to know so much, the soothing, the understanding about Anna and the rage that fuelled Ronson's desire for some measure of revenge. Slowly, she had began to reveal herself, the drugs always playing their part as Halah drew Ronson in before releasing him again. Before he could comprehend what he was committing himself to, she had turned his burning anger into something tangible, a means of avenging Anna's pain, and exorcising his own.

20.00 hours

Rob knew that Jenny was nervous. The knowledge that Max was as close as the next village had been enough of a shock to Jenny, but the idea of inviting him into their house and back into their lives was, for Jenny, a major undertaking. They had had words, tears from Jenny, Latham's insensitivity evident again. He knew it, but he didn't need his wife bringing up the subject of his sister to force the issue home. He was just as nervous, and he knew of Jenny's gnawing anxiety, that he would go the way of Ronson. He feared it to.

Latham made sure he answered the door as Jenny busied herself in the kitchen. The idea for the meal had not gone down well but Jenny had agreed under the circumstances. She knew how much they had gone through together, and with Ronson gainfully employed as well as in a relationship, she had almost been as intrigued to meet the couple as her husband. Still she was nervous. As the front door opened Latham braced himself. Max had made an effort and had scrubbed up well, but was out of his league compared to his escort. Halah Akief wore a figure hugging black dress; her toned and deeply tanned legs accentuated by tall black stilettos. Expensive looking jewellery framed her face. The smile was a million miles from the stern visage at the window of the Mercedes. Latham offered a hand.

'Good to see you Max' The hand shake was firm and the smile seemed genuine. Halah offered a hand and gave a gently discreet greeting. Latham could feel the intensity of her eyes as he took her hand. Was she flirting with him? He attempted a smile but barely disguised a smirk.

'Please please do come in. Wonderful to see you both.' He motioned them into the sitting room just as Jenny appeared from the kitchen. She stopped in her tracks as Max looked up from removing his jacket. He raised a hand.

'Wotcha Jen, been a long time.' Jenny frowned slightly.

'Hello,' was all she managed before she retreated back into the kitchen.

Du Blayac Farm, Brittany
21.34 hours
Rana scrabbled frantically as he searched for the Filofax that he had buried deep within the maze of the silo. The slim torch was gripped between his teeth. The level had changed overnight, an eventuality that had both shocked and angered him. He had studied du Blayac and his staff of three farm hands throughout the past month. The silo had remained unused for all of that time. Now the grain level had dropped. From just inside the hatchway at the base of the silo, Rana scooped great handfuls of maze from the steel panels that made up the sides of the vast cavernous storage facility. The previous week had seen the silo at least a quarter full, causing Rana to access from the second story hatch. Now, with the level no more than three feet from the base, Rana had been able to open the bottom hatch with ease. The small glass porthole in the centre of the steel door had told him all he needed to know. He stopped his search and composed himself,

reaching back to silently close the hatch for fear of prying eyes. Again, he fixed his gaze on the narrow ladder that climbed the internal wall, disappearing into the gloom some forty feet above. At its base, he had wedged the leather bound case behind a rung that was now fully exposed. There was no case visible. He sank to his knees where the ladder disappeared into what remained of the maze and began to shovel with both hands.

Slow at first, the effort increased to a flailing rhythm until Rana was consumed with rage. His scream rebounded off the interior walls and remained in the air for some seconds. He stopped as his hand touched something hard up against the steel of the wall. He sank his arm down to the elbow, the dust in the air causing him to choke momentarily. He shielded his nose and mouth with the other arm in a vain attempt to filter the air entering his lungs. He now had a firm grip and hauled the Filofax from its shallow grave. The clasp was still intact, the seal unbroken. Rana allowed himself a brief, muted cry of relief, his clenched fist raining down hard on the hatch interior. The case secured inside his jacket, Rana studied the courtyard of the farm buildings before exiting the silo and silently making his way out into the darkness of the fields. The dew had begun to form and Rana left wet footprints in the long grass of the meadow. As he approached a high stone wall he stopped again to search for signs of unwanted company. With his back to the dry, dusty flint he sank down into a sitting position and slowly removed the case from his jacket. He balanced the torch on his knees, the light playing across his face. From a pocket his flick knife hissed from its handle and Rana worked at the clasp seal that

had ensured the case's integrity.
He placed the open case down in front of him, his fingers slowly turning the first few loose pages. The next page, made from stiff card, was held in place by a small magnetic clasp. Once removed Rana folded the page back to reveal two glass phials held in a specially shaped foam receptacle. Each container measured six inches in length and was three quarters filled with a clear water-like liquid. Rana carefully removed one of the phials and held it up to the torchlight, squinting as he gazed at the contents. He smiled.

Yasan Rana had remained hidden in the second suite of the Mansur Miliyah Hotel during Kamal's meeting with Uday Hussein, some eleven months earlier. He had been allowed to hear the conversation but had been ordered not to reveal his presence on the day. His own briefing had come later. Transferred from his duties at the Al Nihiya prison complex, Rana had been summoned by Uday personally. The initial briefing had been handled by his immediate superior Hamdani, the over weight sycophant who ran the Al Nihiya. Rana wanted his position in Uday's affections and could not comprehend the fat pig's seemingly continuous presence in heir-apparant's entourage. The briefing had been detailed up to a point; the locations, timing and personnel involved. A demolition job, all that was missing was the target and method of removal. Uday had entered the darkened room at the end of the presentation. He gave his usual short speech, the praise of his father and the greater glory of Iraq and Allah. The money came later. Rana had heard it all before. He spoke only to answer his name and bowed deeply before leaving the apartment, the black leather Filofax

his only possession. He had flown to Syria that night and boarded a flight for Marseilles two days later.
Rana replaced the phial into its foam housing and resealed the clasp. As he rose from his position at the foot of the wall his line of vision caught sight of headlights pulling into the courtyard. As they came to a halt Rana could make out the familiar silhouette of the white van. Kamal and Asil appeared in the cab interior as a light flickered on. Rana pulled himself in tight against the crumbling façade of the wall. The two men sat impassively for a brief moment before Kamal jumped down from the cab and retrieved a large holdall from the rear. Both men moved swiftly into the confines of the stone barn, the darkness of the large doorway swallowing them up. Rana smiled to himself. His package had arrived.

With his eyes adjusting to the dimly lit interior, Rana made for the trestle table at the far end of the barn. Kamal and Latif were hunched over the crumpled, open holdall. A single shaft of torchlight played across the object cradled in Kamal's arms. The now assembled tubular construction was some six feet in length, a pistol grip and telescopic sight positioned half way along the barrel. Kamal turned to face Rana as he approached.

'Your insurance, Rana?' He held out the Stinger missile launcher. Rana took hold and weighed it in his hands. It felt heavy, solid and reliable. Rana could not help but grin.

'Get me a boat off the peninsular and I guarantee you a shoot down, Lightning or not.' The tone was almost sneering. Kamal shrugged his shoulders.

'Fine, whatever. Just do your job at Lessay and you can have your pot shot'. Kamal pointed directly at Rana. 'And only if Steel fails, right?'
Rana shrugged his shoulders. 'Slam as many into him as we can, I say.' Again, the piercing stare.
Kamal drew himself up to his full height. 'You know the drill. The Stinger is back up and no more than that.'
Rana shifted the launcher on to his shoulder in one, violent jerk. Depressing the trigger slightly, a red LED flickered on the side of the sight. A high-pitched whine filled the interior of the barn as the sensor in the head of the missile searched for a heat source to lock on to. Kamal reached out and grasped the pistol grip, his knuckles whitening. Rana held onto the grip before the pain became too much. He released and the whine immediately ceased. He stared at Kamal, his head cocked to one side.

'You want us to fail…sir ?'

'On the contrary, I want us to succeed, and to live. Your time will come, Rana.' Kamal smiled without emotion and released his grip.

Thirteen

Templemere Airfield
March 29th, 09.45 hours
John Reed reached for the outstretched hand.

'I thought you were going to take over the world, sir?' The grin was broad.

'Nah, they had me out numbered John, and less of the sir. I'm a mortal now.' Latham turned to face Ian McCleesh, his hand on Reed's shoulder.
'This old bugger was Chief Tech' for the Wright brothers'. Both men laughed as Latham gripped Reeds shoulder. It felt good to see such a friendly face, someone who Latham had relied on in so many ways in the past. A one time designated member of Latham's ground crew, Reed had overseen the care and maintenance of the Muharrac wing of Latham's squadron in the Gulf. A good tech was the nearest

thing a pilot had to a guardian angel and Reed was among the best.
Latham had been quietly awestruck by the scale of Roly Whittaker's set up at Templemere but the presence of men like Reed emphasised the professionalism that the American's money had bought. Latham had initially taken up Whittaker's offer of some weekend flying, when commitments at Westfields permitted, in order to come on board the Lightning rebuild. Today would see Latham partnering Max in the two-seat Vampire on a thirty-minute test flight. With Max already forty-five minutes late, Latham could not help but replay the scenes of that evening two days before.

The meal had started well enough, both sides feeling their way with pleasantries and platitudes that bordered on the inane. The ritual of etiquette soon ran its course with Max the first to break cover. The glazed eyes were warning enough that old habits were still very much to the fore. He seemed almost determined to pick a fight with Jenny. He broke cover with an anecdote guaranteed to provoke. Latham visibly winced as the tale of two young servicemen prowling the bars of Cyprus was spun. Topless bars and many other establishments all got a look in, in lurid detail. It was unnecessary and far too tasteless at such an early stage of the evening. Jenny just smiled and continued eating. Halah spent much of the first half hour listening attentively and delicately rearranging her food. Very little made it into her mouth. In a rare lull from Ronson's meanderings, Jenny tried to bring Halah into the conversation.

'I hear that you are in antiques, Halah?' She

caught her mid-mouthful, Halah choking slightly before struggling to answer.

'Um…yes,..yes. Cars, aeroplanes, like Mister Whittaker,' she nodded in the vague direction of Templemere, 'I even sold Clark Gables Alfa Romeo once.' She beamed. The smile was warm and she seemed grateful to have been able to change the subject. The mood had warmed as the meal progressed with only Max seeming to carry any edge in his voice the bitterness still never far from the surface. Jenny had cooked light, a calculated ploy in case they needed a quick getaway, the meal taking a little under forty-five minutes to consume. The post meal drinks had barely begun when, much to Max's annoyance, Halah had suggested that they leave in order for Ronson to prepare for the next days flight. Rob and Jenny agreed without too much obvious haste and their guests departed less than ninety minutes after their arrival. As they slumped down into the large sofa that dominated the living room, Latham held his wife tightly. He knew how difficult she had found the experience and silently wondered if his recent discovery was going to bring more trouble than they needed. He decided to give the next day a trial run and gauge Jenny's mood in the morning. As they silently made their way up the staircase, Latham knew that he had a struggle on his hands. The pull of the flying at Templemere was almost seductive in its hold, Whittaker even broaching the subject of money, good money. A nest egg in the making, but he knew also that the only woman he had ever loved, the woman who had followed him across half the known World, had more than earned the right to say no.

Roland Whittaker's face beamed as ran through the hanger entrance. He was waving a letter above his head. Latham looked on from the wing of the Vampire. Max was now over an hour late and the arrival of his boss was not about to do him any favours.

'What's up Chief? You look like Neville Chamberlain. McCleesh jumped down from the wing. The American paused to catch his breath, his face beet red.

'CAA at Gatwick. They've only bleeding well gone and done it.'

Latham smiled at the American's use of English slang. 'Done what?'

'Took just over five hours. Permit to fly, everything. We can go in one week if we wanted to. They took everything. They loved it. Said they were lookin' forward to seeing her fly.' He looked over at Reed.

'This is so much you, John. You realise that? All those hours of paper work, the maintenance, the visits. They told me afterwards that they'd never seen such a thoroughly prepared application. This one's for you.' Whittaker tossed Reed one of his fat cigars. The softly spoken Mancunian carefully pocketed the Cuban and smiled before turning his attention to the Vampire. Whittaker was still bubbling.

'I gotta say guys, I wasn't expecting it so quick. Someone up there must be smilin' down on me today.' He raised his hands to the sky. 'Ian, ya know this means we can start the test programme, what, within a week ?' McCleesh rolled the gum around in his mouth before nodding.

'Aye, can do boss.' Whittaker looked around

the hanger.

'Max, where's Max?'

Latham stepped in.

'Car problem, Roly. He's not long.' He lied. He caught McCleesh's quizzical look but did not look directly at the Scot. He immediately knew that he had crossed a line that he had vowed not to. It wasn't the first time he had had to cover for a Max Ronson no-show. Old habits, he thought.

Having stalled the ecstatic Whittaker with ease, Latham took the opportunity to have another look at the F6. Reed accompanied him to Hanger 2 and, as he chewed on the remnants of a dangerously drooping sandwich, updated him on the progress of the rebuild. The Lightning was now fully flight ready.

'Stunning, John, just stunning'. Latham stood in the shadow of the port wing. 'I'd give my right nut to have a go.' He winked at Reed.

'A bitch to maintain but superb to fly', Reed answered. 'yeah, I reckon you jocks have the shitless end of the stick on that one all right. You never know, the way Max has been lately the boss might just give you a go.'

Latham squatted down and surveyed the large flat oil drip trays that lay under the fighter. Lightnings had been notorious for leaking fuel in their service days, a legacy of the expanding and contracting that the fuselage suffered in the extreme temperatures of supersonic flight. Latham studied the markings that covered the matt grey paintwork.

'Who's buying this again?'

'Some Arab guy. Got his own museum in the desert.'

'I'm surprised that he didn't go for the natural look.' Latham referred to the Lightning's aluminium finish of the 60s. At the height of the Cold War the silver fighters had been a common sight over the North Sea as they were scrambled to intercept Russian spy planes over the Greenland gap.

'This dark sea grey was what we had when they retired. Low visibility. Not exactly a stand out at an air show, is it?' Latham shuffled further under the fuselage as he noticed a black, oval shape painted on the underside of the cockpit. He pointed.

'And this? We never had false canopies painted on.' The matt black image was designed to disorientate an enemy fighter in a dogfight. Fleetingly glimpsed, the false cockpit could confuse a pilot into thinking that the fighter was entered into a different orientation and so buying precious seconds of opportunity. Latham climbed out from under the fuselage.

'We didn't even do that in the Gulf. I know the Yanks painted them on their fighters, but I'm surprised he wants this on. What does Max make of this?'

Reed took another mouthful and continued.

'Arab fella wants it apparently. I don't think Max cares if it's painted in Zebra stripes as long as he can get his hands on her. I know he can't wait.'

'He's a bit keen is he?'

'A bit? He won't let anyone near her other than me. Bit possessive. Bit like that bird he's got.' Reed's eyes lit up. 'What a cracker she is. And she's got the boss wrapped around her little finger. She's only driving his beloved tank around, ain't she? He let her take the Merc over to France few month's back.

Whole bleedin' week. Like a child, he is.' Latham smiled at the mention of Halah. She seemed to be having quite an impact.

DGSE Headquarters, Paris
10.08 hours.
Jubal Al-Rikabi had only made the one mistake. He had clenched his teeth a second before the blow had landed. He knew what was coming. He could see the determination etched in Xavier Pinon's eyes, the sweat-covered face grimacing with effort as the fist drew back. He had heard the crack. They had all heard the crack. His parched lips split as he tried to move his swollen tongue. The broken jaw refused to move any further, the boys scream echoing around the small cell as bone grated against bone. Gilde Tressor, his back against the solid oak door, massaged his brow in frustration. He focussed on the figure slumped in the chair at the centre of the room. The once angelic face a mess of swollen bruises. Pinon, his braces hanging down the sides of his legs, shirt sleeves rolled up over the elbows, was hunched over the prone figure in the chair. He fought for breath, his lungs sending used air rasping into the chamber. Jubal had passed out, his head lolling onto his chest as his body leant forward in the leather straps that bound him. Wet hair dripped fine droplets of sweat onto the stone floor. Another, larger puddle had formed under the chair.

'Play the tape back again, something about a brother in prison.' Tressor spoke towards the single microphone that hung from the centre of the ceiling. His voice carried an edge of anger.

The boy had given no resistance on the Seine

riverboat, Pinon and two other agents escorting him to the waiting car once the ferry had docked on the Left bank. He had protested little in the car, merely asking the reason for his detainment. Pinon had found him unexpectedly calm for one so young, arrogant even. Once in the basement of Rue du Mont the façade had disappeared. Doors echoing throughout the sparse, neon lit corridors. Pinon deliberately held him at the entrance to the interrogation room. Jubal scanned the chamber, his eyes focussing on the single length of electrical flex that hung from the ceiling. Tressor stood at the centre of the room, his long thin fingers resting on the back of a high backed wooden chair.

'Do you know why you are here, Rikabi?' The words echoed off the damp stone of the walls. Jubal stared impassively, his hands twisting the plastic handcuffs until the circulation in his wrists ceased to flow. Pinon pushed him forward, at the same time kicking his feet from under him. He sprawled headlong landing on his elbow, the sharp pain racing up his arm. His cry bounced around the interior. Tressor stepped from behind the chair and motioned towards Pinon.

'Up, pick him up.' Pinon's huge hand grabbed the boy by his shirt collar and hauled him into the seat. Jubal, his eyes closed in a silent grimace felt his hands forced apart and back behind the chair. The plastic cable ties were replaced by heavy, old-fashioned style handcuffs. Ratchets clicked loudly into place. The questions had started immediately with Pinon wasting little time in letting the boy know if he found the answers lacking. A straight right to the bridge of the nose came first, Jubal tasting the metallic flavour of his own blood as it ran down his face.

His lips parted slightly. The words were almost silent as he concentrated on keeping his jaw still. Tressor leant forward, his ear inches from the boys mouth. Again, the rasping exhalation of breath that carried the faintest trace of a voice. Pinon moved closer.

'Sir?' Tressor held up a hand, his forefinger to his lips. Slowly he rose up and spoke clearly into the microphone.

'Vire Estuary by trawler on the 6th. The name Rana and something about a school teacher' Tressor looked down on the now unconscious figure of Jubal. His eyes narrowed as he studied the bloodied features. The once smooth skin was broken in several places, swelling beginning to close both eyes. Tressor turned and left Pinon to clear up the mess. Twenty minutes later the two men listened as Tressor replayed the tape, the boy's spluttering testimony echoing around the high ceiling of his forth floor office. He stopped the tape half way through the third hearing. As he spoke, he spread the contents of Jubal's rucksack across the table.

'We know a day, a place and a method of transport. Who, why or exactly which month is another matter.' Pinon snapped his fingers.

'Could be a get away route, then again an arrival point. We could get Nantes to put it on phone surveillance, sir.' Tressor arched an eyebrow at the suggestion. He fingered the small address book that Jubal had carried. The pages flicked past his gaze.

'Possibly, but that would take a lot of manpower to sift through any leads. Within the city alone, it's a common word. Could try starting with a sixty mile radius and close in. See to it.'

Honiton Police Station, Devon
11.07 hours
Two figures hunched over their respective desks in the brightly lit office, the already cramped interior further compromised by several large file crates. Ronald Thursby had his head in his hands as he studied another document from the case by his desk. As he paused to rap the contents of his pipe into an ashtray, he swung around in his seat.

'That bombing raid that went tits up in the Gulf, you get anything?' Thursby shot his Sergeant a glance. Hart, his desk beneath the large square framed window, raised a finger to his top lip, pausing as he sifted the information. The two men had been processing paperwork for the last three hours and the progress was becoming ever more laborious. He found the relevant page. He rubbed his eyes.

'Sorry sir. I got this over night, same guy over at Swindon. He said it was a bugger to get hold of, so we owe him on this one.' Thursby nodded as Hart continued. 'Seems that Ronson was part of a raid that took out an airfield before moving on to a bridge over the Euphrates in central Iraq. That's were the incident took place. A school bus full of children.'

Thursby winced.

'All of them?'

'Whole bus incinerated.'

'Jesus, no wonder the bloke went schitzo.' Thursby turned his back on his assistant and moved to the window. The late morning light was dimming as the cloudless sky gave up the last of the sun to gathering clouds. Thursby turned back to Hart, pieces of stray tobacco landing on the floor at his feet as he crammed the bowl of his pipe.

'Bloke like that could be forgiven for going a bit gaga. I'd certainly be at war with the world if I'd gone through what he did. And now he's in a relationship with a woman under God knows what suspicion from the French.' Hart leant forward in his seat.

'And working for Whittaker. Talking of which, mate of mine in traffic saw Whittaker with our esteemed MP the other day, out at the Jellicoe.' Thursby let out a guffaw.

'Our very own Cardew the cad? I pulled him once for speeding. Sweetness itself, he was. Talked about the Chief Super, asked after his wife, the usual bollocks.'

'Did he walk?'

'Of course he did. You'd get more to stick to a chromed shovel.' Thursby paused to light his pipe.

'That could be a bit tasty, him and a known felon like Whittaker. Keep an eye out while we're waiting on this Taraz woman'.

Templemere
11.16 hours
Latham was sitting in the Vampire cockpit when Reed appeared from the office interior. The look was resigned as if the news was expected. Old time Max, Latham thought.

'He's not turned up. Halah's just phoned, says he's sick. Food poisoning or something, but he's out of it.'

Whittaker gazed up at the ceiling of the hanger and hissed through clenched teeth.

'Jeezus Christ, is this bird ever gonna get airborne?' He walked towards the Vampire, his arms outstretched. He rested his elbows on the edge of the cockpit, the unlit cigar rolling around his mouth.

'Look Rob, I'll get straight to the point. We've kinda got used to Max getting tired and emotional on occasions. I mean, don't get me wrong, I know you guys go back an' all that but the guy can be a major sonofabitch pain in the ass.' Latham could not help but smile.

'Ah mean the guy's a major jet jock an' all but I need a regular player who I can rely on. You know where I'm comin' from Rob?' Latham pulled the straps of his ejection seat tight.

'Are we talking about the F6, before I make any sort of commitment?'

Whittaker took his time relighting the Cuban before he answered. The cloud filled the cockpit interior as he exhaled. The match was flicked over his shoulder as he fixed Latham with the first serious expression that he had seen from the American

'I can match what your on over at those cow herders at Yeovil. I need someone who I can rely on, someone with experience.' He fixed Latham with a stare, the cigar ash flicked into the cabin with relish. Latham pulled on his flying helmet. As he tied the straps he flicked the ignition switches, the Goblin engine hissing into life. Above the increasing din, Latham shouted to Whittaker, his hand holding up five fingers.

'Give me five minutes to think about it.' The Perspex canopy lowered as the chocks were removed and the small fighter began rolling. The taxi to the runway complete, Latham wasted little time in powering the engine up and releasing the brakes. The takeoff was rapid, the Vampire's wheels folding on the point of departure from the runway. The little fighter leapt from the Templemere threshold, Latham hauling the Vampire into a tight 120 degree turn that took him back over the main hanger and out over the perimeter fence. He kept low, the jet wash from the whining Goblin flattening a trail through an adjoining field of corn. Turning sharply back onto the main runway, Latham made for the distinctive shape of Whittaker's Mercedes. The ground crew instinctively ducked as the twin boom fighter beat up the hanger, leaving a deafening cacophony that echoed throughout the interior. Whittaker watched as the silver fighter Victory rolled across the airfield before lowering its undercarriage for a slow descent onto the main runway. The fighter breaked sharply, the nose dipping before the Vampire settled into a slow taxy back towards the main apron. Slowing to meet the ground crew, Latham raised the canopy as he taxied to a stop in exactly the same position he had occupied four minutes earlier. Whittaker was laughing audibly over the decreasing whine of the Vampire's engine. He slapped the side of the still warm fuselage.

'Son, you got my attention.'

TWO

D-Day

One

Templemere Airfield.
April 2nd 1994, 11.48 hours

With the briefing completed Latham made the final check of his flight suit on the tarmac outside the office building. The rain had begun to subside, the apron littered with vast pools of water that merged, one into another. The sea mist that had enveloped Templemere for most of the morning was starting to lift. With the landing lights cutting through the dank air, the runway was almost fully visible from the apron. Reed tightened the straps on Latham's Mae West jacket and checked the oxygen hook up that would connect the pilot with the aircraft. Latham zipped the flight map into his knee pouch and began his walk around check of the fighter. Various panels were knocked and ailerons swivelled. As McCleesh removed the red panel that covered the engine intake in the nose,

Latham reached the foot of the pilot's ladder. Glancing up at the cockpit that seemed to tower over him he began to climb, arching his back under the in-flight refuelling probe that rose, lance like from beneath the port wing.

Latham eased his way down into the cramped interior, the cockpit edges rubbing tight against his shoulders, it was the smell that he recognised first, the aroma of old, decaying rubber fittings mixed with the pungent bite of aviation fuel. He scanned the instrument panel letting his fingers play over the careworn controls, many of the thirty year old switches long since weathered of any paint finish. As he began the pre-flight checks he could not help but compare the awkward cockpit layout with that of the ergonomically superior setting of the Tornado. Where the modern bomber allowed a pilot the comfort of automated controls, the Lightning seemed positively steam driven by comparison. Reed remained at the top of the ladder tightening the ejector seat straps, before sliding his way down to the tarmac to ready the power generator that would start the engines. Latham gave the start-up signal, his right hand, the index finger extended, circling. Reed replied the signal and, after a brief pause, the starter motor fired. A loud hissing noise filled Latham's ears before he felt the isopropylnitrate liquid propellant ignite in the chamber behind the cockpit. The slow rumble of the Avon engine steadily increased until a single pulsing note filled the cockpit. The procedure was repeated, the Lightning straining against the force of the two powerful engines that threatened to force it from its chocks. McCleesh's voice crackled in the headset.

'Two turning and burning, boss. Chocks are

gone.' Signalling to Reed, Latham dabbed the brakes, causing the fighter to bow briefly before the throttles were increased and forward momentum again achieved. The canopy slowly lowered on its hydraulic rams as the Lightning began to taxi forward, the rumble of the Avons rising in their pitch. In the cockpit Latham made one final check on the canopy before contact with Exeter control was made. As he steered the fighter along the perimeter taxiway, the jet efflux sent a boiling plume of spray from the rear of the aircraft. The ride was smooth despite the bumps and cracks that littered Templemere's ageing concrete apron. Tail plane, ailerons and flaps constantly twitching as Latham continued the pre-flight checks, the passage around the perimeter took a full five minutes before the large fighter found itself turning onto the threshold of the main runway. Latham applied the brakes as he stared down the long expanse of tarmac before him.

Latham ran though the final checks in his head. Pins out, straps tight, harness locked, visor down, oxygen flowing. His own final check was personal. Canopy down and locked – the all too vivid memory of a terrifying incident in his training days. Latham eased the throttles forward, the Lightning feeling like a dog on a leash. Selecting the afterburner control that would send fuel cascading into the jet exhausts, Latham held the fighter in check as the power surge increased. The rumble inside the cockpit could be felt more than it was heard. From the rear of the aircraft the blue white javelin of flame began to pulse. Latham released the brake lever on the control column and the fighter leapt forward. The acceleration was slow at first, the centre

line of the runway flashing below with increasing momentum, Latham being forced ever further into his seat. At 140 knots the nose wheel rose from the tarmac as the stick was eased back. Latham felt the satisfying clunk of the undercarriage retracting and checked that he had three red lights out on the panel to his left. With the threshold rapidly passing below Latham lit both afterburners, sending an explosive fuel mix into the engine chambers.
The effect was immediate. He pulled the stick back as hard as it would go into the pit of his stomach. The nose reefed upwards and threatening grey sky suddenly filled the canopy. The once comfortable fit of the G-suit was replaced by a crushing sensation as the leg and abdominal bladders filled with air. At 5g, blackout would be certain but for the involuntary tightening of the muscles, sending blood to the oxygen starved upper body. Latham heard his own laboured breathing as the fighter climbed through the cloud at 450 knots. Beneath the tightness of his oxygen mask, he could feel his cheek muscles aching from the most enormous grin. It felt good to be back in the office.

The Zeiss binoculars had whirred audibly as they came to focus on the silver grey fighter slowly making its way along the perimeter track. Leaning on the roof of the Saab, Aisha scanned the horizon on either side of the aircraft. Her chest rising rapidly as she fought to calm herself, Taraz had floored the accelerator of her car in the narrow lanes that led up to the airfield. She cursed Max Ronson under her breath. The pathetic figure that she had left at the farm was now heavily sedated, the effects of the Codelphine neutralised by a rapidly acting tranquilliser. The swelling to the left

side of his head would take longer to disappear.
At the far end of the airfield the fighter had come to rest at the end of the runway. In the crisp autumnal air the heat haze from the idling jet engines caused the horizon behind the Lightning to shimmer. Aisha adjusted the focus until the aircraft filled her vision.
Suddenly the air at the rear had become distorted, the elephantine roar taking a second to reach the ears. The momentum was slow at first, the heavy airframe seemingly reluctant to make progress. As the thundering crescendo rolled across the airfield the fighter began to accelerate. Passing the halfway point of the runway the nose wheel rose off the tarmac and was immediately followed by the main wheels, the undercarriage retracting almost instantaneously as the fighter held its minimal altitude. Drawing parallel with Aisha's car the Lightning suddenly forced its way into the near vertical, the thrust vibrating through her body as the air seemed to crackle around her head. It was an impressive sight and, to Aisha, the vindication of many months of careful planning. She had counted herself among the sceptics when the initial delivery aircraft had been proposed. The former cold war warrior was a forty year old design that, although once the most potent fighter of its day, would need the skills of a talented pilot to deliver its cargo. She had personally interrogated a Kuwaiti Air Force pilot at the beginning of the war. He had been captured at a border airfield on the first day of the invasion. His log book indicated that he had flown the fighter in the Seventies. He gave little away before he died but curiosity merited a closer look. She remembered her visit to Kuwait International Airport days after those momentous events of August 1990, and the fleet of retired Lightnings in open

storage at the airfields perimeter. As she walked the line she studied the aircraft at close quarters, little realising how fortuitous the visit would become. The row of fighters stood glistening in the midday heat, their metallic skins mirroring the glare of the sun. She thought them powerful looking, sitting squat on their stalk like undercarriage, and yet, on the ground at least, their hulking presence seemed to belie the enormity of their speed. Passing the airfield some days later she had searched out the line of obsolete aircraft. Only the burnt out shells now remained, the victims of a rampaging invader drunk on its newly acquired victory.

Aisha held the image in her mind as she focussed the binoculars on the rapidly disappearing fighter. The Lightning left a dark trail of vapour in its wake, in sharp contrast to the white vortexes spiralling from the wing tips as it rose ever higher. Soon, it was swallowed up by the cloud base and only the distant rumbling belied any presence. Aisha lowered the binoculars and smiled. It might have been the wrong pilot, but the machine was most impressive, she thought.

'Outstanding' she murmured under her breath.

The cockpit filled with blinding light as the fighter punched its way out of the cloud base and continued climbing. With the airspeed indicator nudging Mach 0.9, Latham held the nose high until his altimeter reached thirty thousand feet. The acceleration still shocked him.

The Lightning levelled out and held a steady course north towards the Bristol Channel giving Latham time to check the aircraft's systems. After shutting down the afterburners contact was made with Exeter Control before reporting back to Templemere.

'She's a bloody gem Roly. You've got yourself one hell of a convertible, over'

Whittaker kept his response brief.

'Take off was stunning. How's she handling Rob, over?'

'Like a dream. Best fun fare ride in the world. I gave her full reheat up to thirty thousand and its like I've never been away. All lights green, over.'

The grey fighter soared between the clouds, Latham working through a series of gentle loops and rolls as he made his way out over the Bristol Channel and up the Welsh coast. One hundred miles short of Cardigan Bay Latham turned out towards the sea, his Air Force training steering him clear of the missile range north of Aberporth. Pushing the stick forward, he took the fighter down towards sea level. At fifty feet the calm surface of the Irish Sea flashed beneath at incredible speed, altitude increased only on sighting the occasional fishing vessel.

The flight was barely forty-five minutes old when McCleesh's gruff voice interrupted Latham's concentration. The check was for fuel. The Lightning had been notorious during its service life for the short flight duration that its meagre fuel tanks allowed. Without the luxury of in-flight refuelling, the average sortie would last under an hour, the use of re-heat shortening the mission further. Latham checked his fuel gauges before climbing to a safer height and turning south. The run in to the Templemere overhead took him over the same terrain that Max Ronson had fought so hard to avoid some two years before. Exmoor soon loomed large in the canopy screen, the ruddy ochre of scrub criss-crossed by the pattern of worked land and roadways. The winter sun was low in the sky, the orange glow playing warm shadows across the cockpit interior. Latham throttled back.

The direct line to the embassy had been clear, the message short and to the point. The Lightning had been impressive. Aisha replaced the receiver on the dashboard of the Saab before returning her attention to the distant horizon to the north. The radio receiver on the passenger seat indicated the imminent return of Latham's Lightning. Within minutes the fighter appeared low over the needle-like Wellington monument before banking sharply to make a low, fast run across the airfield. A graceful victory roll seemed to signal the end of the flight as the fighter slowed and the undercarriage was lowered. After a sedate circuit of the perimeter the Lightning glided over the threshold, tyres biting the tarmac heavily as Latham sat ten tons of fighter down on the centre line, the break chute snapping open in the jet-wash.

Ronson retched as his eyes became accustomed to the piercing light slicing through the gap in the curtains. The Jack Daniels bottle fell from his grasp and smashed on the tiled floor of the bathroom. His throat felt raw as the involuntary spasms convulsed his body. Finally, as his stomach gave up some long since forgotten vestige of food, he vomited into the sink. As he wiped a hand across his mouth, he caught his reflection in the oval mirror. Blood shot eyes stared back. He made the mistake of sticking his tongue out.

The green carpet of fur caused him to wince. It was then that his eyes focussed on the hypodermic that stood in the glass jar on the windowsill. He felt an immediate rush, his senses heightened by the memory of his most recent hit. Halah's face swam into view, her scent filling his nostrils as her presence filled his vision. She was smiling as he felt the sharp sensation in his arm. The memory caused him to grip the edge of the sink until his knuckles whitened. He fought the surge of adrenaline that coursed through his head. As the memory dissipated Ronson forced his hand towards the cold tap and he filled the sink. His hand shook as he struggled to force the plug into the hole.

Plunging his head into the cold embrace of the water, feeling and focus shot back into view with painful intensity. Throwing his head from side to side he showered the walls with spray. He stepped away from the mirror, his feet finding spaces between the shattered fragments of glass that littered the floor. It was then that he noticed the bruising around his eyes. Suddenly, feeling found its way back into his senses and his body began to discover the results of the previous night. A dull ache in his groin stopped him momentarily. As he looked back at the mirror he saw that his right eye was slightly closed, the swelling already turning an angry shade of purple. A series of scratches stretched the length of his left cheek, the skin tender to the touch. He decided to leave the wounds alone.

Making his way back to the bedroom he could see his clothes scattered about the floor. His flight suit lay in a crumpled heap at the foot of the bed. The bone dome helmet had done some serious damage to the dresser mirror. Leaving the curtains closed Ronson felt for the bedside lamp switch and lit the rest of the devastated bedroom. Jeesus, she'd really gone for it this time, he thought. Vague flashes of violence interrupted his thoughts, blows raining about his head and upper torso in an eruption of pain. What had started out as such sensorial pleasure, the bathing, the slow, drawn-out sex had turned with the first puncture of the needle. He had given in again, letting the wave of euphoria wash over his outstretched body. Heat flowed into his twitching limbs and coursed through his chest causing his heart to pound with a thunderous resonance. Halah took advantage, as she always did. The prolonged erection was a side effect he could do little to fight. As his sight began to blur the recognition of the thrashing figure bestriding him merged into a dark mass. He thanked God that he had passed out soon after the punches began.

Latham sat at Whittaker's desk, his flight suit unzipped to the waist. On the table he had stowed his gloves inside his helmet, the smoked visor carefully wrapped in a cloth cover. The grin stretched across his face as he ran a hand through his damp hair.

'Perfect Roly. She's perfect.' Latham stood and began to stow his flight gear in one of the lockers to the left of the office door. Halah entered and draped her shawl across the back of Whittaker's chair. She stared impassively. Latham nodded and continued. 'Slight binding on the nose wheel brake and the fag lighter doesn't work.' He grinned as he pulled his jacket from the locker.

'The reheat OK?' Halah interrupted, the expression serious, the question unexpected. Before Latham could answer she quickly added. 'My client in

Saudi is very much interested by the speed of the aircraft. Boys and their toys, you know.' Her voice lighter now. Latham looked over at a smiling Reed.

'No problem there, it was like being shot out of a cannon. Any sign of damage, Reedy?'

'None at all, I'd say that she was good for Mach 1.5 at a push. Even then you'd still have plenty left in the tank.' Halah looked suitably impressed.

'Sounds fast enough to me.'

Whittaker waved his cigar smoke away. 'Still whip the ass of most things flying today. It was only when my guys got F15s that they had any real competition.'

Halah turned to face the American, her head slightly tilted to the side. The smile was warm.

'Roly, I was wondering if we could have a word?' She glanced over at the other two men, Reed immediately realising that he was intruding. Latham held up a hand as he hurriedly grabbed at his wallet from the locker.

'I'm out of here. Give me a ring at work tomorrow, Roly. Talk about test schedules for next weekend.' With a wave he and Reed were gone. Halah gently closed the door behind him. She waited, watching the two men through the glass. When she finally turned, the smile had gone. Whittaker looked up from his desk.

'What's up cupcake? You and Maxy had a fallout?' Halah swept a hand across his desk, a photo frame flying across the room.

'What the hell was he doing in the F6. Only Max flies, you know the deal Whittaker.' It was the first time she had used his surname. Whittaker began to stand.

'Now wait up honey, I don't know what you

got up to last night but I'm done with waiting for your boyfriend an' his no-shows. It's about time you….'

'Max is the pilot. Unless he flies, the deal is off. I have very strict instructions that *must* be followed. Do you understand?' Halah brought her fist down hard on the desk, her teeth bared. Whittaker backed off, the ferocity of her voice confusing him.

'Okay…okay honey, you got your deal, but you gotta realise that if Max is flyin' this ship, he's *gotta* be here. And I mean in a decent enough shape to cope with a 6g fighter. This ain't no Tiger Moth we're playin' with here.' He could see a change in her stance, the softening of the body language. Halah stopped, her head bowed slightly, calmer now. The voice was slower and more measured in tone.

'Mr Amilnas hand picked Max. He has known him since his Gulf War days. He trusts him.' She wagged a finger in the direction of the door. 'That was Latham's last flight, Roly. Is that clear?' Whittaker held up both hands.

'Listen honey, for half a million bucks, he can have Snoopy fly the goddam thing. What ever you say. But do us all a favour, and get Max in shape. He's a hot pilot, but it ain't right pouring him into that cockpit time after time.' Halah managed a half smile.

'Leave him to me'.

Latham had just passed the perimeter gate when he saw the familiar shape of Max's blue Morgan approaching. He instinctively slowed, the window winding down. As the two cars converged, the Morgan suddenly swerved violently, coming to a halt feet from Latham's bonnet. Through the swirling cloud of dust Max was already out of the car and making straight for

Latham. His fist pounded the door frame, the other hand reaching in to grab Latham's jacket. As he hauled, the door came open.

'You sly bastard. You couldn't wait to jump into my shoes could you?' Now out of the car, Latham forced his arms up to protect his face. Max had both fists up under his collar. 'You'll be trying to poke Halah next, eh flyboy?' Latham was pushed squarely in the chest, the force momentarily winding him. He slumped back across the bonnet. He could feel the surface buckling under his weight.

'Now whoa' there Max. You're well out of line on this one mate.' Latham tried to straighten himself, one hand outstretched.

'Mate? You have the fucking *nerve* to call me mate?' Latham could feel spittle in his face, alcohol fumes sweet in his nostrils. Max shoved harder, pinning Latham across the bonnet, his face inches away. 'My fucking gig, sunshine. The first break I get in years and you want a piece of the action do you?' His right fist flashed upwards, catching Latham's nose. A thin trickle of blood ran down his lip.

Latham had seen enough. He hooked a foot around the back of Ronson's left knee and forced him onto one leg. At the same moment he thrust his body weight forward and unbalanced Ronson in one swift movement. The two men crashed to the ground, Latham's weight winding Ronson momentarily. Before he could react, Latham pinned Ronson's upper arms with his knees and clamped both hands under his jaw. He leant close.

'Do you know how much I've put out for you over the past years?' The pitch of his voice rose higher as he screamed into Ronson's face. 'Do you? The first time I see you in almost two years, and you treat me like shit. Have you forgotten the times I dragged you out of the gutter, the lies and covering I've had to go through to protect you. And for what exactly?' Ronson twisted his body and Latham ground his knees harder. Ronson's arms were on fire. He tried a head butt, his neck straining to reach Latham. He slumped back to the ground.

'Leave it, Max. I'm not after your lousy job and I'm sure as hell not interested in Halah.'

Ronson's head was still, the face impassive. He blinked slowly. Latham rocked back on his haunches and rose from Ronson's prone form, his finger pointing. 'Take care, Max. You're pissing a lot of people off.' Latham spat blood as he wiped his sleeve across his nose. He turned and got back into the Jeep. Struggling to find first, he spun the wheels, flooring the accelerator. In the rear view mirror he watched through a cloud of dust as Max Ronson slowly climbed to his feet.

Two

DGSE, Paris
April 18th, 11.15 hours
Jubal Al-Rikabi was buried on wasteland to the south of the Parc des Princes national stadium in the south west of the city. Under a glowing moonlight, the looming north grandstand had cast a shadow across the rubble-strewn ground. The disposal had been impersonal and swift in execution. Pinon had overseen the operation after the death. He had noted Tressor's discomfort in the immediate aftermath. The Colonel had closed himself off from the events of the night, ensconcing himself in the playback room with the tapes of Al-Rikabi's responses. The orders had been swift and largely non-verbal, a wave of the hand and a silently closed door. Pinon knew but did not question. The death was to be regretted, a hazard of the game. Pinon stared at his hands as neon street lights flashed across the interior of the Citroen. He turned them over,

studying the raised calluses of his knuckles. The boy had been his third.
Entry into the DGSE compound completed, Pinon had made his way back down towards the detention block. Tressor was still in the same seat he had occupied an hour ago. He stared through impassive eyes as Pinon entered the room, the un-spooled mess of an audiotape spread across the table. As he picked at his nails with a penknife he looked up.

'I want you to continue a sweep on everything we've got on Kamal. Lestat has come up with an Algerian connection in the mid-eighties, some dissident coercion centred on the Al Rachaman group. Most of it is on microfiche over at Charenton-Le Pont.'
Tressor rose from his seat and perched himself on the edge of his desk. He pointed at the pin board with the knife.

'Anything' He pointed at Pinon. 'And I mean *anything* that strikes you as a connection with him and I want to hear about it. Twenty-four hour.'

The records facility at Charenton-Le Pont in the southeast of the city was made up of three single story concrete blockhouses in the centre of a drab housing estate. An elderly woman met Pinon at the door, the smell of Gouda strong on her breath, the long ash of a cigarette hanging from the corner of her mouth. The dark corridors seemed endless as Pinon was led down towards the records section. Long banks of computer consoles stretched into the darkness as he was shown to a desk. A single angle poise lamp lit the keyboard. Pinon thanked the woman and watched her shuffle off into the gloom before opening the file that had been placed next to the keyboard. Lestat had been thorough, the folder containing a comprehensive record of Abdul Kamal's whereabouts over the last five years. Photographs, transcripts of recordings and records of video tape held elsewhere, recalled the years up to the Gulf War. After that the picture was less clear. Pinon read through the summery sheet that Lestat had compiled as he inserted the first microfiche film into the projector. The first set of images concentrated on Kamal's last known long term infiltration into French interests; Algeria, in the late spring of 1986. The surveillance had centred on the Syrian embassy compound in Al Jazair and a known safe house of the Al Rachaman group. Reels of film had charted the appearance of a new cell of unknowns to the area. Professional and discrete, the Iraqi's, as they became known, were recorded over a two-month period of little consequence. The frames swam past Pinon's eyes in rapid succession as he searched for Kamal's distinctive features.

After ten minutes Pinon stopped abruptly, his fingers drumming the roller ball in reverse so that the previous pages reappeared. The photograph was a typical surveillance shot, long-range lens close-up, a grainy image, the street side café scene shot through the overhanging bough of a palm. Kamal's bald pate and distinctive dark moustache immediately caught the eye, but it was the presence of the female form sat opposite him that Pinon leant forward to study. He was too close, the individual grains of the film distorting the image further. Moving his chair away to the side, Pinon stood several feet from the screen, his eyes narrowing slightly. The hair was longer but the bone structure was the same. He had a match.

Holding the telephone between his shoulder and cheek, he dialled the number with his pen. The ring tone was answered almost instantaneously. Tressor's tired voice crackled down the line.

'This better be good, Xavier.

'I think I may have something, sir. I've got part of the Algerian unit from the eighties and, although I've got Gaston working on a positive identification, early matches would indicate that one Aisha Taraz was part of that unit.' Pinon paused for effect.

'Do we know her?' Tressor's was impatient.

'I think we do, sir. I am certain that she is also Halah Akief, the woman we stopped at Cherbourg in September. Hair's changed style and colour, and she may have had some surgery around the eyes, but I am 100 per cent on the match.' This time the response was more measured.

'Kamal and this Taraz woman have a previous working relationship?' Tressor cupped the receiver in his hands. He paused as Pinon's response sunk in. The voice was calm.

'I think that we need to find our man, and fast.'

'And the British?'

'Not just yet, I need to be sure before having to rely on their help.' As Tressor replaced the receiver his mind wandered to the interrogation room at Cherbourg. Taraz had been too knowing in her demeanour to go unnoticed. And yet he could not help but feel that if she was a professional, he was being fed a deliberate feint. He needed more. He turned to the console that dominated the left hand side of his desk and flicked the switch that would give him direct contact with London. He cancelled it before the contact was made, leaning forward to study the transcript of Jubal's last words. He needed a connection.

The Admiral Jellicoe Inn,
Churchstanton, Devon
21st May, 11.43 hours

'Roly, my dear boy, how are you?' Sir Giles Cardew rose stiffly from the confines of a large leather armchair that seemed to fill one corner of the smoke filled bar. Roland Whittaker stooped beneath the low ceiling interior of the snug, his head barely missing the ruined oak beams. He stuck out a large hand, the smile revealing expensive dental work.

'Sir Giles, it's mighty fine to see you again, I hope Marjorie is keeping well?' As he sat opposite the MP he glanced over at the small flight case sitting beside the leather chair. In the bar behind him, a few local faces filled their usual locations. Trade was light, a few business lunches mingling with tourist families. A youth busily fed a fruit machine in the corner, the flashing lights and intermittent bursts of sound at distinct odds with the eighteenth century surround. Whittaker leant forward in his seat.

'Is this it?' He pointed, the motion spilling a large drop from the brandy glass in his hand.
Cardew looked down and patted the case fondly.

'The very same, dear boy and, yes Marjorie and the boys are in fine fettle.' On a cool spring morning, the warmth of the fireplace was comforting, the low light of the interior aiding the intimate feel. Cardew had deliberately chosen the isolated pub for the exchange, discretion a speciality of his when the

situation arose.
The diversion of a little excitement had been too much to resist, a distraction from the familiarity of the journey a more than welcome diversion. Jeddah had provided the usual brief but welcome pleasures, the women the expected corporate perks. Cardew had begun to lose track, the blurring of boundaries between establishment courtesy and fraudulent bribery long since dissipated.

'Amilnas has posted you the key, I take it?' Cardew sat back into the warmth of the chair, aging leather creaking under the weight. Whittaker swilled the brandy in his glass before swallowing the contents whole.

'Not yet, Miss Akief has to contact him on the case's safe arrival.'

'Ah, yes. A shrewd operator, our Mr Amilnas.' Cardew leant forward, a glint in his eye.

'He told me that it was some kind of camera.' A wink followed. Whittaker smiled and held out both hands.

'Giles, you're a nosey bastard, I'll give you that. That's what it really is; it's a gun camera, it takes cine footage during mock dogfights. He wants it fitted for the testing and the footage sent over to Saudi. Honest to God.' Cardew was far from convinced.

'Well, in that case I feel rather a fool. I thought this was all hush hush.' Whittaker chuckled.

'Sorry, Giles, I know it seemed a bit James Bond, but you were over there and it just seemed to make sense. After all, you do bypass all that customs baloney.'
Cardew's cheeks were beginning to rouge. His expression of disappointment increased as Whittaker

drained the last vapours from his glass and rose from his seat.

'Leaving so soon old boy, I thought that we were in for the duration?' Whittaker leant down and grasped the handle of the silver flight case. The weight surprised him.

'Sorry. People to see, places to go, know what I mean, Giles? We're not all gentlemen of leisure.' He slapped the MP's arm. 'You must come up to Templemere some time. I'll get you aloft one of these days.' Cardew waved a fat hand, pausing to fight off indigestion.

'……You…must be joking. 747's are one thing, but those crates of string you glue together? Never in a month of Sundays, old boy'

Du Blayac farm,
April 28th, 18.00 hours

The group met in a huddle in the shade of a eucalyptus tree at the edge of the vineyard, the gathering of fellow countrymen causing few heads to turn. Kamal scanned the whereabouts of the other pickers, scattered groups choosing similar shaded seclusion for their evening food. The sun was already hugging the crest of a far distant slope. Dropping down on his haunches in the centre of the group, Kamal wasted little time on pleasantries.

'We are all here?' He scanned the faces before him. Heads nodded.

'We must surmise that our route through the embassy is broken and Jubal has been taken. We are now acting alone. The only contact direct will be for the extraction details. You all have contact numbers and will be expected to use them over the next week.

When you have the details of your own personal route, you will be acting alone from the moment your own personal tasks have been completed. As you are aware, each route is for your own knowledge and no one else. Some of you will be on your way before the main event and others could well be laying low for weeks if not months. You will not discuss this information with anyone else in the group. Is that clear?' There was a pause before heads slowly began to nod approval.

'We have secured the Blind Eye unit through diplomatic channels. The British actually had it on loan to a Middle East manufacturer. It will be installed as close to the day as possible.' Salaam broke off a large piece of bread before moulding it in his hands. He raised a hand as he began to chew at the crust. Kamal nodded and offered an explanation.

'Blind Eye is a small handheld unit that can be carried inside the cockpit. It is still under development but is sufficiently effective to be of major value to us. When activated it transmits a long-range frequency that disrupts the display of any radar monitor within an eighty-five mile radius. Any screen will begin to pulse until the vibration matches the natural frequency of the human eyeball, causing temporary blindness. This is maintained until the aircraft has left the radar's scope of radius.' Rana interrupted.

'This blindness, is it permanent?'

'Momentarily, the operator will see nothing on the screen until the aircraft is out of range and then normal sight is instantly returned.' Rana sat back on his haunches, his hands clasped behind his head. Kamal continued 'Whether the operator will know what he has been through is a matter of how much the

French know about Blind Eye's existence. My feeling is that they will be totally unprepared for it.'

'Why the need for the air show at Caen then? Would he not be covered flying from British airspace?'

'Blind Eye only works effectively over a short distance. It disrupts each radar sector that it flies through, but the pattern would soon be picked up over any sustained distance. Three hundred to four hundred miles at the most, anything more and a switched-on sector controller would scramble an intercept. Caen gives Steel the reason for being in that airspace. Using his speed, he should be in range of Air Force One before any controller gets suspicious.'

'And this unit disrupts any airborne radar as well?'

'Exactly the same, with the added advantage of disorientating any incoming pilot during potentially crucial manoeuvres. The Americans won't know where he has come from until it is too late.' Kamal allowed himself a grin of satisfaction. It died quickly as he saw Rana smiling back across the darkening gloom of the clearing. He was laughing.

'And we got this from the British?'

Blakes Wine Bar
Honiton, 22.44 hours

Thursby cradled his pint glass with both hands. It had been a long and tiring day. On the next stool, Ian Hart settled himself at the bar awaiting an answer to his initial question. The impromptu after work drink had slowly settled into a confessional. Thursby let out a long sigh before giving him his answer.

'Look son, as you know, I'm out of here in a few months. If we've got a nice bit of nonsense going on up at Templemere, then I want to be a part of it, know what I mean?' Hart placed his glass on the bar top.

'I owe you a great deal, sir. You know that. No amount of Hendon training could give the experience you have.' Thursby smiled before downing his pint. Hart continued. 'What concerns me sir, is that this Whittaker thing could get out of hand. Lets face it, we could be so out of our depth, its unreal.'

'Fair point, but this French stuff could be the making of you.' He pointed a finger over the top of his empty glass. 'Your shout I believe.' Hart shook his head as he beckoned the barman.

'And break me before I've even started. No offence sir, but if you leave London out of this Taraz woman connection we could have a major terrorist incident on our hands with minimal backup at best. I mean I trust your ARU guys down here, but they don't exactly get a lot of trade.' He paid for two more pints and took a set of darts from the bar top.

'Granted, I'll give you that, but you need to trust your own instincts more. If we've got trouble, and I mean in over our heads trouble, I'll pull us back. You've got no fear on that score.' He paused eying Hart as he raised the fresh pint to his lips. He had barely begun to drink when he paused again, more urgency in his voice. 'Trust me on this one. It's the woman I'm after. Screw Whittaker. She's onto something and its more than smuggling, I'll grant you, but we need the evidence. At the moment we've got bugger all apart from circumstance and happenstance'
Hart moved off his barstool and made for the dartboard at the side of the empty fireplace. As he threw the third dart he outlined Thursby's motives.

'Going out with a bang is one thing sir, but screwing up a major incident is another.' Thursby grabbed at the cluster of darts.

'Meaning?'

'I mean that we are taking risks in not keeping London fully briefed. This direct line you have with Tressor in France, he seems almost as unwilling to share information as you do.'

'You expect the worst?'

'I'm purely trying to cover all possibilities.' Thursby turned to face the dartboard and threw. Double nineteen.

'Son, if I had covered all possibilities over the past thirty years I'd have nicked under half the number of villains. What ever happened to instinct, good old intuition?' The voice was raised. 'Just bloody well go with the flow, son. Is that too much to ask?'

Hart stroked the stubble on his chin. He wanted to be back with Brenda and the kids. He needed sleep badly. Before he could answer, Thursby held up a hand.

'You probably won't like this, but I've signed you off all domestics for the next week, told them you were going for your promotion stint, got it?' Hart nodded without answering or understanding. 'I want you to monitor Whittaker and the woman from close in. I want movements and meetings, you can have an unmarked motor and a plain clothes with direct access to me at all times.' Thursby paused for effect, his hand holding the darts outstretched. 'You with me?'

Hart bowed his head. He just wanted to be at home. The barman called last orders, the old brass bell ringing three times. The last dregs of his pint downed, he raised his eyes to the ceiling. The lesser part of judgement was about to prevail.

Three

May 10th
Salisbury Plain
Wiltshire, England

The three-ship formation would have turned more than a few heads. Whittaker in the Spitfire, the Griffon running at close to full power, was having less trouble than Max in the F6. The Lightning, nose pitched up, was close to stall as it struggled to stay with the slower piston engine fighter. At the high end, the Spitfire could match the Lightning's lower speed range, but it was in the aerobatic turns and slower passes along the flightline that the WW2 fighter caused the most problems for it's Avon powered successor. Keeping his distance, Latham followed the intricate aerial ballet of the display in the two seat Vampire, his airspeed unimpeded by a need to match either of the display aircraft. High over the Wiltshire Downs, the formation began another run through of the display. The afternoon sortie had seen the aircraft enter their third week of practice flights, each one working up a further addition to what would be a four and a half minute routine.

Whittaker and Ronson had first run through the moves on the ground, to the apparent mirth of the ground crew as the two men wove in between each other on the apron of the main hanger. The routine had a far more serious application as any close formation required meticulous timing preparation and timing. With the Lightning now airworthy, Whittaker had devised a two ship routine with the Spitfire in the months before the Lightning was due to be shipped off to the Middle East. Initial enquiries to the larger air shows that took place during the summer months in Britain had yielded a great deal of interest as well as requests from further a field. With growing interest into the unique pairing several European shows had made contact. Among the first had been the forthcoming D-Day Anniversary display to be held at Caen. Whittaker had watched as the interest spiralled and the money flowed in. He would stand to make several thousand pounds over the next month alone. Whittaker had had Max restored to the flight team after a brief hiatus, the break seeming to produce a more relaxed character. He had also engineered a meeting between Ronson and Latham in an effort to complete the team. For different reasons, both men needed the reconciliation and the session at Whittaker's house seemed to have papered over several cracks. The programme had run smoothly, ahead of schedule in many ways and yielding further interest from air shows and displays as news of the unique pairing

filtered through the aviation world.
Latham watched the pair tail chase far below him. Across the slowly undulating and treeless Downs of Salisbury Plain the two aircraft wove in and out of each other's slipstream, Ronson working the harder of the two as he struggled to keep the heavier fighter airborne. The display was starting to look polished with each aircraft demonstrated as a solo before combining in a mock dogfight and series of passes. This would be some crowd pleaser, Latham thought as he heard Whittaker patch in and call for home. The small fighter rolled out of a slow turn and increased power to form on Latham's starboard wing. Max stayed low and throttled forward without warning. There was no radio contact and soon he was a speck on the distant horizon, the other two struggling to stay with him. From his canopy Latham could see Whittaker shaking his head. Old time Max, he thought.

Max had arrived at Templemere ten minutes after Whittaker and Latham, the lack of contact soon explained, Ronson signalling a radio failure from his cockpit as he taxied in. As usual, Halah was waiting for him, leant against the bonnet of Ronson's Morgan. She lowered the sunglasses from her head and waited for the Avon engines to die before approaching the cockpit ladder. Ronson slid the remaining five feet of the ladder, landing with a spring in his step at Halah's feet. The grin was wide as he removed the matt black bone dome. Without speaking, he threw the helmet to one of the ground crew before kissing Halah. By the time the pair had reached the car, Ronson was out of his flight suit and stowing it in the well behind the driver's roll bar. He spun the wheels sending a plume of smoke from the rear of the Morgan. Ian McCleesh stood, hands on hips, his head slowly shaking from side to side as he watched the car roar off across the airfield.

'So I guess you want us to put your aircraft to bed, eh Max?' He scratched his head before turning towards the still warm Lightning. It would be another hour before he would be able to leave.

Halah waited until the car had passed out of the main gates before speaking. She removed the glasses momentarily, the slipstream smarting her eyes. The warm summer air bathed her face.

'You looked good today. How did it go?' Her hand caressed Ronson's neck, a single finger tracing the line of his jaw. Max shifted into fifth, the Morgan bucking with newly released energy.

'Ran on rails, the display's virtually there and the ship is as ready as it can ever be. Got the first show on the 27th, up at Mildenhall. Straight in and back, then the build up to Caen'

'And your experiment?' Ronson smiled as he glanced at Halah and back to the
road.

'Used the hand held Blind Eye for fifty miles only. Full reheat, took two minutes forty.'

'The coastline route?'

'Started down from the old range at Aberporth. Your contact in Air Traffic should have enough to tell us.' Halah retrieved her cell phone from the glove compartment and keyed in a long number. After a long pause, the conversation was by turn short, her head nodding as she listened.

'Good, good. That's excellent. Thank you very much.' Ronson noticed that her free hand had clenched into a tight fist on her lap.

'Good news?' Halah removed her glasses again, her eyes shining.

'Swanage Control lost you for approximately three minutes. Once radio contact had been made with you, they then began a systems check that is still ongoing. They think that it's their problem.' She let a slow smile play across her lips, tilting her head back in the warmth that flowed around her face. 'You have all the cover you now need. We only now need to fit it permanently in the cockpit. They won't know what hit them.' Ronson floored the accelerator as the Morgan entered a long straight, the canopy of trees on either side forming a tunnel with only the occasional shaft of bright light cutting a path across the tarmac. Halah shifted herself in the bucket seat, one leg folded under her as she faced Ronson, both hands holding onto his arm.

'Listen, I need to disappear soon. The farm is ready and we're close enough to start preparing for any unseen possibilities' Ronson did not face her, his mind still back in the cockpit disseminating the information about *Blind Eye*. Halah continued 'We need a very public argument.'

Ronson's smile was thin.

'Should be easy enough.'

May 28th, Brittany

Asil al-Jenabi drew a weary hand across his sweat soaked eyes. He glanced back over his shoulder at the dusty track that had led from the valley. He was alone. The farm buildings drew ever closer as his aching legs carried him forward. He was coming down with something. That much he did know. That, combined with an over enthusiastic zeal to impress his superiors had resulted in compromising his fitness. His father would have beaten him had he not have lain in an unmarked grave some thirteen thousand miles away on the Iraq/Iran border. Asil had been a malnourished eight year old when he last remembered his father, waving to him from the back of an old British built Bedford truck. The whole village had assembled to watch the fathers, husbands and brothers leave to fight the Great enemy. For his mother, Asil had sensed the loss. And the relief. It was as if the war had given her husband a sense of purpose. The drinking had decreased and with it the beatings. He had not touched the boy for weeks since the call-up had been announced on the radio. The war had entered its eighth month before she heard any news of him. The Ministry official had been curt and uncaring, sat in the sparse living space of their Karbala home. Asil's father had been part of a major push on the eve of Ramadan. His unit had been gassed. He remembered his mother courteously thanking the official as he left before carrying on with her washing. There were no tears.

A large hay cart filled one corner of the barn, its wooden frame visibly sagging with age. Asil glanced back at the empty yard before entering into the inviting darkness. He made for the cart. Moving out of the line of sight from the door, Asil slid down against one of the great spoked wheels. His head slumped forward as he was overtaken by fatigue. He struggled briefly, knowing that discovery would bring trouble. His eyelids flickered slowly as he lost his battle with consciousness.

In the stark glare of a late morning sun, Henri du

Blayac stood on the edge of the escarpment that headed the crop valley. The gently sloping, vine-covered hills stretched to the horizon, only the occasional châteaux grounds punctuating the terrain with their shock of cultivated woodland. Du Blayac could not afford another year like the last. The incessant rain of the past two autumns had hit his crops hard, the September harvests producing a particularly acidic yield causing him to drastically lower his prices. The New World was at Europe's door and the American and British palates in particular, had become over educated. He eyed the long line of pickers that stretched out over several acres. Good boys, he thought. Hard workers, and no trouble. He cleared his nostrils onto the dusty path before turning to make his way back down to the farm buildings. He glanced at his watch, Eleven thirty. Time enough for some pilfering, he thought.

The barn had a faintly scented air as du Blayac gingerly edged his way through the barely opened door. A single paraffin lamp hung from a beam in the loft space, long shadows spreading the length of the interior. He had long since felt any guilt in turning the former pigsty into accommodation for the workers, but it still surprised him at the conditions that some would tolerate. A steep wooden ladder, each step causing the frame to bounce under the Frenchman's weight, accessed the upper floor. The air, although sweeter than before, still overpowered the nostrils. As he clambered onto the rough-hewn floorboards of the dormitory, du Blayac stood for a few seconds, allowing his eyes to penetrate the darkness. Two lines of simple bedrolls lined either wall, rucksacks and sports bags propped against the ancient roof trusses that disappeared up into the darkness. The smell was now pungent, a sweet musty odour that seemed to emanate from the gloom of the far wall. A wisp of smoke revealed the gently glowing ember of a single joss stick, its stem sunk into a small pitcher of earth. Taking a final look at the ladder behind him, du Blayac moved into the shadows that enveloped the closest of the bedrolls. The first three yielded little more than a few worthless possessions. The reading matter seemed limited to a few battered copies of the Koran and a map of Normandy. Du Blayac froze as he heard distant voices. The language was French, the old farmer relaxing as he recognised Grestain's Parisian drawl. He waited as the engine of the tractor faded into the distance. The next rucksack felt heavier. Hands felt in the darkness, fingers feeling the solid outline of a book like shape. The cover felt warmer, the textured surface expensive. The Filofax emerged silently from the rucksack's interior. Du Blayac held it up to the light of the lamp. It looked important. He fumbled with the clasp.

Behind the cover of the wagon, Asil watched as the farmer made his way silently along the row of beds. He was about to move out into the open when he caught sight of a figure at the base of the ladder. He moved back into the shadow of the wagon and waited. In the loft, the single clasp on the leather bound surface of the Filofax clicked open. Du Blayac flicked through the pages until the final page revealed an unexpected content. The interior of the file was hollow, a compartment shaped to hold two glass phials. Clear liquid, save for the presence of a number of air bubbles, filled each receptacle. It was then that du

Blayac sensed that he was not alone. The shadow fell across the farmers' body as he turned to face his assailant. The movement was swift and silent, the blade of the knife slicing through the jugular in one arcing thrust. Rana pulled away before the jet of blood could hit him. The farmer grabbed vainly at his throat as he slid down against the wall, his eyes filled with confusion as warm liquid flowed down over his chest. From behind the wagon, Asil winced with an audible intake of breath, pulling himself back into the shadows. As the body fell forward into the soft straw Rana held his stance momentarily before sheathing the blade in one swift movement. He studied the farmers still form before rolling the body further into the straw. Pulling bales from the stack, Rana quickly covered the body before retreating back into the shadows.

May 30th, Templemere
14.09 hours

Whittaker slapped the brown envelope down on the desk in front of Max, his face puce with anger. He prodded a finger on the table.

'Read it.' He ordered. Max leant forward and removed the letter. He read silently before the flicker of a smile played across his lips. Whittaker exploded.

'Funny? You think this is fuckin' funny? I've just had the Ministry of Defence on the phone for the best part of an hour with my balls in a vice.' Ronson removed his feet from the desk rose from Whittaker's chair. 'Calm down, Roly. Nothing happened.'

'You take off like a bat out of hell without permission and end up on the MOD range at Aberporth. They said you appeared out of nowhere and started an attack run on one of their target drones. You call that nothing?'

'Ease up, Roly. A bit of fun, that's all.' Ronson was holding out his hands, the smile apologetic. Whittaker rounded on him.

'The brass at Whitehall asked me to give them one good reason why you shouldn't be grounded and have your ass hauled over the fires by the CAA, and do you know what? I couldn't. You want to kill someone, you do it in your own time and in your own fucking airplane, mister.'

Whittaker held back, retreating towards the window. He had shown too much emotion, the business acumen revealing a human touch. Bad for business. Ronson took a deep breath before he spoke, the heroin rush fading fast.

'Look Roly, I…I'm sorry, you know? Trading the old Volvo for Mach two still gets me hot under the collar, know what I mean?' His brow furrowed, the sweat collecting above his nose. He wiped his face with a flick of his wrist. Whittaker turned to face him. The look was calm, the voice measured.

'You're off the flight Max, at least until after Caen. You need a rest. You blew it with Rob and now you're falling out with Halah.' Ronson started to panic.

'You can't…you…I mean, I've been in from the start.' His face was desperate, the display unsettling Whittaker, a side of Ronson he had not seen. The look only served to confirm his decision. He held up a hand as Ronson stuttered an apology.

'Look Max, I know about you and Halah splitting up. It's been no secret around here for about a week. You need a rest my friend.' The look was almost apologetic. 'Get yourself away from here for a while and we'll talk again.' The gesture was final. Whittaker lit up a new cigar as he swept out of the office, the door gliding gently shut. The soft click of the lock sounded around the interior. Ronson held his pose, his eyes the only darting presence. His hand clenched, the knuckles whitening. The punch took out the angle poise lamp on Whittaker's desk, the shattered remains snaking across the floor. With a bloodied hand he reached into his jacket pocket for his cell phone. He jabbed at the keypad. Aisha answered on the second ring.

Honiton Police Station
22.40 hours
Ronald Thursby replaced the receiver with a satisfied grin creasing his face, the clipped tones of Gilde Tressor's Parisian accent still fresh in his ear. The conversation had been brief but satisfyingly rich in its content. Thursby scuttled his chair across the cramped office on its runners
He came to rest against the elderly fax machine that nestled in the corner of the dimly lit office. Within seconds the paper feeder was spooling through the printer, a grainy image appearing from the tray. Thursby tore off the paper before it had fully appeared, the torn edge cutting a diagonal tear across the neck of the head and shoulders line-up shot. A side view began to print as Thursby studied the face. He immediately picked up the telephone beside the fax and stabbed a cell phone number into the keypad with his pencil.

'Evening son, are you alone?' Twelve miles away Ian Hart propped himself up on his pillow, the still form of his wife beside him. So much for an early night, he thought.

'Sir?, just the missus and she's asleep.

Thursby bulldozed on.

'Good. Listen, it turns out that our friends up at Templemere are more than meets the eye, or at least one of them is. Our Halah Akief turns out to be a former Iraqi agent who was last seen working in the mid eighties in Algeria. Supposedly gone straight. Now she may be legit, but with her having form, we need to pin something concrete on her actions. Paris needs a connection with a possible cell on their side but it's all circumstantial at present. They're not giving us the whole picture but we need proof of a connection over the water and more than just a couple of social calls before we start earning our corn.' Thursby cupped his hand over the receiver as he reached for the side-on mug shot. He squinted as he held it at arms length, his tired eyes straining to adjust focus.

'I want us in on this one son, the London boys can wait for a while.' He listened for Hart's reply, the receiver momentarily silent. 'You still there?'

'Yes…sir.' The voice hesitant. 'The problem is that our main suspect seems to have gone to ground.' Thursby sat up straight in his seat.

'But you've had contact records over the past week, the phone taps and visuals?'

'Taps, yes, but the sightings actually dried up last week. The last contact was on Thursday evening at Whittaker's house. She's been keeping contact on mobile since then and never long enough to get a lock. I'm sorry sir, but we were hoping that she was going to reappear.'

Thursby pushed a hand through his thinning hair, the ancient office seat groaning as he leant back.

He took a deep breath.

'And the taps?'

'Nothing other than business and social, the usual pattern. Nothing overseas.' Thursby tried to take in the possibilities of the timeframe involved.

'And the last sighting dried up at Whittaker's?'

'After the visit, she lost us in the lanes up around Culmholt. Nothing up at Ronson's house and Whittaker's still driving his Merc. Customs reports no sign of her at any port.'

'Jesus Christ, she could be anywhere.' Hart was now out of bed and starting to get dressed.

'One thing the phone boys did say was that her signal was strong enough to be local, so she must still be in the area. The latest call was this afternoon at three. She talked to an Ian McCleesh, Whittaker's chief mechanic. Something about future orders and a deal in the States.'

It was a vain attempt to soften the blow. Thursby's voice had been shocked rather than angry.

'You'd better come in, son. We need to get on top of this one.'

Four

Admiral Jellicoe Inn
June 3rd, 2100 hours
Whittaker held court at the head of the long oak table, his cigar gently smouldering in the ashtray before him. The full company of Whittaker Aviation were assembled for the briefing. The Caen operation was complex and would stretch the crew to its limit. McCleesh would head up the French operation with Matty Fry and Joe Lissner as ground crew while John Reed would oversee the departure of the Lightning with Whittaker, before the boss left in the Spitfire. After the initial briefing, the mathematics of timings and logistics taking most of the first hour, Whittaker leant forward in his seat and raised a hand for some silence. His face was solemn.

'There is to be one major change of plan,

however. Rob Latham will be flying the F6 on Monday.' There was a brief pause, the silence revealing what most were already suspicious of. 'Max will still be a valued part of the team but we felt that he needed a break from what has been a tough testing schedule.' Again the silence, many heads buried in their pint glasses. It was McCleesh who broke the air with typical bullishness.

'You're letting a Geordie play with your pride and joy, then boss?' It was a blessed relief from the awkwardness of the moment. Fry, an ex Royal navy man chipped in.

'I don't know about letting a crab climb all over my handiwork, what do you reckon lads?' Whittaker took his chance and changed tack.

'Ian and his team will fly out on the 5th in the Devon and make all of the preparations at Caen. The accommodation and fuel is already booked. Myself, Reedy and Rob will depart the F6 first at 12.30 hours, with me following in the Spit approximately fifteen minutes later. The rendezvous point will be over Jersey ready for a run in and slow pass arrival over Caen at 13.20 hours. Any questions?' Matt Fry raised his arm.

'Any chance of an over night, boss?' The grin spread across his face in a flash.

'Sorry Matt, expenses don't stretch that far I'm afraid.' Whittaker glanced over at McCleesh. 'I'm sure you could persuade Ian to take you over in that mobile brothel of his.' McCleesh raised his glass.

'Yous all be laughin' on the other sides of yer faces when I'm entertainin' all of those fair Mademoiselles, and no Matty, you can't have a lift.' The big Scot gathered up all of the empty glasses from the table. 'Whose fer another, Mister Whittakers round, I do believe.' As he made his way between the tables towards the bar, he caught sight of Rob Latham's reflection in a mirror on the wall. He sat alone in the snug bar nursing a bottled lager.

'Us grease monkeys no' good enough for you then?' Latham looked up and smiled as he recognised the figure before him.

'Has he told them yet? Only, I….I didn't want to be there when he did.' McCleesh parked himself on a small stool, his frame dwarfing the round table.

'Ay, laddie. I know what you mean. One or two of the lads have grown used to Max and his quirks. I think we all have.' He lit up a cigarette.

'Trouble is that he's become dangerous recently. It's no fun strapping a man into his coffin, and the last few times I really began to wonder if he'd be coming back, know what I mean?'

Latham nodded as he stretched out a hand towards the packet of cigarettes on the table. McCleesh frowned as he offered up the pack.

'I did'na know you smoked, son.' Latham shrugged.

'I haven't, not for a few years anyway. Trust me, it's been one of those weeks.' He coughed as he exhaled the first drag. Jenny would kill him. 'I guess you heard about my punch up with Max back along?'

'Hand bags at twelve paces, Roly called it. Said that you gave as good as you got and it was all now history.'

'Fucking stupid, the whole thing. And now he's gone AWOL again, I'd chuck the whole gig to see him right again.' Latham downed the remainder of the bottle before the Scot could answer. He rose from the stool and pointed at McCleesh's half empty pint.

'Another?'
The big mechanic held up an oil stained hand.

'Not me son, thanks all the same. I've got to put an F6 to bed. You not going to join the lads?'
Latham declined, the need to be with Jenny suddenly more important. He lowered the empty bottle onto the table. McCleesh rose and placed a hand on Latham's shoulder.

'Give it time son, and he'll come around. He knows it's for the right reasons.' Latham nodded, the look unconvinced. As he made to leave a hand slapped down on his right shoulder, jolting him. Whittaker placed his arm around Rob's waist. The voice was slightly slurred.

'You gotta forget about Max, son. He needs the break. I've offered them the use of my place in Tuscany for the week.' Latham cocked his head to one side.

'And Halah was OK with all of this?' Whittaker smirked and held up both hands.

All right, so maybe she doesn't know and I'm letting Max tell her. Jeesus, Rob, I wanna keep my balls'

'Fair enough. I've got to admit that I have seen flashes.' Latham rose to leave. Whittaker moved to one side, the gentle sway of his frame barely perceptible as he leant back against an oak beam. 'You not staying with us then Rob?' Latham shook his head slowly.

'Its called paperwork Roly, and besides, I've no wish to bump into certain people tonight.'
As Latham rose to leave he noticed McCleesh and two of the crew stood at the bar. It would be a late start for Whittaker Aviation, he thought as he walked out into

the warm evening sunshine that bathed the car park.

22.00 hours

Max had parked the Morgan out of sight of the farmhouse and waited in the lengthening shadows. As the engine cooled, the pinging of contracting metal was the only sound, save for the distant thrum of a late night tractor. Ronson leant forward in his seat, the main door of the house visible between a break in the foliage that bordered the driveway. Still no lights, Halah's new Saab sat on the untidy grass track that led from the dilapidated wooden garage. The house was certainly secluded, he thought. The move had been planned to coincide with Halah's withdrawal from view, the abandoned farm house secured through idle gossip in the local in Churchstanton. The property had been deserted some four years previously and was sufficiently hidden from any main roads to provide the desired seclusion. Ronson's hand instinctively felt along the ledge of the map compartment for his cigarettes. He managed to get one as far as his lips before he remembered his surroundings. Where was she? The telephone call in Whittaker's office had lasted less than thirty seconds, Halah's calm response sending an unexpected icy spasm down Ronson's spine. The voice was measured, the monotone delivery as if she had been expecting the news. Ronson had sobered rapidly as he followed her instructions to make for the farm. He had pulled over onto a clearing at the edge of a wood that skirted their village. On the edge of the Blackdown Hills, Max Ronson stared out over the mist filled Vale of Taunton, the evening slowly dissipating in the angry glow of a harvest sunset. He'd nailed half of the packet of Camels before he felt able to face Halah at the house. Even then, the progress had been painfully slow, the Morgan pulling into the drive at a crawl. He had killed the engine before the dogleg corner, the car gliding to a halt. He winced as the handbrake rasped on its ratchets. The house was dark.

Ronson retrieved his leather jacket from the passenger seat and pocketed what remained of the Camels. He trod the grass-covered centre line of the drive as he approached the house. As he silently fished for the keys in his pocket, the front door glided open. Ronson squinted to make out any shape that hid in the grainy darkness of the interior. Halah stepped forward, her aroma filling his nostrils.

'Are you alone?'

Ronson nodded and bowed inside the low porch.

Halah silently motioned towards the warm light emanating from the kitchen doorway, the newly cropped hair distinctive against the glow. On the table in the centre of the room a map had been laid out, several sheaves of paper lay scattered about the edges. In the half-light Halah pulled a chair out from under the table and Ronson slowly moved from the doorway into the lamplight of the kitchen. He instinctively moved towards the table at the far end, his immediate thought of the two bottles of Teachers wedged tight at the back of the cutlery draw. If she'd found them, he was in for a rough night. He knew how much the alcohol had played its part in Whittaker's decision. He stopped short and turned his attention to the paper unfolded in front of him. The map showed the English Channel, the coasts of Britain and France bisected by red ruled lines. Large coloured map pins acted as locations. Ronson was familiar with all. He looked up at Halah, his hand sweeping across the contents of the table.

'Are we still capable of this?' Halah nodded slowly.

'We had a contingency for your compromise and this is it. We simply remove the equation.' Ronson frowned as he placed his hands either side of the map. His eyes played over the intended route of the display pair over the Channel and on into Normandy. He turned and leant against the table.

'The simple fact is that I am no longer the designated driver.' The smile was sarcastic. He had a feeling that she had been expecting Whittaker's decision. He had felt unable to resist the tide of the last month, the fading of one sortie into another. The spaces in between had been even less defined, the juxtaposition of pleasure mixed with pain. Halah had been in turns, a provider in both senses. She was swift in her summing up of the situation.

'You send him to me. I'll deal with him. We need somewhere out of the way, like a farm out building or barn. Give him a good reason, something solid but a certainty that he will turn up.'
Ronson frowned.

'Deal with him ? You mean kidnapping?'
Halah stared at him, her eyes narrowing slightly.

'What are you like? Too many questions, too many coincidences. Can't you see through that boyish façade. If he doesn't know now, he soon will.'
Ronson looked down at his hands as he realised the finality of her words. He clenched his fist inside the pocket of his jacket. He knew she was right.

'You want me to make the phone call, is that it? Send him to you.' Ronson's head remained lowered.

'Friend or no friend, he could be all that stands between us, and success. You deliver him to me and you *will* be the pilot, do you understand?' Ronson sobered rapidly. He rocked his head backwards and rolled his eyes. Anna loomed large on the interior of his eyelids, the rage building again.

It was his turn to experience clarity, the vision of the rubble of the unit at Muharraq. He had landed forty-five minutes after it had happened, the US Special Forces Chinook circling the airfield before dropping next to the smouldering remains of the impact crater. The daze had set in before the helicopter took off, the obscene request for a personal identification upon landing just adding to the surreal events of the last hour. As he sat, stunned in the cabin of the Chinook, it was Latham who identified the body, the confirmation hitting home before restraining arms could pin him down. In the empty interior, the two men held each other. The following months would see Ronson's rage build from within.

'I'll deliver him.' The words had been empty, unfeeling. Ronson turned his back on Halah and ran a hand through his lank hair. He suddenly felt very tired. As he sank down into the oak chair, he glanced up at Halah.

'Don't kill him.'

Her hands smoothed the back of his neck as she began to massage the tension in his shoulders. Her thumbs kneading the top of his spine, Halah leant down and began licking his ear. Her hot, breathy voice filled his head.

'Just out of the way, that's all. Until we're

finished.' He was still tense, his frame stiffened to await the first blows. He had been lulled before.

'Now I want you relaxed tonight, a good meal, a hot bath, me.' Her hands played across his chest, fingers reaching between the buttons of his shirt. He let his head fall back. He could feel her hot cheek against his. Max flinched as the unseen needle punctured the skin of his forearm.

'Jeez…no..not….' The rush hit him and he surrendered immediately. Any thoughts of the day were swallowed up in the swirling haze that now filled his consciousness. Halah let her hands play across his stomach and down to the belt of his jeans. Her fingers unbuttoned his fly and, reaching inside, she held him tightly.

Du Blayac farm
June 4th,02.12 hours
The five figures huddled about the soft light of the oil lamp. Despite the muggy warmth of the night, the interior of the barn felt cold. Kamal sat at the head of the table. The surface was conspicuous by the absence of paperwork. He pointed first to Salam.

'Once you have created the diversion, your work is done. I want you out of there immediately and onto your rendezvous. No loitering' Salam nodded. Kamal faced the three remaining men.

'The diverted Steel will be approximately ten minutes flying time from the replenishment. We're looking at a ten-minute turn around from the moment he comes to a standstill. The engines will stay running. A two-man team comprising of Latif and myself will load the ordinance. Fuel will be out of the question. We don't want to draw any more attention to ourselves than is necessary. A small van will turn no heads, whereas a fuel bowser asks too many questions. Steel will then have twenty minutes to target engage.'

'We're not fitting another brake chute?' Latif's brow furrowed.

'He won't be landing.' Rana's reply needed no further explanation. Kamal continued

'At the same time as he takes off, Rana and Asil will take out the main runway at Lessay with the mortar. That will make the nearest fighter unit Deuville, and that is a further ten minutes flying time. This should give *Steel* a five minute window in which to engage'.

'What is the latest on fighter escort?' Salam asked. Kamal turned to another page in his folder. He lowered his spectacles to the end of his nose and glanced over the top of them.

'The Americans rely on a high level of security when it comes to the itinerary and the route in question. There will be an escort of sorts but this will take the form of a high level CAP from the USS Ranger in mid Atlantic. The aircraft are on exercise with the British and are in proximity but the proposed intercept area is at the very end of their endurance. With the French escort delayed at Lessay, Steel should have enough time to make it a turkey shoot.' Rana leant forward.

'Countermeasures on the 747 ?'

'As you can imagine we are looking at a comprehensive package of ECM jamming together with chaff and flare dispensers. No armament to speak of but we are aware that the engines are augmented and will give a fair turn of speed. As I said, a five minute window will give him plenty of time.' Kamal paused briefly, his eye's playing across each face.

'Finally, your exit routes are pre-determined and cannot be changed. Our couriers know you all by sight and will only operate on a confirmed identification. After that you are on your own.' Asif raised a hand.

'And Jubal?' Kamal stood and walked away from the table before turning to face the lamp light. He shook his head slowly.

'Nothing, nothing at all. We can only surmise that he is either lying low or been taken by the French.'

'Or dead.' Rana's eyes glinted through the gloom. Kamal nodded silently.

'A distinct possibility, yes, but what I do know is that communication through the embassy route shows no breach. Until such time as an insurmountable obstacle faces us, gentlemen, we proceed.' Asil persisted.

'And if he talks?'

'Six weeks without contact and we are still active. What else can we do but proceed. We must follow through until the opposition is overwhelming. We all have too much to lose at home, not to.' Rana grunted and rose to leave.

'And you place that above loyalty to your President. Women and kids?' He stared silently at Kamal before disappearing into the shadows.

Five

Churchstanton, June 4th
10.07 hours

The early morning sun filtered through a gap in the drapes, the shaft of light cutting across Max Ronson's face. In the far distance of a mist-shrouded morning, working dogs could be heard barking to each other. He turned over onto his back, the deep, welcoming mattress forming a warm embrace around his frame. As he pushed himself up onto the pillows, the bedroom door swung slowly open. Halah appeared with a tray, a full-length dressing gown trailing the floor.

'A breakfast for champions,' she said. Ronson looked up at her.

'The last meal of a condemned man?' Ronson held her gaze as she lowered the tray onto his lap. She looked away.

'It doesn't have to be that way.' Halah sat on the edge of the bed, the gown slipping from her shoulder.

'Meaning? I thought that it would suit all concerned if my act of revenge ended in a fiery act of self-sacrifice. After all, don't your bosses go for all that fire and brimstone rhetoric? Halah's smile was half hearted, one corner of her mouth managing to rise.

'You have Blind Eye, and we could have a relief landing ground ready with a route out.' Halah was holding his leg as she spoke. She squeezed his knee gently. Ronson held her gaze before rocking his head slowly back and smiling. Halah looked confused. She pushed his leg away. She was frowning.

'It's still possible.' She moved onto the end of the bed. Ronson shifted onto one shoulder and sank his teeth into a piece of toast.

'You honestly think that the pride of the US Marine Corps are going to give me a second chance? Don't patronise me love.'

'I'm not trying to. I just want you to know that the last few months have been….'

Ronson interrupted.

'What's this? The professional Ice Queen letting her emotions cloud her judgement. I didn't know you had any.' Halah exploded.

'Fuck you, Ronson.' She pulled away from the bed and walked towards the window before turning to face him. 'I'm trying to give you a way out here. I'll admit that you may have got to me over these months. Is that so bad?' Ronson scoffed.

'Got to you? With the help of a fucking syringe, I may have.' He sat himself up in the bed.

'You'd have done better than to pump me full of that shit. You see, I don't need any false motivation. What burns me, you will never experience or understand.' He struck his chest with his thumb. Halah walked slowly towards the bed.

'I can't ever expect to compete with the love you had for your……' Ronson punched the tray from his lap, the contents crashing against the fireplace, rivulets of liquid running down the ornate Victorian carvings. Ronson's fists grabbed at Halah's throat, his hands closing around the collar of her shirt. In one movement he pulled tight across her windpipe, his bodyweight sending her crashing down on the bed. Teeth bared, he brought his face within inches of hers, hot breath filling her nostrils.

'You don't know the meaning of the word love.' His grip tightened, Halah's hands grasping at his wrists. 'I was fighting your kind long before any of this. Compassion seemed to be a banned commodity on your side.' He loosened his grip slightly and Halah retched violently. She struggled to catch her breath, the words coming in punctuated sobs.

'We......we.. weren't the cause of your grief, you said that much yourself in......in Nice.' She choked back a sob. Ronson grabbed her face with his right hand.

'Your bastard Scuds were the start. If those Yank scum had paid a proper price, I'd be going after your boss by now.' He paused, releasing the grip.

'What ever this may be to you, my destiny is with my Anna. You are a means to an end and that is the *only* way we satisfy each other.' Halah's eyes widened, her mouth slowly creasing into a wide grin. As she started to laugh, Ronson pulled himself away from her in disgust. The laughter echoed around the tight confines of the low ceiling, Halah propping herself up on the bed.

'You're perfect, you know that?' She rubbed at her burning throat. Ronson moved away from the bed and towards the door. He pointed towards her without turning.

'What I have is purely personal, nothing more. You simply give me the opportunity, you understand?' Halah shook her head silently, the smile dissipating. Ronson stood his ground.

'Fuck your ideals.' The voice was lower, the head bowed. He stood and walked through the doorway in silence. Halah stayed on the bed. She called out.

'Exeter at Ten. We need him out of the way.' She listened for the inevitable slam of the front door. She rose slowly, draping a robe around her shoulders, and made her way out onto the landing. Through the circular window at the head of the staircase, she watched the taillights of Ronson's Morgan fade into the early morning mist.

In the dim light of the bathroom mirror she studied the bruising around her throat. The silver hypodermic lay in the soap dish, the needle glistening in the neon light. Halah clenched her teeth as the needle punctured the skin. The rush was almost instant. Her head arched back as she caressed the length of her slender throat. She began to buck and shudder as the Codelphene coursed through her veins. Fists and teeth clenched. The shrill tone of her cell phone broke the brief silence. Making her way back to the bedroom she paused on the side of the bed. She took deep breaths before composing herself to take the call. Roland Whittaker's normally assured tones were subdued, the voice hesitant.

'I've, er..made a final decision on the Caen

show, honey. I don't feel that Max is up to a display flight right now and I'd feel safer with Rob Latham.' He paused, expecting a hostile reaction. He heard the sigh. The reply was measured.

'I know, I know, it's your call Roly. We all know what Max is going through it at the moment, but leave him to me. I'll have him ready for Thursday.' Whittaker paused.

'I…I don't know, Halah. This is a big show for me and I have a big contract in the pipeline with this Amilnas guy, you know?' The silence lasted several seconds.

'We need to talk, Roly.' The voice was conciliatory. 'If we could meet at Templemere tomorrow evening, I would be very grateful.'

'You want to talk about Max, or what?' Whittaker failed to disguise his eagerness. The voice on the other end was almost a whisper.

'Oh, you know. Max, you and me, the future.'

Paris,
13.50 hours

'Thank you very much, sir.' Gilde Tressor bowed slightly as he turned to leave the office of his superior. The seventh floor was deserted save for the Minister and his elderly secretary, the empty corridor echoing to the sound of Tressor's footsteps as he walked away from the office. The instructions had been short and simple to digest. Tressor held his own council in the lift, the temptation to lift the telephone receiver in the carriage resisted. Pinon could wait. Tressor pulled a small address book from his pocket, thumbing the pages as he waited for the elevator to finish its ascent. The response had not surprised him.

He knew that he was dealing with a man of little imagination. As the lift doors opened, Tressor remained inside; his slim frame leant against the vast mirror that filled the rear of the compartment. He stroked the stubble of a daylong growth, the rasp audible within the confined space. He kept his thumb against the OPEN button, the doors repeatedly trying to close. He felt so tired. The lift gently came to a halt. At the end of the vast corridor that stretched out before the open lift doors, Tressor's office door opened, Pinon's unkempt shape appeared from the dimly lit interior. He squinted as he tried to focus on the continuous movement of the lift doors at the far end of the corridor. Slowly, Tressor appeared from between the open doors. Pinon did not need to ask. From his superior's body language, the question had been rejected.

In his office, Tressor thumbed the address book pages. He could still smell a trace of the chemicals from the forensics test. It had revealed nothing.

'The Minister played it by the book I suppose, you'd have to give him that. I know that they all have Marseilles on their minds.' Pinon winced at the mention of the twelve year old operation.

'A long time ago, sir.' Tressor smiled as he looked up.

'Alas, not long enough, Xavier. Funny how one mistake can wipe away an entire career.' He clenched his fist under the desk.

'It's the election, sir. They merely want to smooth the path to it. Any negative publicity is out of the question'. Pinon offered.

Tressor turned his attention back to the book in front of

him. He let the pages of the address book fall open at the calendar, eying the circled dates. As he leant forward, he held the notebook closer and studied the page over his glasses.

'Forensics and the usual Mukhabarat codes all run through, you say?' Pinon nodded as Tressor frowned. 'Are we crediting this youngster with too much?' He looked up at Pinon, a smile slowly appearing. 'We've not seen the wood for the trees. I don't think that these are dates at all. Look at them.' He tossed the book across the room, Pinon catching it at the second attempt.

'Look at the numbers he has circled,' Tressor pointed, 'all of the single digits start with a zero and yet some are circled with and others without. These aren't dates, they're numbers. We pay those eggheads in code breaking God knows how much and it's right there in front of us'

Pinon studied the page closer, his face reddening at the dawning realisation.

'If you take the first three digits, including the first zero prefix, we could have a cell phone number here.' Pinon pointed a large finger at the first numbers outlined in January. He laughed out loud as he stood, papers slipping from the desktop onto the floor. He instinctively grabbed for he handset on Tressor's console. A hand shot out, grabbing his wrist. Tressor held on tight.

'Not now. If we are talking about the closest target, we need to use this nearer to the time.'

Pinon stared down at his boss.

'And not *before* it happens?' Tressor folded the spine of the address book back on itself. He placed it gently on the desk, the small size belying its importance against the vast emptiness of oak. He lowered himself slowly into his seat.

'If this is a number, and we need to be certain of this,' He gazed up at Pinon. 'We need to use it at the right time. If this is the 6th of June, we need to make this a one shot certainty. We know that we need a clear eight second contact for a fix anywhere near accurate, twelve to be certain.' Pinon turned away from the desk.

'When exactly, then?' Tressor swivelled his seat to face the window. He picked up a paper from his desk.

'The main ceremony is at Arromanches at Five, the majority of the dignitaries arriving in convoy at Four forty five. Both the British and US will be landing at Cherbourg at Four and Four-thirty respectively. The only other major target will be Queen Elizabeth arriving from her yacht at Two for the ceremony at Courseulles. I suggest that we make the call at about One.'

Templemere,
18.25 hours

Whittaker fumbled with the large bundle of keys as he approached the main hanger. He dropped them, cursing as he struggled to find the distinctive Chubb key. There was no sign of Halah's car, the place seemingly deserted. The key turned in the lock but the handle only turned half way. It felt stiff. Whittaker pushed hard on the door of the hanger with his shoulder. There was a crack of splintered wood as the door finally gave way. One broken half of a broom handle lay on the concrete inside, the other piece wedged into the door handle. The interior was dark save for the solid outline of the Lightning appearing from the grainy blackness.

He felt for the light control on the corrugated wall of the hanger. He fumbled for the switch. The flashing of the fluorescent lights battled against the dark before illuminating the interior. Whittaker paused to survey the scene. His eye was caught by the silver flight case that stood on a tool trolley beneath the Lightning's cockpit. It was open. The access ladder was against the fuselage, the canopy raised.

He walked slowly towards the case, the familiar outline of a container that was supposed to be safely locked in the boot of his Mercedes. Reaching the access ladder, Whittaker saw that the case was empty. Instinctively he climbed up the ladder. At the top he stretched forward into the cockpit, the interior lit by a solitary pencil torch balanced on the sill of the instrument panel. His eyes played over the familiar controls for several seconds before his gaze was broken by an unfamiliar outline beneath the brake chute release handle. A rectangular box hung from the underside of the panel. A small array of numbered buttons ran the length of the unit with a single LED on the right hand side. To the uninitiated the matt black of the box would have blended seamlessly with the rest of the interior. To Whittaker, it was alien. His hand reached out towards the box. As his fingers grasped the still warm exterior, from somewhere beneath his feet, there came a sudden rap of metal on metal. The sound echoed up into the chasm of the roof trusses. Halah Akief knocked against the steel fuselage again with the barrel of her Glock. Whittaker stared down at her, his eyes taking in the scene at the base of the ladder. She motioned silently for him to come down. Whittaker hesitated, utter bewilderment in his eyes.

'Who the hell do you think you are, lady?' As

he made his way back under the refuelling probe his expression was now one of anger, colour filling his cheeks. Halah backed away as he reached the base of the ladder, the pistol covering him. On the ground, Whittaker moved slowly, his hands outstretched in front of his chest. His mind was racing.

'Listen honey, you know I don't keep any cash here.' His thumb pointed over his shoulder. 'Hell, all the money I got is tied up in this baby.' The smile was hesitant, the nerves on show for a purpose. His palms now faced upwards, the head slightly cocked to one side.

'What's all this about honey?'

Halah grasped the pistol grip harder. Her lip curled as she spoke, the voice an octave lower.

'I would think that this all comes as a bit of a shock.' Whittaker could not help but smile at the understatement.

'You could say that. Is this something to do with Max or is this about us?'

Halah scoffed.

'Us? You poor deluded fool. You can't see further than the end one of those fat cigars, can you? You've been used Whittaker, the car, your business, even your identity.'

'Used for what?'

'As the means to an end, and I must say that you played your part well.' The finality of the statement hit Whittaker, the sarcastic tone of Halah's voice deciding his next move. He edged back towards the crew ladder, the Glock shadowing him as Halah continued.

'The only real problem was that you failed to tell me just how much of an interest the French and

British customs have in you, Whittaker. What was it? Drugs. Porn. Your sordid little smuggling game got me noticed.' She held the pistol tighter, the slight smile disappearing. 'All that you need to know is that you can have the satisfaction of being part of changing history. I just wish that the irony of a Yank being involved was not wasted on you.' Whittaker moved to the side of the tool trolley, his arms outstretched.

'Now, whoa lady. Pulling an iron on a Southern man is one thing, but to accuse him of being a Yankee is another.' As he smiled his left hand felt for the edge of the trolley. In one powerful movement the flight case was sent cartwheeling towards Halah. It glanced her right hip, the force unbalancing her. As she fell the muzzle of the pistol flashed briefly, the Glock bucking in her fist. The shot hit Whittaker square in the chest causing him to stumble backwards. His great frame swayed momentarily before crashing back against the trolley sending tools cascading across the concrete. Halah paused to allow the crescendo of noise to rebound around the walls. Her nostrils were full of the acrid stench of cordite. She massaged the growing pain in her right hip. As the noise died away she climbed to her feet and walked slowly over to Whittaker's body. Her booted heel rolled his head to one side. A second shot rang out.

Six

Brittany, 21.00 hours

In the half-light of the barn Kamal's tall figure was bent over the missile trolley, his hands deep inside the inspection hatch of the Red Top. At his feet lay a neat roll of tools, several of the pockets empty. A large unfolded plan sheet sprawled across the forward half of the fuselage. The work was slow, Kamal deliberately meticulous in his actions, a jigsaw puzzle of disassembled pieces spread out on a tray next to the tool roll. Occasionally, he would squat down, the beam of the small torch that he wore in a headband playing across the worn pages. From the shadows of the barn's interior, Rana approached silently, watching the proceedings for a full minute before announcing his presence.

'What sequence do they go off in?' Kamal spun around in surprise, the voltmeter in his left hand clattering to the floor. He instinctively ducked down in an effort to retrieve it.

'You bloody fool!' he hissed from between clenched teeth. He rose slowly to his feet, breathing deeply in an effort to lower his hammering pulse rate. Rana's interest surprised him. He stooped again to retrieve the meter, the cracked digital reading rendering it now useless. He eyed Rana's still form framed by the moonlit glow of the open barn door. 'I thought that these were supposed to be obsolete compared to your Stingers?' He turned and ran a finger along the edge of the open inspection panel. He could feel his heart beat slowing. 'Starboard then Port, in rapid succession if need be.' Rana smiled before placing a half-smoked Gitane in his mouth. He retrieved a gold cased lighter from his jacket pocket and began to raise it towards the stub. He paused as he eyed the open inspection hatch. He gestured towards the missile.

'How much do these pack?' Kamal gathered up the loose pages of the manual before answering.

'68lb, fragmentation warhead. Why do you ask?'

Rana snapped the lighter shut before placing the unlit cigarette behind his ear.

'Oh, no real reason. Do you think this guy will need both?' Kamal cleaned his hands with a cloth that had covered the nose cone. A question answered with a question. Typical Rana, he thought. The inspection hatch was replaced and the Allen screws slowly tightened into place.

'You're mistaking me for someone who cares, Rana.' Kamal shocked himself with his lack of candour. 'When our task is complete, I for one will not be staying to see the conclusion. There are more important priorities. I don't expect you to understand.' Rana raised a quizzical eyebrow.

'You think that you have more to lose than the rest of us?'

Kamal pointed in the direction of the fields.

'I'm 38, Rana. I am the old man. Look at them. Kids. They are expendable resources with unswerving loyalty, that's what you call them, isn't it? Your faithful Fedayeen. You and I are the only career soldiers here, and only you do this for the money.' Kamal's voice echoed around the interior, the pitch rising as Rana sensed his anger as he continued. 'Or is it that you are starting to enjoy the killing?' Rana smiled.

'I can, how shall I put it, be somewhat over zealous in my work.' Kamal flashed a look of distain. He had heard plenty about Rana's barbarism in the field.

'I hear that those Marsh Arab children were particularly difficult to deal with.'

'They hid terrorists among them.'

'And you believed those lies. Who told you. Hamdani? Straight from the top no doubt. Plant a few grenades among the women did you?'

Rana continued to smile. He now had his information and, pocketing his lighter, he turned and walked out into the night. Out in the courtyard, he kept walking, the snaking gravel path disappearing off into the open land of the vineyards.

The village of St Pol de Leon was quiet; a lone dog moving from bin to bin was the only visible presence on the main road. The small bar was at the far end of a line of shops, the barman hooking a thumb over his shoulder when Rana asked to telephone. The walk from the du Blayac farm had taken a leisurely twenty minutes in the increasing gloom of the dusk. The bar was empty save for an old man sat in a window seat. He seemed asleep, a full glass of claret on the table in front of him. Rana paid for a half of lager and a pack of American cigarettes, leaving them on the bar as he made his way into the dark at the back of the bar. The small wooden cubicle at the rear was glazed on three sides, the forth comprising a shuttered door. Rana pulled the doors after him and leant with his back to the bar. The reflection in the glass gave him a full view of the room. Lifting the receiver, he dialled from memory the twelve-digit number he had secured from Jubal. The youth had given little resistance in yielding the code words for the call. Rana had no faith in a system that withheld information until the last minute and Jubal, his eyes wide with terror under the glinting blade of Rana's stiletto, had soon crumbled in the Paris safe house.

The earpiece crackled as a dialling tone searched for a connection. After fully thirty seconds he could hear the ringing tone and the call was answered. Rana's voice was casual, almost chatty.

'Henri…Henri, is that you? You old goat, I've been calling you all week. Listen, I have news of your uncle.' Rana paused. '

'Is that so?' Again, a pause. 'Me?, no I'm fine. So I'll still see you on the 6th? Good, good. What news of my schoolteacher sister? I thought that she said she was holidaying to the south. Gone a week so far. Otherwise all is well in the family?' He was nodding slowly, his eyes surveying the solitary figure of the old man silhouetted against the harsh neon of a street light. He had awoken and, adjusting the crumpled homburg on his head, got slowly to his feet and shuffled out into the night. The claret remained untouched. 'The Vire Estuary you say, from two onwards, that's good. I'll see you at home then. Bon chance.' Rana replaced the receiver after carefully wiping it clean of fingerprints. He left the lager untouched and swept the cigarettes up from the bar top.

Forty-seven miles away, in a drab three story building on the outskirts of Nantes, an audiotape finished recording, the hiss finishing abruptly as the spool came to its end. The tape began to rewind itself. Three words in Rana's conversation, each innocent in their own way, had combined to activate the recording. Across the other side of the narrow, windowless room a tall, bespectacled woman in her early forties looked up from her book. She had just taken a large bite from her apple when the single tone from the bank of tape recorders at the far end of the room attracted her attention. Placing the battered pulp thriller to one side, she rose from her comfortable seat and scuttled hurriedly towards the tape decks. She swiftly removed the tape and made the telephone call to her superior on the third floor.

Culmhead
22.02 hours
The answer machine clicked into action, Jenny's voice apologising for their unavailability. Latham stood at the door, his hands full with shopping bags. The first message was from Jenny herself. She sounded mischievous, something about some news that would

have to wait until she was back. Latham dumped the bags on the kitchen floor, his curiosity suitably baited. As he made his way back towards the phone the answer machine continued. The message was succinct and direct, if somewhat unexpected. Max Ronson's voice echoed across the hallway.

'Robby boy,......' The pause was brief, the words slightly slurred. 'I've gotta apologise for the other day, guy.' Ronson continued before Latham could answer. 'Can we meet? I'm in Exeter tomorrow with Roly at eleven for lunch, what do you reckon? I'm patching it up with him away from Templemere, somewhere a bit quieter. I know that it's close to the display but I could sure do with some back up from....' Latham hit the button and killed Ronson's voice. He made his way into the kitchen, the bags weighing him down. With Jenny not due back from her mothers until tomorrow, the late night garage at Stop Gate had rescued Latham once again. He took his time in putting the groceries away, Ronson's words playing over in his head. Finally he walked over to the 'phone and, taking a chance, dialled Templemere. After a lengthy wait, John Reed's voice crackled through the earpiece.

'John, it's Rob, Rob Latham. Is Roly in?' Reed sounded puzzled.

'I thought he was with you guys. He's not been up here all day.'

'Listen, have you heard anything about him meeting up with Max in Exeter tomorrow morning.'

'Yeah, I got a message from Roly shoved through my door last night, said to start pre-flight as per schedule and that he would be back from Exeter by twelve. Something about a pow wow with Max. Kiss and make up, all that sort of stuff.'

'And he hasn't called in or phoned so far?'

'He couldn't. I'm looking at his cell phone right now. He left it on his desk yesterday.'
Latham paused. 'I got pretty much the same message from Max last night, about a meeting with Roly. I'm going to go along but what ever happens, expect me back at twelve as well, OK?' Reed's voice showed caution. 'Bit late for a reconciliation, ain't it?'

'What ever it takes, John, what ever it takes. Put it this way, I guess I still owe it to him to try.' Latham replaced the receiver slowly. Inside, he knew that Max would let him down again. He massaged the back of his neck as his mind ran through the next day. He looked over at his flight kit, carefully laid out on the trunk in the porch. Jenny had always prepared him for each flight, his own meticulous planning mirrored by her ritual of washing his flight suit and gloves. The boots had even been polished. The matt green helmet, the visor swathed in a black velvet cover lay on top of the pile. Next to the clothing, an A4 poly pocket contained the flight plans and maps of the route to Normandy, together with a detailed account of the display routine for the authorities at Caen. Latham turned off the hall light and climbed the stairs. He needed a full night.

Paris
22.39 hours
Tressor studied the text of the decoded message a second time before setting the paper down on his desk. The full audiotape of the call spooled through a small cassette recorder at the side of the office. Rana's dull monotone seemed anything but revelatory. Pinon

rewound the tape for the fifth time before pressing the large 'PLAY' button again. The recording started abruptly, the call trace only activated on the use of one of the pre-coded words. Mention of the Sixth had activated the recording. "Good, good. What news of my schoolteacher sister? I thought that she….." The second and third word confirmed the significance. Pinon placed a second cassette in front of his superior.

'The voice bank confirmed a match on one Yassan Rana al Tikriti, a Fediyeen. He's the same Mukhabarat operative that disappeared from Tangier in April of last year.'

'And can we pin any connection with the group in Algeria in the mid-eighties?'

Pinon shook his head.

'Nothing doing. He has no other connection other than being a member of the same organisation. In truth, with his reputation, he could even be rogue.'

'Freelance?'

'There has been evidence of the Mukhabarat haemorrhaging significant numbers of operatives since the Gulf war. I could find evidence of at least seventeen that have disappeared over the past two years alone.'

Tressor shook his head slowly.

'Too much coincidence for my liking. For desperate acts, you need desperate men. He fits the profile.'

'And Kamal?'

'Different, I'll grant you, but motivation can come in many forms. He gazed up at Pinon as the large sergeant raised his eyebrows. The look was confused.

'This Rana's going on the 6th. Why?' Tressor looked down at the map spread out across his desk.

'It's too bloody close.' He rotated the paper knife between his fingers before looking up at Pinon.

'This Rana character is an enforcer, you say?' Pinon nodded.

'Torture, a thug for hire, but no specific specialism to speak of.'

'No explosives interest?'

'Not that we are aware of.' Pinon answered.

'And not a sniper.' Pinon shook his head slowly.

'But he is leaving before any of the heads of state arrive.' He looked away towards the window. 'If he's not the delivery boy, or a shooter, then what?' The paper knife was now marking the surface of the mahogany desk. 'We need this to be a lead on Kamal. I want that estuary staked out at a discreet distance from this moment and all movements to be reported directly to me.' Pinon immediately lifted a dark blue 'phone from the console on Tressor's desk and punched in a three digit number.

The order was brief, one hundred miles to the west of Paris; a helicopter crew immediately scrambled from a drab single story building on the parameter of Lanveoc airfield. The pre-flight checks were brief, the expectation of flight curtailing the usual, meticulous run through of system checks. The rotating rotor blades built to a crescendo, the body of the Aerospatiale Puma twitching as the downdraft increased. Slowly at first, the fuselage lifting from the damp tarmac, the helicopter rose, the nose dipping as the Puma set off across the airfield. Soon, the bright red fuselage of the Air Sea Rescue helicopter was lost among the low hills to the north.

Pinon replaced the receiver in its cradle.

'Aerial team have just lifted off, under the guise of a training flight.' His hand hovered over a second handset on the control panel. 'You want the ground boys in close.'

Tressor held up a hand.

'Not yet, I think we have enough of a uniformed presence to squeeze any villains in the area. I want a discreet presence around the estuary but nothing constrictive.' Pinon nodded.

'We've got Simione and his unit at Brest. I know that he'd appreciate the fieldwork. It could be combined with an amphibious exercise with the aircrew. ' Tressor snapped his fingers.

'Do it.'

Yassan Rana finally located the hexagonal hole of the first Allen bolt. The L-shaped key slotted home and required a sharp twist to get it to move. The eight bolts were removed in total silence, each one placed onto the unfurled cloth that lay on the missile's casing. With the last bolt completing a neat line, Rana located the two finger holes and gently pulled the hatch away. His question was immediately answered, the interior lit by the pencil torch held between his teeth. Although the compartment was largely a mass of circuit boards and wiring, there was a redundant space behind the left-hand side of the opening. It was just big enough. Placing the torch on the top of the casing he reached inside his jacket and pulled out the Filofax. He gave one final glance over his shoulder. Gently removing one of the phials from its housing, he also pulled the foam packing that had surrounded it. Rana cautiously rolled the phial in the padding and slipped a heavy-duty elastic band several times around the package. The shape formed a perfect wedge as Rana gently eased the Sarin phial into the opening. Confident that it was secure, he began to close the hatch and replace the bolts in the same, laboured sequence. As a final precaution he wiped the surrounding area with the cloth. As he smiled in the dim light, a sound caused him to freeze, movement at the rear of the barn, a shuffling sound. He squinted as he struggled to make sense of the grainy murk at the far end. As he edged forward, his concentration was broken by the sound of voices behind him.

Kamal stared impassively as he steadied the swing of the large oak door. A momentary silence, before Salam and Latif appeared beside him, their low, chattering voices cutting through the atmosphere. Rana held his position, as if frozen. He turned back towards the gloom. Silence.

Kamal paused, his eyes playing over the interior. He studied the Red Tops, the tarpaulins still secured. Silently, he signalled for the other door to be opened and the sound of a gently revving engine filled the barn. In the cool of the evening, the tailpipe emitted a steady stream of exhaust as the Peugeot was backed slowly towards its intended cargo. Rana stood on the periphery as silent figures began to load the two missiles into the back of the van, the interior swathed in the luminous glow of the red taillights. The operation took a full and wordless seven minutes, the remainder of the time spent clearing the barn of any evidence of their occupation. With du Blayac's farmhouse showing little sign of life, the three-van convoy made slow progress over the gravel drive, only the lead Citroen using its lights. It was not until they reached the tarmac of the main D58 highway that the vehicles moved into higher gear, Latif unconsciously spinning the Peugeots wheels as they left the soft gravel of du Blayac's land. Kamal glared at him as he sheepishly held up a hand to acknowledge his mistake. Early on Sunday morning, the road to Morlaix would be quiet.

Seven

Exeter, June 6th
11.15 hours
Latham checked his watch and rose from the small round marble table. A half empty grapefruit juice lay next to his cell phone. He gazed around the darkened interior of the room. Save for a few early lunchtime drinkers the wine bar was empty. He glanced out into the cobbled street, the narrow thoroughfare busy with shoppers as he strained to pick out familiar figures in the crush. Latham felt a growing doubt gnawing away inside, instinct telling him to get out of a situation he should not be in. For one of them to be late was expected, but for both felt very wrong. It had been Whittaker's whereabouts that had concerned him more, particularly so close to a major display. A barman was wiping down the counter top as Latham approached. He had heard of neither of the missing men or had any messages to relay. Pausing to take one

final look around the interior, Latham made his way out into the street and fumbled his jacket pocket for the keys to the Jeep. Alone in the car park he sat in silence contemplating his next move, anger rising at another wasted effort. A call to Templemere proved fruitless, Reed as confused as Latham at Whittaker's whereabouts. With the rest of the flight crew already in Normandy it was down to him and the two pilots to launch the aircraft that afternoon. With Whittaker's cell phone still on his desk and Max not answering, Latham spun the Jeep's wheels as he began to descend through the levels of the multi-storey.

In the choking Monday morning traffic, his anger welling up, he made a silent vow to end any association with Max. A clean break was what was needed. On the outskirts of Exeter he floored the accelerator and headed for the Blackdowns. He would just have enough time for a shower before getting changed into his flight gear.

11.38 hours

Max paced slowly around the edge of the clearing, his footsteps crunching through the deep gravel. He fingered the cell phone deep in his coat pocket; drawing deeply on the cigarette cupped in his other hand. At the far edge of the gravel, the Morgan stood against a backdrop of towering conifers. The private land was at least a mile from the main road, the forest covering over fifty acres of the north-eastern ridge of the Blackdowns. He had been there many times, a chance to hide, to be totally alone. The rusted padlock to the gate had come away easily enough the first time. He had sought to escape the confines of the farmhouse and more importantly, her. It was always short lived, however, something stronger drawing him back. This time, he knew that there would be pain before pleasure. As his mind ran through the explanation, the shrill tone of the cell phone broke the silence.

Ronson's nervous fingers fumbled in his pocket and punched the keypad. Halah's voice carried an edge.

'I'm at the farmhouse. He hasn't shown.'

'I know.'

'What do you mean you know?'

'I sent him to Exeter. He's supposed to be meeting me in a city centre bar. He'll be at least an hour before he realises I'm not going to show.' The response was instant and sharp.

'You bloody fool. I want him eliminated, not merely distracted. He'll return to the airfield as soon as he knows it's another no-show. What the fuck do you think that you are protecting?

There was silence from the other end. Halah continued. She struggled to sound calm.

'Get yourself over to Templemere for twelve. Tell Reed that they are both delayed and that you'll help get the F6 started. I'll meet you there. Now move.'

Ronson ground the remains of the cigarette under foot.

'What about Latham?' The dead tone at the other end reverberated in his ear. He pocketed the phone and made his way over to the Morgan. He slumped down into the bucket seat and immediately sparked another cigarette. He needed another fix badly. There was only one person who could satisfy that need and she was pulling him in like a magnet.

11.46 hours

The heavy Mercedes left tracks in the gravel as Aisha

edged slowly along the drive of Granary Cottage. She winced at the sound she was making. Coming to a gentle halt, she removed her sunglasses and placed them next to the large bouquet of flowers that covered the passenger seat. She had been prepared for this. She knew Max too well. From the dark interior she could see Jenny Latham in the garden at the side of the house. She was lifting a laundry basket when she turned to face the drive, a brief pause before she waved and began to walk towards the Mercedes. The smile seemed slightly fixed if not a little surprised. It was to be expected.

'Hello, nice to see you again.' Jenny closed the small wooden gate behind her. She looked at the bouquet as Halah emerged from the car. There was more warmth in the voice.

'I hope you don't mind me calling by without ringing first.' The flowers seemed to dwarf her. Jenny stepped forward to help but then stopped herself. Halah saw the hesitation.

'Yes…yes these are for you. I just wanted to say sorry about Max again.' The tension in Jenny's shoulders dissipated and she rested the wicker basket on her hip.

'Honestly, Halah. There was no need, really. I've been putting up with flyers for far too long now, to be upset by a bit of jousting.' Halah's hesitant smile broke into a full beam.

'Oh, thank God for that. I thought that Max had burnt his bridges this time. I gave him such a telling off when we got home.' They both laughed.

'Come in, come in. I was just about to have a coffee. Would you like one?'

The two women walked through the entrance hall and

on into the kitchen. A kettle steamed in one corner. Jenny took the flowers from Halah and began to search beneath the sink for a vase, the aroma was already filling the room. Halah leant back against the worktop, her handbag to one side. As Jenny began to fill a large glass pitcher, Halah asked of Rob's whereabouts.

'Exeter, I think. He said something about a meeting, but I know that he wanted to call back here before heading for Templemere. He has a routine thing, you know, superstition and all that. All flyers have it apparently.' She grinned over her shoulder as the water-heavy jug clumped down onto the draining board. Halah nodded.

'Max is the same. He has some of my fishnets that he insists on wearing.' She winked before continuing. 'Are you going to see him off?' Jenny turned and gathered the flowers from the table.

'Fishnets? Under his flight suit?' Her eyes were wide in mock horror. Halah shook her head.

'In his dreams, maybe.' The laughter was easy and unforced. Jenny began to cut away at the stems with a pair of old secateurs. She turned to face Halah. The flowers partially covered her face.

'I said that I'd watch the take-off, but I'm due in Bath at three' She stopped. The figure on the other side of the Kitchen was in a different stance. The feet were planted firmly apart, the arms outstretched. Halah brought the Glock to bear, her fingers tightly entwined in a two handed grip.

'Keys to the Volvo.' She flicked her head towards the hallway. Her teeth were bared.

'Get them'.

Templemere
12.05 hours
Ronson had pulled the Morgan into an exaggerated skid as he stopped, the sound from the tyres suitably conspicuous. John Reed appeared from beneath the Lightning's port wing, ear defenders hanging from around his neck. As Ronson bounded from the bucket seat the breathless delivery completed the illusion.

'Just phoned, Rob's had a flat on the Jeep. He's on his way, says to fire her up now. I'll do the honours' Ronson motioned towards the apron, the Lightning squat on the shimmering tarmac. Reed responded with a hesitant thumbs-up and hauled the ear defenders over his head. He yelled after Ronson's sprinting frame

'Where's Roly?'

Ronson ignored the call and made his way up into the cockpit as the portable generator roared into life. The two men communicated with hand signals above the din, and soon the two Avon's were starting in rapid succession. With the Lightning idling on half power Ronson was quickly down the crew ladder and made for the main hanger. Reed called out as Max disappeared through the office doorway.

'I ain't seen nothin' of Mr Whittaker yet, either.'

He shook his head slowly and turned back towards the idling fighter to continue the flight preparations. After a full five minutes Reed looked up from the shadow of the starboard wing and caught a glimpse of Max re-emerging from the hanger office. He was in full flight gear. As he strode towards the apron, Max donned one of Rob Latham's matt green helmets, the oxygen pipe and straps hanging down from the side. Reed finished checking the tyres on the port undercarriage and stood up. His brow furrowed as he walked slowly to meet Max.

'Unless you know otherwise, Mister Ronson, I'm not expecting anyone other than Rob Latham to be flying this afternoon.' Max continued walking towards the crew ladder, the black visor now lowered over his eyes.

'Just keeping her warm for him, John.' He patted the chest of his overalls. 'No use in taking risks, though.'

Reed stepped in front of him at the foot of the ladder, one arm grasping a rung. His face was set.

'I've seen you run engine tests in shorts and tennis shoes before this, why all the safety clothing now?' Ronson stopped and wordlessly pointed over Reeds shoulder. From the eastern end of the airfield, Roland Whittaker's Mercedes was making its way around the perimeter track.

Once outside the cottage, Halah had hurled the car keys into an adjoining barley field. She then turned her attention to the Volvo. The dull thud of pistol fire was followed by the sound of high-pressure air escaping from the cars tyres, Halah taking careful, methodical aim at each one in turn. Jenny was forced into the drivers side of the Mercedes, Halah climbing into the rear. As Jenny struggled with the automatic shift she felt the barrel of the gun in the small of her neck. Halah motioned forward and the car began to roll. At the end of the village Halah signalled for Jenny to turn down a rough farm track, the Mercedes jolting violently as it hit deep potholes. The pistol was pushed harder into her neck, a signal she took for increased speed, her foot jabbing down on the accelerator. Jenny kept her eyes fixed on the track ahead, her hands grasping the steering wheel tightly. Too fast, she thought. Another bend like that and we're going to roll. Her foot eased off the accelerator. A sharp pain jabbed at her neck.

'Slow down and I shoot. Now fucking *move*!' Jenny felt the spittle of Halah's breath. The tone of her voice was much different now. A harder edge. Soon the track began to wind its way down into a wooded valley. The Mercedes passed through a large farm, the tyres rumbling over the bars of a rusting cattle grid. The farmhouse was not unknown to Jenny. She remembered the outline from a previous walk she and Rob had taken in those early months on the Blackdowns, the flat lines of a Devon longhouse that had seen better days.

The journey took an agonising ten minutes, the rusted fencing that surrounded Templemere looming into sudden view at the brow of a hill. As Jenny took the Mercedes past the main gatehouse she could see the Lightning parked in front of the main hanger. Halah pressed the barrel deeper into Jenny's neck as they got closer. She winced as the barrel ground into her flesh.

The helmeted figure at the steps of the fighter certainly wasn't Rob, she thought. Too short. As the car drew nearer the pilot climbed up to the cockpit and eased himself into the ejector seat. Jenny pulled the Mercedes into the hanger gliding to a halt alongside the office. John Reed was walking briskly towards them, an oil stained cloth cleaning his hands. Jenny was told to lower the window.

'Hi Jen. Rob's on his way luv. You come to see him off ?' Reed leant on the sill of the door, his eyes searching the dark interior for Whittaker. His voice tailed off as he saw Halah appear from behind Jenny. Sun glinted on the barrel of the Glock. Aisha removed the sunglasses allowing him to see the eyes. The sudden thud of the pistol caused Jenny to start as Reed's body was thrown off its feet. Jenny screamed.

Granary Cottage
12.13 hours
Latham walked into the kitchen and flung his keys onto the table. The traffic had fouled up again on the outskirts of Honiton and he was now late. The open front door was not unusual. It was the pile of unwashed dishes that caught his attention. Jenny hated clutter. She shared her husband's sense of organisation and order and this stood out. In the centre of the long pine table lay a single coffee mug next to an open newspaper. Latham dipped his finger into the mug. Luke warm. He call Jenny's name again as he surveyed the back garden through the heavy framed window above the sink. With no note apparent and with the clock indicating he was already late for Templemere, he needed to get moving. Pausing to note that the answer machine was not on, he returned to the hallway, grabbed the pile of flight gear from the foot of the stairs and made his way back out into the sunlight of the drive. It was then that he noticed the Volvo's tyres. The car was parked in front of the open garage. He dumped the pile on the open tailgate of the Jeep and dropped down by the side of the Volvo's rear wheel arch. Each deflated tyre showed the same tell-tale entry point. Latham felt around the inside of the first tyre, his hand searching for evidence of an exit wound. The shredded rubber told him all he needed to

know. He made for the Jeep, slamming the tailboard shut. Latham punched the numbers into the cell phone on the dashboard. He cursed as he made a mess of Jenny's number, he'd rung it enough times to know it by heart. Three rings before she answered. He was about to interrupt her when he realised. The voice was the answer facility on her mobile. He hung up. Where the hell was she?

Templemere,
12.20 hours
The scene in the hanger seemed to freeze. Jenny had stopped screaming, her hands clamped to her mouth as she stared in horror at Reed's still form. A dark stain of blood had started to spread its way across the shoulder of his flight suit. Jenny fought to keep her body rigid, afraid to move for fear of drawing attention. She could hear Halah's rapid breathing behind her. As she stared through the windscreen, she caught sight of the Lightning reflected in the rear view mirror. The helmeted figure stood motionless in the cockpit of the fighter, his hands grasping the frame of the windshield. Slowly, he lowered himself back down into the ejection seat. Jenny wiped tears away from her clouded vision as she looked back to the interior of the hanger. The silenced barrel of the pistol nudged her neck again as she heard Halah's passenger door open.

'Out.' Jenny struggled to suppress her sobbing as the barrel of the Glock motioned her towards the rear of the car. The boot lid swung up. Roland Whittaker's lifeless eyes stared up at Jenny as she was pushed up against the bumper of the Mercedes. Aisha was grinning. That same sing-song voice.

'Take a good look. He doesn't give me any trouble now. Much more compliant with nine millimetres of steel in his head, don't you think?' Halah laughed as she motioned towards open boot. Close-up, Jenny could see the blood shot whites of her eyes.

'Like to keep him company?' She did not wait for an answer. 'I thought so.' A booted heel rammed the small of Jenny's back and she was sent sprawling. As the lid slammed shut, darkness enveloped her eyesight. The interior was devoid of all light. Jenny could smell Whittaker's powerful aroma, a mixture of aftershave, sweat and another more metallic scent. She forced her knees against the solid weight of the corpse and pushed her way into the corner of the boot. Her head pressed against the upholstered interior as she struggled to make anything of her senses. Feeling with the top of her head she wedged her ear against the opening of the lighting unit. Muffled talk in the distance, the slight echo placing it somewhere inside one of the hangers. After a short pause she heard the Lightning engines throttle up, the rumble vibrating through the car. She felt the Mercedes rock as the driver side door was slammed. A brief pause before the engine was gunned, the noise much louder than expected before the blackness erupted into neon red. The brake light shone through a missing inspection panel beside Jenny's left ear. She blinked as the interior was briefly lit. Whittaker's staring eyes were bathed in a demonic glow before the boot was plunged back into darkness. The wheels spun on the tarmac sending stones ricocheting into the wheel arch. That was when Jenny lost it.

Eight

Templemere
12.32 hours

As the airfield came into view Latham strained to see the hanger complex over the rise in the perimeter fence. A car could be seen, the front half hidden by the darkness of the hanger interior. A single, anonymous figure lingered at the rear. As the Jeep raced towards the guard house at the northern end of the field, a glimmer of reflected fuselage metal flashed across Latham's vision. The Lightning had just turned into the threshold of runway Two-Six. The familiar nod as the brakes were applied.

'Who the fuck!!..........' Latham gunned the engine and hauled the wheel of the Jeep sending the 4x4 skidding across the opposite lane of the perimeter track. The rusted frame of the link fence gave way with little resistance, several metres of barbed wire becoming trapped under the bull bars of the Jeep as it bucked its way onto the rough scrubland of the airfield. The tyres bit deep into the semi-soft earth, the four-wheel drive eating up the terrain. Latham made straight for the nearest section of the runway, his eyes constantly darting from the windscreen to the prone figure of the fighter at the runway's end. The Jeep left the ground momentarily as Latham hit the small rise that marked the edge of the tarmac and he immediately slewed the Jeep across the centreline, the engine still running. Latham jumped down on to the tarmac and began to run towards the roaring cloud of spray that was building at the far end of the runway. It was the change in engine pitch that stopped him in his tracks. Full throttle. The Lightning was rolling.

The shimmering at the end of the runway increased, vaporous spray enveloping the eastern end of the airfield as the grey silhouette gained momentum. Latham was fully thirty feet from the Jeep, his mind racing. Who it was, was now irrelevant. Getting the hell off the runway was. As he reached the open drivers side door, he looked back at the gathering maelstrom behind him. Hauling himself into the seat, Latham gunned the engine and shifted into reverse. His foot hit the accelerator pedal, the large tyres biting into the tarmac sending clouds of blue smoke billowing from the front end. As fast as he reversed the Jeep, the windscreen was filled with the onrushing mass of the Lightning. Latham's foot slipped as he brought his arms up to shield his face, the impact inevitable. At the last moment, the fighter leapt from the runway, its undercarriage retracting the moment it left the surface. The ventral fuel tank glanced the roof of the Jeep, the Lightning bucking slightly before correcting its course.

Inside, Latham ducked, the interior seemed to erupt with the impact. It was seconds before he forced his eyes open, the receding roar and swaying of the cab telling him that he was still alive. In the rear view mirror he watched the fighter leave a smoke trail as it climbed out of the Templemere airspace. Slowly, the rocking of the Jeep subsided. Latham kicked open the driver side door and hauled himself out of the interior. The Lightning was briefly glimpsed, the roar of the engines now resembling distant thunder, before being swallowed up by the low cloud base. Latham studied the damage to the Jeep. The windscreen was completely shattered, a jagged gash cutting its way along the length of the roof. Another few inches lower, he thought, would have done for both of them. He glanced back over his shoulder at the hanger buildings. Nothing moved.

Pulling up under the shadow of No 1 hanger doors, Latham searched for signs of life from the unlit interior. The sound of a radio echoed around the roof trusses of the hanger. Reed was nowhere to be seen. Latham called out as he ran between the various aircraft parts that littered the interior floor. As he entered the main office his eyes caught sight of the crew gear locker behind McCleesh's desk, or rather the coat that hung from the door. The faded green Barbour looked too familiar. It was Jenny's. As he unhooked it be recognised the perfume from the collar. He opened the locker door. John Reed was wedged tight between the sides of the interior; his crumpled body slumped to one side. The left shoulder and chest of his light blue overall was soaked with drying blood, his hands tied by electrical tape. A piece of lined notepaper had been pinned over the stain. As Latham approached Reed opened his eyes and groaned. Frowning before recognising the figure standing before him, he managed to free himself before falling into Latham's arms.

'I…its..it looks worse than it is, guv.' He managed a strained smile, the perspiration masking his face. Latham dragged the dead weight of his body and gently slide him down into a sitting position. He began to gently unzip the overalls.

'Who the hell did this?' His mind was racing as his blood stained fingers pulled at the note paper. Before he could decipher the scrawled message, Reed grabbed at his wrist with a grip that surprised Latham with its strength.

'They got Jenny, Rob. They wanted the F6. Jenny's with Halah. She took her when Max flew out.' The effort clearly caused him pain as he spoke. Reed hauled himself up into a sitting position as Latham worked on the wound.

'That was Max?' Latham asked. Reed winced as the dried blood was pulled away from the wound. He took a breath before continuing.

'He said you'd been delayed. She fuckin' shot me, can you believe that?' His eyes were wide in bewilderment. 'I must have passed out. Found myself in here when I came round. I heard them talking about some rendezvous point, about some airfield called Coudeville-sur-Mer, or something. Whats…whats in my top pocket ?' At the centre of the bloodstain a pocket bulged slightly. Latham reached in and retrieved a bunch of mangled Allen keys. The cluster had taken the full force of the bullet, directing it's path up into Reed's shoulder.

'Feels like its still in there. Christ that hurts.' Reed reached inside the overall and pulled out a soaked rag. The cloth had staunched most of the flow.

'Jenny? What the hell was she doing here? Where is she?' Latham had to stop himself from grabbing Reed by the shoulders. The man was weak from the loss of blood. He passed out before he could answer. Latham reached up and pulled the telephone from the desk. Cradling the receiver with his shoulder, his free hands smoothed the crumpled, blood stained notepaper against the concrete floor. The message was short but chillingly succinct.

Latham,

We've got your wife as insurance. If you want her alive you will not make any attempt to contact the authorities. You will receive details of her whereabouts at 12 noon tomorrow.

Any Security Forces, and she's dead.

The final, underlined word drained the blood from his cheeks. He momentarily felt completely overwhelmed and alone. As he slumped back against the wall Latham's mind began to race. He leapt forward and shook Reed violently by the shoulders. The mechanic moaned as his head lolled on his chest. He was out cold. Latham composed himself and allowed the unconscious man to settle back against the foot of the radiator. Again he studied the note, the panic of confusion starting to subside as he began to sift through the equation. The Lightning was ten minutes gone and most probably Max Ronson with it. What the hell was he doing?

Latham unconsciously pushed nine on the 'phone in rapid succession. As the dialling tone began to sound he rapped the cancel button and looked again at the note. As he read the words again, he looked up through the office window. The open hanger doors framed the solitary silhouette of Whittaker's Spitfire, the cockpit hood partially slid back, a pair of goggles hanging from the rear view mirror. Latham scrambled to his feet. He flung open Whittaker's flight locker, a battered leather jacket hung from the back of the door together with a parachute harness. Flying gloves and a leather helmet were stuffed into the left hand pocket, the musty odour of machine oil and sweat passed Latham's nostrils. He paused to check Reed. The bleeding had stopped and his pulse was steady. He would have to take a chance on him.

Latham leapt onto the Spitfire's wing and hauled the canopy further back. Sliding down into the cockpit, memory took over as he flicked switches and checked dials, familiarising himself with the layout of the control panel. He stopped, frozen as the realisation hit him. Frantically he searched behind the seat, his hands reaching into the tight space behind the armoured panelling. His hand closed over the cold shaft of the steel starting handle and he hauled it from it's housing. With no one to start the engine for him, Latham would have to hand crank the Griffon himself. Sliding out of the cockpit and down the wing, he fitted the handle into a hole on the starboard side of the engine cowling. The crank locked in position and Latham rotated a full 360 degrees before clambering back onto the wing. Reaching into the cockpit he opened the fuel cock, set the throttle at open and flicked the electric ignition switches before sliding back down to the ground. He grasped the handle with a firm two-handed grip and

swung. The rotation was slow, the gearing making the crank hard to move at first. As the momentum increased, the sound from inside the engine cowling resembling a slow turning dynamo, the first splutters of life shot from the exhaust ports. Yellow tipped flames danced briefly before being engulfed in blue exhaust gasses. The propeller whined as it gained momentum, the four blades quickly blurring.
The Griffon was alive.

12.43 hours
It was the bass rumble that caused Ronald Thursby to check the gear stick, the engine suddenly seeming to surge, the roar of excess power vibrating through the car. Over the top of the perimeter fence a grey shape filled the windscreen. The unmistakable silhouette of the Spitfire shot over the Templemere threshold, a nanosecond before the car was rocked by the shockwave. Thursby instinctively ducked, throwing the Orion sideways before it slewed to a stop against the barbed wire of the fence. His wide-eyed stare appeared over the dashboard as he pushed himself out of the foot well. The Spitfire climbed rapidly as the fighter pulled itself out of the station's airspace. Thursby scrabbled for the handset of his radio as he watched the aircraft disappear through the cloud base. He clicked the Send button and opened his mouth to speak before slowly releasing his grip. He peered hesitantly over the bonnet at the wide expanse of runway that began on the other side of the rusting fence. What was he going to do, book him for speeding?

12.50 hours

Latham had allowed the Griffon the luxury of a slow ascent in order to allow the engine to maximise its power. The relatively low altitude would offer more resistance to the fuselage and so slow the aircraft, but Latham needed time to re-introduce himself to the Spitfire. He scanned the control panel dials, the importance of engine temperature being uppermost in his mind. He gave himself the time to complete instrument checks, time he did not have on the ground at Templemere. Various needles hovered reassuringly free of their respective danger zones and the fuel gauge indicated full tanks. As the airspeed indicator nosed past the 200 mph mark the fighter broke the cloud cover into the vibrant blue of a summer sky. The sunlight invaded the small cockpit space with an intensity that caused Latham to shield his eyes. Glancing around the cockpit interior his eye caught the folded sheaf of maps tucked into a storage space next to his left thigh.

The first map was labelled 'Normandy'. He held the control column between his knees as he smoothed the folds of the map out on his lap. A crimson red pencil line dotted its way across the Channel, bisecting Jersey and Guernsey before heading inland towards Caen. It was not the fastest or more direct route but any deviation on a day like this would probably get him shot down. With ninety minutes of flying time he had a loiter capacity of thirty- five minutes in his tanks. At the edge of the map he pencilled the name 'Coudeville-sur-Mer' and circled it several times. It was as he returned the map to the storage compartment that his first contact from air traffic control was made.

'Unidentified aircraft on One Seven Three,

this is Exeter Sector. Please identify, Over.'
Latham paused briefly. He needed to sound relaxed. His thumb flicked the radio transmit control on his oxygen mask.

'Roger, Exeter. This is Spitfire Golf Whiskey Tango Mike, out of Templemere bound for Caen air show, Over.' The voice was steady, calm as he read out the code printed on a small plaque over the control panel. There was another pause.

'Roger, Spitfire. We make you thirty two minutes behind schedule, Over'

'Cold start problems, am attempting to make up time.' Latham then tried his luck. 'Request that you contact Jersey air sector and warn them please. I wouldn't want the attention of those air defence boys, Over.'

'Will do, Spitfire. Enjoy your day, Over'.

That would buy him valuable breathing space, he thought. Normandy would be heavily patrolled from the air and all aircraft would need to be registered, in order to be identified. Whittaker's submitted flight plan should give him safe passage as far as Caen, any deviation courting trouble.

He suddenly felt very alone again. His mind raced over Reed's last words and the note. He fished for the crumpled piece of paper he had hurriedly stuffed into his jacket. Smoothing the creases flat on his knee, he read the words again. Why did they need him out of the way? His fist closed into a tight ball and he punched the inside of the canopy. What the hell was he doing?

If the engine had been reconditioned as Whittaker had promised, Latham reckoned that it should be good for at least the 350mph mark. His left hand eased the throttle forward and the pitch of the engine increased. There was a slight buffeting of the fuselage as the fighter forced its way through a patch of turbulence, the airspeed needle flickering briefly before registering 345 mph. Latham throttled back to 300. Over and over in his head, he calculated his potential journey time. He wedged the map into the storage compartment, allowing Whittaker's route to be clearly visible. He tried to flex the muscles in each leg, difficult in the cramped confines. It was as he was rolling his head to try to alleviate the stiffness in his neck, that he caught sight of a gap in the cloud base. Far below, the English Channel seemed alive with a multitude of ships. Latham gazed out over the elliptical wingtip and down upon a miscellany of ships. Small private vessels were mixed with larger cruise liners and naval warships that were ploughing a steady furrow towards Normandy. It was an impressive sight but still nothing like the scale of the original armada in 1944.

Latham soon lost sight as the cloud closed back over. His thoughts returned to Ronson. Even if he found the Lightning there was little he could do other than talk, and what state of mind was Max in? His thumb felt for the original gun button at the top of the control column. He pressed. Nothing. He smiled to himself. Not even armed and chasing a Mach 2 monster. Again, the urge to pull the aircraft around and head home swept over him. Wherever Jenny was, she wasn't with Max and there was no guarantee that he could be found. Latham cut the throttle and pulled the stick over. The slow arc took the Spitfire down towards the cloud, the speed decreasing rapidly. He thumbed the radio button to open a channel. As static hissed gently in his ears he tried to compose his thoughts. Who should he contact first? Police? Air Force? And what exactly would he tell them? Latham pinched the bridge of his nose as he screwed his eyes tightly shut. That impulsive nature that had always paid off was now in danger of losing him everything. He winced as the indecision welled up through gritted teeth. It was the spluttering of the Griffon that hauled his senses back into focus. He was stalling. He screamed.

'Fuck it!' The throttle pushed hard forward, the Spitfire bucked as the engine roared back into life. A cold sweat chilled Latham as his instincts took over. He fought with the sluggish controls as the increased power began to haul the aircraft back into the sky. The small fighter slowly regained its momentum. Latham pushed the stick hard over again and, with the moving sunlight playing shadows across the cockpit interior, brought the Spitfire back on course for Jersey Sector.

After ten minutes of level flight, patchwork fields began to emerge through the clearing cloud cover, the jagged Channel Island coastline made vivid by the foam of breaking waves. Further inland, the clutter of St Helier broke from the grip of the vivid green countryside that surrounded. Above Latham's head, the deep blue of the sky seemed endless. In his headset, he heard the signal from the Jersey Sector beacon and began a slow turn to port. He retrieved the map from the stowage compartment and smoothed it out over his legs. A red china-graph pencil line bisected the two Channel Islands before heading over the French mainland east of Cherbourg. Again, the name of Coudeville-sur-Mer stood out at the edge of the map. His eyes played across the various gauges that required regular monitoring. The oil temperature had stayed constant throughout, the only movement coming from the steady decline in the contents of the main fuel tank. Latham calculated that he would need to switch to the reserve tank in just over twelve minutes.

Nine

Blackdown Hills
12.51 hours
Halah trained the Glock on Jenny as the boot swung open, her tear-streaked face squinting in the sudden rush of light. She needed little encouragement to escape the confines of her prison, Whittaker's glazed eyes staring at the back of Jenny's head. She immediately recognised the courtyard, the Devon longhouse in the background. Halah pointed to the farmhouse.

'Keys above the door.' Jenny stumbled over the stony ground towards the doorway. She fumbled for the key before working the ancient lock. The musty odour complimented the dank interior of the kitchen; the entrance had turned out to be the rear of the house. The tiled room was sparse, a single table dominating. On it was an oil lamp together with what looked like a portable telephone set. Afternoon sunlight broke through the large window above the large sink, the rays of light accentuated by the dusty atmosphere of the interior. Halah hauled a chair from around the table and grabbed Jenny by the shoulder. She was shoved into the seat and a length of flex produced from a draw by the sink. The wrists were bound tightly behind her, Halah pulling the flex through the slats of the chair back until it bit into the flesh. Jenny clenched her teeth, fighting the urge to cry out. Turning towards the table, Halah pulled the large rubber handset from its housing and extended the pack's aerial to its full height. She looked at her watch before turning to face Jenny.

'You've got three hours before I decide what to do with you.'

Jenny instinctively let her eyes flicker briefly to the clock on wall behind Halah. As Halah looked up from her watch, Jenny held her gaze.12.55pm. One small victory.

DGSE, Paris
12.59 hours

The three men were squeezed into the sound booth that was situated at the end of the communications room. Tressor, Pinon and the call trace operator were sat around a small octagonal table above which hung a microphone boom. The tiny room was sound proof and extremely hot. Pinon mopped his damp brow as he gazed at the large clock above the door. With one minute remaining before the call would be made, Tressor carefully laid the small address book on to the table surface. He creased the spine and leant forward, gazing down through his spectacles at the ten-digit number he had written across the top of the opened page. He eyed the clock silently, watching the seconds hand make its slow, agonising way towards the twelve. He nodded to the operator who began to dial the number into the digital console that made up his side of the table. As he lifted the handset to his ear, Pinon started the audiotape.

The number sequence completed, there was a pause, the line crackling with static. Pinon clenched his fist under the table, releasing it only when a ring tone began to sound over the speakers. The phone rang six times before it was answered. The woman's voice spoke in heavily accented English. She asked who was speaking.

'One moment please, I am connecting your call. Please hold.' Tressor spoke in English. Holding his hand over the mouthpiece, he nodded to Pinon. He took hold of the handset and waited for several seconds before speaking.

'Good afternoon Madam, I am calling on behalf of your service provider. This is a courtesy call to ask if you are.......' The line went dead. Both men looked over to the console operator. Tressor pleaded.

'Tell me you got that?'

Lessay Naval Air Station,
Normandy
13.03 hours

Rana adjusted the focus of his binoculars. From blurred vision, a view of the main runway suddenly filled the frame in sharp focus. Pin pricks of white light ran either side of the expanse of flat concrete, both lines converging on a point on the distant horizon. To Rana, the dazzling landing lights seemed at odds

with the brightness of the daylight. He pulled the binocular grips slightly apart, allowing his brow to nuzzle into the rubber sights. The scene was crystal clear as he slowly panned across the airfield.
The journey from the vineyard had taken just over two hours, Rana and Asil splitting from the rest of the group on the outskirts of Avranches. The parting had been wordless, each member of the team fully briefed during the final hour before leaving du Blayac's. The two men had parked in a lay-by close to the naval air station waiting for the sunrise before moving on. The morning had passed slowly, pre-prepared meals eaten on the move, the dashboard littered with the contents of newspapers. The van had toured the locale, never using the same road twice, never stopping for longer than was necessary. Rana was immediately aware of the military presence together with the increased numbers of police in the area. All towns and villages seemed full of tourists, many elderly, many obviously revisiting the area for the first time in fifty years. American, British and French flags flew from every available flagpole, Canadians, Polish and other nationalities occasionally visible. The van passed convoys of historical military vehicles as well as more modern examples stretching along the country lanes. The road to Lessay seemed strangely quiet to Asil, the nature of it's location taking them away from the main arteries that led to the landing beaches. Once a complete circuit of the perimeter had been made, the van pulled up at a clearing at the northern end of the airfield. Rana carefully backed he Peugeot into the shadow of the dense gorse bushes he had discovered during his reconnoitre of the site some weeks before. Then, he had viewed the location through a pair of

night vision goggles. In daylight, the gorse offered a perfect hide for the van.

In the shimmering heat haze, Rana focussed on the squadron of aircraft sitting line abreast in the shadow of a large hanger. A solitary fuel bowser weaved its way between the elderly Crusader fighters, the sole evidence of life on the flight line. It was the four Mirage fighters parked at the far end of the apron that most interested him. Rana could sense Asil edging closer. The crushing of the surrounding grass seemed to fill his ears. He held up a hand.

'Quiet'

'What can you see?' Rana could hear the edge in the boy's voice. Why did they send these kids? He refocused and continued to scan. His concentration turned towards the control tower at the eastern edge of the flight line. The narrow, three story building was topped by large outward sloping windows that allowed the control tower a panoramic view of the airfield. Behind the smoked glass a number of stationary figures could be seen silhouetted against the brightness of the morning sky. It was several minutes before Rana saw anyone move. From behind him, he could hear Asil's rasping breath as he struggled with the weapon components.

The mortar barrel itself was four feet in length and would be anchored to a heavy steel base plate partially imbedded into stony soil that made up the surrounding landscape. Two telescopic legs protruded from half way up the tube and were themselves firmly rooted in the scrub. Rana took little time in positioning the barrel, small adjustments made using two calibrated wheels at the base. Behind him, Asil flicked open the

catches on the long trunk that contained the ammunition, and lifted the lid. Six rounds, each thin tubular casing ending in an aluminium fantail, lay side by side in its own foam housing. Asil gently eased the first round from the trunk. Rana could see thin beads of sweat forming in the oily grime on his brow.
He glanced back at the van and cursed that he had locked his drivers' side door.

13.07 hours
The rubber housing was not enough to protect the handset when it hit the stone wall of the kitchen interior. Fragments of shattered components spilled out onto the floor. Halah had screamed with rage as she stared at the smashed remains of the receiver. She turned her attentions to the table, the back of her hand sweeping the radio pack over the edge. The call had lasted mere seconds, but she knew how much precious time had been spent. She had been compromised.
Jenny watched the scene from her chair, the sudden burst of rage causing her to jump the chair back several inches on the flag stone floor. The woman seemed unhinged. The call had obviously been unexpected and had caused her to lose control. Jenny was terrified as she watched Halah pace the kitchen floor like caged zoo exhibit. Muttering under breath, Halah seemed to snap out of her torment and quickly walked out through the back door. As the sound of her footfalls subsided, Jenny quickly surveyed the kitchen interior in her absence. The telephone, she reasoned, would now be unusable and whatever message she had been waiting for may not arrive. Nausea overwhelmed her as the realisation of the loss of contact could decide her fate. She slumped forward, her head

pounding as she fought to control the retching in her stomach. She looked at the clock through watery eyes, wanting Rob badly. She snapped her head back as she heard what sounded like the door of the Mercedes being opened. She strained to listen for more sound. Nothing, the silence never sounding so utterly ominous as it did now.

Using the clock, Jenny timed Halah's absence. A full five minutes had passed before she heard the slam of the car door. Halah appeared in the doorway, Jenny immediately seeing that she was unarmed. She stood motionless for a moment, her bloodshot eyes surveying the remains of the transmitter. She swayed slightly before walking towards the sink. The tap complained briefly before giving up a hesitant stream of water. Halah gulped greedily from the cup.

'Someone get the wrong number?' Jenny shocked herself with her bullishness. Goading an unarmed Halah could be her only way out, she thought. Halah turned slowly, her eyes boring into Jenny. The cup swung in an arc, crashing just in front of the chair, shards of broken crockery spraying against Jenny's legs.

'Shut your fucking mouth.' The voice was slurred, only the eyes showing an edge of clarity. She waved a finger at Jenny. 'I was going to kill you anyway but now it will be sooner rather than later.' She then seemed to realise that something was missing. The Glock was still in the car. As she turned, she heard Jenny laugh.

'What, a drugged up bitch like you?'

Halah rose up to her full height, her fists clenched at her sides, teeth bared. She leapt at the chair, her head down in a charge across the room. Jenny instinctively hauled herself sideways, toppling the chair, the back braking as it hit the tiled floor. The wooden spar gone, Jenny wrestled her hands free of the rope. From the floor she reached out for the downed aerial that lay close to the remnants of the transmitter. In one swift movement she brought the steel rod whipping through the air in an arc that cut full into the side of Halah's head.

The crack of the aerial making contact with exposed flesh echoed through the room. Halah crashed headlong past Jenny's sidestep and on into the wall. She landed in a crumpled heap. Blood began flowing freely from her cheek before she could bring a hand up to feel for the wound. For a fleeting moment confusion played across her face before her eyes focused on Jenny, stood in the centre of the room. She seemed frozen to the spot. The wound was deep, stretching from just below the left earlobe to the corner of her mouth. Halah surveyed the scene briefly before feeling behind her for the wall. She slowly edged herself up and into a standing position, all of the time her eyes darting about the room. Jenny felt her legs weaken but stood her ground. She was in shock and hesitant as to her next move. Halah let her hand drop to her side. A smile appeared from beneath the straggle of hair that covered her face.

'You should have finished me when you could, you bitch. The radio means nothing.' She reached inside the leather jacket and pulled out a knife handle. The blade flashed from its scabbard with a sharp click. Jenny felt her throat drying as she attempted to swallow. She began to back away, the aerial whipping from side to side in an effort to keep some distance between them. Halah now fixed her

gaze and began a slow movement to the right as if circling her prey. Despite the gaping cut across her face the frozen grin remained. She edged further forward, her knife hand passing slowly from left to right. Jenny swiped hard, the aerial missing by two feet as Halah leant back out of range. Immediately she was on the offensive. Dropping down on her haunches she swung a low kick that caught Jenny by the left ankle. The impact was enough to unbalance her. As she hit the floor her vision was filled by Halah's leaping form. The dead weight crushed her chest, her arms burning as Halah's knees pinned each bicep.
Jenny gripped at the choking hand that dug into her windpipe. She could feel her lungs bursting with pain as she struggled to remain conscious. As she began to black out she saw the raised arm, the glint of light on metal. The kitchen window exploded into a million fragments, the same instant a plastic baton round snapped Halah's head sideways. Her body remained upright momentarily before Jenny felt the release of weight from her chest. Before she could gulp in vital mouthfuls of air, a smoking canister sailed through the shattered window frame and rolled to a stop against the skirting board at the far end of the room. As the tear gas billowed into the air Jenny rolled slowly onto her back and blacked out.

The interior of the ambulance smelled of disinfectant and stale sweat. As she opened her eyes, the bright neon glow caused Jenny to squint, her head immediately starting to throb.
A smiling face filled her view. The moustache twitched as the corners of the mouth turned up.

'You back with us love ? Just you take it easy

and we'll have you in Musgrove soon.'
A younger man came into her vision and the questions began.

'Jenny' The voice was too loud. 'Jenny can you hear me. Can you tell me what happened back at the farm house?' The memory came back with a jolt, the throbbing in her throat an all too real reminder. As she began to look around, her head turned on its side. Across the narrow isle the serene form of Halah lay in the second berth. A large gauze pad had been taped over her cheek and the blood that caked her neck was being sponged away by a yellow-jacketed paramedic. Further down the body Halah's hands were handcuffed with what looked like oversized plastic cable ties. At the far end of the berth a black uniformed police marksman sat at Halah's feet, a snub-nosed machine gun trained on her still form. Jenny turned back towards the soft features of the younger man. He repeated his question. Jenny opened her mouth to speak. The acrid taste caused her to retch. She struggled to sit up, hands supporting her weight as she was helped upright. As the coughing subsided the fog of her memory regained all of its clarity. She gulped deeply at the cup of water that was held to her lips. Her throat muscles relaxing, she swallowed and began to speak in a rasping whisper. It was painful at first.

'Sh…she t…took me from my home. Roland Whittaker. He's in the boot of his car. He…He's…..'
Iain Hart held up a finger to Jenny's lips and placed a reassuring hand on her shoulder. 'Shhh, don't you worry Jenny, we know all about Whittaker. Now slow down and tell us about the farm house.' His eyes seemed warm and friendly. Jenny took more gulps of air and tried to steady herself. As she sifted through the

last two hours she nervously looked over at Halah.

'Don't worry love. We've got her sedated' Ronald Thursby winked reassuringly. When Jenny spoke it was with measured and deliberate clarity.

'I don't know what exactly, but she was waiting for something to come through on that radio. Something that would happen in three hours.' Hart grabbed at his wrist.

'Think very carefully Jenny. When did she tell you this. Do you know what time it was?'

'Twelve, just after twelve. I'm certain.' It was the older man who spoke next. His answer was immediate.

'Three o-clock, and it's now one thirty. We've got ninety minutes to get it out of her.' Thursby pulled a radio receiver from inside his coat. 'Challinor, get onto Musgrove. We need a secure room. No windows, nothing. Just a table, chair and clock. Over.'

Jenny held up her hand. 'I can also remember hearing a jet starting up when I was in the boot, and a gun shot. Who was it? Where's my husband?' A look of panic masked her face. 'Rob, tell me it wasn't Rob. Where is he…?'

This time Thursby held Jenny's shoulders.

'No, no love. It was one of the mechanics and he's only slightly wounded. We can't find any trace of your husband but we do have two missing aircraft and the only two blokes who were qualified to fly them. We think your husband may have taken off after Ronson. My guess is that where you will find one, you'll find the other.'

Ten

Caen Airport
13.15 hours

The flight had been uneventful, each communication with air traffic control on time and Ronson flying the Lightning through a textbook pre-ordained flight route. The only unscheduled moment came in the form of a curious Dutch F15 pilot in-transit to the same display. Ronson reeled off the friendly banter, the two experienced jet jocks trading compliments before the fighter climbed away to the south. He watched as the contrails spiralled from the American built fighter. In less than two hours he would meet the cream of the USAF flying the same aircraft. Ronson settled the Lightning onto a slow glide path over the French coast reaching Caen overhead a minute ahead of his scheduled time. After two passes along the crowd line he brought the fighter in for a landing, holding the

nose wheel off the deck for longer than was strictly necessary. As he taxied towards the display flight line, he could see McCleesh's large frame, ear defenders perched atop his head, as he stood by the stand-by generator. Three of the ground crew were with him.
Max went over his explanation of events, the delays and no-shows needing to sound convincing. As the Lightning's wheels were chocked, the Scot appeared from under the port wing, the top of the crew ladder appearing beside Ronson's head. Even before the canopy was raised, he could see that McCleesh had recognised him. He was at the top of the ladder before the fresh air had hit Ronson's face. Max held up a hand and shouted over the din of the spooling engines.

'I know, I know, I'll explain later. Roly's about thirty minutes out but is on his way. Lets get this one fuelled up.' Before McCleesh could respond, Max had unbuckled his harness and was hauling himself from the cramped cockpit. At the base of the ladder McCleesh beckoned him away from the noise of the aircraft. Putting an arm around his shoulder, he yelled in Ronson's ear.

'No disrespect son, but what the fuck are you doing here?' Max nodded and answered him, smiling.

'Bit of a shock, eh?' He shouted. 'Rob didn't show at Templemere, turns out that he had a shunt on the way to the field. He's OK but he was too shaken up to do this.' Ronson hooked a thumb over his shoulder at the Lightning. 'I was with Roly at the time and told him I'd fill in.'
McCleesh's brow furrowed deeper.

'But what about the display, the moves. Do you….' Max held up a hand and nodded.

'I know it inside out, remember? Most of it's

mine anyway. Look, we'll be fine. I caught up over the channel but it's Roly who's going to be late. Where's the operations centre, I've got to get our flight plan confirmed.'

By now the two men had been joined by the rest of the flight crew, the news spreading among them. The Scot shrugged his shoulders.

'Rob's OK ye say?' Ronson nodded. 'Well in that case we better get started lads.' He slapped Max on the back and pointed to a distant control tower emerging from the clutter of tail fins that littered the flight line. 'That's it laddie. You've got about twenty five minutes until you're on, Roly or no Roly.'

Ronson had submitted his display confirmation to the control tower before losing himself in the crowd. The French controller had patiently listened to the same story before agreeing to a possible solo show from Ronson should the Spitfire not make it in time. An initial attempt to contact Whittaker's radio had failed and Ronson had made his way back towards the static park. Back on the flight line Ian McCleesh was busy fielding questions to a growing crowd of enthusiastic punters, eager to see the F6 at close quarters. Whittaker had had an information board made up and this was placed at the front of the cordon that surrounded the fighter. The air display had yet to start, the only activity being the arrival of the remaining aircraft due to demonstrate in the afternoon. Ronson strolled along the flight line of static aircraft. Out of his flight suit, he mixed easily with the thousands who thronged the main causeway. The aircraft were a varied mix of old and new with many nations represented. Ronson allowed himself a sly grin as he stood before a Luftwaffe F104 Starfighter. As he turned to walk away, two flight-suited US pilots passed by him, the accents cutting through his consciousness. He paused momentarily, before forcing himself to continue on. His time would come soon. For now he needed somewhere, somewhere private where he could refuel his own needs.

Musgrove Hospital, Taunton
Secure Wing, 13.42 hours
The ambulance had used a side entrance on arrival at the hospital, the two patients hurried into the unit on trolleys. With Jenny taken to a side room for treatment on her injuries, the armed unit were led to a secure room at the far end of the main corridor. The by-now conscious Halah was hauled from the trolley and onto a plastic chair. Her body twisted to the side, her hands were cuffed to an ancient radiator. A desk was then placed between her and the door and a second chair brought in. The door then slammed shut and she was alone.
In the corridor Thursby was pacing the linoleum with intent. He rounded on Hart who had just returned from Jenny Latham's bedside.

'A few scratches and a parched throat……..' He was cut off. Thursby wagged a finger under his nose.

'Now listen son, you keep those Government twats off my back and I'll break this one. Just run with it and deny all knowledge of our whereabouts. I need an hour. Got it?' Before Hart could answer Thursby disappeared inside the room and slammed the door shut.
The welt on the side of Halah Akief's head had risen to

an angry shade of purple. The blindfold removed, inquisitive eyes immediately searched out the interior of the room. Finally, her gaze settled on Ronald Thursby sat opposite her, his arms folded on the tabletop. He was playing with an opened packet of American Camel's. He looked up.

'No crap, love. Who, what, where, when and how? That's all I want to know. Now I could let the goons over at Portsmouth have you with all their exotic methods, the drugs, the Chinese water torture and their direct connection with the National Grid'. The sarcastic smile was dropped in an instant before he continued.

'Now, me?' Thursby pointed to himself. 'I'm just a small time copper hoping for an early retirement but what I do object to is the likes of you upsetting my biorhythms.' His fist slammed down on the table, the Camels jumping. The smile again, and the packet of cigarettes sliding back across the table. Halah looked up from between a straggle of messed hair. Thursby turned away and walked towards the door. 'You see love, I'm not a very patient chap and if I don't get results my governor tends to get in a right strop.' He turned to face her. 'Budgets and financing, he'll say. Got to run a tight ship, threat of redundancy, cost effectiveness, all that malarkey.' Thursby held out his hands in front of him. 'So you'll appreciate my lack of decorum.' He leant forward and brought his face within inches of Halah's. He turned his head as if listening. 'Anything to declare?'

Before she could answer, the suddenness of Thursby's movement caused Halah to jolt in her seat. He wheeled away and yanked at the door handle. Thursby roared into the corridor.

'Hart. Get her out of here.'

The last she saw was Thursby's disappearing form before the blindfold was replaced.

The radio had started to play up over Jersey Sector, the garbled static of voices barely discernible over the constant drone of the Griffon. Latham scrolled through the channels of the modern receiver unit, the dead airwaves momentarily giving way to the occasional snatch of garbled American chatter. The French coastline broke through the cloud cover above Cherbourg, several large ships visible through the haze. Latham studied the map on his lap, one hand tracing the coastline as the control stick was held between his legs. A finger followed a line down the Western edge of Normandy until the name of Coudeville-sur-Mer appeared, an airfield symbol not half a mile inland from the small village. Latham grasped the stick and hauled the Spitfire through a slow turn to starboard, at the same time lowering the nose and putting the fighter into a shallow dive. Instinct was taking him away from Caen and with it, the protection of the pre-ordained flight plan. Within three minutes of deviating from his route, Caen Sector made contact.

'Spitfire Golf Whiskey Tango Mike, this is Caen control, over?' Latham thumbed the mike control on his oxygen mask.

'Receiving, over.'

'You are charted as inbound for Caen overhead. Your present location has you due west of St Lo on a southern track, please explain your movements.' Latham was quick in his reply.

'Roger Caen, am experiencing an oil pressure problem and would appreciate time to rectify it and a possible relief landing site should I need it, over.' There was a brief pause before the French controller replied.

'Your nearest relief is Lanveoc to the west, please maintain a regular contact as to your situation, over.'

'Roger, Caen.' Latham flicked the switch and held his course towards the coast. He needed a enough of a story to keep the combat air patrol boys off his back, he had seen a number of CAP fighters on the flight across the Channel, their contrails weaving patterns across the deep blue of the sky high above. Any doubt on the part of the controller would result in an armed escort into the nearest airfield. Oil pressure was enough of a grey area to buy time, the unpredictability of an aging museum piece aiding the charade, but Latham would need a believable update on a regular basis to keep the CAP boys off his back. The distant haze of the Normandy coastline slowly began to emerge over the nose of the Spitfire, the yellow tips of the propellers encircling the Chausey Islands, a landmark that told Latham that his target was close

Caen
13.44 hours
In the cold darkness of the shower room Ronson let out a stifled cry. The single storey blockhouse was situated to the rear of the control tower, access only to display pilots and their ground crew. Ronson had found his way into the empty changing rooms, the rusted bolt scraping home as he sort solitude. He

backed his sweating frame up against the cool of the tiles, slowly sliding down until he was slumped on the floor. Tearing at the arm of his flying suit, he tied the tourniquet off, pulling at the rope with his teeth. Veins pulsed through his bare arm, the needle quickly puncturing the skin. He called out again as he pulled the back of his hand across his eyes, the salt tears stinging as he struggled to focus. Unzipping the kneepad of his flight suit he pulled a tightly folded letter from the pocket, the last he had received from Anna. With sickening irony it had been delivered three days after her death. She had been so optimistic, so fresh, the words tumbling with ease from the paper. Ronson had only read it the once, the pain of those words enough to last him a lifetime. In the distance, a Tannoy announced his name, his final call to the flight line. He turned the folded paper in his hands, his vision blurring. He would know when the time was right.

Ronson had three and a half minutes to display the Lightning to its full. The plan he had submitted to the Caen committee had been markedly subdued for such a potent fighter. Ronson had excused this by citing the fighters fatigue life. No one would expect any fireworks from such a recently restored airframe and Ronson would need to conserve his fuel carefully. From high up in the cockpit he had seen McCleesh's confused expression as the Scot glanced at the fuel gage on the refuelling tanker. As the Lightning began to taxy forward, Ronson watched as McCleesh leant into the cab and began to question the driver. The refuelling had taken longer than McCleesh would have expected, the very reason for his enforced absence in search of a spurious phone call. Ronson had overseen the filling of all of the fighter's tanks, the over-wing auxiliaries being the last to fuel. The remaining ground crew of Matty Fry and Joe had had little reason to question the action. Ronson had suited next to the aircraft with a small crowd forming at the barrier to watch the departure. The pre-flight checks had been rapid, the cockpit radio link being broken as Ronson waved the nose wheel chocks away. The Avons' had started first time and had spooled up to 60% power when McCleesh's large frame reappeared alongside the bowser. In the emerging sunlight the Lightning rolled, slowly at first, as Ronson edged his way out of the flight line. In his mirror he caught sight of the Scot remonstrating with Fry.

The Lightning had pitched up on leaving the runway entering its trademark vertical climb, Ronson giving the afterburners a short burst of power before rolling off the top of the climb at five thousand feet. Thunder rolled in waves across the surrounding countryside. Staying within the perimeter of the large airfield, Ronson then pulled a series of tight g-turns in front of the crowd-line before turning away to the east to line up a high-speed pass. Condensation spiralled from the wingtips as the fighter powered its way along the runway centre line at fifty feet, the shockwaves setting off a chorus of car alarms in the vast park that made up the southern end of the airfield. Ronson concluded by throttling back for a slow pass, the nose high with the undercarriage lowered and the airbrakes deployed. He gave the wings a waggle before cleaning up over the threshold and increasing the power. Soon the Lightning was little more than a dirty smudge on the horizon, the rumble slowly dying away on the wind.

13.53 hours

Salam gently unscrewed the bolts that held the aluminium frame of glass in position before retiring back into the interior of the van. In the bright summer sunshine the opening would blend perfectly with the smoked glass in the other half of the rear doors. Salam knelt on the seat cushion and allowed his body weight to lean against the back of the wooden chair. He brought the rifle to bear and nuzzled his left eye into the telescopic sight. Through the clutter of the crowd and the melee of tents and stalls, the main runway suddenly appeared in stark clarity. Three small acrobatic biplanes of the Royal Jordanian Air Force display team; the Falcons, were lined up at the far end of the runway, their engines idling as they awaited confirmation from the control tower. Suddenly there was a surge of power and the lead aircraft began to roll. Salam played the cross hairs of the sight across the under carriage of the lead aircraft before allowing it to pass through his vision. As the second Falcon came into view Salam held the momentum in his sights and followed the near side wheel. He took a slow, deep breath and gently squeezed the trigger.

'Allah al ahkbar', he silently offered as the rifle bucked in his shoulder blade. Through the sight, a millisecond later, the tyre exploded in a shower of shredded rubber. The Falcon immediately slewed across the path of the third biplane narrowly avoiding a collision. The pilot fought to control the skid but could do nothing as the port undercarriage faring collapsed sending the aircraft spinning back across the centre line of the runway. As suddenly as the incident had happened, the Falcon came to rest in a cloud of dust and debris. The pilot lost little time in vacating the grounded aircraft, mere seconds passing before the howling of sirens punctuating the silence as the crash rescue teams swung into action. Salam calmly surveyed the scene for a few brief seconds before slowly and methodically disassembling the rifle and replacing it in the floor cavity. Closing the window frame, he slid into the drivers seat, started the engine and at a leisurely pace, made his way towards the car park exit.

13.55 hours

Ronson had calmly waited for the contact from the control tower as the Lightning loitered towards the south of the airfield. A full forty five seconds early the contact was made. The controllers voice betraying little of the situation at Caen.

'Whiskey Tango Kilo, be advised we have an aircraft down, I repeat aircraft down. Main runway is not optional. Please hold your station, over.'

Ronson calmly selected the Send channel on his radio and answered.

'Roger tower. I have a potentially critical fuel situation here, so am advising cut and run to Deauville relief, Over.' Ronson was referring to the satellite landing ground some thirty miles due east of Caen that in the event of an emergency could be used as a bolt hole for display aircraft.

'Roger, Lightning. Will contact Deauville to expect you, good luck, over.'

Ronson swung the large fighter east and plugged in both afterburners. The airfield was soon in view on the horizon and Ronson made ready the Blind Eye unit. Flying at just under five thousand feet Ronson over flew Deauville and flicked the switch. Immediately, at the Cressy Air Traffic Control Centre some twenty miles to the southeast, the signal that had been Ronson's Lightning disappeared to the human eye.

Ronson punched in the afterburners and felt the acceleration course through his body. A three- minute burst would give him a fifty mile distance from Deauville. The turn south would then take him in a wide arc back towards the west coast and then finally up towards the former Luftwaffe fighter base at Coudeville-sur-Mer.

Eleven

Exeter
14.09 hours
The three car convoy swept into the main holding area, located at the centre of the head quarters of the Devon and Cornwall Police on the eastern outskirts of the city. The journey from Taunton had taken a little under thirty-five minutes, the cars forsaking the more direct route of the M5 motorway, for a breakneck slalom through the back lanes of the Devon-Somerset border country. Thursby had the door of the lead Ford open before the car had come to a stop. Halting outside a side entrance to the cell block he was met by a group of plain closed officers and an armed escort. Akief, her head covered by a blanket was bundled inside and through a series of corridors before she found herself slumped into a hard-back chair. A door was slammed somewhere behind her and then silence. It was a full

five minutes before she realised that there was another presence in the room. A rhythmical rasp of slowly drawn breath was eventually audible over the low throb of the air conditioning. It was Thursby who removed the blindfold. He smiled gently and pushed the same packet of Camels towards her. She immediately took in her surround. The room seemed identical, the same table and chairs, the same clock, strip lighting and even the tiled floor. Akief blinked as her eyes fought with the stark lighting overhead. The plastic handcuffs registered pain for the first time as she tried to twist her wrists under the table. Thursby leant back against one of the walls and placed one hand casually in his pocket. With the other he held a ballpoint pen, the top being clicked by his thumb in a slow, mannered way. He licked his drying lips before speaking.

'Ever been to France, Aisha?' The use of her real name caught her attention. Thursby sensed the flicker of recognition.

'Thought so. You see, I've got an associate over the water, who'd *really* like to get to know you a lot better. Says that you're up to no good on his patch.' The eyebrows raised, again the head slightly turned to one side. He cupped a hand to his right ear. Taraz worked her mouth but the parched throat caused her to wince with pain.

'I'm sorry love, you'll have to speak up.'

Thursby rapped twice on the door and after a pause Hart appeared with a jug of water and two glasses. She took three great gulps before stopping herself suddenly, as if mistrusting the cup in her hand. She looked up at Thursby who had straddled the backward facing chair opposite her. He rested his folded arms on the back.

'You were going to say?' Taraz drew on the moisture in her mouth and sent a well-practiced gobbet of spittle across the table. Thursby sat impassively as the phlegm hit his right shoulder. Removing a neatly folded handkerchief, he began to mop himself down as he rose to his feet. The smile remained. He stood at the table's edge and stared down at the fierce eyes looking back at him. He picked up the cigarettes, turned on his heels and silently walked out of the room.

In the corridor outside Taraz could hear raised voices. Almost immediately Hart reappeared and the blindfold went back on. She was roughly hauled to her feet and pushed out through the door. In the far distance the sound of revving engines could be heard.

14.10 hours

As the flat grey expanse of the Atlantic appeared through the mist, Ronson began to search for Coudeville-sur-Mer. Lying only half a mile inland from the coast, the airfield had been a former French Naval base until the outbreak of the WW11 when it had been used by the Luftwaffe as a forward staging post for the recovery of downed aircrew in the Channel. One of the three runways was still serviceable, a small parachute school in operation at the weekends. Today it would be deserted. Ronson swung the fighter out over the sea and back over the shoreline before heading south towards the airfield some eight miles away. The small pattern of runways showed up light against the darker ploughed fields that surrounded the station. He soon recognised the familiar outline of the main runway, the hours spent studying photographs of the airfield proving invaluable. As the fighter lined up on the final approach, Ronson caught sight of a small white van, the only speck of colour against the green of the surrounding bocage.

At the far end of the runway Ronson taxied towards the waiting van. He flashed his landing lights in rapid succession and received an immediate reply. He throttled the engines back to 45 percent, a flame-out at this point would prove disastrous. As Latif ran forward and positioned chocks in front of the nose wheel, Kamal got down from the passenger side of the cab and pulled the large head phones that rested around his neck onto the top of his head. He tuned his hand held radio receiver as he looked up at the cockpit, the pilot returning his gaze as the smoked visor was raised.

There was a brief crackle of static before contact was made.

'Lioness confirming position, copy?'

'Confirm. This is Steel, over.'

Kamal gave a thumbs-up and waited for Ronson to acknowledge the signal before returning to the van. He kept the earphones in position, the rumble of the idling Avons a constant sensory presence. On the Starboard side of the fighter, Latif was busily attaching a winching brace to a hard point on the underside of the wing. After opening both rear doors of the van Kamal pulled aside a grubby tarpaulin to reveal the two Red Tops concealed in their containers. Latif was soon at his side, the two men manhandling the first missile onto the tailboard. Cradling the round in their arms they carefully made their way around the front of the aircraft. In the cockpit high above, Ronson's eyes scanned the control panel for any signs of trouble. The JPT gauge registered 750 C indicating a stable temperature from the engine exhausts. Satisfied that the fighter was ticking over Ronson allowed is eye to scan the horizon about him.

The bocage flattened out towards the edge of the field, being in close proximity to the coast. Again, the pain behind the eyes brought Ronson sharply into focus. He pinched the bridge of his nose as he reached for the pouch pocket on the left leg of his flying suit. He swallowed the capsules in one, his parched throat managing to produce a modicum of saliva to aid the passage. As his left hand settled back down onto his thigh, he could see the shaking. He clenched his fist several times before he was snapped from his torpor by the crackle of static in his headphones. He looked down at the face gazing up from the tarmac. Kamal again signalled with a raised thumb.

'Port round loaded.' Ronson managed an uninspired mock salute as the Iraqi disappeared beneath the wing. With his left hand he brought both engines up to 55 percent and began to tighten the straps about his shoulders. He rolled his head from side to side, easing his taut muscles.

Outside, the raised pitch of the engines seemed to unsettle Latif. He grabbed at the second Red Top before Kamal had reached the tailgate of the van. The fibreglass container slid through his hands and crashed down onto the concrete of the runway. Both men froze. High up in his cockpit, Ronson remained unaware of the situation outside, the increased pitch of the engines filling the cabin interior with a constant tone. Only the slight clunk of the missile locking into position gave Ronson any indication that the stores were loaded. He waited for the second green light to illuminate the weapons console. There was a brief flicker as connections were made before the console glowed with confirmation of the two loaded Red Tops. Kamal held both thumbs up and then one outstretched palm as Latif disappeared into the back of the van. Ronson lowered the visor of his helmet and gently increased the throttle further. Both men stared silently at each other as they waited. After a full thirty seconds, Latif's head appeared from the van door, his left hand thumb and fore finger gesturing an 'Okay' to Kamal. The Iraqi adjusted his microphone.

'Latest confirmation has target ten minutes behind schedule. You will need to fly a loiter pattern to avoid fighter cover range, copy? Both rounds are now live. You are clear to go, Steel. Over.' Kamal stepped back from the aircraft, wary of the imminent crescendo of noise. He was not disappointed.

'Roger. Cover me. Over.' The reply was short and businesslike. As the fighter began to roll both Kamal and Latif turned to scan the perimeter of the airfield. Staying close to the open rear of the van Latif now began to clear the clutter of tools and to dismantle the winching brace. Moving away from him, Kamal's fingers tightened around the pistol grip of the AK rifle he now held beneath his coat. Even if Ronson's landing had failed to alert the authorities, the cell had, at the very least expected a modicum of curious locals. The airfield, apart from the occasional microlight, had long since seen any real activity.

Glancing back over his shoulder Kamal saw the Lightning turn back onto the main runway and come to a halt. Again he scanned the horizon. As he held the rifle tight against his body, he slipped a hand into the coat pocket to gain a tighter grip along the barrel. His fingers brushed against a tightly folded square of paper in the furthest reaches of the pocket. Instinctively, he retrieved the paper and unfolded it with one hand. He instantly recognised Asil's juvenile scrawl. Before he could read the writing, Kamal was distracted by a movement away to his left. At the far end of the airfield, as the ground began to drop away towards the coast, Kamal picked out the sight of a head travelling at speed above the neatly trimmed top of the perimeter hedge. He cocked the weapon without revealing it.

'We've got company, a cyclist I think.' Latif froze just as he was loading the van with the brace. Kamal did not point but nodded in the direction of the now still visitor. He glanced back at the grey fighter. Now powering up, the hedges behind the runway in the throes of some unseen maelstrom, the engines reached maximum thrust. The brakes were released and F6 began to roll. The head at the far hedge was now standing higher in an effort to get a better view. Kamal held up a hand to Latif.

'Leave it, we need to get out of here fast. We've got boats to catch.' Both men calmly got into the van as the Lightning leapt off the runway and immediately pulled into a steep vertical climb. The head at the end of the runway rapidly disappeared beneath the roar overhead. On the other side of the field, the white van had left nothing but a cloud of dust hanging in the newly disturbed air.

14.22 hours

Colonel Dale Steiner, commanding officer of the 89th Airlift Wing of Air Mobility Command eased the throttle lever gently forward, the Boeing 747-200B banking slightly to starboard as the power surged through the four Pratt and Whitney engines. The climb was levelled at forty thousand feet, the wings reflecting the low sun as Air Force One settled back on course. Below and three miles to stern, a large KC135 tanker aircraft began a slow turn for home. Some three hours and twenty minutes out of Andrews AFB, North Carolina, the 747 was one hundred miles north of the Azores when contact with the tanker escort was broken. From the cockpit, Steiner watched as the pair of Navy F18 Hornets drew alongside. The leader, his face masked by the glacial black visor, snapped a salute before he and his wingman broke away low to starboard. Steiner's gaze followed them down until he lost sight of them in the low cloud base. His headset crackled.

'Cutlass One and Two to Two-Six-Thousand, it's been an honour, sir. Over.' Steiner flicked the intercom.

'Roger Cutlass, Two-Six-Thousand inward bound. Outstanding service, gentlemen. Out.'

Fully replenished, the 747 began the slow turn to port that would put it on course for the north western coast of France. Steiner relaxed as his co-pilot took control, the tanking rendezvous always being the responsibility of the captain. It would be another fifty minutes before he would be required for the landing. He carefully unbuckled his seat straps and left the cockpit.

The agent at the doorway nodded slightly as Steiner passed, the tall Texan ducking to miss the low frame. Passing through the corridor that took him around the side of the Presidential staterooms, he paused momentarily at the open plan meeting room that filled most of the forward cabin space. The boss was in relaxed mode, a football game playing on the large screen that hung behind his desk. The most powerful man in the world was in shirtsleeves, one hand in a bowl of pretzels, the other fist slamming the tabletop at another missed field goal attempt. Steiner continued along the corridor until he came to a small door in the centreline bulkhead. Tanking had always played hell with his bladder.

14.23 hours

It was as the Spitfire began its dive towards the coast that Latham caught sight of the Lightning climbing away from the long expanse of tarmac at Coudeville-sur-Mer. He pushed the fighter lower, the altimeter showing five hundred feet as the Spitfire flew over the village and began a slow arc out over the sea before heading back inland. As he strained to follow the line of the F6 he realised that he had lost sight in the turn and cursed the slowness of the fifty-year old fighter. Ronson was gone, a tell tale diamond shockwave pattern appearing from the number one upper jet pipe as the afterburner was activated. Latham levelled out over the airfield and headed for the sea, the nose pitching upwards in an attempt to keep the speck of Ronson's fighter within the frame of the windscreen. He pushed the throttle as far forward as it would go, the Griffon at full power now. Latham scanned the control dials, his attention constantly divided between the slowly rising oil temperature and the air speed indicator. He knew that the newly conditioned engine had not been tested at this speed, but was placing his trust in well tried and tested Rolls Royce engineering. The question was just how long could the Griffon could keep up this pace. He studied the airspeed needle as it crept past the 370 knots mark. He had never

pushed a piston-engined aircraft harder.
His fist clenched tighter in a ball on his lap, Jenny filled his minds eye, her face becoming harder to visualise above the din of the roaring engine. His fathers face swam briefly into view, a chill shuddering through Latham's back as he contemplated being alone again. He began to wind his way through the radio channels on his transmitter set. He had to make contact. He had to know why Ronson was now carrying missiles.

Devon
14.40 hours
The journey had seemed longer than the others, the stop-start nature of the final few miles had, together with the sounds outside the car, given Taraz the impression of a town or city. The earlier drive had seemed smoother and faster. Motorway, she thought. The handling was less rough and once out of the car, a much shorter walk to her new room. The blindfold removed, Taraz immediately hunted for a clock. Thursby was sat in his usual position across from her, the stoop of his shoulders somewhat accentuated. He seemed weary. Again the room was virtually identical save for small rectangular window above the door. Only the sight of slowly moving clouds could be seen. The light seemed somewhat darker. Again she glanced at the clock. The time showed six minutes past three. At that moment, Hart burst through the door. He fought to catch his breath.

'Reuters are reporting a major incident, sir. No news on what or where but the network just lit up like a bleedin' Christmas tree.' Thursby wheeled away from the table, his clenched fist thumping the wall. He turned to face Aisha, a look of resignation written across his tired face. She was smiling. He slowly turned the chair forward and lowered his frame into the seat.

'So you win.' The voice carried no trace of the previous bravado. The head was bowed as his thumb and forefinger massaged his eyes. 'Where was it? Which poor bastard got it this time?'

The teeth were bared as she writhed in her seat. Again the manic, low chuckle that seemed to rise from the depths of her lungs, her head rocked back as she laughed out loud.

'You ignorant scum.' She roared, spittle running down the side of her chin.

'Your murderous butcher is now dead. A glorious act of revenge has been struck in honour of those thousands of souls destroyed by your pathetic war.' Thursby relaxed his arms and calmly placed his hands in his pockets. He repeated the question slowly, his eyes staring at the tiled floor.

'Where and who?'

She remained impassive, the smile fixed like a corpse. After some thirty seconds, she spoke. The voice was calm yet mocking.

'Six minutes ago the leader of your so-called free world was blown out of the sky. That murdering frat boy is at the bottom of the Atlantic.' Hart moved towards the table.

'The President? You mean the US President?'

The sneer was confirmation enough.

It was Thursby who now began to smile. Slowly, he held out his hand, the palm up turned. Suddenly the fist snapped shut.

'Hook, line and bloody sinker.' He grabbed at

the handle and threw the door open.

'You heard it boys. Air Force One. Heading for Normandy. Get onto the French at Brest and use my name. Now *move*!' Thursby rounded on Aisha, his left hand clamped firmly around her cheeks. He squeezed hard.

'Twenty minutes early love, we country boys have always been twenty minutes behind London, see?' Aisha stared at the policeman, her brow furrowed. She looked up at the clock.

Thursby sat on the edge of the table and retrieved his pipe from his jacket pocket. He took his time in lighting up. The first cloud of smoke billowed into Aisha's face. Thursby turned and walked over to the far wall and took the clock down off the wall. He retrieved a second watch from his inside pocket, studied it and moved the clock's hands back twenty minutes. He looked up at Aisha.

'Trouble is love, I can never remember if the clocks go back or forward this time of year.'

Twelve

Lessay Naval Air Station hours

The first round came down some twenty yards to the right of the main runway with a dull, almost unobtrusive crump. The column of earth that spewed high into the air had barely begun it's decent when Asil dropped the second mortar round down the firing tube. Rana had already made a slight adjustment to the aim. Knowing what to expect Asil clamped his hands over his ears and turned away from the imminent percussion wave. A hollow thud again signalled the mortar's exit from the barrel, Rana able to follow the trajectory with the naked eye. The round climbed through a slow, looping arc that gained momentum as it began to descend. A split second before impact, the piercing shriek of a siren echoed across the airfield. This was instantly cancelled out by the explosion of concrete that erupted from the centre line of the runway. A direct hit, Rana hissed through clenched teeth, his hand rapidly signalling to Asil to load another round. This time no adjustments were made. As the round left the barrel, Asil screamed, his fists punching the air. He ran to the edge of the scrub and thrust a middle finger in the direction of the perimeter fence. Rana yelled through the rumble of the explosion at the defiant figure. He scrambled over to the trunk and loaded the forth round himself. Through the haze of falling debris, the sirens were now accompanied by the flashing lights of vehicles approaching from the direction of the control tower. Asil seemed to freeze in the sensory onslaught before him. His throat parched by cordite, he ceased his ranting and turned to run back to towards the mortar. The single round hit him above the left eyebrow, his head snapped back by the force, the body following as he crashed down among the bushes. Rana quickly holstered his pistol before turning and sprinting towards the Citroen. Behind him the debris from the forth mortar had already started to clear as a convoy of security vehicles approached the craters in the main runway. Fumbling with the keys, Rana the wrenched the door open and rammed the key into the ignition. He gunned the engine, the narrow tyres biting into the dry ground beneath them. Grinding through the gears at rapid pace, the small van bumped its way onto the perimeter road. Above the din of the thrashing engine Rana could hear the clatter of small arms fire from behind. A quick glance in the rear view mirror revealed the muzzle flashes of several weapons through the wire fence. Only one round found its target, the driver's side wing mirror shattering with a loud crack. Rana put his foot down and headed for the coastal road to the north.

14.44 hours

At fifteen thousand feet the Channel Islands could be seen in close proximity, their jagged outlines surrounded by the wakes of numerous vessels. Latham passed directly between the islands and the coast of the mainland, the Griffon maintaining its steady roar over the sound of the slipstream around the Spitfire's cockpit. A sudden, if brief stab of brilliant light from below caught Latham's eye. Barely discernible among the myriad of reflections that sparkled from the sea's surface; experience told him to hold his gaze. Again, the pinprick of a reflection. Far below, a small shape was flashing across the surface at wave top level on a northerly course. Against the charcoal grey of the Atlantic the outline of the Lightning was well hidden by camouflage, only the occasional reflection and white, arrow straight wing tip contrails betraying its existence. Latham had found him and he watched as Ronson began a slow turn to starboard, as if making back to the mainland. The turn continued through 180 degrees until the fighter levelled off on a southern tack. Latham began to recognise the standard racetrack pattern of a fighter loitering for trade . Through sheer luck, he had chanced upon Ronson waiting to rendezvous with his intended target. Latham wasted little time and began to lose altitude. He flicked through the channels of his radio again, the simple message repeated after each pause for an answer.

'F6, F6, This Templemere Spitfire, Over.'

Each time the airways stayed silent, Latham running out of channels as the dial clicked clockwise through one full rotation. He reached the final notch. Still nothing. He was either shut down or not responding. Latham went back to the beginning and started again.

Ronson pushed the stick forward and the nose lowered. He flicked the off switch on the radio, the static dying in his ears. Latham's voice had been a shock, an unexpected, unforeseen possibility that even Aisha's meticulous planning had not foreseen. The radar-scope showed several faint contacts within a fifty mile range and only two of those were on his course. Ronson scanned the horizon, his large shoulders struggling to turn as he surveyed the sky behind him. No visuals. He knew why Latham had followed and almost felt relieved that he had escaped Aisha's attentions. The Spitfire would prove little in the way of trouble, the F6 capable of almost 1200 knots at a push. His fingers hovered over the transmit switch as he briefly contemplated a reply.

He was beginning to sweat again, his face feeling clammy beneath the oxygen mask. He smashed his head against the canopy frame three times, the pounding of each blow vibrating through the helmet. Through welling eyes he caught sight of the dog-eared photograph that had been tucked into a recess on the control display. Anna smiled back at him. He could feel the rage building again. He pushed the control column forward, the slight swell of the Atlantic was soon flashing beneath the belly of the fighter as it held steady at sixty feet. Ronson kept the speed at just under 400 knots and checked his fuel gauges. He counted off the seconds as the over wing fuel tanks drained their last precious drops of Kerosene. The fuel gauge needle finally died as the Lightning now switched to its own internal fuel supply, those tanks registering full on the control panel. Raising the nose slightly, the fighter gained an extra hundred feet. Ronson flicked the safety cover from over the fuel tank jettison switch and, with a final glance over either shoulder, released the cigar shaped cylinders into the slipstream. In his rear view mirror he could see the tanks cart wheeling away towards the surface of the Atlantic. The Lightning immediately felt lighter in his hands, the 4500 lbs of fuel and ferry tanks gone, the fighter no longer restricted to subsonic speeds. Diving for the wave tops again, Ronson slowly eased the throttles forward and felt the surge of power ripple through the fuselage. The target was closing at 65 miles. Ronson switched on his radar again and, with his visor pressed tight up against the rubber cowling, immediately began to scan for a contact. His hand was no longer shaking.

14.45 hours
At 25,000 feet, Air Force One left an arrow-straight vapour trail that cut through the azure blue of the afternoon sky. Colonel Dale Steiner had just taken control from his co-pilot when the first contact from French air traffic control came through on a scrambled channel. The welcome was cordial, the controller at Cressy estimating contact with the French air force escorts at seventeen minutes, the planned rendezvous with the Armee de l'Air Mirage 2000's to pre-empt a flypast of the US cemetery at St Laurent before a landing at Paris Orly. Steiner searched the sky ahead for any tell-tale contrails, a blue visor shielding his vision through the canopy windshield. He flicked the intercom control to the Secret Service control room in the rear.

'Mister Tuchner, sir, I believe *Warrior* requested to be present on the flight deck when the French escort arrived. Be advised that rendezvous is in

approximately fifteen minutes. Thank you'
Steiner allowed himself a sly grin as he re-selected the scrambled channel on his receiver. Kastner, his co-pilot beat him to the thought.

'Training yahoo's in the Air National Guard in Alabama sure beats a tour over Cambodia, eh boss?'
Steiner's smile widened.

'Whatever, the guys still a fellow pilot and if he wants to see the French fly boys then that's what we'll give him.' He tapped a display on the console above his head. 'Besides, you know the black suit boys play back all cockpit recordings after each fight, don't you?' Kastner waved a dismissive hand as he pointed at the stripes on his arm.

'Last tour, boss. By the time it comes to trial, I'll be fishing in the Keys and this guy will be giving lectures at Harvard.' As Steiner secured the restraining straps of his seat harness
he called over his shoulder for a radar check.

'Gin clear with four contacts still to show. ETA should be thirteen minutes, sir.'
As he smiled, Steiner's attention focussed on the radio console, a red light flickering. He switched the receive on his headphones, the French accent different than before.

Latham had seen the tanks jettison, the increase in speed immediately discernible as the Lightning, free of the shackles of extra weight, seemed to leap forward. Banking vertically, Latham let the nose drop and ruddered into a shallow dive. He pushed the throttle open and pulled the Spitfire into level flight at fifteen thousand. The aircraft would need the thinner air to maintain any speed. The Griffon was roaring, 405 knots registering on the airspeed gauge, the sound in the cockpit now a continuous cacophony of engine noise. Latham realised what he had seen, a loitering fighter turning out of its orbit and accelerating towards an acquired target. The question was still, what target? Below, the pin-prick shape of the Lightning was becoming smaller by the second, only white wing tip contrails caused by the fighters proximity with the sea aiding Latham's vision. He held the Spitfire level in the thinner air and, feeling for the base of the throttle lever, his finger located the remaining space in the groove that told him how much more power he had. Slowly, he edged the lever forward until it would go no further, the only discernible change being the increased pitch of the Griffon. He watched the airspeed indicator as the needle laboriously flickered through 410 and up towards 420 knots. Latham could feel the dampness in the hollow of his back. He had never taken a piston engine to this speed before and he knew how much he risked blowing the Griffon completely. He shuffled back into his parachute, tugging hard on the straps. With a blown engine at this height, it would be a long descent into a cold Channel. He flashed a gaze at the airspeed. Steady at 438 knots, the Griffon sounding stronger. The oil temperature had also increased but had stabilised just short of the red zone. He again toyed with the notion of making contact through Cressy control, but the final line of the scribbled note in his knee pad pocket scrolled over and over in his head. Conflicting emotions created an indecision that Latham knew threatened Jenny's safety as well as his own. As his head began to drop, the radio channel burst into life.

Vire Estuary
14.52 hours
The track became increasingly rough as the van bounced its way towards the mouth of the estuary. The roads from Coudeville-sur-Mer had been continually congested, convoys of tourists mixing with assorted military personnel along the narrow lanes of Normandy. On the outskirts of Carentan Kamal pulled the van over at an isolated bus stop. Latif had his own rendezvous to make and there were no words exchanged by the two men as the drop was made. The van circled the small town before heading towards the coast along single-track lanes. Kamal put his foot down as the River Vire appeared alongside the road, the banks widening as the tributary approached the mouth of the estuary. Kamal could see several small vessels moored out in the middle of the channel. Small fishing boats mixed with private gin palaces, many of them ocean going, the estuary contained any number of possible methods of escape. It was then that he caught sight of the white Citroen parked at the waters edge, a coastal crabber moored fifty yards out. The deck seemed empty. As Kamal drew closer, the rear door of the Citroen opened and Rana appeared. He hauled the Stinger case from the interior and shot a glance at the approaching vehicle.

Kamal brought the van to an abrupt halt, a shower of stones landing at Rana's feet as the wheels locked up. He stood his ground, the emotionless stare that waited for the next move. Kamal groped around beneath his feet as he held Rana's gaze. On the floor of the passenger foot well, an adze naval axe lay wrapped in an oily cloth. Kamal unfurled it and ran his thumb along the blade edge. It was reassuringly sharp. He pocketed the small axe and got slowly out of the van.

'The Sarin? Where is it?' he shouted. Rana began to smile.

'And I thought it was only family that you were interested in.' Kamal walked forward towards him but halted at the sight of the pistol emerging from Rana's waistband. His stare intensified.

'Family and the lives of innocent people.' Rana began to laugh, gesturing with the pistol as he spoke.

'How the righteous man has spoken. You hypocritical bastard.' The laughter died as Rana steadied the pistol.

'Your gun.' He gestured the ground immediately in front of Kamal. 'Throw it away from yourself.' Slowly and deliberately Kamal removed the pistol from his jacket pocket and, holding the barrel between two fingers, threw it onto the ground. Out on the estuary the presence of the two figures on the bank had drawn the attention of a passing motor boat, the two crew straining to see the shoreline through the afternoon haze. Kamal held up his hands as he noticed the captive audience over Rana's shoulder.

'Yes, I have done my share of killing, but never the innocent. If you release that Sarin, you kill thousands in this area alone.' Rana shifted his stance and raised the pistol higher.

'A few thousand peasants is nothing compared to the death brought to our country.' As Rana sneered, Kamal pointed to the two figures standing in the now becalmed motorboat.

'You have an audience.'

Rana held his stance. Slowly, he pointed the pistol over

his shoulder and fired a three round burst. The shots missed wildly, the crack of the pistol fire echoing across the waters surface. The two figures dived for cover. Kamal could see a crouching figure frantically reaching for the boats controls. The engine roared into life. As the boat rose on its wake, Kamal brought his gaze back to Rana. He stood motionless as the motorboat disappeared into the mists of the estuary.

'Alone again. You'll have to do it yourself now.'

Thirteen

14.53 hours
Latham jolted as the voice cut through his consciousness, the heavily accented English breaking through the roar of the Griffon.

'Spitfire Golf Whiskey Tango Mike, this is Cressy Sector, over?' The voice was French, the background noise sounded, to Latham, like the interior of a helicopter. The voice continued.

'Rob Latham, if you can confirm, over?' Latham's name caused a flinch. What came next, was shock of another kind. 'Please confirm, Mr Latham. Your wife Jenny is safe, I repeat safe, over?'
Latham lunged at the transmit switch, his reply stuttering.

'Yeah…yes this is Latham in…' In his confusion he had to read the aircraft's code from the small plaque above the control panel. '….Golf Whiskey Tango Mike, who is this please, over?' There was a pause of static before the voice broke in.

'My name is Colonel Tressor of the French Security Service. I am approximately 170 miles to your east over the Normandy coast.' The voice was shouting above the noise of the helicopter's rotor blades. 'We have been contacted by the British police to say that they have your wife in safe custody, Mr Latham.' He let his head sink back against the armoured headrest, his eyes welling up as Tressor continued. 'We need to know your intentions, Mr Latham. We have a missing Lightning F6 fighter, possibly armed and with the intention of engaging an extremely high profile target. Do you have any information, over?'

Latham composed himself before answering. He throttled the engine back, the nose immediately dropping slightly as the Spitfire cruised at 350 knots.

'I made contact with Max Ronson leaving an airfield at Coudeville-sur-Mer on the east coast about 25 minutes ago. He was carrying Red Top AAMs, I repeat, Red Top air-to-air missiles over.'

'The course, Mr Latham?'

'My last sighting was directly astern, at approximately 3000 feet and a due west heading, over.' There was another pause before the line crackled back into life.

'We have no radar or radio contact with Ronson's Lightning, but if his course is correct, it would put him on a direct heading for a US aircraft. We have had to divert air force escorts to your course but they are a full twelve minutes from ETA. You are the closest visual contact we have at present.' Latham sensed the intent in Tressor's voice.

'You want me to try and find him?'

'Until we have fighters on station, you are the only eyes we have'. Latham allowed himself time, his elation in danger of engulfing him. The clear blue sky ahead of the Spitfire suddenly seemed welcoming, the logistics of finding a needle in a haystack fast diminishing. He realised that his cheeks were wet with tears, the old leather of the oxygen mask soaking up most of them before the salt taste reached his lips. He swallowed hard as Tressor cut back in.

'Mister Latham? Time is vital, sir.' The reality was too stark to ignore. Latham could certainly stay at a safe distance from any action. He felt his confidence returning as he flicked the send switch.

'I'll give you your eyes, Colonel but I want your fighter cover with me, over.'

There was a calm authority about Tressor's voice.

'Eleven minutes.'

14.55 hours

Ronson kept low as he searched for the target, his head buried in the cowling of the radar scope. Conscious of the fighter's proximity with the surface, his eyes occasionally flicked to the altimeter to his left as the wave tops flashed past below. After a full two minutes, a large contact broke onto the screen from the West, the ceiling at 20,000 feet. It was alone. Ronson calculated the speed of the target as he searched the scope for any further contacts or signs of an escort. Latham no longer registered as a signal. Satisfied that his calculations were correct, Ronson folded the cowling of the scope to one side and lowered his smoked visor. He caught a glimpse of Anna's smiling face and the angered burned. He had played this moment over and over, the probabilities and the possibilities.

He had wanted to see the whites of their eyes before the kill. He had even toyed with a slow pass alongside, the possibility of a terrified face at a window. That face. He knew that all of this decreased the possibility of a clear shot. Years of intensive training had prepared him for all eventualities, but in the best analysis a lock on from line astern of the target would give the missile less to do and a much higher probability of a kill. Ronson would under-fly his target before turning on a 180 degree course some twenty miles behind the Boeing, all of this undetected by radar and only the remotest chance of a visual identification by the American crew. He gazed up through the highly polished Perspex of the canopy. Some twenty thousand feet above him, Air Force One cut a single white line through the cloudless sky.

Ronson went back to his instruments to calculate how much time he had before the turn. At eighteen miles distant from the target, he throttled back and began a slow roll to port, at the same time climbing away from the buffeting air stream caused by the surface of the Atlantic. At this distance he no longer had a visual contact and, lifting his tinted visor, Ronson again squinted into the radar cowling. The contact appeared again at the very edge of the screen, the small green blip glowing against the pitch black of the scope. Ronson immediately throttled up and pulled the nose higher.

Vire Estuary
14.56 hours

Rana paused before answering Kamal's question, the pistol gesticulating before him.

'The Red Tops? Yes I did think of them, but when it came down to trusting an alcoholic Englishman, I would rather place faith in my own ability.' Rana smiled slowly as Kamal held his ground, unable to move. Swiftly, the hit man dropped to one knee and placed the Stinger case in front of him. In one movement the catches were open and the anti-aircraft missile was over his right shoulder. He pocketed the pistol. Kamal heard the familiar whine of the seeker head as Rana depressed the trigger, the Stinger aimed directly at him. He held his ground. From inside the casing Rana produced a small glass phial and held it at arms length.

'This what you're looking for?' He cocked his head to one side, one eye closed as he held Kamal in the cross hairs of the sight. 'Asil told you tales, did he?'

Kamal stretched a hand out and pointed at the Stinger. He edged forward.

'You won't hit it with that, you don't have the range.' Rana pulled back from the eyepiece of the sight. He paused, the reply slow and measured.

'He's only one man. I want more than an individual.' He pointed towards the east. 'That beach contains every major head of state in Europe. I only need to be within ten miles and I take out all life.'

From the mouth of the estuary a helicopter swept low across the surface of the water, the blades thudding through the mist filled air. It banked sharply as it drew parallel with the crabber. Rana turned, and Kamal took his chance. In a stooping run, he grabbed at the rough earth and aimed a handful of dirt at Rana's head. It caught him as he turned to face the onrushing figure, the momentary flinch enough to give Kamal the advantage. He caught the midriff with his left shoulder and sent Rana flying. As his body fell, the Stinger crashed into the mud of the bank. Rana scrambled onto his knees, his empty hand fumbling his pocket for the pistol.

In one swift movement, Kamal brought the adze down hard across Rana's wrist severing the hand in one motion. The scream cut through the air as Rana frantically grasped at the stump of his arm, blood now pulsing from the wound. The hand, fingers outstretched, dropped the phial into the mud, both immediately beginning to sink beneath the surface. Rana scrambled down the shallow bank and slumped into the water, his remaining hand thrust into the mud. Moving in on the prostrate form, Kamal aimed a well placed kick to the side of the head and sent Rana sprawling onto its back. He slid down the remainder of the shallow bank coming to rest in the festering mud. Rana's eyes narrowed as he struggled to focus on the figure above him. Kamal hesitated. From the prone figure before him, a flurry of movement.

The shot caught Kamal full in the shoulder, his upper body jerked violently sideways until he lost balance and crashed backwards into the grass. Rana was now on his feet, the glint of the pistol shining from his mud soaked fist. He roared as studied the mangled stump of his hand.

High above the two prone figures, the helicopter had settled into a hover, the downdraft from the rotors flattening the rushes below. His body buffeted by the maelstrom, Rana began to stumble over the long grass towards Kamal's still figure. The shoulder wound burned as Kamal tried to raise himself up. Hauling himself onto his elbow, his arm touched something. Partially hidden by a large clump of reeds, the Stinger lay on its side. A red LED flickered at the base of the sight. With his right hand, he dragged the launcher towards him, gripping the handle with all his remaining strength. Rana fired again, the round catching Kamal's right ear. He screamed as warm blood began to flow down his neck. In one final effort he hauled the launcher onto his one good shoulder. Rana stopped in his tracks.

Pulling himself into a sitting position, Kamal trained the Stinger on Rana's swaying form some thirty feet away. His vision struggled to remain focussed. Uday Hussein's henchman bared his teeth. Above the din of the helicopter, Rana shouted his defiance.

'This is what holds you back, Kamal.' Rana shouted, his one good hand pointing with the pistol.

'With me, it's money, power, personal gain. With you?' He sneered. 'Duty? Family? You even allow a conscience to fuck your judgement.'

Rana raised the pistol. His finger started to squeeze the trigger. In the distance, an amplified voice was trying to cut through the clatter of the rotor blades.

The Stinger roared from its launcher, the recoil sending Kamal sprawling. The missile tore across the short distance of ground and straight through Rana's stomach, carrying his body fully thirty feet as the round continued its path out into the estuary.

Kamal watched, as Rana's lifeless, smouldering body cart-wheeled out over the water. In the distance, the

Stinger spiralled out of control and plunged into the far bank of the river. The missile hit the ground sending up a huge plume of earth, the un-fused round failing to ignite. Only the wild, snaking exhaust trail remained, gently dissipating in the still afternoon air. Kamal sat, frozen momentarily, the launcher falling from his grip. He stared at Rana's corpse as it disappeared beneath the surface of the water. Slowly, he staggered to his feet and walked towards the waters edge. Lying at his feet, Rana's pistol lay half submerged. Kamal winced with pain as he stooped to retrieve it. Wiping the mud away from the barrel, he turned to face the still figure of Gilde Tressor.

14.58 hours

The Lightning moved into a direct line astern of the giant, some five miles distant. Even at this range, the turbulence from the four Pratt and Whitney engines buffeted at the nose of the fighter, causing Ronson to compensate. He held the Boeing in the cross hairs of the missile sight and began to close the contact down. He could hear his breathing as he consciously tried to relax himself, the tenseness in his neck and shoulders now agonisingly apparent. Through the sight, the four contrails snaked over his head as the heavyweight grew in his vision. At four miles, Ronson paused for a deep breath. He switched the safety on the control column, his thumb pressing lightly on the fire button. He ran the final checks through his head as he had a hundred times before. As his grip slowly tightened around the control column, the view through the cross hairs suddenly changed.

The port wing of Air Force One dropped sharply sending the Boeing into a steep dive, simultaneously a cloud of chaff appearing from beneath the tail-plane. Ronson roared as his fist pounded the sill of the control panel. The photograph of Anna disappeared beneath his feet. They were onto him. His eyes focussed onto the Blind Eye unit, the green indicator showing it was still active. They must know from the ground. He frantically searched the full 360 degree field of vision, his mind immediately assuming he had company. The radar still showed only one major contact, the shower of chaff spreading like a haze across the screen. The missile lock burbled briefly before cutting out, Ronson knowing instantly that the countermeasures had compromised the shot. He re-set the safety and punched in the afterburners. Rather than rolling away for another pass, Ronson held course for the Boeing, the fighter passing close enough to create a turbulence that rocked the heavy airliners frame. He cursed his lack of guns.

In the cockpit of Air Force One, Steiner fought with the controls, a grey blur flashing across his windshield. As he struggled with the whiplash of the control yoke, his eyes followed the trajectory of the spiralling fighter. Before it dived out of view he thought he knew the shape, his hand instinctively reaching for the send button on the radio. Oxygen masks dropped from housings above both pilots, the violent manoeuvre of the aircraft having activated emergency procedures. Before Steiner could speak, Kastner screamed through his oxygen mask.

'I got one, no two contacts on my tail closing fast.'

As he reached for the tail defence unit control, Steiner's earpiece made static.

'Two-Six-Thousand, this is Cutlass One and

Two. Repeat, Cutlass One and Two inbound. I believe you have trade, sir. Over?'

The F18 Hornet passed close over the starboard wing, immediately pulling across the nose as if shielding a vulnerable prey. Steiner held the aircraft steady, his eyes fixed on the exhaust trails of the navy fighter as the jet efflux buffeted the 747. The second fighter appeared from port and took up station alongside the cockpit, the nose raised in order to match the heavyweights slower airspeed. Again, Steiner's eyes darted about, the distinctive grey shape of the aggressor out of visual and still not registering on the radar.

'You are truly a sight for sore eyes, gentlemen. We've got one aggressor who is not, I repeat not making a signal. It has British markings but it looks older, copy?'

With no showing on his radar, the lead F18 pilot took his fighter higher to gain a greater view over the target area, his wingman holding station alongside the Boeing.

Far below, an unseen radar contact began to rise through the low cloud base, the speed increasing as aircraft accelerated in a near vertical climb.

As Ronson rose to meet him, the US Navy pilot made a last second visual contact, the darting shape briefly registering as from a bygone age, before the tell-tale plume of a launched missile arced up towards him. Ronson felt the Red Top run off its rail, the loss of weight necessitating and instant re-trimming of the controls. The Lightning bucked slightly before regaining level flight. The missile exhaust climbed rapidly away from the fighter, a great plume of white vapour trail arcing its way upwards. Ronson pulled the

Lightning onto its back and wheeled away towards the sea. Over his right shoulder he followed the exhaust trail as it snaked its way towards the target. In the F18, klaxons wailed their warnings, the pilot simultaneously launching countermeasures as he threw his aircraft violently to port. The flare canisters exploded aft, one passing agonisingly close to the Red Top but unable to tempt it from its path. The F18 pilot stood little chance, the missile slamming into the underbelly of the twisting fighter, the impact tearing the starboard wing clean off. The two Sidewinder missiles ignited a second after the Red Tops own warhead. The Hornet was engulfed.

The threat neutralised, Ronson hauled the Lightning around in a tight turn. Flames clung to the burning debris as it made its way down through the cloud base. Ronson passed close, the 747 clearly visible through the smoke as it reeled away. The turn completed, Air Force One was now climbing away from the dogfight. Ronson throttled forward to maximum power.

Fourteen

14.59 hours

The Griffon was hot, the oil temperature needle hovering dangerously close to the red as Latham struggled to play catch up. The throttle had been wide open for a full five minutes, fuel visibly disappearing from the main tank display gauge. The Spitfire had risen steadily towards the thinner air, the increased speed creating a crescendo of noise in the cockpit. Latham struggled with the headphones over his ears, the hiss of the open radio channel growing faint in the struggle against the outside noise. He pulled the goggles above his eyes and wiped the sweat that had collected in his eyebrows. The heat from the engine was making life uncomfortable in the cramped confines. Latham saw the twisting contrails first, the sight immediately reminding him of wartime footage of wartime dogfights over London, the swirling pattern of aircraft fast losing altitude. The larger aircraft was diving, the manoeuvre instantly looking at odds with its size. Latham recognised the shape of a 747, the blue and white of the livery strangely familiar as he dropped the port wing into a shallow dive.

The explosion flashed with a white heat that momentarily blinded, Latham's head snapping sideways as his eyes struggled to adjust. The F18 disappeared in a broiling inferno, the intensity of the explosion engulfing the aircraft in an instant. An oily cloud of smoke quickly gave way to descending fragments of wreckage. Latham kept the Spitfire in a dive, the Griffon momentarily protesting at the sudden change of altitude. Ahead, the Boeing continued to fall, the descent pulling to port as the heavyweight struggled to lose height. Latham pulled his goggles down over his eyes and transmitted the position of the aircraft over the open channel. Tressor's reply was a curt acknowledgement and confirmation of the French escorts ETA. Four minutes. A brief flash of sunlight on metal revealed the second F18 as it dived towards the Boeing, Latham quickly realising its role as escort to the heavyweight. Ronson was nowhere to be seen.

15.00 hours

The second F18 seemed to have taken flight, Ronson's radar scope revealing a small contact either in retreat, or preparing for another attack run. He now had vital seconds. Ahead, the aircraft's contrails now resembling a pattern of Morse code stutters, Air Force One was now weaving through a zigzag pattern of evasive manoeuvres, the tail intermittently sending out a cascade of phosphorus countermeasures. Ronson closed in, bringing the fighter up from below on the port beam. At eight hundred yards he gently squeezed the missile lock button. The high-pitched growl in his ears revealed a strong signal, the seeker head of the remaining Red Top acquiring an infra-red lock on the Boeing's heat source.

As his thumb hovered over the firing button his forward vision suddenly filled with the mass of a climbing Spitfire. Arcing across the Lightning's nose, the piston engine fighter screamed into view. The reaction was instant, the control column all but wrenched from it's housing as Ronson fought to avoid a collision. The tone of the missile lock was momentarily broken before re-affirming it's target, the high-pitched whine again filling Ronson's ears. The large fighter bucked as the rear airbrakes were deployed, spilling the thousands of valuable strips of chaff into the slipstream, and violently reducing the airspeed. The contact was fleeting; Latham's tail plane taking a glancing blow from the Lightning's nose. Ronson felt the impact shudder through the fuselage, his hand instinctively shielding his face. High above, the Spitfire levelled out and entered a wingover, placing it directly between Ronson and Air Force One. As the F6 struggled to regain momentum, Ronson punched frantically at the missile lock control for confirmation of contact. The shrill tone indicated a target but with the Spitfire directly ahead it was near impossible to confirm which aircraft it was.

Inside the Spitfire's cockpit the Griffon's tone abruptly changed as the tail began to disintegrate. Latham felt the drag increase the strain on the already protesting engine. An almighty bang from directly in front of the

windshield heralded the engine's final roar. Glycol coolant fluid flooded from the cowling and over the canopy; the cockpit immediately plunged into darkness. Latham gripped the control column with both hands as his world turned pitch black. The Spitfire flipped onto its back, fragments of the engine cowling breaking off in the slipstream as the overstressed fuselage began to disintegrate. Latham's hands grasped at the handle above his head as he struggled to haul the canopy back on its rails. It would not move. His hands grasped at the column again. As his world span about him, Latham caught a glimpse of the Lightning through his canopy, the grey fighter spinning away towards the sea. He wrenched his hands upwards again. The grasp was firm.
The canopy shot back with a jolt, the force catching Latham's knuckles on the handle. He wrenched his hands free and punched the harness release. Nothing. He panicked, his fingers pulling at the straps that trapped him.

'Noooo'. He bellowed his protest, his minds eye catapulted back through time as his father had fought to save his own life. Clasping his fists together, he brought the full weight of his shoulders down across the release. It shot apart, the harness straps releasing Latham from the tight confines of the bucket seat. He forced himself up into the slipstream and grasped the edge of the windshield. The g-force snapped his frame back against the armoured headrest, his temple catching a glancing blow and pushed him back down into the seat. He felt for the windshield edge again and hauled himself into the whirlwind that tore over the canopy. The Spitfire began to roll. Latham waited until the aircraft was fully inverted before allowing gravity to take over. His body tumbled from the grasp of the cockpit, narrowly missing the disintegrating tail plane by inches. He was winded as the snap of the drag punched into his rag doll form. Through a cart wheeling vision, Latham saw the blurred outline of the Spitfire as it continued its roll towards the sea, the left wing now fully severed and trailing debris as it made its own separate way down. His head thumping, Latham managed to pull a hand across his chest. Battling the slipstream that had already torn his gloves off, his outstretched fingers searched for the D-ring of the parachute release. He found it and pulled hard. The second long delay was expected but seemed like an eternity. Finally, the small drogue chute rippled from the harness, dragging the lines of the main chute free of the backpack. The orange and white canopy cracked open over Latham's head, the drag instantly slowing his body by over one hundred miles per hour.

15.01 hours

The Lightning spiralled through the sky, losing fifteen thousand feet in just over a minute. Ronson struggled to stay conscious under the enormous forces the spin had induced. The collision, minor in its actual contact with between the aircraft, had had a violent effect on the Lightning's momentum. The nose had risen briefly as the fighter fought against stalling, the throttled back Avons on the verge of flameout. Gravity took control as fifteen tons of metal began to spin earthwards. In the cockpit, Ronson felt his g-suit expand cutting the supply of blood to his lower body. His breathing rasped through the oxygen mask as he fought to stay conscious, his vision a maelstrom of kaleidoscopic colours. Instinct forced the control column to port to counter the spin, airbrakes deployed to slow his airspeed. Still the fighter plummeted, he needed to lose more momentum. Ronson forced one hand away from the stick and desperately forced his outstretched fingers towards the undercarriage down switch. He made contact. The effect was almost instantaneous, the fighter bucking as the landing gear lowered into the slipstream. Slowly, the spin began to subdue, the pressure in Ronson's g-suit subsiding as the Lightning regained level flight.

There was another shudder through the cockpit as the undercarriage was torn from the underside of the fuselage. The Lightning felt light again in his hands as Ronson began to search the sky for a visual contact. High and to the left, through stinging eyes he spotted Latham's canopy some two thousand feet higher and slowly descending. A mile beyond, Air Force One had now levelled out from its dive and could be seen heading eastwards towards the mainland coast. Only three of its engines were emitting a contrail. Ronson roared through his facemask as he hauled the fighter into a tight turn, Latham's parachute swinging into view directly ahead. He selected the Red Top fire sequence and focussed his vision on the optical sight through the windshield. Beyond the slowly falling canopy, the 747 was straight and level. Ronson quickly acquired lock, the growl in his headset steady and loud. He throttled up and pulled the nose higher. He just had one more task before firing.

Latham struggled in his harness as he desperately tried to turn and face the rapidly accelerating fighter. The Lightning was closing fast and beam on, Latham in no doubt as to Ronson's intentions. His fists burned as he grasped the canopy straps tighter, the shocking realisation that he was utterly powerless to resist. He let go and let his arms hang limply at his sides, his eyes locked in a terrible fascination at the growing sight of the onrushing Lightning and the building crescendo of noise. He threw his arms over his face in the final seconds.

The Lightning was wrenched from its path with a crescendo of rending metal. A third of a second elapsed before the warhead of the AIM 9L Sidewinder ignited taking most of the rear fuselage with it. Pitched nose down, the fighter's engines surged to full throttle, severed controls having little effect. Game over, was Ronson's only thought as the distant surface of the Atlantic spun into view. As the increasing g-forces began to black out his vision he heard the whooping cries of the American F18 pilot in his headphones. The cart wheeling wreckage spiralled down towards the sea trailing the black plume of a funeral pyre. His head reeling from the acrid fumes that burned his lungs, Ronson struggled to grasp at the fire button on the control column in one final vain attempt to launch the last Red Top. His hands where constantly thrown back into his chest as the cockpit seemed to disintegrate around him. With his last vestige of strength Ronson forced both hands together into a fist and rammed them down towards the ejection handle between his knees. The delay seemed endless as the canopy was given a vital second to clear the cockpit. Restraining straps hauled his legs tight against the seat as the firing sequence was activated.

Max Ronson was not conscious when the rocket motors of his seat propelled him some sixty feet above the burning wreckage of his aircraft. A small drogue chute automatically deployed, the larger silk canopy snapping open above the prone figure still strapped to the seat. Below, what remained of the Lightning continued its blazing arc towards the sea, the rear fuselage enveloped in a furnace of molten aluminium and aviation fuel. High above, the remaining F18 began a slow, arcing turn towards Ronson's chute as it made it's slow decent.

Latham had felt the force of the explosion, his canopy coming dangerously close to collapsing as the percussion blast rippled through the silk envelope. He swung his legs to pull the canopy open. Far below, he could make out the trailing wake of several small motorboats snaking about a larger, naval looking vessel, one inflatable making towards the splashdown site of the Lightning's wreckage, a boiling mass of foam slowly spreading over a wide area. As he prepared him self for a difficult landing, he caught sight of Ronson's canopy high above. The slumped form spun slowly under the larger parachute, the descent significantly slower.

The sea rapidly rose up to meet Latham, he releasing his harness the moment his feet touched the water. As he surfaced he could hear the sound of an outboard motor chopping its way through the slight swell. The French navy Gemini was immediately upon him, rough hands hauling him on board as French voices filled his ears. He struggled to sit up in the well of the boat as he strained to see Ronson's canopy. His temple was pounding, a thin stream of blood streaking the side of his face. The chute was some five hundred yards off the stern, its descent taking it close to the remains of the Lightning. Latham watched as the prone figure disappeared beneath the surface, the canopy collapsing over Ronson's head as his body was rapidly forced back to the surface by his lifejacket. A one-man raft automatically inflated and bobbed up next to him. The sea stained bright green by marker dye from the life raft, Ronson's body lulled in the foam of the swell caused by the crashed fighter. All of the other inflatable craft had come to a halt, engines at idle, with no attempt being made to approach the crash scene. As Latham was wrapped in a large grey blanket he stared blankly at his rescuers. The nearest, a large sub-lieutenant in yellow oilskins noticed Latham's puzzled expression. He stood to block the Englishman as he struggled to rise to his feet. Latham stumbled over the wooden seat, his parched throat trying to form a shout. All he managed was to hook an arm over the Frenchman's shoulder before his strength finally gave way. The bellow was long, rasping from his aching lungs.

'Max !, Max…..' A large hand clamped down on his shoulder and held him off. The lieutenant pointed with a single finger and slowly shook his head. His accent heavy, he growled just the one word.

'Sarin.'

Fifteen

Cape Wrath, Scotland
18th January 1995

The casket was empty. Only three other members of the congregation knew. Latham bowed his head Max Ronson's coffin was carried down the isle of the small church. Outside, a gale swept in off the Atlantic, the tall reed grass of the unkempt graveyard flattened as a chill wind raced across the headland. This forgotten stretch of the jagged northern Scottish coastline had long since passed out of the public consciousness, for fifty years its sheer cliff faces and uninhabited islets had served the nation as a bombing range for the British, as well as numerous visiting armed forces. The rusted remains of a target hulks were the only reminder of the range's past, most of these relics slowly succumbing to the tides and eddies of the shifting sands. The range had covered several thousands of acres in its heyday, two villages swallowed up at the stroke of a Whitehall pen in the late autumn of 1939, with entire populations uprooted and re-housed. D-Day was rehearsed on the nine hundred foot cliff faces in the build up to Normandy, while the inland gunnery ranges served as targets for the experimental weapons facility at nearby Durness. It was this single storey complex of blockhouses that were now the sole occupier of Cape Wrath, the only other structure, the tall, white stone of a Robert Stephenson light house now an empty relic. As land had been reclaimed in the early nineties, the local wildlife began to thrive in the now peaceful surrounds.

On the edge of a cliff face that ran along the southern end of the range, St Breoc's had stood, untouched for over seven hundred years. The Norman church had remained closed to the public throughout the war years, on into the uncertainty of the Cold War and beyond. In the decommissioning of vast tracts of land in 1992, the church, much to the disgust of campaigning locals, had remained within the boundaries of the retained range. For it served a purpose.

Although no regular services ever took place, the church was used for burials. The small graveyard contained over a dozen gravestones, many tilted at lazy angles as subsidence undermined their foundations. None of them pre-dated the late thirties, and many contained inscriptions in languages other than English. Inscriptions that were never meant to be read.

Latham walked out into the bright light, the watery winter sun fighting its way between ever darkening skies. Although the churchyard was some five hundred feet above the churning rocks below, he could taste the salt spray on his lips, the swirling spray dampening all about. A couple of brass hats followed him through the porch, in the distance their official cars waiting at the entrance to the churchyard. Latham recognised few among the small congregation. Ronson's former Squadron Leader from the Marham Wing had been allowed to attend, but the tiny church had looked virtually empty. Latham had heard about this church. A resting place where the dead would be forgotten, closed to the prying eyes of the public and out of the consciousness of whichever government had been embarrassed. The graves of escaped German officers were mixed with those of traitors and criminals, a half decent end for those thought not worthy of remembrance. It was here that Max Ronson's parents had been told that he wanted to be buried. Latham squinted through the drizzle.

They looked smaller than he had remembered, the stooped figures, almost brow beaten in their demeanour. It was hardly surprising, in the circumstances. Ronson had seldom mentioned his parents in all of their service together, Latham having to prise any information from him during less guarded moments. They had been told of an accident, a test flight that had been their son's final sortie. No mention in the papers and no wish for a public funeral. The months that had separated the accident with the final service had only heightened their sense of confusion. Together with the public, they had no idea of the true events that had led to their son's death.

Air Force One, a damaged engine fire extinguished and shut down, had stabilised at ten thousand feet and, under escort from the single F18 and five French Rafale fighters, had made an emergency landing at Landivisiau Air Station in northern Brittany. With only minor injuries to report, and with an assurance from the security services, the President and First Lady had continued their itinerary for the afternoon; the veterans' parade at Omaha Beach followed by a mass drop by men of the 101st Airborne Division; the 'Screaming Eagles'. A convoy of heavily armed vehicles had then taken the heads of states to Paris for a reception at the American Embassy.

In a swift damage limitation exercise, the governments of France and Britain had imposed news blackouts served on all forms of media, the attempt to stem the embarrassing lapses in national security. It was scant consolation that the DGSE had Abdul Kamal in custody after the event. Salam Mawsil and Latif Nadar were quickly rounded up within an hour of each other, the former just minutes from boarding an unsuspecting trawler as a hired deck hand, the intended destination; Cadiz in western Spain. Both had quickly surrendered, the realisation that they were overwhelmingly compromised, compounded by the shear volume of security forces that had swamped the area. They were presently being held at Lorient naval base awaiting trial on charges of terrorism against people and territories of the French Republic. Behind the scenes accusations were made through diplomatic channels, Iraq charged with promoting an act of state sponsored terrorism. Tariq Aziz, the deputy Prime Minister, strenuously denied any involvement, dismissing the accusations as yet another hysterical attempt by the West to demonise his country.

Despite the efforts of a Royal Navy salvage team, Ronson's body had simply disappeared, the vessel unable to enter the contaminated area for twenty-four hours. With the Sarin threat dispersed by the Atlantic swell, the salvage team had lost little time in recovering the wreckage of the Lightning, the British government desperate to retrieve the stolen Blind Eye unit.

Abdul Kamal had been moved with rapid speed from a holding centre in Brest, his incarceration barely lasting 48 hours before the high-speed transit to Landivisiau airfield. On the tarmac, the small Dassault business jet was waiting, engines whining as the small party boarded. Kamal was hooded for the duration of the three-hour flight, unable to hear through the heavy ear protectors and shackled hand and foot. He felt the jolt of the landing, the warmth of the Cyprus climate filtering through the hood as he was led down the steps. What he could not see was the similarly shackled figure stood some fifty yards from the aircraft. Several armed men surrounded the prisoner, the final guard emerging from the driver's side of the transit van that had held the captive. The two groups had eyed each other warily before a silent signal began the choreographed switch of prisoners. Jules Rochforte stumbled forward, a nudge in the back and a few quiet instructions enough to send him on his way towards the plane. The French agent passed Kamal in silence. The hooded figures reached their respective destinations, Kamal stumbling as he was manhandled into the back of the van. With the jet powering up, the Mukhabarat driver span the wheels of the van and headed towards the coast road. It would be a long journey.

Latham stood back from the small procession and watched as Ronson's elderly parents followed the coffin down the single path to the open grave. A freshly dug mound of earth lay alongside, a carelessly placed shovel struck at a lazy angle. The ceremony was short, almost obscene in its haste, Latham wincing as the priest hurried back along the path in the rain, the grieving parents left to mourn alone. As the held each other, Latham could not help but think how fragile they looked. Jim Ronson, in particular, was a spent man. Latham tried to block the vision of his own father from his consciousness, turning away from the Ronsons. As he made his way up the path a familiar figure stepped forward.

Gilde Tressor stuck out a hand.

'You have far to travel?' He nodded towards the grey clouds massing on the horizon. 'Force eight tonight, apparently.'

Latham grasped the outstretched hand.

'Not far, making a break of it actually.'

Tressor smiled, the corners of his thin lips rising slightly. He tapped Latham on the shoulder with his rolled umbrella.

'Try to stay out of the limelight. A chap like you could attract undesirables.' His eyes twinkled in the gloom. 'You have, I take it, been informed about the Taraz woman?'

Latham nodded.

'Suicide, I was told.' Tressor snapped open the umbrella and turned the collar of his coat up. The tone of his reply was one of mild disappointment.

'Yes, yes, a great pity. We'd have liked to have talked to her ourselves.'

As Tressor walked away, Latham turned for one last look at the mound of earth. The rain was heavier now. He shook his head slowly and thought of Jenny.

The drive to Kinochbervie took Latham through the Oldernorshore Mountains, the underpowered rental car struggling with the steep inclines. The twenty-four miles seemed endless, the winding road snaking it's way down into isolated fishing villages before climbing inland again, the route following the jagged edge of the coastline. The threatening clouds finally delivered, the lashing rain causing Latham to slow further, the wipers struggling to clear the deluge from the windscreen. On the crest of yet another hill, the lights of Kinochbervie sparkled through the spray, Latham carefully made his way down towards the harbour front. The Thistle hotel stood at the farthest end of the narrow high street, the last building before the granite finger of the harbour jetty stretching out into the Atlantic. Although the large basin was cluttered with trawlers gently ebbing with the swell, the walkway was empty. The predicted storm had swelled the safe haven by nearly a dozen visiting trawlers, their crews warming themselves in the three bars in the village, the Thistle included. Latham parked the car at the harbours edge and made a dash for the hotel lobby, his coat hauled over his head. He raced past the small reception desk and took the stairs two at a time. The door to his room was not locked.

Jenny smoothed his hair away from the bruise on his temple, a finger tracing the line of scar tissue, the jagged gash healing slowly. He winced.

'Careful, you're not the only one in a delicate

state.' With both hands he slowly caressed Jenny's swollen belly. She was eight months gone, a boy they had been told, the scans revealing a healthy infant. Latham smiled as he parted her bathrobe. The skin felt smooth, his hands feeling the firm roundness of her stomach. A kick, then two in rapid succession. Jenny's eyes widened, her face lighting up. Latham pulled her close breathing in her aroma.

He didn't want to let go.